Critical Injuries

Joan Barfoot

KEY PORTER BOOKS

National Library of Canada Cataloguing in Publication Data

Barfoot, Joan, 1946–
    Critical injuries

ISBN 1-55263-347-0

I. Title

PS8553.A7624C74 2001   C813'.54   C2001-900981-X
PR9199.3.B37C74 2001

THE CANADA COUNCIL | LE CONSEIL DES ARTS
FOR THE ARTS | DU CANADA
SINCE 1957 | DEPUIS 1957

ONTARIO ARTS COUNCIL
CONSEIL DES ARTS DE L'ONTARIO

The publisher gratefully acknowledges the support of the Canada Council for the Arts and the Ontario Arts Council for its publishing program.

We acknowledge the financial support of the Government of Canada through the Book Publishing Industry Development Program (BDIPD) for our publishing activities.

Key Porter Books Limited
70 The Esplanade
Toronto, Ontario
Canada   M5E 1R2
www.keyporter.com

Electronic formatting: Heidi Palfrey
Design: Peter Maher

Printed and bound in Canada

01 02 03 04 05 06 6 5 4 3 2 1

Contents

An Unfamiliar Disobedience   5

Nobody With Any Sense   13

Tied Up, Bound Down   20

A Strange, Faraway Sky   29

All the Time in the World   43

Rewind   51

A Simple Plan   61

Mrs. Lot and Mrs. Job   73

Winging It   94

Cops and Robbers   105

Pretty Good Punishment   130

The Short Book of James   147

Like a Secret   168

Catapults and Boiling Oil   183

A Clear, Steady Gaze   213

A Great Deal of Coming and Going   220

A Few Good Words   232

Not Too Much Buddy-Buddy   243

The Useful Mother   257

Belles Lettres   276

Various Monstrosities   284

Her at the Wheel   302

Necessary Sensation   319

An Unfamiliar Disobedience

"**H**OP IN," LYLE SAYS, and in Isla hops. He does a little number on her thighs: "tickling the ivory," he calls this. It still delights her to climb into his old dented green pick-up, so large and high, sturdy and work-manlike. Not like the toy sports car he uses for work, or even like her own practical compact, but a serious vehicle designed for serious pursuits.

Although they haven't always been serious in it. Once, they made love in the bed of the truck on a well-used old mattress Lyle was about to take to the dump. "One last time," he said then, from his own Lyleish combination of immediate lust and permanent sentiment. That was a couple of years ago.

This journey is for some other purpose, celebratory and impulsive. Something to do with ice cream? At the far, far end of it, that much trickles back, but there's a problem: a profound interruption after that hopping-in moment; something like an electrical outage.

Isla perceives an absence of memory, and right on its heels an urgent longing for memory, along with a powerful, simultaneous desire not to remember. How odd. She's pretty sure she doesn't ordinarily give much thought to memory, that it doesn't usually loom so consciously large. She notices then the concept of consciousness: that something, anything, might or might not loom large in it. Also that she has, having lost it, regained it. Which has to do with memory, the desirability of it, or the importance.

This distress, this disorientation, is annoying; like something itchy she should be able to scratch. Petty, when there's something large that ought to concern her.

Something itches and it seems she can't scratch. That could get maddening fast. She fidgets, and mysteriously feels herself failing to fidget. "What the hell," she thinks, meaning to speak but hearing her words fail to arrive in the air.

This is peculiar, very troubling, but perhaps the cause will come clear if she's patient and waits. That usually works, although sometimes things take their own sweet time about coming clear, and sometimes they do so in ways she would not have chosen.

Well, if she knows that much, she must have memory; and suddenly so she does, a great swoosh of scenes, voices, words, sensations, events, years and years worth roaring back into her head like a train in the night, brightly lit windows, faces pressed against glass, tearing through darkness full-tilt.

Banging into the hard wall of Lyle saying, "Hop in."

Where is Lyle, and where, for that matter, is she? In this darkness she can't make anything or anyone out, and has no sense that there's another soul in the room. At least it seems like a room, an enclosed, stable, solid feeling to the air. She must be lying down—how else could she achieve this quality of stillness?—but she isn't absolutely certain of even that much.

She is certain, though, that there must be other things she ought to be doing besides lying around in, presumably, a room for, presumably, some reason. What should she be doing? Depends what day it is, and what time.

Oh. She hadn't realized she doesn't know what day it is, or what time.

It's possible she's in a dream. That happens: layers of dream peeling away, resistant to waking, so that there's a dreaming awareness of dreaming a dream. That kind of dream is especially hard to rise out of. So this may only be an excursion into the unconscious that's unusually hard to rise out of.

Usually she dreams in colour, and in motion, and in some activity, however senseless and strange. This, if it's a dream, is a most silent, dark one.

She can remember quite a lot now; just about everything, she thinks, she could remember before.

Before what?

There's the missing memory: whatever that elusive *what* is, that leaves her without a clue where she is, or what day it is, or what time, or what she ought to be doing. Her days are filled, her schedule packed, and this, whatever it is, sure wasn't marked on it.

If she understood exactly how she might be lying down, she could likely figure out exactly how to get up, and get going. As it is, an unfamiliar disobedience seems to be occurring. Her brain orders, "Move," and nothing, apparently, happens.

This is ridiculous.

But say it's a dream: the trick in that case is to fall back into its full embrace, let whatever it is dream itself through, so that when she returns to the surface, the dream whole and completed, her real world will be there in all its colours and capacities, just as it always is when she's been sleeping and wakes. It's satisfying to find a sensible solution to a quandary, a puzzle, a dilemma. This is among the skills she's learned, sometimes in hard ways, in which she takes, therefore, some pride.

Although this time, it does not work that way.

This time, with return of consciousness there's light, thank God, a relief that she hasn't gone inexplicably blind, and there are also nearby but out-of-view voices. "What's happening here?" she tries to say. Not to mention, where exactly is here? Once again words don't emerge. Instead of dead silence, though, there's garbled sound that is chilling. She sounds like an idiot. Seriously. Or like somebody fresh from a terrible stroke. Someone whose eyes roll, and whose tongue lolls, that's what she sounds like, someone damaged either by implosive or explosive, internal or external forces.

Still, she knows those words: *implosive, explosive.* She can't have turned into an idiot, and how likely is it she can even have had some brain-damaging event like a stroke if she still knows words like that, even if she can't say them?

She recognizes Lyle's voice, although not the other man's and not, quite, the words, a sort of tumble-rumble in her ears, not unlike her own sounds. Which they must have heard; which perhaps even meant something to them because here they suddenly are, one youngish stranger, one Lyle, looking down at her, and it's good, reassuring, to see that she can see them. Senses, some of them, functioning.

Lyle is wearing the gardening shirt he had on as he sat in the truck saying, "Hop in": an old, soft, blue and black checkered thing, gone at the elbows, worn at the neck, cuffs rolled up his ropy forearms, whose tendons she is excessively fond of, enjoying the play of them working when he's doing something muscular, or just stretching, like reaching up to change a ceiling light bulb. But passion is not her mood at the moment, nor, it seems, his. His narrow features are drawn down and frowning, the tendons of his arms flexing with what looks like tension of a kind that is distant from pleasure.

She hopes he's not still wearing the heavy old boots and the worn blue jeans, as well as the shirt, in which he usually kicks around in the garden. They'd be muddy. She could swear she is straining to raise up her head, turn it to look, but the view doesn't change. Something hard and serious seems to have clamped itself to her head.

"What?" she inquires again, and the word sounds clearer this time, although she wouldn't know that from Lyle's face, which looks more scared than anything else. She would like to smile at him, just so he'd feel better. For all she knows, she is smiling. Perhaps in some scary fashion. The thought may be the deed, she can't tell, but she also can't see a reason she'd be better at smiling than at turning her head. This is all puzzling, and surely no dream.

Whatever it is, Lyle will fix it, she can rest easier with him at hand since he's a reliable fixer of practically everything, from Jamie's drug charge to the toilet when it wouldn't stop running. She's never seen him look quite this way before, though; as if he has no idea where to begin, and moreover is afraid of the task. From this angle, too, she can see how crumpled and worn his throat's skin has become: tissuey, fragile.

She is forty-nine, he is fifty-two; not old, either of them, but also by no means young. Saggy events have been occurring with her flesh as well, although in her case it's been more a matter of rippling than crumpling. "What is it?" she attempts, one more time.

She sees his lips move, hears him say "Isla," and then also for some reason hears "ice cream," and "You run in, I'll keep the truck running," although his mouth doesn't move beyond "Isla."

How ridiculous the two of them sound: Lyle and Isla, Isla and Lyle. There's no way to gracefully put those two names together. They're a tongue twister, lyrics to a gibberish song. They didn't actually notice this, or at least she didn't, until his older-by-five-minutes twin son William was toasting the newlyweds at their wedding six years ago and sounded so silly doing it, slightly pissed, that the whole room burst out laughing. Including Lyle and Isla, Isla and Lyle.

Why, when she can perfectly well see his hand reaching down to what must be her arm, or some real part of her, anyway, can she not feel his touch? Why won't he touch her? Why would he leave his hand hovering over her skin? That's almost cruel, in a way. It's not like him to hold himself back.

Oh. They were celebrating, that's what the ice cream is about. Another piece of information fallen in place: that Lyle's arteries were not after all about to explode or his heart to clench closed, because in just over ten months he'd ratcheted his cholesterol down from seven-point-something to five-point-something, and was in a mood to throw caution briefly aside.

Naturally at their ages they're aware of the possibility, moreover the likelihood, of encroachments from the inside: indiscernible nibblings by stray cells going exploring at the edges of organs, testing conditions for their own omnivorous, destroying survival. Lyle, especially, knows about this. Both of them would be horrified but not startled, exactly, by cancer or heart attack or kidney collapse, anything invisibly internal like that. Although they also know about the possibilities of accidental, external doom, these seem so random as to be faint and not worth considering, but never mind anything that came before—in just the eight years Lyle and Isla have been together, including the six married years, they've been to a number of funerals involving natural causes, as these things are termed. Friends. Colleagues. They rule out mere acquaintances. "I don't think it's something we want to do recreationally," Isla told Lyle. "Going to just anyone's funeral is a hobby we might want to hold off on for a few years."

Maybe she's dead. That would account for Lyle looking so unhappily down at her. Although it would hardly account for her looking back up.

They'd taken his spiked and unwholesome cholesterol count seriously. "I don't want to lose you," she'd said, tenderly because it was true, he has been something of a miracle, not to say revelation.

She imagined his arteries like the mysterious events that regularly occur on expressways: you're booting along nicely just over the speed limit, happily singing to the radio or a favourite CD, looking forward to an agreeable destination, and all of a sudden there's a whole line of brake lights ahead, a blockage, a jam that slows everything to a crawl, ages and ages spent creeping until finally there's a couple of cars twisted together in the left lane, or construction narrowing the right lane, and sometimes there's no visible reason at all and the traffic just clears and you're back to booting along nicely, humming along. She'd imagined, when he came home reporting those high cholesterol levels, his arteries just like that, flowing smoothly and then suddenly clogging up, moving sluggishly, moving, fatally, not at all.

They ate salads, low-fat cheeses, egg substitutes, lentils—dear lord, they now have a whole stack of recipes for various lentil manifestations. Naturally when he came home from the doctor's, happy as a kid with a good report card, with his five-decimal-something cholesterol count, he wanted a treat. "Ice cream," he said. "The real thing. Just once, I promise, but I want a big Rocky Road. Or double chocolate, with thousands and thousands of chips."

She saw traffic parting in front of them, the driving clear and easy, returning to cruise control, only more watchful now, more alert.

They are responsible, she and Lyle, to each other's lives. That's what marriage now means; to her, anyway. She hopes, if she is not managing to smile as she would like to, that her eyes send this warm message to him. He looks so unhappy! She can't see beyond the unhappiness, although his face usually has a capacity for layers and layers of expression, if she watches closely enough. She can on occasion, for instance, perceive anger behind gentle concern, or vice versa, and often enough there's some kind of laughter, and some variation of affection in the lines of his face, the set of his lips, the tenor and shape of his eyes.

If he laughed right now, she would feel a whole lot better. If he even just smiled, she would be reassured.

He was laughing when they left home for the ice cream, laughing at her because he'd swept her into his light-hearted whim without giving her time to change from her work clothes, which happened to be the midnight-blue linen suit with the snug, fitted skirt that's tricky when it comes to manoeuvring into the truck. It rucked up around her thighs, and he helped her pull it down, although not right away.

What comes next?

Driving out the lane, she supposes. Down the road. Into town. But that's not a particular vision, it's not something she sees but something she's done so many times her head can re-create each dip and turn, every culvert, roadside rock, fence and crop.

She sees Lyle bending over her, she sees whiskers and pores. She hears the younger man on the other side of her talking. "The damaged vertebrae," he is saying, the end of an incomprehensible sentence.

Lyle says, "What does that mean? What will it mean?" Bless him, he speaks for her, takes the words right out of her mouth and in addition, more than she can do at the moment, apparently, makes sense of them, makes them come out right, not mangled, like her.

"There's a lot of variables. It may work itself free, so we'll give it a little time, I think. Either way, probably surgery a bit down the road. To get it out, one way or another. In any case there are many possibilities, a lot of levels of outcome, plenty of room for hope, you know. It's tricky, with the damage that's already been done and the bullet fragment lodged where it is, but we should know soon what direction we're heading."

From too little information, suddenly too much. Vertebrae. Surgery. Bullet. Not an ending to something strange and confusing, but the beginning of something too awful to contemplate.

One of those moments when life turns completely ass-over-teakettle, in no good way, no good way at all.

Nobody with Any Sense

RODDY IS SO COLD, SO COLD. Even though it's a stinking hot night, and everybody's windows are open, and people have been going around all day with hardly any clothes on, Roddy cannot stop shivering. He's not dressed for this, is just wearing jeans and a T-shirt and sneakers, not even socks. He would give anything for a fireplace, a fleece-lined jacket, heavy boots. He can hardly remember how warmth feels, although he was sweating when he woke up this morning, and maybe that was partly from knowing what he planned for the day to contain, but it was also just stifling. His grandmother doesn't have air conditioning. It would have been nice to do something about that. People are going to think he's a bad person, and will feel sorry for her and for his dad, too, but some of Roddy's ideas weren't selfish or greedy at all.

Buster, Roddy's grandmother's old part-collie, part-shepherd, was just lying on his side this morning on the kitchen floor tiles, unwilling to move although Roddy tried to coax him. "It's all right," his grandmother said, "he's been out. He won't feel much like a walk today. Nobody with any sense would." Then, all that heavy fur looked kind of horrifying and cruel. Now Roddy would give just about anything to have his arms around Buster, his face shoved into Buster's coat, smelling that slightly rank, warm, friendly, familiar, old dog smell.

Roddy misses a whole lot of things. For one thing, he misses this morning. Time shouldn't be like this. A person should be able to go back and start over if they find out something that looked okay is a huge mistake. There should be a few hours' leeway.

If he was home, his grandmother would set out with blankets and hot chocolate to get him warmed up, but he's seen enough shocked, horrified eyes for one day. He couldn't stand shocked, horrified, disappointed, betrayed eyes.

Maybe he should just kill himself: try to sneak off to the river and walk straight out into the water. Or there must be something sharp lying around someplace close that he could slice himself open with. Then he wouldn't have to see anyone's face. Also then if he was cold, he wouldn't have to feel being cold. He wouldn't feel anything if he was dead.

Except what if he changed his mind? Waded in one footstep too far, or lost one drop of blood too many, no way back, floundering or seeping his regretful way out of life? Which would completely figure, on a day when he hasn't made a single good choice. So maybe till he can work out a few things, he'd better keep lying low out here in the tall grass, shivering and watching the early glow of town lights and stars. Darkness takes forever to fall this time of year. Usually it can't stay light long enough to suit him, but tonight he is a mole, a bat. An owl, except that he's hiding, not hunting.

In full darkness he could probably navigate out of here pretty easily. He knows this turf well, has spent hours of his life following fence lines and ditches, tramping through fields, not doing anything much, really, except seeing what's there. Which keeps changing: frogs, daisies, dead dried-up snakes; then all of a sudden a strip mall. Fox tracks, sometimes, in winter. Groundhogs and different kinds and textures of grasses and grains; then a new clump of houses. On the other side of this field is a bare and brittle dead elm, its limbs an eerie sort of landmark even in full light. Now it's both eerie and comforting. He knows where he is. If it were dark he could maybe get somewhere else.

How did he even get this far?

He never pictured having to hide, any more than he pictured being so cold. He's so stupid! All the stuff he didn't expect, when he thought it was all simple and his cleverness was just figuring out its simplicity.

By now everybody must know. His grandmother will probably be telling everybody how wrong they must be, but underneath he bets she knows. Underneath he bets her heart is in pieces. He wouldn't hurt her for anything, but he has. Why didn't he see that this morning? How could he not have understood?

His dad'll probably be sitting in his chair in the living room, downwind from the TV, shaking his head, looking mournful. Nothing new there, he looks mournful a lot of the time. This time he'll have something to look mournful about. Roddy can just hear his father's limp voice saying over and over, "I don't know," and sighing. "I really don't know."

Once a few years ago, in Roddy's last year of public school, his dad didn't show up for the play Roddy had a pretty big part in, even though he'd promised. Roddy's grandmother tried to smooth it over. "Your dad's had a lot of disappointments in his life. Sometimes he just doesn't manage everything very well."

"Why should I care?" What Roddy meant was, it wasn't fair, if his father'd had so many disappointments, for him to go around spreading disappointment to other people. If he'd had so many himself, he ought to know better.

Roddy's grandmother is totally different. "You'll be a fine man," she tells Roddy, and "Set your sights high, you can be whatever you want in this world." Only, she wouldn't have dreamed this could possibly have been, even briefly, even for the few thrilling weeks since the idea cropped up, what he could want.

Now he most fervently doesn't want it. He cannot believe this has happened to him. He doesn't want to think about that woman, either. Oh God.

Just a little bit darker and he can try making a run for it. For what? But he can't just lie here freezing and waiting for somebody else to make the next move.

It might be nice if somebody did, though. It might be nice not to have to make any more decisions and choices. He's awfully tired.

He curls onto his side. He wants to make himself small and, if possible, cozy. He has no spare flesh. That's maybe partly why he's so cold. His grandmother's big, there's lots of extra to her, and in the winter she laughs and says the bulk helps keep her warm. This time of year, though, she really suffers, sometimes looks as if she can't breathe deep enough, isn't getting air through all that flesh. Last summer for the first time she didn't do any baking, and not much cooking either, during the real hot spells. "I'm getting too old for all that," she said, although actually she's only sixty-two which, while fairly ancient, isn't like the end of the road.

This could kill her. Now and then, just for a few seconds, Roddy forgets why he's lying here. What has he done? Why didn't he think? He pounds a fist into his forehead. Pain is what he deserves. In a matter of one day, or one night, he has stupidly, carelessly, thoughtlessly changed his whole, entire life.

That's too strange: that everything that happens from now on has to spin off from this single day.

He wonders how Mike is doing, how Mike has done. He wonders what happens to buddies in very bad times. Mike has been Roddy's best friend forever, right from when he and his mother knocked on Roddy's grandmother's door the first day Roddy and his dad came there to live. Roddy was seven, upset and skinny, Mike was eight and stocky and had a weird short spiky haircut and bold eyes. The grown-ups sent them out to ride their bikes around the neighbourhood together. "Be careful," Mike's mother warned. "Show Roddy the stop signs and lights. Show him the school, too, why don't you?" That was ten years ago, more than half their lives. Now their interests have suddenly, after all this time, gone in different directions. Mike, although not innocent, isn't quite guilty, either, at least not of how things turned out. When it comes to that one huge, grave moment, Roddy was, is, on his own.

It made sense at the time, their idea. How could it have?

They nurtured it, admired it, went over and over together how sleekly it would work, how smoothly events would follow one after another. It was like in other summers when they'd figure out some trip out of town on their bikes, or last year in Mike's parents' car when he got his licence, and even if they were only going to be gone a little while, they went over routes, good stopping places, what food they might feel like. Planning was part of the whole thing, talking about it beforehand wasn't separate from the excursion itself. It didn't mean they ruled out surprises. They took surprises for granted. Surprises were why they went.

Maybe they didn't think so much about surprises this time because they weren't planning something that would be fun, exactly. They did practise, though, more than usual, because this project had a real thrilling edginess to it, a new sort of adventure. They grew attached to rehearsing their moves. They refined the words over and over although the plan looked so simple, just another walk in the country. Roddy's pretty sure Mike started it, and it was just a laugh, a bit of a joke between them at first. Who made it start to be serious? How did that happen, and when?

Maybe Roddy did that part. Sometimes Mike, who's eighteen, which makes a difference, slugs Roddy's shoulder when Roddy's been actually trying to think something through and says, "Lighten up, don't be so serious."

He keeps seeing what happened. The little quick unwanted pictures flashing on his eyelids are bad enough, without putting words to them.

There were sirens, lots of them. By the time he arrived in this field breathless after walking fast and straight through a few streets where there might be people, then starting to run, and running doubled down for quite a while, and dodging behind trees, into ditches, over fences, scrambling and panting and very near tears, even the echo of sirens had stopped. In the distance, though, when he peered back, he could see red whirling lights, going slowly up and down streets. They must have called in cops from outside the town, too, the ones that patrol in the country. The lights are still out there.

As soon as it's pitch dark he'll start moving again.

He only has a couple of bucks on him, and no food, nothing to drink, no wheels. He and Mike never went off so unprepared, not even when they were little kids. Once it's dark he can start moving again, but where'll he go, and what'll he do when he gets there?

It's just, he can't think of anything else.

Unless he could sneak home, creep upstairs, get hold of a whole pile of blankets and burrow in till he was warm again. Except he's never going to be safe. The house'll be crawling with cops; or they'll be watching it, anyway.

He's kind of mad at Mike now. He shouldn't have to be out here alone.

Well, he is. And it's almost dark enough to get moving. Past the shadowy elm there's a fence, then another wide field, a pasture with short, exposing grass, and then another fence, a ditch and a big wooded area, not quite a forest. Once he gets there, there's a creek, even though the water's probably full of shit, and some walnut trees and probably berries.

Right, like he'd know how to live off the land. But it's something, anyway. It's the start of some kind of possibility, maybe.

Two fields back the way he came, from out by the first concession road out of town, he hears barking. Has that been going on long? It's like sometimes he tunes out, gets tuned into just his own head. The barking sounds deep and focused. Two dogs, maybe. Not small ones. Eager ones. Kind of excited, sort of happy-sounding, like Buster when he was younger and got a squirrel up a tree.

Oh shit, oh Jesus. Roddy's up on his feet and running. His arms pump like a whole track team put together, he flies through the thigh-high grain with his eyes on the elm, and past it vaults one-handed over the fence. The pasture is stony and rough. Are there cattle, is there a bull? The barking doesn't diminish, it gets closer and louder and acquires a thrilled sort of tone. Then it stops, which is worse. Nothing else stops, though. Roddy keeps flying, so agile and young and light, so desperate and exhausted and grief-stricken, tears and sweat mingling and blurring until finally, mercifully, there's a whoosh through the air behind him, a large form leaping, careful jaws closing around one of his arms, tilting him off balance, bringing him thumping, bruisingly, down, and he's on his back looking up into stars and a solemn, pointed, alert face on one side, a matching one on the other, and he hears the shouts and thuddings of men and closes his eyes for a moment because everything's over and whatever happens now will be happening to somebody completely different, with a completely new life, all of it that quick, that sharp, that unbelievable.

Tied Up, Bound Down

THE DOCTOR'S NAME, THE YOUNGER, dark-haired guy she saw hovering over her, across her bedside from Lyle, is apparently Grant. "Thanks, Dr. Grant," Isla hears Lyle's ragged voice saying from, it must be, a doorway which she cannot from her angle see. "I'd like her children to be able to talk to you tomorrow. What time works best?"

Good Lyle. Knowing that would be important, and then making it happen, forcing it to. She knows, although not very personally, about the rushed lives of doctors, and their reluctance, too, to get very involved with families. They have a point. She isn't sure herself that she wants Jamie and Alix hanging over her, disrupting further what is already an odd and awful disruption. But it's necessary, among family, to bear anything; and maybe they'll rise to the occasion, who knows? Depending, perhaps, on what the occasion actually is. Or on how weary they are of their troublesome parents' distressing events.

Well, though, it's her turn, isn't it?

At least she can assume she's not dying. If Jamie and Alix don't need to see Dr. Grant till tomorrow, it implies there will be a tomorrow, and that there's something to talk about. She would like to know what that is. Jamie and Alix aren't the only ones in the dark.

She would like at least not to be scared; not *this* scared.

When she says, "Lyle?" the word comes out plain. So she is making some progress here, unless of course it's only plain in her ears and not in the room. But if it is clear, surely next thing she knows she'll be swinging her legs over the side of the bed, standing up, getting out.

Getting out of where? Hospital, obviously, but which one and what sort? Lyle must have gone off with the doctor. Within the range of her vision, there's only off-whiteness, broken by chrome. A creamy, pitted tiled ceiling. Something nearby is making slow whuffing sounds, like the breath of a giant. There's also something stuck into her nose, although it doesn't impede breathing, which seems strange. The actual terror, though, lies in this business of feeling nothing, except in her head. She can't figure it out, a circumstance in which there's no sensation, not even pain. If she is lying down, which she obviously is, there should be a feeling of flatness, of her spine, shoulders, legs, and arms actually resting on something. If she is in a bed, she should also be able to feel some weight and pressure, even if it's only of a sheet tucking her in.

Oh please, she wants to be *home*. She wants whatever this is to be undone, so that she can go back with Lyle to their miraculous life. This isn't fair, she has had, in the scheme of things, barely a taste of this reward, this well-earned achievement. She is owed so much more! She wants to go *home*.

Eight years ago, the first time she saw Lyle's farm, or at least the house and the property directly around it on what isn't quite a farm, more a country place, she thought she'd died and gone to heaven. "But this is perfect," she said as they joggled the final potholed metres in his truck up the laneway. "Perfect."

Previous to meeting him she would, mistakenly and urbanly, have called the laneway a driveway. She was nervous then, too, about travelling into what as far as she knew was a wilderness, like a movie, like *Deliverance*, something like that, with a man she'd only known a few weeks. Because who knows what can happen in a man's heart when he's removed from influences, controls? There was something good in his features, both kindness and sharpness around his eyes, but who really knew?

So she drove with him up that long driveway, laneway, wondering and slightly fearful. Then was struck in the heart by what she saw. "It's a classic, all right," he agreed. It was early days. Isla mistrusted the business of getting to know each other, perhaps he did, too, because it would simply, likely, mean moving towards outcomes in which she had no faith and for which she mainly thought, after James, she'd lost heart. "Takes a lot of work, though." She could feel Lyle's pride as he watched her regarding the place.

"But it must be worth every minute. It's beautiful." So it was. *Beautiful* was inadequate. Even *perfect* fell short. *Sanctuary* might have come close.

For him, too, he said. He had lived there for three years by the time he and Isla drove up that laneway. He had spent almost all his spare time in those years improving it, tearing down, building up, making it his. If Isla was already inclining, dubiously, in favour of affection for him, she fell in love with his home. As far as she knows he has never been jealous of that, or suspicious of motives. In fact she has thought that if she hadn't fallen in love at first sight with the place he'd cared for and worked on so hard, he would have thought less of her. His home was not exactly a test, but it was still something that could be failed.

The laneway was lined densely and arced over with big, leaning old weeping willows and maples. "It washes out every year," he said, explaining the potholes and ruts. "Takes a few loads of fill and gravel, late spring." Then abruptly, what was revealed at the end, around a slight curve, was a two-storey, yellow brick house, solid and plain except for its copper-toned roof and intricate corners designed with extra interlaced bricks. Dark green shutters sheltered spare, rectangular windows, and a deep-green-painted porch wrapped itself around two sides of the house, one side at that moment in full sunshine, the other shaded by another arching maple. Curved wooden and wicker chairs and tables, a roll-up sailcloth blind at one end, also deep green.

This was where he came after his wife Sandra died, of breast cancer, which had led to clusters of other cancers, more than rampant enough to eat her alive, and after he'd shepherded his two nearly grown sons, twins, whom Isla hadn't yet met, through adolescence and grief, and after he'd recovered his own balance and begun looking around, observing what his solitary desires might be, and had gone out in pursuit of them, coming, finally, upon this place.

"What I decided I wanted," he told her, "after all the years in the city, was space. Just elbow room. Perhaps it's partly longing for something you haven't had, but do you find that in one situation, you sometimes have dreams of another?" Oh yes. Isla nodded, but although he paused, eyebrows raised, she didn't begin saying why, or how, or in what circumstances that had occurred.

"All those years I'd lived with Sandy, and then very shortly the boys, and I had no idea what being alone would be like. Frightening, of course, I expected that in a way, trying something that would seriously require some effort, but a challenge. And a kind of triumph if it turned out. I made a couple of real estate agents nuts showing me this, showing me that, when all I knew was that it had to be within driving distance of work and that I'd know when I saw it.

"And then the agent called, said something had just come on the market, an estate sale, she hadn't seen it but it might be a good deal, although she'd heard it was also fairly rundown. I came out on my own, mostly out of guilt by then about wasting her time. Couldn't find the place to begin with, went back and forth past the laneway, because it doesn't look as if it goes anywhere, but finally I gave up and turned in. Hit bottom a couple of times on the laneway, bounced around, got pissed off and then—there it was. Coming around that curve and that was it. I didn't care what it cost, or how much work it was going to take, or what I'd have to do. It was the most amazing thing ever happened to me in my life. Well, except for the boys being born, but that's different. This was mine. It was just me. And it was a surprise, even a shock. The boys were totally right, and so was this, but it was an entirely different thing." Isla had thought of the births of her own kids: magic, yes. Shocks and surprises, indeed.

So many aspects to be leery of, with a still-unfamiliar man who came with a jam-packed history: a dead wife growing, perhaps, increasingly golden with time; the naturally passionate attachment to offspring, which Isla herself knew something about; even a susceptibility to miraculous places. Isla wondered why he had taken her there, what reason she'd imagined for going there with him. "And now you're here," he'd said then, "and that seems right, too."

So it was. And oh, she wants to be there. They should not have left, they should not have stepped from that porch, climbed into that truck, gone off for ice cream. They could have been safe.

But instead, here she is; and now here he is, too, back in this strange off-white room. He is lowering himself beside another hospital bed, leaning carefully over another wife, his features looking pinched, the lines that run from the side of his nose down past his lips deeper than normal. He looks, this man to whom Isla edged closer and closer before finally giving up, giving in, falling into faith, weary now; nearly old. God knows how she looks. "Mirror," she says.

He is clearly alarmed. "Oh no, not yet. You're still kind of wonky." *Wonky*: which means distorted and skewed. Which may also mean scary.

He can't realize it's not just about seeing her face, it's seeing that she has one; that she's still real at all. "Mirror," she repeats, and he sighs and stands and moves out of her line of vision.

In a few moments he's beside her again, holding a round green-plastic-framed mirror to his chest, arms folded across it. "Listen," he says, "it'll probably look worse to you than to anyone else. It's too soon, you're still puffy and bruised. Partly because of the tubes. So don't be shocked, okay? You're going to be fine." If she could, she would gesture impatiently. He sighs and steps forward, turns the mirror away from himself, aims it directly above her.

Oh. He should have warned her. Somebody should have said.

This is a gargoyle. Grey-skinned, except for some bruising near her nostrils. Tubes, a nasty yellowish colour, holding those nostrils wide above a plastic span joining them. Eyes, her wide blue eyes diminished to slitty, peering things in a bed of charcoal flesh. Her skin is stretched thin over cheeks, chin, jowls— she has jowls!—that have bloated, look full to bursting. Her curly, cropped auburn hair, discernibly grey at the roots from this angle, is spiked and dirty. And clamping the whole thing, a metal frame, curved and padded. Which accounts for why her head doesn't move, and why she has to look straight up into this mirror or slant her eyes as best she can sideways.

Oh. This is the horror Lyle's been looking at. For how long? If she could do one thing, one single thing, she would put her hands over this face.

"Tell me," she says, and watches Lyle's lips turn briefly inward, as he takes a difficult breath. She is relieved that she can see and hear even minor events exceptionally clearly, and wonders if that's supposed to be some sort of compensation for loss, for what she can't put her fingers on.

For what, if she could put her fingers on it, she wouldn't be able to feel.

Where are her fingers? What are they doing? Lyle's hands are down there somewhere, around where hers should probably be, his clever deft hands she would like to be holding. When they were in court, in the moments before Jamie's verdict was announced, Lyle's hand was the strongest, most comforting, sturdiest and most reliable set of bones and flesh in the world. She wondered right then how she would have managed to sit there without that hand, and what on earth she'd hung onto before it came along. She squeezed it, he said later, numb. Maybe now he's squeezing hers numb.

She not only looks grotesque, it seems she exists now only in her head. This is like an old horror movie: a laboratory run by a mad, wild-haired scientist, with a disembodied head in a jar, a battle between the proud but horrified scientist and the furiously calculating, raging brain. The scientist is a victim of his own sacrilegious ambition to create. The head, reliant on wits and ruthlessness, is also a victim of that sacrilegious ambition. Nobody wins. Everything is destroyed, for the error of hubris, the mistake of going too far.

They were only going for ice cream, not far at all.

"Tell me!" Because terror does not improve for its causes being unknown.

Vertebrae. Surgery. Bullet.

In bitter moments James used to look at her, narrow-eyed, narrow-lipped, threateningly low-voiced, and say, "Don't ask anything you're not ready to hear the answer to." It eventually became obvious what he must have meant. Isla would say there are some questions for whose answers there's no such thing as being prepared, but which there's also, as with the mirror, no option about asking. She also thinks that her outlook always was more complex and interesting than James's, who turned out to be disappointingly simple-minded, really.

"Do you remember any of it?" Lyle's voice is low, slightly trembling, determinedly gentle. And oh, of course, he'd have no way to know what she knows and what she does not. He has no idea where gaps begin and end, and where he should start filling them in. Funny how she must have assumed he would know. Funny how much she has come to imagine he understands.

Perhaps his deepest desire at the moment is to run out of the room. Or to rage, or to weep. At any rate, likely his deepest desire is not to sit here regarding her, looking old and speaking further words she's pretty sure she's not keen to hear, but must. "I'm sorry," she says, meaning in a general sort of way, sorry for imposing, taking his energy, time, generosity of spirit, for looking hideous and for being a burden in a way she doesn't yet understand, and which she has to rely on him to make clear. Even that, the explanation, is something he signed up for, marrying her.

Mere love doesn't encompass burdens like that. Marriage does. Lyle and Isla are tied up, bound down in ways that are not necessarily permanent, but which do apply, without doubt, to this moment. Just as Jamie and even Alix, who are irretrievably permanent, surely have no real choice but to come.

"Cholesterol," she manages, although the word comes out somehow backwards. "Ice cream." Even that's slurred.

"Really? That's what you remember?" He sighs slightly again.

If a sudden traffic jam had occurred in the freeways of his arteries, would she have sighed? Would she even, maybe, have felt trapped, or doomed, to have him entirely reliant on her, and her goodwill? Now she can't look at him. What if she saw in him that kind of despair?

"Dr. Grant said you might not remember," Lyle says. "He said that often happens with shock. I mean, some shocking event, not that you're *in* shock. That it goes blank, but might all come suddenly back."

"What else?"

"Did he tell me?"

"Yes. What will happen. To me." Words are exhausting, she is getting worn out.

"Well, nothing really, right away. They want to wait, do more scans and tests, see what happens. They think it might work its own way out, which would be the best thing. If it doesn't show signs of doing that, or if the tests start to show differently, then surgery. Likely surgery anyway, even if it does work itself free, but in that case it wouldn't be as difficult. It's a good thing you're healthy. Well, healthy, you know what I mean. Strong to begin with. Anyway, they'll see. We'll see. They're really good here, and they have high hopes. They think your chances are good."

Has she never noticed before that he leaves out crucial words in just about every sentence, or is this newly acquired, a dodging and weaving response to whatever this is? What is the "it," would it be the bullet the doctor referred to? And what are the "hopes," and what are the "chances" they have in mind?

She looks for a word she might be able to say, and comes up with "vague."

Lyle nods. "Yes, well, it has to be, for a while, anyway. They don't like committing themselves, too many lawsuits, probably, or warnings from lawyers like me about saying anything's a sure thing. But you and I know this isn't permanent, and of course you'll be moving and walking again. Very soon. This is just an interruption, but we'll get through it, and you'll be back to normal in a flash."

Her listening stops after "permanent," when he gets to "moving and walking." Although she catches the "we" and is grateful.

His determined optimism sounds not only incomplete, but ominous. And also undependable, which from him is a blow in itself. "Tell me," she says again. "Now," she demands, and he bows his head, and takes another deep breath.

A Strange, Faraway Sky

RODDY CAME TO THIS TOWN, to his grandmother's house, kicking and screaming. That was ten years ago. Now, lying flat on his back in the tall grain, watched over by two alert dogs and a thousand stars, he is dumbfounded by loss: that he cannot go home.

He finds things out too late. His rhythms are clumsy, he's too often a beat or two off. That would account for today.

Some of his most momentous, although not always best, moments have been spent just like this: lying on his back, very still, looking upwards.

It's how, when he was seven, he spent the first night of his and his dad's long stay at his grandmother's house. He never threw tantrums, but the day they moved, his dad's loaded car leading the small moving truck that was enough for all they had left, Roddy screamed the whole way. When they reached town, he started kicking the dash. When they pulled up in front of his grandmother's stuccoed grey house, he gripped the steering wheel, then the door frame, as his dad hauled him grimly out of the car. He even kicked at his grandmother, who held her arms around him hard.

By the time the three of them finally had supper, he was worn out. He was packed off to his new bedroom at the top of the house, while his grandmother and his dad made room downstairs for the things Roddy and his dad had arrived with. Roddy's grandmother left a blue, teardrop-shaped nightlight plugged in by his bed, and its faintly reflecting light made the ceiling look like some strange, faraway sky.

He was very angry. About being uprooted from everything that was familiar; but also, if his mother went back to their little house in the city, and they weren't there any more, how would she find them?

One morning his mother was there, giving Roddy a hug and a pat on the bum as he went off to school, and then when he got home the front door wasn't locked and when he let himself in, nobody was there. Well, sometimes she wasn't home, so that wasn't strange for a couple of hours, even though she usually said if she was going to be out, maybe off to a movie, or on what she called one of her rambles.

Usually his dad went away in the mornings and came home at night and ate supper and turned on the TV and, sometime after Roddy did, went to bed. He'd tap Roddy's shoulder sometimes, or ruffle his hair, call him "pal," and if Roddy wanted or needed anything, he took care of it, like he brought home Roddy's first two-wheeler, even though he wasn't around much to help him learn to ride it. It was Roddy's mother did that, running up and down the sidewalk holding the seat, keeping him more or less steady. She was fun. Like, she put up a pup tent in their tiny back yard so she and Roddy could camp out together, and they stayed up late while she told scary stories and made shadows with her hands on the canvas walls. At the park down the street, she screamed and laughed louder even than he did while she pushed him as high as the swings would go, higher than he could have ever gone on his own.

But then sometimes she got really tired and sad, and wouldn't get out of bed, or off the sofa, day after day. "I'm sorry, sweetie," she'd say, "I'm just not myself today."

Except if somebody wasn't herself half the time, wouldn't that be herself too? It was kind of confusing, but also dependable. He knew she'd be one thing or the other. It sometimes felt, in his friends' houses, as if the adults were unreliable because even though they could smile or speak sharply, it didn't always feel true, either one. Like they were wearing Hallowe'en masks. His mother wasn't like that.

Sometimes she bugged Roddy's dad until they went out, to a movie or dancing, even though his dad usually didn't want to. When they went out, Roddy's mother got all sort of glittery in the eyes. She looked happy.

When she still wasn't back that day by the time his dad got home, and when his dad wasn't surprised and was carrying pizza and started putting it out on two plates, that was strange too. He put a hand on Roddy's shoulder and said, "Come into the living room, son, I've got something to tell you."

Roddy was narrow and everybody said he looked like his mum, who was little and thin and had hair nearly as short as his, except curlier. In the living room, he perched on the edge of the sofa, like he did the days she was lying there with a blanket over her, just watching TV and sleeping, the days she wasn't whooping around making up things to do.

"I don't know if you understand," his dad began finally, "that your mother has had some problems. You know how sometimes she's happy and sometimes she isn't?" Roddy nodded. "Well, look." His dad leaned forward in his chair, his elbows on his knees, letting his big hands hang down loose. Look at what? His dad wasn't even looking at Roddy, he was sort of staring into a corner, or maybe at the blank TV screen.

"Look, what that is, it turns out, is, it's a kind of sickness she has. Most people don't feel as good as she does sometimes, and for sure most people don't feel as bad. It's been hard on her going one way, then the other. Well, it's been hard on us all." Roddy shook his head; not hard on him.

"Anyway, today was a really bad day and what happened was, she hurt herself because she was feeling so terrible. So where she is, is in a hospital. She's been to two hospitals today, actually. The first one was because she made her wrists bleed pretty bad, so we had to get that fixed up. And then she had to go to another hospital where they're going to take care of her for a while and make sure she doesn't want to hurt herself any more. You see?"

No. Roddy stared, but he sure didn't see.

How did his dad know all this, for one thing? He worked all day. "She phoned me," his dad said, as if he could hear what Roddy was thinking. "I called an ambulance and met her at the first hospital. See though, that's a good thing, that she called. It means she didn't want to, uh, she didn't want to hurt herself too bad. And she didn't want you to be scared when you came home from school. Because she was real sick today, but she was thinking of you and that's a good sign."

Roddy slid off the sofa and stood in front of his dad. "Let's go see her."

His father shook his head. "We can't, I'm afraid. The hospital doesn't want us to. Anyway she's too sick."

"Has she got bandages?"

"Some, yes. Just on her arms."

She'd cut herself? On purpose she made herself bleed? When Roddy skinned his knees, or had a nosebleed, his mother got a wrinkly look while she put on the antiseptic and bandages or had him tilt his head back and wrapped ice cubes in tea towels. She didn't like blood. Why would she make herself bleed? His eyes narrowed. Could his father be lying? Had he made up this story to hide something different, or worse? "I want to go see my mum."

"I know you do, son." His dad sighed. "But we can't. I'm sorry, but we can't." He did look sad. Not the way Roddy's mother could look sad, like her face had gone dead, but like he might cry. And then he looked right at Roddy and put his face into another arrangement and said in a new, louder voice, "So it's just us boys, we can do what we want, so what do you feel like? We could go bowling, or a movie, whatever you'd like. Or we could make popcorn and watch TV till bedtime. What do you say?"

What Roddy would have said, if he dared, was how come his dad didn't always go to movies or whatever with his mum when she wanted? He shrugged. "I don't care. When's Mum coming home, tomorrow?"

"Not tomorrow. I don't know. We'll see."

"We'll see" was never a good thing.

Who turned up the next day instead of his mother was his dad's mother, with a couple of suitcases. She didn't live all that far away, only in a town instead of the city, and Roddy liked her but only knew her from visits, really. She kept hugging Roddy. Watching TV, she'd reach out and draw him into her cushiony side and they'd sit together on the sofa like that. But days went by, and she couldn't tell him enough about his mother, and he still wasn't allowed to go see her. "I know you miss her, honey," his grandmother said, "but she's too sick to have company."

He couldn't figure out what *sick* meant. Was she throwing up? He kept trying to find different ways to ask because maybe he just wasn't saying it right, so nobody knew how to give the right answers.

"No, honey, she's not throwing up, they could probably fix it more easily if she was sick that way. She's sick another way, inside her head where it's harder to fix."

"Is she going to die?" The first time he asked that, it took all his courage, but after that it got easier because the answer was always the same good one. "Oh no, it's not the kind of sickness that makes people die, don't you worry about that."

"Is it catching?" Like measles, or mumps, which would explain why he couldn't go see her. When people had things other people could catch, they had to stay by themselves, except for whoever looked after them. Who was looking after his mother? She'd be scared if it was strangers.

"No, it's not that kind of sickness, either. Honestly, Roddy, it really is that she gets too happy sometimes and then she gets way too downhearted. You know that yourself, I know you do. But it's hard to fix because the doctors don't understand as much as they do when it's just something in the body that's not right."

Wouldn't it make his mother happy to see him?

Didn't she miss him?

"Where's your mother?" kids at school asked.

"In the hospital. She's sick." They treated him nicer, like they were impressed. Teachers, too, nobody got impatient when he didn't know the answer to an arithmetic question or stumbled when he was reading out loud in class. He kind of liked that part of it, and tried to keep looking brave.

From the drawer of the dining room sideboard where photos were kept, he sneaked a couple of pictures: one of her and him in the park, the other of her and him and his dad in front of the Christmas tree. He hid them under his sweater until he could get upstairs and stick them under his mattress. After that he could take them out all he wanted, as long as his dad and grandmother were safely downstairs. He wasn't sure why having them close should be a secret, but it was. He stared and stared at her face. She was laughing in both of the photographs, and when she laughed, her mouth was the biggest part of her face. He wondered if he took the pictures because he might forget exactly what she looked like. He hoped not.

"Does Dad see her?" he asked. "Doesn't she want to see me?"

He was pretty sure the answers would be *yes* and *yes of course*, and so they were. "Your father has been twice," his grandmother said, "but she's still quite sick so they don't really think it's a good idea. And yes of course she wants to see you, she misses you, but she's not ready for visits."

Who was the *they*? There were people he didn't even know who got to say not just what he did, and his mother did, but what his dad did, too. *They* must be very big and important. If he didn't know them, how could he know if they were good people, or if they really cared, or if they were doing awful things to her? Like on TV when important people did bad things to other people for no special reason.

"Will she come home sometime?" he asked in despair. He no longer imagined *tomorrow*, but he wanted to know a day would arrive and there she'd be, carrying a suitcase because she'd have needed a lot of stuff to stay away for so long, and she'd be laughing on the doorstep, swooping her arms around him, her mouth the biggest part of her face.

"Well, they're certainly trying. They're trying more new medicines, so we'll just have to wait and see how it goes." He hadn't expected that. He wouldn't have asked if he'd imagined getting an uncertain answer like that.

He came home from school and there was a for sale sign on the lawn. His father said, "Roddy, we've decided we need to make a few changes." His grandmother hugged him and said, "You know, poor Buster, I've left him far too long with the neighbours. He'll be so happy to see us again." She said, "You can take anything of your own that you want. Whatever makes you feel right at home."

It was a matter of money, his dad explained. He'd be selling the house and a lot of their things because there were new bills he hadn't expected and there was still a big mortgage on this place. "What's a mortgage?" was what Roddy thought to ask then, at the moment.

The sort of thing he asked later was "Can't Grandma sell her house and move here?" and "But what about Mum? What if she comes and we're not here any more?" Flatly, clearly, helplessly and pointlessly, he said, over and over, "I don't want to," and "I'm not going," and "You can't make me." But of course they could.

All that kicking and screaming the day they moved, it felt good. It felt like something useful and helpful, like if his mother did it, it would cheer her right up. His grandmother held her big arms around him and would have kept them there except he kicked at her and wrenched free. "Don't worry," she told his dad, "I'm fine. You can't expect him not to be upset. He's best left alone for the time being."

His dad hauled in boxes and lamps, a couple of chairs, stuff like that, and it piled up in his grandmother's little front hall. His grandmother took his father a beer and said, "Just leave it all for a while," and "I know it's been hard for you, but oh my, I am glad to be back in my own house."

After a while there were smells from the kitchen. They had supper, and then Roddy went off to bed, in his new room at the top of the house, with the blue nightlight casting a faint, reflecting light upwards. He lay on his new bed, furious until the moment, he guessed, he fell asleep.

The next day he made his first, best, real friends: Buster, who woke him up bouncing onto his bed, and Mike, who turned up at the door with his mother.

Other than that, well, this is a small town and people know things. So they knew why he and his dad moved in with his grandmother. When he started school, it was different from his other one. Like, people looked at him weird, like they were waiting for him to do something strange. One bold kid, who was in fourth grade, marched up the first day at recess and poked a finger into his chest and said, "Your mother's nuts. Bet you're nuts, too." A bunch of littler kids started chanting, "Nuts, nuts, your mother is nuts," and running in a circle around Roddy, reaching out as they ran, touching him and dodging away, screaming as if he was dangerous and they were real brave.

He had a choice of things to do. What he did was grab the grade four kid who was standing around watching what he'd started, and take a hard, fast shot at him. He aimed at the nose and didn't miss. Blood, gushers of it, made the circle stop dancing. A howl made everyone silent.

Roddy got sent home for two days. On his very first day, he got sent home. "Don't take any crap," was his father's advice, which was Roddy's idea, too. His grandmother only looked worried. After that he learned to walk with a sort of roll to his hips, his legs widened, eyes narrowed. It seemed to work. Nobody messed with him much. There was Mike, too, and that helped, the two of them a team, pretty much.

He and Mike have spent a lot of time together, roaming around, exploring in town and also out here in the country.

Sometimes they've got tired and dropped their bikes in a ditch and wandered into a field, and crashed for a while, lying side by side with their hands behind their heads, chewing over some event or idea and looking up into the sky.

A lot of good times. Roddy has often come out here on his own, too. Mike isn't so interested in some of the things that fascinate Roddy. Like watching the purpose and intention of bees, or the progress of a snail traversing the length of his arm, or an ant tugging another insect larger than itself back to its community, for the whole community to devour—this sort of thing he could spend a lot of time on. Because up close, none of these creatures was disgusting or weird. They were amazing. Antennas and hairy legs waved, dark faceted eyes kept watch for danger and prey. One might have a blood-red body, another an iridescent green shimmer. The best were the ones that over time and through stages became some completely other thing. Something that crawled or slithered wound up with wings. Tails fell away. Skins changed their colours. Dead things were ruffled, disturbed, distressed by last moments.

At home he used razor blades to slice pictures of tiny shelled and segmented and many-legged and antennaed creatures from library books, carefully, carefully, so that absences were not apparent. Also, sometimes, from books he and Mike shoplifted. He loves his room at the top of the house, where the ceilings slant and if he sits straight up in bed he bumps his head. He took those radiant photographs from the books and hung them low on the walls. Some of them unfold in strips showing the shifts of the most special creatures from earthbound to aerial life.

His dad called them ugly. Mike said, "Gross," but that's because in the photographs they're blown up so big. His grandmother said it was nice Roddy had such an interest, and maybe he'd be a biologist or some other kind of scientist someday.

He liked the small grey desk for doing homework that his grandmother said was his grandfather's when he was young, and the adjustable light that leaned over it. Once he wasn't so angry, he liked that his grandmother told him, "This is all yours, Roddy. You can do whatever you like with it," so a couple of years ago when he painted the walls black, she didn't say anything. He thought the pictures would look more dramatic, and anyway he liked the idea of it feeling like night in there all the time. His grandmother didn't say anything either when he saw the room looked awful, and totally depressing, and started trying to paint over it yellow, with mixed and muddled results.

His poor grandmother. She wasn't planning on having her son and his son move in with her and never move out again, and looking after them like nobody ever grew up and went away. His dad never says much, even to her. He and Roddy still have some kind of language, though. Passing by, he pats Roddy's shoulder, skids his hand across the top of Roddy's head. Or, "All right!" he yells if they're watching hockey and there's a smart pass, or a goal, and he and Roddy grin at each other. Roddy figures that inside, they're shaking hands then, giving high-fives, pounding each other on the back.

Words don't matter so much anyway. His grandmother says it's what people do that counts. His dad works and watches hockey, and his grandmother bakes and tells Roddy to eat up so he won't be so skinny, and neither of them can be totally trusted. And his mum buggers off. Really, absolutely buggers off.

When Roddy was fourteen, in the summer between public and high school, they finally told him. "You're old enough," his dad said. Maybe his grandmother insisted. Roddy still bugged her sometimes, still had the idea he could go find his mother because when he thought about her, or pulled out those two old photographs, he knew she had to be wondering what had happened to him and was even probably looking for him and feeling bad. At night, when all the lights were out and he could lie in bed looking into the top branches of the tree on his grandmother's front lawn, he sometimes pictured his mother roaming dark streets, looking in windows, buttonholing strangers, in search of her son. He could even make himself sob briefly, picturing that.

Also there was something he'd wanted to tell her, to maybe save her, although he could no longer totally remember what it was, any more than he could truthfully remember what she looked like, beyond those two happy snapshots. Still, even if she'd changed as much as he had, and he guessed his dad too, he'd know her if he saw her. Would she know him? If it was a movie she would.

Anyway, none of that happened. Instead, after supper one night his dad said, "You're old enough," and he and Roddy's grandmother stared at him for a few seconds as if they were deciding if that was true.

In the city there was a particular bridge. There were lots of bridges, over rivers and railways, but this one arced high over an expressway instead of over anything soft, like water. It was where people went when they were very sure they wanted to die.

Roddy's mother was very sure.

More than a year before they told him, she had been very sure.

"I'm sorry, son," his dad said. "Oh, Roddy dear," his grandmother said.

"It was," his father continued, although Roddy wasn't hearing so clearly now, had whole other words and pictures going on in his head, "nobody's fault. They couldn't find quite the right drugs, or she wouldn't always keep taking them, and I guess she just got to feeling too bad to go on. It's something in the body, to do with the chemicals in it, it seems."

"Things were just out of whack," his grandmother added.

Roddy was thinking again of that mysterious *they*, who got to decide things about other people and try things on them and then, finally, fail. If he ever met them, he hoped he'd be quicker and luckier than his mother. "How come," he asked, "you never said?"

His dad looked down at his hands, his fingers spread out flat on the dining room table. "It didn't seem necessary, right at the time. We wanted you to get through public school without being upset, but now, like I say, you're old enough. Going into high school, it's time to know these sorts of things."

"I know it's very sad, Roddy," his grandmother said. "Your mother was a fine, bright woman, and she was so happy with you, oh, you have no idea. When you were born, she kept holding up your wee hands and making people admire your fingers. She thought you were perfect. And so you were. And she was a very good mother. Well, you remember how much she cared for you. This other thing, though, she just couldn't beat it. She tried so hard for your sake and your father's, and she hated it when she felt bad. I remember her saying that when it was coming on, it was like somebody pulling a big black cloth over her head that she couldn't get off. What I mean is, she would have given anything to keep on being able to look after you, and she did the very best she could. Do you understand?"

No.

"Yes," he said. Then, "Did she have a funeral?"

His dad looked uncomfortable. "Yes, there was one."

"Did you go?"

"Yes."

"Did you?" turning to his grandmother.

"Yes. There weren't many people who still knew her well enough to pay their respects but yes, your dad and I went together."

"Where was I?"

"It was a school day."

It had been some ordinary day, then. And behind his back, without giving away anything, his dad and grandmother had sneaked off to his mother's funeral. That was almost more shocking than anything else, that they could do that, hide it, carry it off so he never even guessed they'd been someplace important. Roddy stood. "Okay," he said.

He went to his room and lay on his bed, on his back, very still. He was something other than angry that night, but he couldn't put words to it.

He put pictures, though. He saw her figure, small and distant and wearing a coat, walking slowly, slowly, in the darkness. He saw a high bridge, deserted at night. Way below, on the expressway, which wouldn't be deserted at any hour, day or night, headlights followed each other one after the next. The rough sounds of speeding motors and tires rose upwards.

He saw her lean against the ironwork of the side of the bridge, listening to the rough sounds, watching the headlights sweep by beneath. She would think—what?

That all those headlights meant people with places they needed and wanted to go, with or towards people they needed and wanted to see, maybe that's what she'd think. While she was up there in the dark on the bridge all alone.

Maybe she missed her son. He imagined that, too, although also considered that maybe her son was the farthest thing from her mind; that maybe she'd forgotten her son. Her heart, anyway, was heavy as lead. Maybe it was so heavy she could hardly climb up the iron bridge fretwork. Maybe it was so heavy she thought it would smash easily when she hit bottom. Maybe to her that sounded best.

He saw her falling, like a dummy, like a mannequin, like a person who does stunts for a living. But he couldn't imagine her heart. He wondered what her last thought would have been, flying downwards. Maybe, "Oh no." Maybe, "Finally."

Now, lying on his back in the tall grain, staring up into the starred, darkening sky, and into the remote, watchful faces of two German shepherds who show no signs now of malevolence, listening to pounding boots coming closer through disturbed, rustling grass and words being called out between male voices in cautious tones, Roddy thinks, "Oh no."

He has done everything he could. Even if nothing worked and this moment arrived anyway, he did everything he could think of. "All a person can do is their best," his grandmother likes to say, although she would not have meant anything like this.

So in that way he also thinks, "Finally."

It's a funny thing, though. Roddy supposes this moment of lying here watched by two dogs and a thousand stars, and with probably a million insects and other small things unseen and unfelt underneath, is real. He guesses it's a very particular, suspended moment between one thing and another entirely different thing. The funny, surprising thing, though, is that suddenly it feels good now, being suspended between one thing and another like this. Kind of weightless and free, like being in space.

He's not cold any more, either.

It's amazing, how totally contented he is with this moment. Perfectly satisfied. This is so new, and so fine, he wouldn't mind at all if it just went on and on, forever. He sighs, he smiles upwards, he would say he is nearly, right this second, happy.

All the Time in the World

A S LYLE STARTS SO RELUCTANTLY recounting the missing event, Isla finally sees it unfolding. Although not in his words, or his way. "Hop in," Lyle says, and in she hops. He does a little number on her thighs: "tickling the ivory," he calls this. It still, after several years of doing so, delights her to climb into his old dented green pick-up, so large and high, sturdy and workmanlike. The ruts and potholes of the laneway are easier on the truck's tough suspension than on their cars, although inside it, humans tend to bounce around. Isla feels like quite a tiny person in the truck, with its wide seats and distant floor, as if she's a kid briefly reliving childhood; although not her own childhood.

The laneway ends at a busy county highway, and sometimes it takes a while to pull onto it. It's always a wonder that there's this rush of life so close to the house and yet also so distant. People come to visit, and even if it's not their first time they're likely to remark at some point, with flattering astonishment, "You'd never know this was here! It feels like a whole different world."

So it does. But still an easy drive to town, and then a long, slow expressway drive into the city, and work, and a different kind of whole different world.

They turn left at the foot of the lane for the eight-minute trip into the town whose outskirts, which have been creeping in their direction, include a couple of car dealerships and strip plazas followed by a few streets' worth of frame or stucco or aluminum-sided bungalows, some sliding into decrepitude, others tidy and trim. The core of the town, home and business, is brick, old and original and apparently permanent, in structure if not content. Stores fall vacant, change hands, houses also now and again, and there appears to be a diminishing interest in, or money for, upkeep and maintenance, for keeping things thriving-looking and bright. But Lyle and Isla do their part and shop in town just as much as they possibly can: for basic groceries, for the tools and nails and fertilizers that keep Lyle occupied. They are good citizens, not the kind of newcomers who take it upon themselves to complain about change. "We're just commuters," Lyle tells visitors. "It's easy for us."

They do what they can to encourage local businesses, so in their journey for ice cream there's no need to discuss where they're going, which is of course to Goldie's Dairy Bar.

Goldie's was a real dairy bar at some point in its history, and apparently there was even a Goldie attached to it a few decades ago. Now it carries cigarettes, newspapers, stamps, some staple household products and foods. It would be almost a mere variety store, if the original long transparent-topped ice-cream freezer didn't still run along the front, glass-lidded, bulky and squat. The dairy is long gone, but the high school kids who staff Goldie's on evenings and weekends still scoop single, double, and triple-dip cones from the deep vats of flavours, of which there are, according to the blackboard sign out on the sidewalk, thirty-four. Nice old-fashioned touches, the sign and the freezer, although the staff themselves are often enough pierced, dyed, and tattooed.

Goldie's is now owned by a widow named Doreen, about Isla's age but otherwise not like Isla at all. She bought the place after losing her job in the window factory just outside town in the other direction from Isla and Lyle's, using some of the proceeds of her husband Jack's life insurance after he died of a heart attack leaning over a pool table—or, some said, reaching for a waitress's rear end—in a bar down the block. "I was adrift," Doreen likes to tell people. "I didn't know what to do. Then I thought, 'Ice cream,' and it seemed like the answer." It certainly was for Doreen, who has been transformed from the relative anonymity of factory work into an actual town character, brusque, entertaining, lively-tongued, a woman growing larger and larger, not in size but in presence, with each ice-cream season.

Isla finds this progression appealing, because wouldn't it be grand to grow vivid and large in the minds of others, not to mention one's own mind! Isla might manage grandiosity in a pinch, but thinks she's short of the swollen benevolence that's required, the assumptions of good-heartedness underlying Doreen's reputation.

For all Isla knows, she is herself a town character. Most likely, though, she's just a character drifting through town, an even later latecomer than Lyle, and attached in people's minds mainly to him. When she began living with Lyle, so that people began to take her existence somewhat seriously, and they asked what she did, and she said she worked in an ad agency, attentions wandered and lapsed. It could have been worse, she could have admitted to being part owner and vice-president of an ad agency, facts they probably know by now, but even working at one was so irrelevant, so distant from any normal concerns, that eyes glazed, heads nodded, conversations moved on.

Isla thinks, and not in any patronizing way, that this is exactly the correct attitude. She did not necessarily think that in the early days, but she does now.

It's been interesting, and no doubt salutary, to be an important person in one world—at least important in the sense of having power over a number of people and responsibility for a number of risky, big-price-tag ideas—and to be, here, not exactly a nonentity, but someone on whom nothing in particular rests. No one here, except perhaps Lyle, relies on her. She is generally liked, she thinks, at least certainly doesn't seem to be disliked, but she could vanish to no particular notice.

She considers it this way: if her funeral were held in the city where she works and where most of her life has been led, it would get a pretty good turnout, on grounds of etiquette or respect from some people, affection, she can hope, from most, a creepy curiosity, perhaps, from a few who still connect her with James. Here in town the turnout on any of those grounds would be meagre, and on that last one, non-existent. Here it would mainly be based on people's respect for life, and moreover death, in general, not for attachments they know nothing, thank heavens, about, and not really for Isla herself.

She rather envies Doreen, whose funeral would be huge and heartfelt. Lyle, when she mentions this, says, "My God, you have a morbid turn of mind sometimes. Funerals!"

It's hard sometimes to explain images, symbols, to a man, a lawyer, with a literal turn of mind. Then again, she depends on his literalness, his straightforwardness. "It's only," she tells him, "that funerals are so useful for making assessments. The last summing up."

"But have you noticed that the people who do the summing-up at funerals generally talk mostly about themselves? Like the dead person's just been an incidental entry in their own lives?" True. But again it's the funeral-as-metaphor she's talking about, not real funerals.

Anyway, the discussion takes them happily to town. Do other people run out of things to say? Well, yes. She and James did. Or they had done so much, and gathered up so much to say, that they went far beyond speech. But she can't imagine she and Lyle can ever get to the end of chatting about this and that in the thirty-odd years they have, with luck, remaining to them. The reason for ice cream, and maybe how her mind comes to wander off in the direction of summations and funerals: this outing a celebration of renewed prospects for thirty-odd years. All those words, all those ideas, all those details!

"You run in," he says. "I'll keep the truck running. Then if we're quick we can go sit on the riverbank and eat before they melt."

"What kind of cone? And do you want single, double, or triple?"

That sort of detail.

"Triple, of course, I think I deserve a big one. Double-chocolate chip? Then if I still have some room, maybe we can come back for something fruitier. For dessert, as it were."

As it were. As it is, dressed in her blue linen suit, she will be juggling two cones, one triple, one double, in the truck for the two-minute ride to a riverbank bench. Easy. Suits can be cleaned; husbands, good ones anyway, can't be replaced.

As it is, she walks in on a robbery.

As instantly as she sees this, it is instantly too late. Just through the door, waving back towards Lyle, turning then towards the checkout counter, the freezer, and the young man with the gun is already turning her way, already startled, already recognizable.

Isla's mouth falls open; perhaps she is preparing to say his name, which is Roddy. He is a nearly shaven-headed, fair-almost-red-haired youth, a resident of one of those stuccoed, less-than-trim houses a few blocks away. He can be seen sometimes on street corners, wandering on weekends with rough friends, apparently aimless, punching each other's shoulders, speaking loudly. Ordinary high school kids, really. By Isla's standards, if they are disaffected, they are disaffected in ordinary ways. So she has assumed until this moment when Roddy's startled eyes meet her own shocked eyes, and the terrible thing happens.

She turns, although there's no point. His finger jerks on the trigger, although there's no point in that, either.

She thinks how instantly and thoroughly events become unreal. That this is like a movie, not like her own real life. She wonders what people did when something unreal happened before there were such things as movies; how they identified unreality then.

How did they regard the frame-by-frame unfolding of a sequence of movements, smooth but infinitesimal shifts of bodies through space and time, before they could possibly recognize and identify such a technique as slow motion?

She has all the time in the world for these questions as her torso continues to twist, her right foot turns on a dime, her hips dodge slightly left, as her body recognizes reality, snaps to action, behaves in automatic defence of itself, making its own instant decision to flee; even as Roddy's chin jerks up, his eyes widen—and what long lashes he has in the midst of otherwise unenchanting features—his spine straightens, his shoulders pull back, his knees give slightly so that he achieves the faintest hint of a crouch and his weight shifts to the balls of his feet, his arms extend up, and out, the sudden, rigid steadiness of shock making him detailed and large, someone new, huge, foreign, with barely a relationship to a soft-boned, soft-charactered adolescent, but someone instantly and surprisingly formed.

Either of their bodies, Roddy's or Isla's, could topple, or trip, or stumble with their respective alterations in balance, weight, attention, direction. But neither does. Roddy does not smack forward onto his face as he moves onto the balls of his feet; Isla does not crumple leftwards, but continues her swing towards the door. She can see sunlight and concrete through the glass. She cannot see Lyle, or the truck, because they're parked to the left of the entrance. She knows innocence lies just outside the door, out in the light, out where there is no young frightened man with a gun and she is not a panicking woman whose timing is off. A few seconds, a few minutes' difference and this would not be happening. How does it work, that such a thing can happen because at some point earlier in the day she moved too quickly, or too slowly, and got here just too early, or too late? Roddy may be wondering similarly. Where is the clerk? What can Roddy want?

It probably no longer matters what Roddy wanted, which would have to have been money, any more than it matters what Isla wanted, which was two ice-cream cones to eat down by the river with Lyle. Now Roddy's and Isla's original intentions are lost. They have new moments to endure. She sees quite clearly that this is as true for Roddy as for herself, and imagines this capacity to know about a number of people at once is another effect of the movies.

She is very angry, very bitter. Not with Roddy so much as with Lyle. She has come to rely on him. He has made himself virtually indispensable. But when she truly needs him, in the instant she is in genuine, terrible trouble, he's nowhere to be found. He's sitting in a truck listening to music, or the news, or maybe waiting in silent anticipation of ice cream, at any rate something irrelevant and stupid, instead of being here, where she needs him to be, doing what she needs him to do, which is to save her. How could he, how dare he, pick her up, hold her up, and then let her fall this way, so hard and far?

It's a little late to remember Jamie and Alix, and when she does it's with no particular impression in mind, neither anger nor, perhaps surprisingly, any dazzle of maternal love. In this moment they are simply irrelevant. She expects nothing of them. Not as she has, mistakenly it appears, come to assume salvation from Lyle.

He didn't even give her time to change her clothes. So now she's spinning towards escape hampered by shoes that have heels, and a blue linen suit that hugs tight to her dodging hips.

Roddy's finger is tightening. She is turning, but she can see him as clearly as if she had eyes in the back of her head. "Don't imagine you can get away with something just because you think I'm not looking," her mother used to warn. "I have eyes in the back of my head."

Perhaps this is inherited.

What has Roddy inherited? A willingness to risk? The sort of physical tension that, in the right circumstances, causes a finger to grow tight on a trigger? A pure, blind, dumb tendency towards anarchy, moral, emotional, physical?

She doesn't know the boy. She has nothing to say to him. It seems there's plenty of time for a great many thoughts, but not a moment for speech.

What if she cried out, "Don't!" or "Please!" or "No!"

But it's too late. There's only time for one sound after Isla's gasp and Roddy's sharp intake of breath, and it isn't the sound of words.

She thinks there ought to be a correlation between something important happening and the length of time it takes. Tiny, stupid things, like driving home from the city, can take forever. Mowing the lawns, weeding gardens, can consume an eternity. Even watching a video on a winter's night, feet up on the coffee table, bowl of popcorn between her and Lyle, drinks in their hands, takes at least ninety minutes, sometimes a couple of hours.

This, though—for a long moment the world is suspended, her body is adrift in mid-air, a little pinprick of darkness grows larger and larger until there's only a sliver of light left, then even that sliver vanishes and there's no distinguishing between darkness and silence, it all amounts, and diminishes, to the very same thing.

Rewind

LYLE'S VERSION IS DIFFERENT. Not necessarily less volatile or catastrophic than hers, but—he wasn't there. His account has to be second-hand, third-hand, picked up from running from the truck into the disarrayed scene in Goldie's, then from experts: ambulance attendants, cops, nurses, doctors. He is, it seems, doomed to observer status in the shocking events of his wives. Perhaps frustrating for him, maybe enraging. Possibly a guilty relief. In any case he now seems reduced, with his anxious eyes and fretful mouth: a recounter, a teller, not the actor, or the acted upon.

Perhaps he's just lucky.

"You'd just gone in," he says. "We thought it'd be quick, since for once there didn't look to be anybody around, no bikes or cars in the lot. You were only out of the truck a few seconds. You kind of waved at me in that back-handed way and I heard the buzzer as you went through the door. I was thinking what a good life, sunshine, summer, off to eat ice cream by the river, good health, you, home—I guess those are moments you live off, sort of golden ones that carry you through."

He'd better hope it carries them through. Nice for him, having a golden moment while she's getting shot.

"Just for a second, I couldn't figure out what the noise was. I thought something had maybe exploded. A propane tank? I don't know. Close and loud, and not a car backfiring because it obviously came from inside Goldie's. I jumped out of the truck, ran in. And, you know, there you were."

No, she doesn't know. For a lawyer, he doesn't tell a story very coherently.

"I couldn't believe it. I mean literally, I didn't believe what I saw. I've heard clients say that before, and I thought I knew what they meant, but it turns out I didn't. It's like a whole different level of consciousness, where everything is all of a sudden stark and bright and totally silent. And still. And completely not real. That could have lasted forever, that moment. I didn't know how to end it. I just wanted it not to be real, I wanted to rewind the day."

Maybe she manages some small sound of impatience; at any rate, he glances at her, says, "Sorry."

"You were lying on your side, at my feet, just inside the door. Your head was so close I could have tripped over it. There was blood. You'd think I'd have seen blood before, violent blood, but I haven't. And even if I had, it wouldn't have been the same. It wouldn't've been yours.

"There was a kid. Sort of freckled, and real short-cropped blondish-red hair, we've seen him around town. Just a kid, except he was holding a shotgun. Pointed at the floor, though. Or not so much pointed as just hanging off his fingers. He was staring at you. I don't know if he even noticed me. He looked as if he was going to faint, not a drop of blood in his face.

"I don't know what I was thinking; maybe that if I didn't move or say anything, it wouldn't be real. Like a nightmare, you know? Maybe it was the same for him. It sure didn't look like anything he'd meant to do, or set out to do, and maybe he couldn't believe it, either.

"The cops asked me later how long it was before somebody called them, and I had no fucking clue. We could have been standing there looking at you for a few seconds or a few hours, for all the sense I had about time. But it could only have been seconds. Seems to me now the sound of the door buzzer was still in the air when the clerk's head started poking up from behind the counter, and as soon as there was a movement, even that small one, the moment was broken. The clerk was just a kid, too, I've forgotten his name. I've forgotten everybody's name, I think, except yours and mine. Except hang on, I remember him saying something like, 'Shit, Roddy, what did you do?' so that must be his name, Roddy. The big kid, the clerk, was shaking like crazy, but he came around the counter and reached out and took the shotgun away. Just like that. So he had more presence of mind than I did. And I guess he was brave. It's a wonder the goddamn thing didn't go off again, his hands were trembling so badly.

"The other kid, Roddy or whatever, he didn't even try to hold on to the gun, or do anything with it. When he'd let go of it, he doubled over and threw up. And then he ran. Turned around and bolted through the back, we heard the door slam behind him.

"I didn't care where the hell he'd gone, or what happened to him at that point. I got my voice back, and I yelled at the clerk to call the ambulance, the cops, the fire department, anybody, and I was on my knees checking you out, calling your name. I could see you were hurt, but while there was blood, there wasn't really a whole lot of it, up close. I mean, not pools or anything. And you were alive, you were breathing. I couldn't see what was damaged, but I knew to be careful not to go shifting you."

He himself shifts in his bedside chair. Lucky him, sitting up, leaning over. Moving. Being capable of discomfort.

None of what he's saying rings a bell; but then of course, as he points out, she was unconscious. She guesses she can spare him some sympathy, for being the one to almost stumble over her head, to be frozen by blood, to go through the process of becoming unfrozen.

When will that happen to her?

"It felt like forever before anybody turned up, although I understand now it was under four minutes. An eternity at the time. The kid, the clerk, was crying, kind of wailing away at the counter. I wanted to lie down on the floor with you and hold you, but all I could safely touch was your face. I think I was talking to you, but for sure I remember stroking your forehead, and smoothing your hair. I didn't know if you could feel anything, or if you were right out."

He looks, briefly, uncomfortable; as if he has blundered. Which of all those words did he not mean to say?

"The ambulance screamed up first. I didn't want them tearing in on top of you, so I stepped outside to show them in. The cops arrived a couple of seconds later. The two of them jumped out of the cruiser with their guns drawn, which was a bad moment. I don't think they get a lot of really heavy experience around here. They looked kind of wild-eyed, anyway, so before they took a notion I was the bad guy, I waved them down, told them you'd been shot, the gunman was gone, the clerk was a witness, and I was sort of a witness, and I guess I was being so calm, because I thought I needed to be, that one of them said, 'You're pretty cool for a guy whose wife's just been shot,' like I might have done it myself."

"Oh, who cares?" Isla would like to cry out. "Who the fuck cares? Get to me!" But she can only whisper a protest, which Lyle evidently doesn't hear, or can't interpret.

"By the time the cops got inside, the ambulance guys had you strapped onto a board and were lifting it onto a gurney. The cops looked mad, like they should have just left you there. But maybe I'm wrong about that, I was kind of hyper-sensitive right then. Like everything was real bright and real clear. Not loud, but clear.

"I said I was riding along with you, and the one who'd got shirty in the first place said something like, 'You're a witness, we need to talk to you,' but the other cop said, 'We can catch up to him later, we got the clerk to interview anyway, a lot of other shit to do.' Like it was a chore. He was looking at the floor, where you'd been. The blood." Lyle shivers.

How long ago did all this happen? Recently enough that Lyle might be in shock? Do witnesses and loved ones go into shock, or is it mainly just victims themselves?

Isla isn't in shock. She doesn't seem to be in anything except a rage.

"I said, 'There's no big mystery, you probably know the kid that did it, the clerk does. He ran out the back, but I can't see he'd be hard to find. About five-eight, freckles, thin. And scared, okay?' I wanted them to know he was scared, which maybe meant he was sorry. I didn't know if being scared would make him more or less dangerous, but the shotgun was on the counter so he probably wasn't armed any more, and I didn't want them getting excited and blowing him away when they found him."

This seems excessively merciful. What about vengeance? How about loyalty? Isla would shoot the son of a bitch herself, if it would undo what happened. If it would just get her up on her feet, she would shoot him. If for no other reason than simple, straightforward balance: this for that.

She hopes that boy's conscience, if he has one, eternally vibrates from the persistent, wide-eyed haunting of those few bright seconds in Goldie's when he, something in him, an instinct or a desire or a terror, made a decision. Because these things are decisions, no matter how swiftly or incoherently taken. Decisions are responsibilities, she believes that, not whims; at least not solely whims.

Do people like that think people like her go around armoured and bulletproofed? Do they dream no one will be hurt? If they don't deliberately set out to cause harm, do they suppose harm is unlikely? Impossible? Do they imagine their intentions are true? Oh, she is angry. Unspeakably furious. All the real disasters and true betrayals of forty-nine years—not so many, perhaps, but each one monstrous to her—and now Goldie's.

"I felt," and Lyle sounds puzzled, "that it would be bad luck for you if things went wrong with the cops and the kid. Like it was all a mess, but if we could keep it from getting any messier, it might still be repairable, somehow."

And will it be? Repairable? For God's sake, Lyle!

"I don't know much about what's happened since. I haven't heard if they've caught him. We took off in the ambulance, stopped at the hospital just long enough for them to say we'd better keep going, so now we're at Northern where they say the best specialists are. So you're in really good hands." He smiles at her in a hopeful sort of way; or he is making an effort to look endearing.

One question answered, though: the inessential where. So she's in the huge teaching hospital in, obviously, the north part of the city, not that far, as a matter of fact, from her office. She regularly drives past Northern, and sometimes reads in the newspapers about its research projects and various miracles, but has never had occasion to enter it. Now and then it conducts fundraising projects of one sort and another. She should, perhaps, have contributed.

"When?"

"When what?" But how much clearer can she be, for God's sake? "You mean, what time is it, or when did it all happen? It's morning now. You were out for quite a while, and then they gave you something to keep your system shut down while they did more tests, poked around." She would shudder, if she could shudder, at the notion of people testing and poking around while she was helpless. Not that, apparently, anyone couldn't do anything they wanted to her as she is, awake and conscious.

Morning. She has meetings, although at the moment has no idea with whom or why, and who cares? All that was probably vital yesterday, but it means shit today. Lyle's supposed to be in court first thing. He must be exhausted. A small, forty-watt bulb of compassion flickers on briefly: she would, after all, like to reach for his hand, to thank him for being here.

For all she knows, they are holding hands.

"The cops will want to talk to you whenever you're up to it. They need to nail everything down."

What the fuck does she care about cops and what they might need? "Doctors," she whispers irritably. Surely to God a lawyer knows what is important to a narration, a case, and what is not. In her business of advertising, she wouldn't make that mistake. In her business, there's a little space or a little air to make the point and that's it, time's up.

He looks hesitant, his eyes shifting. This is not the look of a man offering any form of good news. "I've already told you pretty much everything the doctors had to say: we wait, then there'll likely be some kind of surgery, and plenty of hope everything will go right. It's just really a matter of getting strong and being patient, that's all."

Well no, that's hardly all. "Exactly," she says. "Details," she manages.

It's interesting to see somebody actually coming to a decision. She watches his face open up and grow clear, a small, relaxing movement of mouth, and then a drawing down of the nostrils, a widening of the eyes, lifting of eyebrows. Little lines in his forehead iron out, larger ones alongside his mouth deepen. He looks at her with something resembling the way he often looks at her in difficult or tenuous moments. This is an expression likely to contain more respect than, at those particular moments, affection.

Which is reassuring. She's the human Isla again in his eyes, not the patient, or wife, or responsibility, or burden, or problem.

Not quite a cripple.

Where did that forbidden word come from?

"Okay," he says. "What they know so far is that the bullet nicked into your spine. Fairly high up. And that you're lucky, really, in a way, because just a tiny difference in the angle and it could have gone through soft tissue and drilled right into one of the vital organs. Or angled higher the other way, it could have gone into your brain." As if her brain is not one of the vital organs. "It's a very good thing you were turning just as you did when he shot."

Then presumably a very bad thing that she didn't turn just a tiny bit farther, twist just that little bit harder, or faster. Then the bullet would have smacked harmlessly into the door frame, or the freezer, or the floor.

"Anyway, when it nicked your spine, it obviously did some vertebrae damage, but they don't know about that exactly yet because the bullet itself fractured, or whatever you'd call it, so part of it, just a fragment I guess, is still lodged in there. But it may ease out on its own as you get more stable, we'll see."

It doesn't seem to Isla that she could get much more stable than she already is. Immobile must be just about as stable as stability gets, short of death. She frowns, or thinks she frowns, intends to frown, at him.

Still, once again he said "we." Here he sits, with his face full of grief, his heart surely likewise.

Still again, he can say "we" all he wants, but he's not the one, is he, with part of a bullet in his spine, vertebrae damaged with paralyzing results.

"Paralyzed?" she inquires.

He does not meet her eyes. "For the time being. But like I said, try to be patient. Get yourself strong. Then we can find out a whole lot more than we know now. Have some answers."

Be very careful with questions, she remembers again. Because the answers may not be the desired ones, or even bearable. That true thing she learned with James, and which she learned well, right into her bones, and which may now constitute something like a motto, or a creed.

"It's a good sign," Lyle goes on, "that you can speak. It means something to do with lungs being more or less okay. And that your face muscles work a bit, that's good, too. I mean, you can do things like blink. You could even," and how sweet and hopeful he looks, "probably smile, if you wanted to."

She can also narrow her eyes, she believes. He's lucky she can't raise herself off this bed. "What the hell do you think I should smile about?" is what she would like to say. "Why?" is all she can manage. Enough to make him look embarrassed.

But he is here. He is trying. She should be grateful for that.

No. Gratitude is pitiful, she cannot reduce herself to that. Neither can he, in the long run.

There can't be a long run. This doesn't happen to her, to people like her.

But it does. All the time people get plucked, randomly as far as anyone can see, out of the relatively untroubled crowd and plopped into true disaster. Why not her?

Because. Because is there not some sort of quota on catastrophe? And has she not already had hers, Lyle, too? Because she was just getting started on joy again, has only had a few tempered years of it, really, with him. So who's keeping score here, some sadist who doesn't count or assess very well? She would shake her head in disbelief, except of course that's one of the many, many things she can't do.

Well then, what can she do? She can rage. She can remember. Some rare and special shocks stay resolutely in the present—something else she learned from James. The electric knowledge about him still has enough voltage to surprise her over and over again. People speak of earth-shattering moments and may mean anything huge or atrocious. Massacre, they may mean, or murder, hurricane, birth, revelation. Revelation in some almost-biblical, certainly apocalyptic sense. Judgement day. Like a bullet.

Now the moment just inside the door of Goldie's Dairy Bar. Apocalypse for sure.

Softer, more elusive events get recalled for no particularly obvious reason: a conversation, a movement, a colour, a shape; others because an internal directive says, *Do not forget. Remember exactly how this moment is.*

She has to believe this is temporary. She has to bend herself in that direction.

So when she's back up on her feet, she will have to remember this: that even merely treading through an ordinary, predictable, regular day is a blessing. She will have to keep in mind—*be mindful of*, as Alix has taken to saying—what she

59

had that she earned and deserves and desires, and has for this moment lost.

She will set herself to remembering to remember all this. It's a small project, but in this circumstance it's almost a miracle to have any kind of project at all. This is one she can get her teeth into; if she could feel her teeth, if she could sink them into anything. For the time being she can bare them, smiling, at Lyle, like the wolf in Red Riding Hood's grandmother's bed but looking, she really does hope, somewhat kinder.

A Simple Plan

THEY KEEP ASKING WHAT HAPPENED. "Tell us what you did, son," says the bigger, older one. He's the same one who, out in the field, as Roddy stared up at impassive dogs and into the stars, happy as hell, suddenly appeared at the edge of his field of vision, arms outstretched and rigid, in his hands a gun aimed right at Roddy.

"Don't move, son," he said. "Just stay perfectly still. You understand what I'm saying? Tell me you're not going to move a muscle. Right now. Tell me."

"Okay," Roddy said.

"Hold," said another voice, and the two dogs shifted away, out of view. They didn't go far. He could still hear them breathing.

The other guy, younger, knelt carefully beside Roddy, eyed him warily. He passed his hands carefully, remotely, all over Roddy's body. He nodded at the bigger guy, who said, "Okay now, stand up, real slow."

It was like he was old. It was almost painful, rolling slightly and getting his hands and feet in position to push himself up. It didn't help that while he was still sitting, the younger guy took his hands and pulled them behind him and fastened his wrists together. There was no click. The binding felt like plastic, not metal. Roddy guessed things were different than they were on TV. The cop took one arm and lifted it upwards. Roddy almost bounced when he hit his feet finally.

The other cop, the one who called him *son*, stepped back. He was still aiming his gun: a black hole. Roddy wanted to say nobody needed a gun, but he thought maybe he shouldn't say anything. He couldn't tell what they might do. He wasn't scared, exactly, because this couldn't be happening, it wasn't real enough for fear. Just, it was so strange, out here in the field in the night, the young cop holding a flashlight on him like this was a stage, a spotlight, a play.

"Let's move."

Returning through the fields to the road, two flashlights now directing their steps, wasn't easy. Especially with his arms behind him, it was hard to keep his balance, not stumble. In this small way the fields, their slight humps and hollows, their hidden pitfalls and stoninesses, became strange to him; unfriendly.

The two cops grunted now and then, one on each side of him and slightly behind. He could hear the hard breathing of the bigger, older one, and the dogs padding along. Nobody spoke. Nobody spoke when they got to the car, either. The younger cop put his hand on top of Roddy's head as he eased him into the back seat, braceleted and alone.

The roads looked like new country, like nothing he'd ever travelled before. The outskirts of town, the rows of houses, the street lights, everything might as well have been in some other country, in Europe maybe, where he'd never been. Passing the corner of the street that led to the street where he lived right up till a few hours ago, he thought, "Grandma's there, a block away, right this second, and my dad," but it felt like where they really were was in a parallel universe.

Anyway, where they really were was at the police station: his fat, distressed, red-eyed grandmother, his pale burly father. They rose off their chairs the same way the same second, like they were tied together, like they were puppets. Except then his dad stood still, while his grandmother took a step towards Roddy. But the cops said, "No," and guided Roddy right by, each of them holding one of his arms. He didn't even try to look back. What was the point? They were here, but they must think he was nobody they knew.

Now he's in a room with the two cops and some other guy his dad called in to be his lawyer. The guy told him, "You don't have to say anything, I suggest you don't say a word." Roddy just shook his head.

When the cop says, "Tell us what you did, son, tell us what happened," Roddy isn't silent because he's refusing to speak. He's silent because he has no idea what to say. It was so clear before, when it was only a plan.

The woman. Her face. Mike's voice, finally. Too late, the way everything was too late, like time got out of synch and for a few seconds things were happening backwards, or inside out.

Now he's back in time, but it's a whole different time.

"Where'd you get the shotgun?"

That'd be easy. It's his dad's. His dad takes a week every year and goes hunting with a bunch of guys from his work. He never shoots anything, though. He probably tries, but he never hits anything.

Not like Roddy. Suddenly he's very cold again, and shivers.

"You got something to put around him?" his lawyer says. "A blanket? I don't think he's well."

"No shit," says the younger cop. "And no, we don't."

The lawyer shrugs. "If he's sick, if he gets sick, it's on your watch, you know. On your shoulders. In fact I'm not sure we shouldn't be calling a doctor. He could be shocky. That could be dangerous."

"Get him a blanket, Tom," says the older cop.

Roddy's attention swings from one man to another. It's like watching a play. Mr. Siviletti, Roddy's English teacher, just about the only teacher Roddy likes, says every word in a play is supposed to do something. Move things ahead somehow. It doesn't seem to Roddy as if this talking among the cops, the lawyer, is getting anyone anywhere. On the other hand, he has nothing, himself, to add. It's not like those moments out in the field, though. It's not like he's happy and wants everything to stop right now so he can keep on being happy. The lights are too bright, the chair too hard, the faces, even his lawyer's, too harsh.

He thinks all this started, in another, innocent lifetime, with Mike and him, at the start of summer, sitting around the pool at the park. They were making their plans, or dreaming their dreams, whatever. They were at the pool but not in the water. It was a cool day, so they were wearing sweatshirts and jeans, just hanging out, more than anything.

Mysteries and longings build up. Which means other things need to end. Mike said, "If we wanted to leave in September, how could we get enough money by then?" Roddy's almost sure it was Mike who said that, although it could have been him. They talked about leaving a lot, back and forth.

They would have an apartment in the city where Roddy came from in the first place. They had a high-rise in mind, someplace that looked out over miles of bright lights. Roddy liked the idea of a high-rise. It seemed clean and glamorous to ride an elevator to get home, to go out. They would get some kind of jobs. The lights alone would keep them dazzled. There would be alleys and streets, bars and concerts, new people. Girls. That was one of the main things: the great sinuous, mysterious, welcoming variety of girls there would be.

But Roddy didn't know how they would get there, either, two or three months down the road. He must have supposed something like magic. He had odd-job commitments for things like mowing lawns, weeding gardens, and imagined that could add up. Mike was working his second summer of shifts at Goldie's. His mother was a friend of the woman who owned it. "The money's shit, though. Even minimum wage practically kills her, like, when she hands over my money, it's like I've been stealing it off her. Pisses me off. It's not like I just stand around. If there's no customers we're supposed to clean the floors and the storeroom, even dust the shelves, and man, if you don't get it all done, she'll really light into you."

"Yeah, well, at least you've got a job. You know what you're making, anyway."

"But you're working for yourself. And, you know, if you're getting paid by the hour, all you have to do is mow real slow, right?"

Mike was joking, sort of. Roddy said, "Yeah, right."

"The thing is, either way, we're neither of us making real money. Not enough, anyhow. We gotta figure out something better, or we'll never get out of here."

They fell into gloomy silence. They often did. The thought of never getting out of here was unbearable, although there wasn't much that was actually bad they could point to. Just, being so restless was in its way actively, acutely painful. It hurt.

Mike's never had to start over. He's always lived here. His idea of a new life was that it would be totally new, almost like he didn't expect to have memories. To Roddy it seemed that yes, everything about it would be new, but also a variation on how his life should have gone in the first place, if nobody'd had to move, if he'd got to stay where he started.

Everything would be different than it was here. They'd be free, mainly. Roddy thought he might even decide to look different, under those different circumstances. "Maybe I'll grow a moustache," and although Mike snorted, he also nodded, as if he knew what Roddy was talking about.

It wasn't just that he was not looking ahead in any clear fashion, it also now seems to him he was not looking back very well. Sure it was irritating sometimes, living at home, and lately his grandmother's been getting more impatient than she used to be, and he's been more impatient back. Like, how often did he have to say, "It's nobody's business, just mine"? The *it* being anything from whether his homework was done to where he was going, or where he had been. "Out," he said. "Nowhere." And if his father spoke ten words a day to either of them any more, Roddy'd be surprised. Like he'd run totally out of words, and all he had left were those pats on Roddy's shoulder as he passed by, the affectionate skidding of his hand over Roddy's head.

But look: there was his grandmother bandaging his knees when he was a little kid falling down, there she was reading to him when he was home sick from school, there she was in the heat of the kitchen, baking up something sweet, there she was saying, "Feel like a round of cribbage, Roddy, before you go out?"

There were her eyes, looking wounded, and her lips getting tight when he wouldn't talk, or when he snapped at her. Really, she hardly ever snapped back. She mostly made a habit of turning away. What he sees now are her shoulders, her back: bent a bit under his weight.

Feeling bad made him want to be someplace where he didn't have to feel bad.

What a jerk. What a dumb asshole.

It is suddenly clear to him—and he sits up straighter on the chair, startled by this abrupt, certain knowledge—that he and Mike wouldn't have left. They would have gone back to school in the fall, and kept on building their word-pictures of the future, and it would have stayed the future, on and on, until, maybe, the time really did come. He'd have graduated from high school. His grandmother and even his dad would have gone to his graduation. He's never exactly at the top of the class, but he's nowhere near the bottom, either. They would have taken pictures of him. He and Mike would have had double dates for the party afterwards. He would have worn a dark suit. His grandmother would have had tears in her eyes. She's always getting tears in her eyes for one thing and another, even sometimes sentimental TV commercials. She says, "A bit of a weep makes me feel better, is all."

Now she's been weeping for real. He must have been insane for a couple of months, in a dark, cool, closed sort of way. Like he could only feel his own skin and pictures; like he was hunched in a chilly, rough box all by himself, inside his own head. Like there was nothing outside it.

Now, in the light, he has blood on his hands. He looks down at his unshackled hands. There are actually tracings of blood, although it looks like his own, from the scratchings and stumblings of his wild pell-mell run.

His hands have hardly ever done anything, really. A few times they've touched a girl's breasts, that's about it, a few tense, nervous dates that have gone more or less well, but promised much more, with freedom. His fingers have wrapped themselves around lawnmower handles and rakes, turned pages, done dishes. He has nice fingers, long. They've hardly been used.

One of them curled tight on a trigger, though. He'd cut it off, if he could, if it would unmake what happened.

"I'm a kid," he would like to tell these men. "It doesn't count. I didn't mean it. Doesn't it matter that it was just stupid and I didn't mean it?" He can see from the spareness of this small room, from the bright light, from their faces, that it counts, all right.

Right about now he was supposed to be in his room, in bed, the money safely tucked away underneath. He was supposed to take it straight home, and after everything calmed down in a couple of days, Mike was supposed to come over and they'd say they were going to watch videos in Roddy's room and then they'd finally pull out the money from under his bed and count it and figure out how long it would last them in their new life. "We won't be able to take off right away," Mike said wisely. "That'd look suspicious. All we have to do is keep on doing what we usually do for another few weeks and we're free."

They made solemn promises not to betray each other, and not even to hint their intentions to anyone else. They pledged not to do anything dumb, like get tempted to spend even a dollar, and to split the money right down the middle, although Mike wouldn't have any of it till they left. It would be dangerous, obviously, for him to be anywhere near it.

Those were easy promises. They wouldn't dream of screwing up for some stupid reason like using any of the money for a movie, something like that. Neither of them would be tempted to take more than his share. That was the sort of thing they were sure of, just because neither of them could imagine it any other way. They've done a lot of stuff together, they know a lot of things about each other.

They were also sure there'd be a fair amount of money around, because this was the last day of a four-day trip by Doreen, who owns Goldie's, to visit her sister. "Everything just gets put in a cash box under the counter till she gets back," Mike reported. "That's what happened last summer when she went away for a few days, because she said she likes checking it herself before she deposits it." He shrugged. "Stupid. Tough luck."

Roddy supposes Mike thought of the money as fair payment, since he considered his wages unfair. What did Roddy himself think? Not that he was owed it, exactly, of course not. But that Doreen hadn't earned it herself, hadn't even earned Goldie's since she bought it with insurance money when old Jack keeled over, so in a way money just sometimes fell into people's lives, and gave them something they wanted, that made them happy, and it could fall into his, too.

He guesses he saw it as some kind of evening up, although now can't think what imbalance he was setting out to correct.

Their plan, so honed, so fine, was simple.

Mike would go to work for his usual three o'clock shift. Everything would be normal. Customers would drift in and out. At five the day clerk would take off and Mike would be on his own. He would begin biding his time.

About the same time Mike was showing up for work, Roddy would be quietly moving his dad's shotgun from the basement cabinet where it was kept, and the ammunition from his dad's bedroom bureau drawer. At that hour, his dad was at work and his grandmother would either be out shopping and visiting, or in her own room having a nap. Roddy would take the shotgun and the ammunition to his room. A couple of hours later, Mike well into his shift, the whole town heading indoors to supper, Roddy would be leaning out his bedroom window, out over the low roof overhang, dropping the gun into the petunias below. His grandmother and dad would still be at the kitchen table, finishing their dessert. Roddy, eating fast, would have excused himself before they were done.

The ammunition would be in the back pocket of his jeans. He would go downstairs, out the front door, calling out, "See you later, I won't be long."

Outside, he would go around back, retrieve the shotgun, and shove it down one leg of his jeans. He would walk, with whatever ungainly, stiff-legged but not especially noticeable gait was required, the three blocks to Goldie's.

The back door would be open. In the storeroom he would haul out the shotgun. He would load it. He would listen for voices. If he heard any, he would wait silently. If he didn't, he would give a little whistle: the first notes of the theme of *The Good, the Bad and the Ugly*, an old flick he and Mike like to rent. If everything was ready to roll, Mike would whistle the next few notes back. Roddy would step into the main part of Goldie's. Mike would be behind the counter, like normal.

All this worked exactly as foreseen. Smooth as a dance. Even walking the three blocks to Goldie's with the shotgun under his jeans didn't feel too awkward or remarkable.

What was supposed to happen next was that Roddy would go almost right up to the counter and—this was the dicey part—let off one shot, into the shelves behind. Inevitably this would be loud. The thing was, Mike said, "There has to be a threat, some reason I'd hand over the money and let myself be tied up." Because that was the other step. While Roddy was doing his thing with the gun, Mike, having already put the cash box into a plain shopping bag, would be binding his own mouth with a handkerchief and taping his own ankles together. He would be on the floor, all ready for Roddy to tape up his wrists.

They rehearsed and rehearsed this. They got it down, from shot to wrists, to twelve seconds.

Racing back to the storeroom, Roddy would stash the shotgun back down his jeans and take off home, with the grocery bag. In a matter of minutes, he'd have dodged his grandmother in the kitchen, his dad in the living room, and be in his own room. The money would go, uncounted and untouched and still in its box in the bag, under his bed. The shotgun also. Tomorrow, once his dad was at work and when his grand-mother went out, Roddy would return it to its cabinet in the basement. Nobody would know. Nobody would even know to look. Who would dream?

Meanwhile, behind Goldie's counter, Mike would wait. When, eventually, somebody came through the door, making the buzzer go, he would scuffle his bound limbs and moan. He would be found and unbound. The cops would be called. Mike would be upset and dazed. He would say the robber wore a ski mask, and work boots, jeans, black T-shirt. He would describe him as being about six feet, big-shouldered, a paunch. "Maybe he should have a tattoo, or moles," Roddy suggested. Not only to make the man more interesting and unique—there were times, discussing him, when this assailant grew real and almost visible to them—but also to keep somebody innocent, who roughly fit the description, from getting nailed.

"Good idea." They gave him a dark green snake on his right forearm, and a black mole on the back of his left hand. His eyes, through the plain navy mask, would be dark blue, they decided.

Mike would be questioned over and over. He would tell the same story over and over. "Don't add details," Roddy warned. "Keep it simple." His folks would probably want to take him to the doctor, or even the hospital, to be checked over.

They each had interesting parts to play, Roddy beforehand and during, Mike during and afterwards. It was like two sepa-rate acts, as they rehearsed. Roddy took the roles of discovering customer, cops, parents, doctor, questioning Mike. There were different directions those conversations could conceivably go. They practised every one they could think of. They were smooth, and prepared. They saw it all perfectly.

Even at the first step, going down to the basement to get the gun, Roddy was struck by the difference between the words and the action. It's not that he thought of backing out. If noth-ing else, he couldn't back out on Mike, they had a commitment, and everything was inevitable now because of that. But still, it was a weird feeling, going down those stairs, going back up. Then all the rest, getting through the remaining afternoon hours, through supper like nothing was different, and finishing fast, and all the way to the storeroom.

Exactly how they had planned.

He got as far as the counter. He could see that Mike had the cash box in the bag, ready to go, the handkerchief to bind his own mouth in his hand, a roll of masking tape waiting to be whipped around his ankles and wrists. In Mike's eyes he saw the same scared, thrilled look of being in the middle of something big that Roddy imagined showed in his own eyes.

They didn't speak. Mike jerked his head towards the shelves behind him and off to one side, and Roddy began raising the gun. This was the trickiest part: having to move very fast afterwards because of the sound of the shot.

He saw Mike's eyes widen and grow bleak, looking over his shoulder, at the same time he heard the door shifting inwards, the buzzer. Mike's mouth started to open. Perhaps his own did as well. He was turning as he was still raising the gun. The woman in the tight wrinkled blue suit was turning, too, but not before he saw her eyes. Perfectly blank eyes. Whatever expression they might have had as she opened the door to Goldie's was wiped out and replaced by nothing at all. The sound of the buzzer was still in the air.

Why hadn't they thought: *Lock the door?*

His own body was rising onto its toes and then slightly crouching. He could feel every muscle: calves, thighs, stomach, shoulders. Finger, too, tightening. This took forever, and no time at all. There was no stopping it.

She whirled and whirled and then she was on the floor like the air had gone out of her. Something began turning red. There was a man in the doorway. This was too much, too much vision, too much to see. He heard Mike's voice, familiar and strange at the same time. "Shit, Roddy, what've you done?" He saw Mike's eyes. He felt Mike's hand removing the shotgun from his. He realized it was the gun that had been weighing him down, and without it, there was nothing to hold him. He leaned over and lost his early, fast supper all over the worn Goldie's floor. Then he was light and could fly. So he did. He flew, and flew, out the back door, through streets, over fences, across fields. He was the wind, he was a bird, he swept, for a little while, over the earth. For a little while he was frantic. Then finally he had those few happy moments that could have lasted forever, but didn't. This is not what he meant. It's not who he is. It's a long time since he's cried, but he could weep, just weep, for everything lost; so he does.

Mrs. Lot and Mrs. Job

ISLA HAS BEEN A WOMAN with hankerings for lean men. Also a woman who leans towards words like *hankering, craving*, words with intensities ranging from hungry to ravenous and which apply to other things, too: to burying her face in her babies' marshmallow bellies; to hurtling her own hot skin into frigid lake water; to hanging from her dad's railwayman arms out into the space between speeding train cars, rushing air pinning skin so hard and cold to her face that tears came.

To any extreme and happy sensation.

A most bitter loss, then.

She would, if she could, jump clear of this pale skin, leap free of these useless muscles and bones, these mute nerves. Veins and arteries, down to the narrowest of capillaries, must still be opening themselves to blood, but she can't feel it. Could she before? Before, she must have been paying insufficient attention. Now she would know better. Oh, she's learning at quite a clip, that's for sure. She is already exhausted by learning. There is too much to know.

Men begin for her with hankerings: seeing James stride out of university into his father's office supply store where she was a young girl working part-time; and many years and much experience later, tangling with Lyle, slapstick-style, at the revolving door of a hotel. With each of them, hankerings grew into cravings, blossomed, blew up, inclined themselves even towards addiction; then with James lapsed into inattention, then into—well, into loathing, although that is also, it seems, a passionate addiction of sorts.

Lyle is sturdier stuff. He sustains craving quite nicely.

It's reachable ribs that do the trick. Long thigh bones. Fine feet, an elegant turn of collarbones, shoulders with not only breadth, but discernible bone ridges just under the surface of skin. Her particular taste.

Taste is salty more than it's sweet. Taste is blue blocks of salt set out years ago for her dad's parents' cattle in summer, great thick rough tongues licking troughs into them, licking them patiently thin. Taste is jazzed-up french fries at fairs, it's sunshine washed off in a winter tub, a summer lake. Taste is her mother's sweat over the iron and the tangy perfume she wore going out for an evening, and it's her father's sweat wrenching pipes into place beneath a new sink and his discarded uniform in a pile for the laundry. Taste was, now to her horror, James's tongue on her, and vice versa. Taste is also her tongue on Lyle, and vice versa.

So the best taste is salty. The story of Lot's wife never made sense to her, and certainly didn't frighten her into learning what she took to be its instruction: don't look back, have no regrets, abandon familiar companions, forget customs and comforts, lose longings. Aim instead stalwartly and—most importantly—obediently forward.

Her sympathies were with Lot's wife.

Anyway, if the pillar of salt Lot's wife became were finally eroded and worn away by the elements, it's not as if that was a different fate than she would have endured if she had aimed stalwartly, obediently forward and never looked back. She would have been eroded and worn away by the elements anyway, by her husband Lot, and by her children, and by duties and hardships and chores, and by various joys, and by years.

If Lot's wife had kept her eyes forward on that long trek away from her home, what would the view have been but black rock, steep mountain, bleak desert, strange rough men, strange weary women? No wonder she looked back instead.

Of course she would have regrets, of course she would glance behind her with certain longings. Isla can regret that she ever met James. She regrets hopping into and out of Lyle's truck, swinging her happy way into Goldie's. Who would not?

Was Lot's wife angry at being transformed into a pillar of salt just for the sin of regret, for being human?

Isla is furious.

This is hardly the restful state of mind she's supposed to be in for encouraging a bullet fragment to release itself from a bone cranny, and gaining strength for surgery that's likely to be both tricky and critical and which will mean everything. On the other hand, rage feels very salty, not at all sweet. This might be exactly the right moment to be wheeled into surgery, on the theory that furious, she's as tough as she's ever likely to be. Except she also knows the roots of rage lie in grief, a weak, collapsing sort of emotion. "Pick your poison," her dad used to say when her parents had company and he was mixing the drinks. Isla picks anger, every time, over sorrow.

Isla's mother Madeleine, despite a general opposition to gloom, now and then lapsed into it: mainly that she had wanted many children, an armful of small bodies to embrace, but something was wrong, or missing, in her or Isla's father, Isla was never clear which, and as a result, "you," her mother said, "were a miracle." This was a large and cherishable thing to be, of course; although it could also be hard, sustaining miraculousness.

Isla's father was a trainman, a conductor, often away, a man who came home with a rhythm in his walk, a certain way of planting his feet. His glamour lay in invisible adventures, racketing over the land, meeting strangers, taking care of them, listening to them. Sometimes when he got home he said he was tired not only of being on his feet, but of smiling. Often he brought home stories, which he could tell in different voices and tones and as if they were happening right in front of their eyes. His words seemed large to Isla because he knew things, good and bad, that occurred out in the world. Sometimes it was strange that he knew these things and these people while she and her mother did not, never would, and part of this strangeness was that he came home anyway to her and her mother, as if they might be the interesting ones, the real story.

There was a nice one about a woman giving birth on the train, and how a whole carful of people cheered, and disembarked laughing and happy about being in on the beginning of a surprising, unscheduled life. She remembers also that her mother was not smiling when he finished that story, and that her father didn't notice. It wasn't, Isla saw, that he didn't care about her mother's feelings, because he did, but that he just plain didn't know. How was that possible?

Awful stories came home with her father as well. Trains were so big, and people so small. They hit people walking alongside the tracks, amputating various limbs, sideswiping their lives. Cars and trucks stalled on tracks. Some people deliberately aimed their cars and trucks at the trains, pressing hard on accelerators for last screaming, hair-raising rides. "The sound," he said, shaking his head as if that would shake it free of the sound. "It's something to hear." Trains were so loud it didn't seem possible to Isla that much could be heard over their engines and wheels, but he said it was. He said you could hear metal and, if you listened carefully, flesh.

"Engineers are worst off, they see what's coming but can't do a thing about it. They say you don't get over that, ever, sliding into a crash." Well, no. She had nightmares sometimes in which large objects rolled slowly but irredeemably into other large objects. Sometimes the sounds of her dreams woke her up.

When she was very little, her father swung Isla around by her arms until she hardly knew which way was up. He carried her on his shoulders when there were distances to walk. Her mother preferred holding hands, and at crowded places like a fair she held tight because there were so many strangers and Isla was her miracle. They all rode together on the Ferris wheel, but steered separate bump 'em cars, slamming wildly into each other. At beaches they swam and watched sunsets. Sometimes at night she heard her parents argue, but not very often. Often they hugged, or just touched.

Honest to God, that's what she thought families were like. No wonder she assumed that kind of happiness, took for granted that if there had to be endings they'd be tragic, wasting-away ones like her father's when he got lung cancer and died when she was sixteen. No wonder James was a shock. Followed by a series of other shocks, courtesy of her cherubs, her ballasts, her Jamie and Alix.

Now this.

The story of Job reflects even worse on God, in her view, than the tale of Lot's wife. No loving creator there, but a prideful, cruelly playful child. What really pissed her off even as a kid first hearing of Job was that although it was Job's faith being tested in the stupid wager between Satan and God, everyone around Job suffered too. His children. His wife. As if they meant nothing at all, were only abstract losses in a tug-of-war for Job's loyalty.

And that Job saw it more or less that way, too, except he didn't know about the bet, he didn't know all his losses were meaningless.

She had no sympathy for Job.

Still, she has seen lives go downhill. She certainly knows that that happens: one mistake, one surprise, and other mistakes and surprises start following until it seems nothing good is going to happen to a person again; that no matter what, any decision or shift or change is going to have bad results. She has not felt this happening to her, but it's possible the past happy eight years have been only a bump in a generally downhill trajectory.

No, she can't believe that. This is a hard situation, but not one she won't bounce out of.

Well okay, not bounce, exactly.

"Isla?" Lyle's face looms over her. Jesus, it's startling when people do that.

"The kids are on their way. You ready to see them?" What, he expects her to nod?

He means her kids, not his. His have no particular requirement to rush to her side; whereas hers do.

Poor Lyle, who not only has to deal with this new nightmare, but with her exceedingly trying children, who are not his fault and who should not be his problem. They would be quite different people, Jamie and Alix, if Lyle were their father—or maybe, too, if Sandy had been their mother, who knows? Lyle's own boys, Bill and Robert, those twins who were still young when their mother died, the same age Isla was when her father died, are now solid citizens. Bill is a physicist at a research institute, and Robert is pursuing a doctorate in the multi-layered relationships between various media and various aspects of politics. Isla can have interesting conversations with Robert. Talking to Bill is a lot like talking to Alix: a deep involvement in a mysterious and unfathomable subject, with its own mysterious and unfathomable language.

The point is, Lyle's boys didn't screw up. They are sturdy, not credulous. They do not expect quick returns, or something for nothing. They do not see something hard in front of them and look for an easy, soft-headed route around it. Their virtues must be difficult for Jamie and Alix to tolerate. They're a bit hard on Isla, as well.

"How do I look?" she whispers to Lyle. "Awful? Scary?"

"You look fine." She'll have to speak to him again about lies. Lying is about the worst thing he can do, he knows that, and however kindly intended, this is no time to forget. She must still look like hell, particularly in this pitiless combination of fluorescence and daylight. Also, oh God—what grotesque, nasty system is in place to empty her body? Or for that matter to fill it. She loves food, it's surely strange not to be hungry. Or, maybe she is hungry. Just one of the multitude of things she can't feel.

Much to think about, a good deal to wonder. Did she leave behind enough clean sheets and towels for the kids she didn't know would be coming? Unfamiliar shoes will be kicked off inside the double-bolted front door, strange creams and shampoos will appear on bathroom shelves. Alix's thin Serenity Corps dresses will maybe be rinsed out and hung over an impromptu clothesline to dry. Lyle and Isla's beautiful house will be invaded by anxiety, crisis, confusion. He will mind that, too. He likes his sanctuary.

"Really," Lyle says, "I wouldn't let the kids in if you looked upsetting. Trust me. You know, they're out in the hall now, they're waiting."

Oh. Well then. That's a bit more abrupt than she expected, kind of a shock. Also she is sharply reminded that the small gesture she would make with her hand to say, never mind, go ahead, is no longer possible. All that silent, eloquent language is gone.

So how can she tell her children then that she loves them, and that no matter how she looks, they shouldn't be frightened? If she can't put her arms around Jamie, or stroke Alix's wild and brilliant red hair, so much like Isla's own at that age, how will they understand that everything is going to be fine, and this is only an interruption, terrible and upsetting and annoying but really only an interruption? No matter what, she has always embraced them, although for sure she has also shouted, argued, pleaded, slammed doors. But always, always she has tried to put her arms around them. Because even people with irregular lives need regularity. They need to know some things for sure.

She hardly knows what to expect. Her children are full of surprises. Other young people endure catastrophe without falling apart, why not hers? Jamie is twenty-five years old, and as old as the hills. His beautiful little-boy's face won't ever unline and uncrease itself back to innocence. The things he has done! The things that have been done to him!

And Alix—gullible, foolish Alix has pledged herself to serenity. Literally, she has pledged herself to something called the Serenity Corps, and obedience to, reverence for, a tubby middle-aged fellow with excessively blue eyes who calls himself

Master Ambrose. Alix now calls herself Starglow, although outside the Serenity Corps no one bothers. Even taking all their upheavals into account, Isla can't think how she raised someone who would call herself Starglow.

At any rate Alix cannot make it sound reasonable to Isla. Alix has waved her thin, long-fingered hands vaguely, widened her absorbing eyes under that riveting fall of red hair, and spoken of universal powers and forces, a community of support, purpose, and love. But what is that purpose? What kind of love? For three years now, Isla has half-expected a phone call, a knock on the door, a stranger's voice announcing that Alix has been discovered, toes pointed to heaven, dead in a hopeful migration to salvation on a far better, kindlier, more golden planet.

Something like that.

Alix is twenty-two. She is too old to believe in stupid shit, and she is far too young to die.

How the hell did this happen to those sweet, clever, most adorable babies, toddlers, children? A family weakness, perhaps. A grave need that may exist in anyone, but in them happened to be precisely located and drilled into, bringing forth gushers of trouble. James happened, he tapped those gushers in his children's tenderest, wariest, clumsiest years. Oh, Isla could kill him, she really could.

Why didn't she, then, when she had the chance? With a little effort she could have tracked him down and killed him any number of times in the past decade or so. Easy to say she could kill him now, when she so clearly can't. Well, mothers don't have time for murder, do they? Nor would it have exactly improved the situation.

Now that she can no longer rise, at least for the time being, to any occasion of theirs, it will be interesting to see if they rise to this occasion of hers, these two young people, her babies, who have sought oblivion, or salvation, in some strange and terrible places.

Maybe mere escape is what they've been after. She wouldn't mind a touch of that herself. A touch of anything, for that matter.

Ready or not, here they are. "Mum." Alix is abruptly leaning over her, huge-eyed with fear, skin translucent with pity. "Oh Mum."

Or maybe her skin is translucent with hunger. She has always been thin, but now looks gaunt. That son of a bitch Master Ambrose, is he starving Isla's daughter? Alix's fly-about hair sweeps her cheeks and whips the air. Its flamboyance is her own, its shoulder-blade length however, part of the uniform of female corps members, intended to reflect, presumably, serenity. The rest of the uniform is a brown cottony garment, loose and nearly transparent. A strange, lost, yearning soul looks out of those large eyes, Isla thinks. When Alix moves, stepping forward to lean over her mother, stepping back to make way for her brother, the word *waft* comes to mind.

Jamie's eyes are brittle, his features fixed and difficult to read. "Ma! What the hell did you think you were doing, getting yourself shot like that?" Oh, she sees. He has set out to be hearty, jocular; as if an injection of gusto into the room could raise her up, hoist her back onto her feet; like Jesus, if he'd performed his Lazarus miracle using only his own zest and energy.

Jamie was a little boy who ran everywhere, all the time. As soon as he found his toddler-legs he was off: tearing around furniture, tottering through rooms, climbing stairs, nipping through screen doors, pelting across lawns and down sidewalks. Isla ran and ran after him, catching him up, clutching some movable part of him, hauling him home.

Was he running towards some desire or away from something that scared him? Asleep, his little legs moved under the sheets like a dreaming puppy's, his little arms flailed. He had nightmares and woke crying. What images could so distress a boy she could swear had no waking experience of fear? Isla lay beside him, holding him until he grew calm and fell back into sleep. Sometimes she fell asleep herself and in the morning

James would be irritable. "You'll spoil him," he said. "You'll make him soft."

If only she had.

"He's just a little boy. He only wants comfort. There's no such thing as spoiling a little boy who wants comfort." In the contest between a husband's desires and the needs of a child, no question arose in her mind. Although it took some time to realize that it was, as James saw it, or failed to see it, a contest. Who would dream such a thing of a grown man? Not Isla.

Jamie ran and ran and grew hard rather than soft. His plump cheeks pared themselves to the bone, and his large, long-lashed eyes grew even larger, more like Alix's, in his narrowing, less and less innocent face. Now he is firm-bodied, and probably good-looking, although that's a difficult thing for a mother to discern about a son. He still has those lashes, which women must love. Both her children are immensely attractive and appealing from this angle, looking up slant-wise, even though Alix is so thin and Jamie so hard. Neither of them looks entirely like their father, nor entirely like her, nor quite like each other. She's glad there's no major resemblance to James, and doesn't care if that's because her features and James's got mixed and combined in new ways so that hers were lost, too.

Once, briefly, the subject of their father was obsessively interesting. Perhaps it still is, but he doesn't come up in family conversation; certainly not since Lyle. Do they ever talk to him? Surely not. They must talk *about* him, though. He is hardly an entirely scrubbable stain. There's no erasing someone, and anyway, like good dogs kids keep hoping for love.

"Careless of me, yes," she says to Jamie, hoping she's smiling and that her eyes show some reassuring merriment. "But it's going to be fine. Lyle must have told you."

"Yeah," Jamie nods. "Where's the peckerhead that did it? Is he busted?"

He would mean the boy. Jamie bends over her, uneasily gentle, dodging, she supposes, whatever apparatus she's attached to.

But determined to embrace her; that's nice, that's brave. His arms go around where her body must be, and his cheek is laid next to hers. Her son, her weak-willed, desiring Jamie who for a time, at least, didn't know what he desired and chose the wrong things.

Oh, she has produced a tear! Can feel it rolling down her skin, into the pillow!

Jamie's breath, so close, is slightly stale; unantiseptic, which is oddly refreshing. "If the cops haven't got him, I'm going to. I'll take the prick out."

There's the spirit.

But the spirit only. Without awful, hot-headed drugs, he wouldn't hurt anyone, would he? He has surely done penance and moreover been healed—still, who is he to call another young criminal *peckerhead, prick?*

At his worst moments he didn't have a gun. At his worst moments he was no Roddy.

Lyle steps forward, puts a hand on Jamie's shoulder. "No," he says calmly, "the police either have him or will have him. Everybody knows who it was, there's no secret about it. So we'll just leave it in the hands of the cops and concentrate on your mother." This is exactly right, of course. Lyle knows both the importance and the techniques of defusing. There is something to be said for Jamie's loyal, vengeful passion, however, and something passionately desirable missing from Lyle. "We're all upset and angry, but the only thing that really counts is your mother, we have to keep focused on whatever helps her, makes her strong." He is wise. She is fortunate.

Well, sort of fortunate.

Count on Alix for the unexpected. Suddenly she is responding as if Lyle has spoken some kind of revelation, beaming down at Isla with eerie radiance. "Yes," she says, "exactly." She looks—can it be?—happy. As if Lyle has reminded her of something good that had slipped her mind.

Much slips what passes at the moment for Alix's mind. At least Jamie is recovered from his affection, his desire, his evident need for drugs with awesome, horrifying names. At least he has been successfully frightened and punished and loved into a sturdier, if less vivid, less rollicking, less desperate frame of mind. But Alix—she has hooked herself to belief, faith, an addiction that may be even harder to kick.

This is what Isla means about Job, doom, fate, luck.

Lyle finds it hopeful that they can still get through to Alix, at least in certain specific, physical ways, and in a sense he is right. A good sign, for instance, that he could get word to her about Isla, and that Alix has been able to come here. The Serenity Corps may be a cult, as in Isla's view it certainly is, but so far it hasn't quite managed to amputate families from followers.

It's three years since Isla and Lyle first heard the name "Master Ambrose," three years of hardly understanding a goddamn word the girl says. "Ah, don't sweat it," is Jamie's advice, "It's just a stupid patch. I came out of mine, she'll come out of hers." But Jamie might remember that he did not escape his stupid patch either undamaged or solely under his own steam. It's not as if he suddenly decided the jig was up and he had to get clean, all on his own. Or that it was easy, and did not involve not only lawyers and jail time and suffering, but his own sweat and vomit. All that.

When Alix announced herself pledged to Master Ambrose, Isla drove straight to the Serenity farm, seventy or so kilometres north, well out of the way and hardly promising for even Serenity's subsistence farming and gardening. Alix said, with her awful new expression of bliss, "It's about loyalty to each other. A whole community of people dedicated to the same end. Really dedicated. Because once you have serenity, you've achieved life's highest goal. But it's complicated, so it's necessary to pursue it together. Well, maybe not necessary, exactly, but it's the best way because everybody helps keep everybody else focused on serenity all the time, whatever we're doing."

Alix came to the unmarked farm gate to meet Isla. "Please be nice, Mother," she said, "I know it's strange to you, but try to see it the way we do." She looked nervous and proud both, introducing Isla and Master Ambrose, who was waiting, brown-garmented and smiling plumply, in a garden. "I regret," he said, "that we do not invite outsiders indoors. The quest for serenity is carefully undertaken, and we cannot have the balances of our community's home disrupted in any way." He offered her tea, though. She refused.

Once there, she wasn't sure why she'd come, except to see the place. It would not help her cause with Alix to leap at the man's throat, which is mainly what she wanted to do. "Starglow, you know," he told her, smug bastard, "has never been truly a child in your life. Her spirit is ancient, she is a very old soul."

How dared he?

He went on in that way, Alix's eyes on him wide and adoring. "You evil little toad," Isla wanted to say, and something melodramatic like "Unhand my daughter." But Alix, she could see, was not inclined to be unhanded. She was entranced, bewitched, beguiled, suckered. And so Isla drove away speechless. She and Alix did not embrace when she left. Alix stepped back from Isla's arms and said, "I'm sorry, but I feel your anger and it's too soon for me to come too close to anyone not in touch with serenity. I'm not strong enough in my own serenity yet."

Well.

But who wouldn't like to be told their soul is quite old and therefore, by extension, quite wise? A nice compliment, Isla could see the appeal, but—consider the source: a man who, if nothing else, had a choice of any name at all and chose Ambrose, which said something about him, but what? Besides that when it came to beauty and euphony, he had a tin ear?

Isla's first journey was pointless and later ones no more successful. The unbudgeable Alix continues to speak of Master Ambrose in the tones Isla imagines Jamie might have used to speak of his drugs, if he had felt able at the time to talk about that most fervent and focused attachment. Alix also speaks of things like internal flames burning radiantly. "The depth," she has remarked. "The pure knowing." In Master Ambrose's eyes, Alix apparently sees redemption and love, purity and peace and salvation. Isla sees a voracious, glittering appetite for young souls. She doesn't want to think about the appetite she assumes for young bodies.

She is prejudiced, of course. Just as she was prejudiced against whoever first fed Jamie drugs.

Now here's this young woman beaming like a lunatic over the bed rails. The fact is, Alix at twenty-two calls herself Starglow and has given herself over to a load of spiritual junk. Isla could slap her silly. She could grab and shake and embrace her until the poor little thin lost thing felt her mother's goddamn love right into her nerve endings and bones. For Christ's sake!

Unable to do any of this, Isla tries to return her daughter's blissful beam with the severest frown she can conjure.

Apparently it is unsuccessful, or insufficient.

"Let me tell you what happened," Alix says. "When Lyle called and told me about all this." She waves her hand over Isla, meaning, Isla supposes, "all this."

"I was so upset. It was an awful shock, and so sad." So it was, so it is; not most for Alix, not least for Isla. Still Isla is, after all, touched. She pictures Alix weeping, pulling at that glorious hair, making a great, grieving scene among people to whom virtue evidently involves never caring enough to make a scene.

She tries to apply an expression of willing benevolence, but then Alix goes on to say, "And then I thought, what have I learned from Serenity if I get upset so easily?"

Easily! Isla's mouth, she believes, falls open.

"Anyway, somebody must have gone for Master Ambrose. And he came! He came right to me. And he spoke to me, took me aside, and that's such an honour, you know." Alix glistens as if she expects Isla to appreciate what a big moment it must have been. Well, no doubt. To her.

"And he took me to the Calm Room, just the two of us." Good lord, what's the calm room? And what would be the names of the Serenity Corps's other rooms? "He sat down with me and held my hands and told me to sit quietly for as long as it took, breathe in and out, count my breaths. That's an exercise for beginners, really, so I was almost upset again, that he thought I was just a beginner, but then when I did it, it worked, I got a grip on myself, just like when I really was a beginner."

Is she trying to tell Isla something? About origins, maybe?

"So we sat for a while with me breathing and looking into his eyes, and finally he nodded and asked me what happened. So I told him and said you were paralyzed and, you know, that you're not old enough to just have to lie there, here, for the rest of your life, forever."

As if there might be an age when such a thing wouldn't matter?

The rest of it—the rest of it, Isla will refuse to absorb.

"I said I had to come because, you know, you're my mother." Oh, triumph! "I mean, mostly we're supposed to overcome attachments like that, so we're sort of attached and unattached at the same time, for everything the same way. I was kind of scared he'd be disappointed in me, but he was really nice. Well, I mean he's always nice, but he just nodded like he understood. About being attached after all. Because you're my mum."

Now she has tears in her eyes. So, oddly, does Isla. Hearing Alix use the word *mum* in that intimate tone, that's one reason. The other is rage: that people, anyone, her own child, could imagine that overcoming attachment, or becoming attached and unattached to the same degree, or feeling attached or unattached in the same way for everything, or anything, could be a goal, or any kind of achievement.

This is so stringently celibate and sterile a notion, and at the same time so radically promiscuous, and must require such a corkscrewing and compressing of emotion and thought that it has to be crippling. So this is how Master Ambrose keeps his followers: he leeches onto them when they're casting about, sadly or desperately, for safety and peace for their hearts, then gives them impossible ways to achieve safety and peace.

He must take them for everything they've got; by which Isla does not mean money.

Did she not quite know this before? Whatever Alix has said about the Serenity Corps, Master Ambrose, it must have been caught in the net of Isla's own failure. Because when Alix spoke of *love* and *support* and *community*, it was as if she'd never experienced such amazements before. Quite a blow.

There may be some virtue, although a very bitter virtue, in having to lie here and listen.

"He said he understood, and that sometimes it was important to learn more about the quality of attachments by acting on them. So I could come." Could? That fat bastard needed to give Alix permission?

Jamie says, "For God's sake, Alix, who gives a shit? This isn't about you and your goofy friends, it's about Mother." There was a time he and Alix were close. Maybe they still are, in their ways. Maybe only a brother—certainly not a mother—can say things like that.

Alix shakes her head, making her hair fly up slightly. "Starglow. And I know it's about Mum. That's one reason I'm here. Because of what Master Ambrose said, about why it might be so wonderful that this happened."

Master Ambrose and Alix have rendered Isla speechless again. She is having some trouble breathing. Something in the nearby machinery is changing its tune also, starting to stutter. "Oh fuck," Jamie says.

"No, really. Listen. When he started talking, it all began to make sense. Of course I should have known it would, I'm just not advanced enough to know for myself, but I keep learning and getting better at figuring things out because sometimes you just need to hear something said and you know it's the truth, and next time you can get closer to that on your own."

Next time. There's a happy thought. Isla is catching her breath again, the machinery is resuming its rhythm. Was that a dangerous moment? Does she have to take special care? Does she, for instance, have to coolly count breaths in the interests of sustaining serenity?

"He said this doesn't need to be awful. That it's actually a huge opportunity and a person can be blessed, really, by sorrow or trouble. And how if you can't move, it can make you go into yourself instead and find the truths of the spirit. Because to feel the eternal flame of true serenity, a person needs to be still, and here you are, set in the midst of stillness even though I know you don't mean to be, but you are, and you could use it, not be hurt or damaged, that it's not awful but a possibility, you see?"

Alix has made herself breathless. No wonder. This might be funny if Alix were somebody else's daughter, raised a fool by some other person. How does that young fellow's, that freckled shooter's, that Roddy's mother feel at the moment? As if her child, too, is no one she knows, has gone far beyond foreignness, become truly alien? Here are these clasped white hands, this intense face with its familiar features, this expanse of sweet daughterly skin Isla has touched and caressed and bandaged and marvelled at, and it has become something else altogether.

Even Master Ambrose must have a mother. A peculiar outcome for her, as well, a son of such strange, compelling needs and such resulting strange, compelling powers. But perhaps it's no surprise, perhaps he learned what he knows at his mother's knee. Perhaps she is evangelical in her own ways. It's hard to imagine Master Ambrose's mother.

"He said stillness, however you achieve it, is necessary for lighting the flame of serenity. In a way, you're luckier than me because I keep trying and trying and I haven't been still enough yet, I've never quite got there. So if you look at it that way, this is really a blessing because here you are, you walked right into it."

"Alix," Jamie says. He is tugging her arm now, trying to move her, remove her. "For Christ's sake."

"No, really." She pulls free. They used to wrestle in the living room and out on the lawn when they were little, when he was maybe eight and she was five, nine and six, ten and seven. Then they stopped. They became, maybe, more conscious of bodies, differences, awkwardnesses. "It's important. What he said, it's so perfect and right. I'm not evolved enough to explain it very well, but he said if I could remember his words, because he reached the other side ages ago, anyway, he said that could help pull you over to the other side, too. So honestly, Mum, all this could be incredibly lucky. Being touched by the flame without even trying, that's really something."

It sure is. There's quite a silence. Because, Isla supposes, there is really nothing to say to this particular, relatively innocent, insanity.

Finally good Lyle steps forward. He puts his large hands, with their long and talented fingers, on Alix's shoulders. "I think," he says fairly gently, "that might be enough. Your mother needs to rest as much as she can. Why don't the three of us take a break, go for coffee?" A break? As if Isla is hard work, difficult to endure, like coal mining or building a railway? But why pick at Lyle? He's not the one going on about how lucky she is to be touched by the flames of paralysis.

He and Jamie are exchanging glances behind Alix's back. They must be close, in their way. Isla wonders if Jamie ever feels angry with Lyle, just for knowing so much? It's hard not to be rescued, but it must be difficult in other ways to have been rescued.

"But," Alix tries to insist, "this is the moment."

"I think perhaps not," says Lyle, and turns her more firmly away.

"Mum," Alix cries. This is familiar: Alix the toddler who's tripped over a curb, banging her round perfect knees; Alix the little girl who's fallen off her two-wheeler, scraping a tender elbow and gashing a smooth, straight, vitamin-enriched leg; Alix the teenager gape-mouthed with grief for her father, her brother, herself. All those Alixes crying out, "Mum."

Isla breathes in and breathes out, counts the breaths up to ten, and then again. An exercise for beginners? All right. And something to be grateful for and attentive to because she so easily might not be breathing, but for a centimetre here, a centimetre there? That's really something.

"You go with Lyle, sweetie," she says, "and I'll count my breaths for a while. It's a nice peaceful sort of thing to do, isn't it?"

Look at that careful, tentative smile, look at that leap of hope in the eyes, that tremble of gratitude—so large a return for something so small. How did Alix learn hope, where did she learn about yearning?

Jamie bends over Isla again. "Sorry. I didn't know how to make her stop. But poor kid, eh? You rest and forget all that shit. We'll see you later." He touches, or appears to touch, her right hand, or something down there past her vision. She guesses he doesn't quite have the hang of things yet; that she really can't feel a thing.

One night, long after James, and after meeting but before marrying Lyle, when it was just Isla, Jamie, and Alix together in that spare rented duplex she'd moved them into, and while Isla was loading the dishwasher after a dinner her children had only picked at, Alix came howling downstairs, hurtling into the kitchen, throwing herself into a chair, throwing her head down onto her arms.

Because she had walked in on Jamie, in the bathroom, with a syringe, a small trail of blood trickling where he'd tried, and failed, to shoot up. Isla was loading the dishwasher at the same moment Jamie was loading his arm. That's how little she knew, how out of touch she was then. Isla heard him yell, "Get the fuck out of here," dropped a plate, and then Alix was there, weeping at the kitchen table.

The shattered plate, the weeping Alix, Jamie upstairs with a needle going into his arm—Isla called Lyle. That must have been the first time she ever called him for help. And he came.

By dawn many phone calls had been made and Jamie was bundled into Lyle's car, speeding towards a private rehab centre thanks to Lyle's contacts. By dawn Alix was finally asleep upstairs in her room, and Isla had crashed downstairs on the couch. Maybe she should have stayed awake. Maybe she should have kept Alix awake, kept them both talking and breathing, talking and breathing until something was clear enough. Maybe she has made a habit of losing steam at critical moments, sleeping through turning points. That wasn't the first time.

"Love you," Isla says as they leave. She means all three of them. Lyle comes back to her bedside, gives a thumbs-up. He is kind, he is good, there's no way not to keep knowing that.

One thing for sure, Alix and Jamie aren't the children middle-class mothers, ex-wives and wives, vice-presidents and part owners of their own clever, creative concerns anticipate having. If women like Isla expect extremes in their children, it must be extremes of goodness or brilliance. They anticipate sturdiness, capability, security, confidence, all the natural results of their own good intentions and without severe penalties for their failures. They certainly do not expect to raise children with psychic holes in their sides large and open enough to stick whole fists into.

Breathe carefully, breathe slowly and count.

A nurse hustles in. Everyone who works here is always in a hurry. Lucky them. "Good, you're on your own. We want you to rest, so I'm going to give you something to help you sleep, all right?" As if a woman who can neither feel nor move has a choice.

At least in this circumstance another needle causes no pain. Does that count as looking, in some Alix-approved way, on the bright side?

How strange it would be to believe in something, anything, the way Alix does. What kind of blind leap would it require? Because of her work, Isla knows a good deal about theories of belief, but that's really only to do with methods of persuasion, not faith. Faith is peculiar. Faith is beyond her.

How about hope, then?

How about sleep? Her vision is blurring, a strange but appealing, cozy, warm blanket of peace descending over every skittering thought in her head. Maybe like Jamie during those terrible years. Except he grew thin and wild, he shook and trembled with his violent desire to be tranquil. Isla, perceiving remotely how easing and enfolding and protecting this feels, and how a person might never want to emerge, thinks that Jamie must, after all, have been brave and even quite strong to crawl out. She must remember to ask him about that. She thinks, "Oh, this is nice, no wonder he loved it so much," and slips quietly, darkly, under again.

Winging It

R ODDY CAN'T BELIEVE HE CRIED. In front of people. Men. He hasn't cried since they told him about his mother, and then okay, he did, but in his own room, alone. Partly for her, or what he remembered of her; but mainly for the too-lateness of everything: her finding him, him finding her, them explaining and saying things. Her being, then, permanently all the way up, finally happy. What was no longer possible.

When he was little, he supposes he cried sometimes. He must have with her, little kids do. Then a few times with his grandmother, but that was more when he did something like fall off his bike, like the time he busted his arm flying over a curb. Not when it was just hurt feelings, and never in front of another guy, like a vice-principal, or even, maybe especially, Mike. Not his dad, either. It would have made his dad awkward if he had to do something, or say something, about Roddy in tears.

Now he's fallen all to shit in front of two cops and a lawyer. Like he's a baby. When shit, what he is, is an armed robber, think of that!

"I'm an armed robber," he thinks, imagining that will make him swell and grow tall in his chair; but *armed robber* is a way bigger thing than he ever set out to be. Another thing he didn't think of before: the words. They are serious and large, and he isn't either serious or large.

Mike was large, and he sure sounded serious in the planning, but then, so did Roddy, and neither of them meant it to be as serious as it's turned out. Roddy here. That woman. And

Mike—where is he? "Your friend," says the bigger cop as if he's listening to the inside of Roddy's head, "your buddy in crime, he's just down the hall, in case you're interested. Also if you're interested, he's saying he had nothing to do with all this, it was your idea, your fuck-up. What do you think about that?"

What Roddy thinks is "No." Then, "Can that be true?"

Mike's been his friend forever. They even got teased about it one time last year. "Faggots," said a guy whose dad was a soldier who'd just retired and moved to town off a military base. The new guy'd grown up on military bases. Maybe that made him stupid. Hardly anybody ever messed with them, especially with Mike due to his size, but Roddy, too, because he could go in low and hard and mean when he had to. Mike started getting major big, not only tall but bulking up, too, when he was about fourteen, and Roddy already knew, for want of size, to be fast, so—they're a team. Mike whipped around and decked the guy, a clean right-hand punch. When the guy got up, Roddy head-butted his gut. Roddy and Mike touched fists in the air. Because they're not faggots, they're buddies, like the cop said except not with that edge the way the cop said it.

They look after each other. They know some stuff.

They both got suspended. Two weeks that time. "You have to learn to ignore some people," Roddy's grandmother pleaded. "Just don't react. Walk away." But she didn't know what she was talking about. If he just walked away, he'd be fucked. Mike said his parents went on about maybe not letting him and Roddy hang out any more. Like, Mike said, they could decide who anybody hung out with.

When they were young, everybody in their families used to say it was nice they were friends and a good thing they had each other to hang out with. Nobody minded, everybody figured they were safe and taken care of if they were together, and didn't worry when they took off exploring, prowled country roads, picked up beer bottles to turn in for money, or even found dead birds to bring home and poke at, take apart, and then bury.

Could Mike really be just down the hall now, telling other cops he's totally innocent and it was all Roddy's idea, nothing to do with him? That part was in the script, that it was nothing to do with him, but he was supposed to say the guy was a stranger with a tattoo on one arm, a mole on the back of his hand. Roddy's name wasn't going to come up at all, no reason it would.

"They'll check me out," Mike said, and Roddy nodded. They watched TV, they saw movies, they knew that much. "But there's no way to connect me. They can suspect me, I guess, for a while, but they won't get anywhere."

Roddy would be long gone, the money under his bed, the gun back in its rack in his basement. "What about that we're friends, though?" Roddy wondered. "If they check you out, won't they do me, too?"

"So what? They won't look very hard. They come to your door and you're all yawning, just getting up." The script called for Roddy, hearing the news, to ask worried questions about his friend Mike: was he okay, was he hurt, did anything bad happen to him? "Nothing to it. Just what you'd say if it was true anyway." This was also part of their rehearsals, Mike playing cops, Roddy expressing concern for his pal.

Wasted, all wasted. They're really winging it now.

They've had those punch-ups together, they've swum and biked and smoked up together, gone to movies and dances and for that matter shoplifted together. CDs, mainly. Nature books, for Roddy's pictures of tiny, beautiful creatures. They hang out with other people too, sometimes, but always at the root of it, it's the two of them, and maybe it started just because Mike and his mother were the first on the doorstep when Roddy and his dad came to town, but that doesn't matter. Those moments just happen. Good and bad moments, Roddy is beginning to see.

So if Mike ratted him out, that'd be pretty incredible.

If Mike ratted him out, it'd mean Roddy couldn't trust any- one. He'd have to look at everything in some different way.

He probably has to do that anyway.

When he and his dad moved to town, and Mike and his mother came to the door, how come Mike wanted to be friends? How was it he didn't already have friends? Roddy knows why he took to Mike, but how come it worked the other way, too?

"So what do you think about that?" the cop who isn't so big is asking. "Your buddy saying the whole thing was you, and he's as surprised as everyone else. You know what he says? He says he's real upset because you took advantage of him having that job. That you knew there was money because he mentioned it, just talking to you like a friend would. And also, by the way, that he took the gun away from you. Which also by the way the husband of the woman you shot can confirm."

Mike did take the gun, Roddy has a recollection of Mike lifting it out of his hands. But it wasn't the way the cop makes it sound, like they wrestled for it, like Mike was doing some brave thing.

The woman you shot.

Imagine if *armed robber* isn't all he is, imagine if there's worse words for him.

There were her eyes. There was blood.

There was that guy in the doorway. He must be the husband, who saw Mike take the gun away.

Even with the rough, red and black striped blanket they've brought him, he shivers.

What the cop says Mike's been saying, it's what somebody desperate to get clear likely would say: that Roddy took advantage, that Mike was surprised as anyone else.

They didn't rehearse for getting caught, that's the trouble. Getting caught didn't seem possible. But it would make an awful kind of sense if Mike laid the whole thing on him. Because Roddy's already fucked, and Mike can still save himself.

He shrugs. "Whatever," he says.

The younger cop turns red and slams his fist on the table between them. Roddy and his lawyer both jump. He imagines good-cop, bad-cop, everybody knows that routine, but can somebody make his own face go red on purpose? "You little punk, what do you mean, *whatever*? This is deeper shit than you've ever imagined, so don't give me *whatever*, you little asshole."

"Hey, hold on," says Roddy's lawyer. "You can't talk to him that way."

"The fuck I can't. Listen," and he leans forward over the table, with his skin all tight and a vein in his neck popping, which it doesn't seem possible he could make happen if he wasn't truly angry, "you know how much money you were going to be getting? Three hundred and forty-two bucks. Guess that's a lot of popcorn and dope for a punk like you, but for three hundred and forty-two bucks, which you didn't even get, you shot somebody. How about that?"

Mike had figured there'd be a couple of thousand, maybe more. What happened?

"Guess you didn't know Doreen called in and told the day clerk to take everything in the box so far to the bank. So all you would've got was the take from part of a day. Different from last year, right? Different from what your buddy told you when the two of you were setting this up?"

Roddy stares into his lap. He has nothing to say.

Of course the cop calls her Doreen. Everybody knows everybody in this town. That's probably the biggest reason he and Mike wanted to leave: so they could have lives without everyone knowing. Even the good stuff's hard to take. Having some woman stop him in a store and say something like "Your grandmother tells me you're doing very well in school," that's the kind of thing makes him and Mike crazy. Or having some guy from her church go past on the street and say "Quite the haircut you got there, young fellow." Like it's anybody's business if Roddy wants stubble with his scalp shining through. It's a cool look. Sleek. Sort of dangerous. Anyplace else, people might notice, but nobody'd say anything because they wouldn't know him. They wouldn't know his dad or his grandmother, either. He'd be free. Mike, too. Mike says people keep their eyes on them more than they used to in stores, like they know the two of them have a little distraction routine when they shoplift, but aren't doing anything about it, just watching.

Anyway, they don't take anything huge or expensive, never clothes or other kinds of stuff that get bought for them anyway. It's just little things they've ever stolen, well, that and money a couple of times from purses a couple of the rich girls left lying around at school. Not much money, no big deal, although he guesses it would have been if they'd been caught. Which they weren't, although the vice-principal called them separately to the office to ask questions, and phoned their homes to say there might be a problem. For himself, Roddy said to his grandmother and his dad, "I don't know why they'd think it was us. Mr. Dougherty's a jerk anyway, and he doesn't like us, and the girls who lost the money are rich and we're not, so maybe he figures we'd be easy to blame."

Nobody likes rich people. Nobody cares what happens to them. Mike said, "It's not like they'd miss it," meaning the rich girls, and also the stores. Even Doreen, if it hadn't all got fucked up, she wouldn't have lost anything. "She's got insurance," Mike said. "They just pay her back. It's nothing to them."

All small stuff. A little excitement, kind of a game, nothing really bad, nothing to take very seriously, even though people like Roddy's dad and his grandmother would have taken it seriously, if they'd known. If they'd got caught, his grandmother would have been really embarrassed.

Oh Jesus, he keeps forgetting. Here he sits, and he still can't keep a grip on knowing what's happened.

"Right, then," says the younger cop, checking the tape recorder, looking hard at Roddy, a real down-to-business expression. "It's your turn to start talking. From about noon. Everything you did. Step by step. If you made a ham sandwich for yourself, we want to hear about it. Down to did you use mustard and was the bread whole wheat or white. Understand? Every goddamn move you made."

Have they charged him? There's some kind of difference between getting arrested and being charged, but he's not exactly clear what it is, and he can't remember what-all's exactly been said. That's what his dad got the lawyer for, he supposes, to know that kind of thing; except when Roddy looks at him, searching for some kind of clue, the guy just nods. He's serious-looking, middle-aged, thin, not a very good haircut. He doesn't look successful, is what Roddy means.

He also doesn't look glad to have Roddy as a client. He doesn't look sympathetic. He doesn't look as if he likes Roddy, or as if he cares much what happens to him.

Shit, if that's his own lawyer, what about everyone else? He'll never be able to go anyplace in this town ever again. People will whisper, they'll stare, they'll be like the cop who called him a punk. Some of them'll be scared. *Armed robber.*

He's lost track again. Like he'll ever be wandering around town any more. It's his grandmother who'll have to do that, and his dad.

And Mike?

Okay, he can go step-by-step through his day. When he gets to about suppertime, eating fast, leaving the table, going up to his room, something will start coming to him, somehow he'll get himself from his room to that field without any detour to Goldie's. Because what can they prove?

Oh. Probably everything. Never mind Mike, there was the guy in the doorway. The husband.

Maybe the woman, too. Oh God, he hopes so.

He looks around wildly, sees only men and grey walls and bright light. No way out, no way in the world. All three men go tense. He can feel their muscles filling up more space in the room.

Think. Think.

Well, he guesses, fuck it.

Mainly, fuck it. Never mind whatever Mike's saying, there's no really good reason to drag anybody else into the shit, Roddy

can be that much of a good person. He would like to be something not bad, anyway; something that, even if it's just to himself, says he's not totally bad.

It's like he's two people, or three, being here. One's watching
this, like from up in a corner or off to the side, and the other
one's sitting on this hard metal chair, right in the middle of it.

The lucky one is following the plan, asleep in his room,
everything warm, well, and safe.

"Start talking," the older cop says.

"You don't have to," the lawyer says, although he nodded
before and seems to want Roddy to. It's late. He probably wants
to go home.

Anyway there's no way out now. Not talking wouldn't help
that. So he begins. He thinks his words make sense, one following another, on and on through the day, every move. He's listening to be careful he's not screwing up, but it doesn't feel like he's
actually speaking, himself. His own voice buzzes slightly in his
ears. This is weirder than dope. Mainly dope makes him sleepy,
but he's wide awake now, just split into speaker and listener.
Plus the one who got free. Really strange.

Maybe he's insane.

Maybe he should have thrown himself off a bridge.

Too late now.

He tells even what he and his dad and grandmother had for
supper, which was pork chops and mashed potatoes and peas.
Now and then one of the cops interrupts to ask things like "And
what time was that?" or "When you dropped the shotgun out
your bedroom window, how could you be sure nobody would
see you?" or "Describe where that bush is that you went behind to
put the gun down your pantleg." Mainly they just let him go on.

He has to be careful once he gets himself to Goldie's storeroom. He can't, for instance, say a word about whistling the
first notes to *The Good, the Bad and the Ugly*, has to make Mike
look pleased to see him at first, assuming he's just dropping in,
and then shocked by the gun. He has to make it sound as if

Mike could really be scared of him. "I don't know what he thought. But he looked like he figured I'd shoot him."

"Would you have?"

Roddy feels himself shrug again. "I don't know."

"He was willing to hand over the money?"

"I don't know. It didn't get that far. I just know he looked real upset."

That's the best he thinks he can do for Mike. He wonders what Mike's doing for him. But then, what can he do? If he wanted to, he couldn't save Roddy.

He'd just like to know how bad Mike wants to.

"Then what happened?"

He sees Mike's eyes widen, at the same time hears the first small doorway movement. He's whirling again. He's hearing the buzzer and seeing the woman's face, flattened by shock into no expression at all. He sees the blue suit, the wrinkles across the lap. She's turning and his hands, not part of his body, removed from his brain, are bringing the gun up. His betraying finger is tightening. "I didn't mean it," he cries. "It was an accident."

Accident isn't quite the right word. He can't think what the right one might be. Just "I swear to God, it wasn't supposed to happen. She startled me, and I kind of jumped. I don't even know how to use a gun, really. I didn't know. I didn't mean it." He hears his voice rising and rising. If he can make them hear, if he can only get through, they'll have to see he's innocent in a way that should count. They're looking at him like they're thinking, "Man, are you stupid." And he's not! Haven't they ever done an awful thing sort of by accident? Haven't they ever been in some situation they're desperately wishing hadn't happened, but did happen, that they can't fix or undo?

"Right then." The big cop stands up suddenly, so that his chair scrapes back. "That's it."

Roddy looks from face to face. His lawyer and the other cop are standing as well, but more slowly. Nobody seems to notice that Roddy doesn't know what's going on. "What?" he asks.

"Huh?" says his lawyer. "Oh. You're going to the cells. I'll see you in the morning, at court. I'll talk to your folks about bail, but I wouldn't hold out a whole lot of hope. With charges like this, the chances aren't very good."

When Roddy was younger, he and his grandmother and his dad used to sit on the sofa watching TV and eating popcorn. They fit tight, one on each side of him. His grandmother used to pat his knee now and then, or dig her elbow into his ribs if she thought something was funny, or should catch his attention. He'd be in his pyjamas. He hasn't thought about that for a really long time. And maybe they didn't really do that so often, maybe it was just a few times that stick in his mind now. But it was nice, sitting crunched in between them, he remembers that pretty clearly.

He would do everything different, just about everything.

Maybe what his mother could see was futures. Maybe when she was safe, or even high up the way she would get, she could look down and see bad changes coming, good things getting all twisted and out of hand. So she jumped, instead.

"Charges?" he manages.

"Armed robbery," the smaller cop snaps. "Attempted murder. We told you all that to begin with." Did they? He guesses they must have.

"Don't you remember?" his lawyer asks, as if he's interested in the answer. Roddy shrugs. His lawyer sighs. One of the cops starts hauling on Roddy's arm. Roddy tries to shake free. The cop tightens his grip and everybody goes tense again, all those muscles expanding.

They must misunderstand. They must think he's dangerous.

Somewhere in all that there was good news: that the word *murder* wasn't just all by itself, that it's *attempted murder*.

The woman in the blue suit, with the blood, is alive. He hasn't killed anyone. He could sit right back down, his whole body gone weak and watery, if that tight hard hand wasn't holding him up.

"Let's go."

"Any chance," the lawyer asks, "he can see his folks before you take him out?"

"They can see him in court in the morning. They can bring him whatever he needs then, too. You know the drill."

He's grateful, actually, that he can't see them right now. He'll have to sometime, but at least not tonight.

"Don't forget he's a juvenile," the lawyer says with a kind of warning in his tone.

"Oh, don't worry. We won't fucking forget that." So much disgust. It's hard.

Out in the hall Roddy looks around, into doorways, for Mike, but there's no sign of him. Maybe he's home by now. Maybe he got himself off the hook.

With Roddy's help. Maybe Roddy's an armed robber, even an attempted murderer, but he isn't a traitor. He can't tell anybody, and it may not be much compared with everything else, but he thinks it's got to be something good, anyway.

Cops and Robbers

THERE WAS A TIME, LONG AGO, when Isla's only two experiences of police were when she was stopped once for speeding, and once when she failed to totally halt at a stop sign. That was an innocent time. If not exactly friendly, the cop-faces she encountered then were not hostile, nor worryingly blank. Today the police at her side are—how would she say?—business-like, but sympathetic. Their eyes contain a deplorable pity, their voices rise and fall with humanity. They are trying to tell her in these ways, it seems, that they're on her side. Which is nice. She has no reason to be angry with them, except that they fell down on what's supposed to be their job: preventing people from being shot in the first place.

Looking up, she sees hair curling out of the nostrils of one of the cops, wavering along with his breath. "We've arrested the suspect," he says. "He tried to run, but not in a very smart way, and he didn't get far. We've charged him with attempted murder and armed robbery, and he's fairly thoroughly confessed, at least to his own part in it. He's good friends with the clerk at Goldie's, and we have some strong suspicions he was involved, too, but so far the kid we've charged won't give him up. But we wanted you to know that the one who shot you is safely in custody."

Safely for her or for him?

Attempted murder. Yes, she supposes. It didn't look as if he was actually attempting anything, but no doubt there isn't a specific charge that covers being startled, frightened, shocked into shooting. The kid's eyes, as she remembers them now, looked ferocious and terrified: an unfortunate combination. She guesses it's good to know he's been caught, is tucked up in jail, out of harm's way. It sounds too comfortable, though. She might have preferred a longer, more dangerous, more frightening, menacing hunt.

"What's he like?" she asks, and sees them exchange glances, these two men in their blue uniforms with all their badges and belts. The older, bigger one shrugs slightly. The word *beefy* comes to mind. There are people she thinks wouldn't look out of place on a butcher's chart: broken into flank steaks, loins, roasts. Juicy, this one. Lots of high-quality marbling.

Unlike the kid, all skinny, flesh-and-bone youth.

"He's been in minor trouble before," the big cop says. "Suspected of this and that, theft, shoplifting, a few fights, that sort of thing. No charges, though, and no serious violence. Nothing that would have pegged him for something like this." Her impression as well, seeing him lounging around town with his friends. Just a kid who was going nowhere special, including anywhere especially bad.

"I think he's, uh, *surprised*, mainly. By how badly everything's gone. How much trouble he's in." And does the boy imagine at all Isla's surprise? How badly everything has gone for her also, and how much trouble she's in?

"How old?"

"Seventeen. Something happened with the mother, and he and his father moved here to live with the grandmother. They didn't see it coming, either." Isla knows the feeling. Some people can be held too close to the eyes, causing blurred vision. Creating assumptions and, perhaps, carelessness. And consequently, surprise.

"Basically, since he's confessed to most of the facts, we won't likely need to trouble you much. We just wanted to let you know the kid's in custody and the case is in hand, so you can relax on that score and just work on getting better." He looks uncomfortable; perhaps has realized how many words, such as *relax*, are not relevant and are beyond her capabilities. Everyone's struggling with language right now, noticing, often too late, that any verbs implying action, even muted action like *work on*, or *relax*, are currently unusable. She has been through circumstances before when people have not known what words could be safely, inoffensively used. James, specifically, drove most people to silence, at least around her.

Was that disaster more shocking than this one, or milder? Well, apples and oranges, really. If James, not she, had been shot, that might have been apples and apples.

"Thank you," she says to the cops. "For coming."

"Yeah, well, we'll be in touch. Good luck, eh?"

At seventeen, people are stupid. They can barely make out, in the distance, the ridges and hollows of long terms and consequences. Certainly they don't discern mortal injury, even if, like Isla for instance, their fathers die practically in front of their faces. If they perceive hope, it's blurred, rosy hope. And seventeen is pitiless. The rest of the world does not truly exist. Some people grow out of that, others do not. At the moment she, too, is like a seventeen-year-old, most interested in herself, and not much interested in any other soul in the world.

Well, though, that kid, who's been caught, and confessed, and is currently, she imagines, sitting around feeling shocked by events—she has some curiosity about him. Some recollection. A connection if not, of course, an attachment.

The trajectory of a bullet hardly constitutes an attachment.

By the time Isla was seventeen, her father had died. He did so slowly, painfully and, at forty-five, much too young. Isla, during this process only fifteen and sixteen and inexperienced with disappearance, never mind loss, was curiously, stupidly taken by surprise. Things crept up. Symptoms and conditions overlapped and overlaid each other. Isla resisted believing. She had some idea, a confused, arrogant, adolescent idea, that a refusal to acknowledge something prevented it, warded it off.

Obviously she was wrong.

Her father began having to sit down on occasion and cough for a while. Then he was coughing so hard bits of himself came up into the tissues he took to carrying everywhere. Then he wasn't going to work, and spent whole days in bed. Sometimes his eyes got wide and wild with the effort to breathe. And even so it was unexpected to be sat down on her parents' bed and be told it was time for him to go into hospital. They were surprised by her surprise. She didn't understand what they meant by *time*. He took her fingers and his hands were bony and frail. There were a lot of things she didn't have a very good grip on.

Most days after school she visited him in the hospital and saw his efforts to smile or speak or even rouse himself fail and then disappear into a haze of drugs. Finally she was called out of class to the school office. Her mother was there waiting. She put her arms around Isla and said, "I'm sorry, dear. Your father has passed away. He had a heart attack. That was unexpected, you know. We'd thought there was still a bit of time, with the other." *The other* being the cancer.

"What?" Isla was staggered. She *did* stagger, out of Madeleine's arms, because what had she been thinking? Why hadn't somebody said, "Look, this is what's going to happen here. Look. Look. Look."

Maybe somebody had.

"The end was very fast," Madeleine said. She wept, of course, but also seemed rather soon lightened, unburdened of something unbearable. Isla was shocked by that, too.

Still, listening to her mother weep in the night, Isla saw she didn't know much about her own parents. Their own life, she meant, the one just between them. This was a new idea to her.

It was a magic trick, his death: the one where a tablecloth gets whipped with a wrist flick from under a whole elaborate setting of china and cutlery, leaving it rattled but still sitting there, barely altered. Although she knew this wasn't how it had been. She knew it hadn't been swift, and that she was the only one so amazed.

Life was *unsturdy*. This was hard information to learn, and she went around for some time stone-faced, remote, cold. She could not seem to get irretrievable loss into her head, but apparently had to.

As her mother did, too. "Life goes on," Madeleine said eventually. She looked older, and thin. "It has to. There isn't a choice." Suddenly she was working in a women's wear store selling dresses and blouses, sweaters and slacks, scarves and brassieres. And then, in a year or so she was looking at seventeen-year-old Isla over their Sunday night dinner for two, saying with a remarkable look of astonishment, even happiness, "Do you know, I enjoy it? I really like being with people all day, and helping them find what makes them look good or," she laughed, "at least not too awful. I like hearing why they're looking for a new outfit: if they're going to a wedding or a conference or starting a job or going on a date for the first time with someone, and I like watching them when they look at themselves in the mirrors, trying to decide, one outfit over another." She was looking trim herself. She had her hair done every week, and resumed painting her fingernails. She made special friends with a nice man named Bert from the bridge club she'd joined.

It was true, and seemed faithless on both her mother's part and Isla's, that life did resume. There were huge holes and gaps, absent customs and habits, lost embraces and stories and sounds and moments to recover from, but for Isla there were also classes, exams, dances, friends. At seventeen she began working part-time herself, in James's father's office supply store although she had no notion at the time that the main thing about him would be that he was James's father.

She sold pens, notepads, paper clips, file folders, and also school supplies such as little cartooned backpacks for children. She liked the feel of paper, she found, and of file folders and notepads. She continued working there part-time in university, while she vaguely studied in preparation for some vague career. She would need, her mother told her seriously, and her mother would certainly know, to be prepared to look after herself. Be responsible for herself.

Isla realized that. She was waiting, and she figured this would come about in a classroom or at an unforeseeable job interview before graduation, for something to present itself as a capturing, interesting pursuit. Her father's life in the world, the stories he brought home—she leaned towards words in one form or another, but was content to wait to see what emerged. She could also see, though, that as her mother said, there was no time to waste, and was impatient for her own unanchored, real, free life to begin. "Your father and I might have done a few things differently if we'd realized how short time would be," Madeleine said. She mentioned farther-flung, more adventurous holidays, a more scrupulous attention to day-to-day life. "Appreciate the moment," she advised, and Isla thought she more or less did.

Isla worked in the store every Saturday. Then one Saturday, and always afterwards, there was James.

He'd been at a university on the other side of the country, getting a business degree. He came home a cocky, on-the-cusp-of-things graduate. He was lean and at work wore suits that fell flat over his bones. Isla hadn't before considered there was any appeal or beauty in suits, but now saw that there was. He was five years older than she and moved through the store in his suits like languid, dangerous water. When he asked her out the first time, he didn't exactly ask. He said, "I'd like to take you to dinner on Friday."

They went to a restaurant with white linens and humble service and glass-shaded candles burning on intimate tables; a *serious* restaurant, she thought. He talked about his plans for his father's business, which he did not express as hopes, or even intentions, but as plans. This confidence was amazing to her, and when he said, "And what are you going to do?" she was embarrassed by her uncertainty.

She'd shrugged, her shoulders shifting under the delicate, nearly sheer fabric of her new dress. She'd bought the dress through Madeleine, who got discounts at the store where she worked. It was mainly a boutique for the middle-aged, but now and then carried nice things for the young, and this dress, pale blue, unbelted, with a tiny pattern of pale yellow flowers, was among them. "I'm not sure yet. I like words, I guess, and persuasion." Probably neither of them quite knew what she meant, although there was truth in it. Probably neither of them was especially interested, either.

It's well known that power is an aphrodisiac. Even James's small power in that business was large to a girl, young woman, who only worked there. Anyway he had a chin to be stroked like a cat's, lush dark hair, intent eyes, and those long, long thighs. He struck her as a man of variety and extremes. His attentions to her included not only his serious, intent regard, but his pale sculpted chest, those long thighs, all the rest of him. And his appreciation of her, captured in all the apparently delighted ways that he touched, stroked, and reached into her. "You're beautiful," he told her and it seemed to her that under his gaze she was actually beautiful, not just pretty, or merely attractive. She took this praise, and a powerful sort of desire, as sufficiently different from anything she'd experienced before that it had to be robustly adult. It felt extraordinarily real, being touched by him.

Life was short. Love was precious.

While Isla continued her slow passage to graduation and some kind of future, James pursued his own rather swift passage. At work, more abruptly than gradually he pushed his father aside. The world of the office was changing. James understood this, and argued that his father did not, could not, that only the young could expect to keep up. His takeover didn't strike him as brutal, nor did it seem especially brutal to Isla, only necessary, as he said. She was loyal to him anyway, as a matter of principle and of, by then, love.

It seemed brutal of course to James's father, who refused to allow James in his house, and maybe to his mother, who was hand-wringingly anxious, wanting to make happy both husband and son, and perhaps worried for her own safety, financially speaking. A few of their old allies and friends, the odd supplier and banker, offended on James's father's behalf, caused some difficulties, but James said, "It'll pass. Meanwhile I have to keep my eye on the point of all this." He also said, "The old man'll get over it, he'll see I'm right," and seemed untroubled that he was not welcome in his parents' home for a time. He was right, they did get over it. Or if not over, at least beyond it. When James and Isla were married, Madeleine's friend Bert cheerfully walking her down the aisle, James's parents were there. His mother wept, as did Madeleine. This was natural for the mothers. At the reception James's father shook his son's hand, and put his hand on Isla's shoulder. "Good luck, young woman," he said.

She was young. She was extremely happy to marry James.

And when Jamie came along, she was tickled stupid. That skin! Those tiny round tugging lips! That sleek, soft, dark hair! The family gathered back around, too, the wonders of Jamie the lure.

"What will you do when he's old enough?" asked Madeleine, who seemed always more intent on Isla than on Isla's family.

Isla shrugged. "Maybe advertising," she said for want of anything else, but felt, still, far too young and certainly unready. She did watch television and read magazines, though, often with a keener eye on the ads than on the programs and articles. She watched structure, design, different appeals; what was funny, what sentimental, what plain and workmanlike. She felt as if, in a desultory way, she was still learning, still pursuing some future beyond her house.

They had brick walls with chocolate-shaded trim around windows and doors, graceful gardens and shade trees. They were tucked nicely away, for such a young family. Some people put that another way, said "set up nicely." It was like playing house, roaming stores, sometimes with James, looking for the right furniture, picking up vases and candles and placemats and little sculptures and other small touches. It felt like making something together, in addition to Jamie. Coming home from the supermarket, groceries in the trunk, Jamie locked into car seat, pulling into the bricked driveway, reaching for the garage door opener, Isla sometimes saw the house as an unusually attractive fortress, perfect for warding off the unpleasant, the distressing, anything very unhappy or painful.

James's business flourished. He was moving much faster than his father would have into computers, new kinds of software, bidding on supply contracts for offices and schools with a boldness his father would not have dreamed of. He wore his lean suits but no longer moved languidly, liquid as water, was too busy now for such grace. She admired the risks he was taking. "We grow or we die," he liked to say. He wanted, all the time, new, larger challenges. Stimulations. As for herself, she was waiting. Meanwhile her days felt captivating enough; if also sometimes, alone with Jamie, amazingly dull and dull-headed.

When James turned towards her some nights, energetic and ambitious and with his eyes confiding and tender, or she touched and stroked him into turning towards her, she thought that was a good conversation, speaking of the fundamental part of the deal, which would have to be love. Having supposed they were understanding what each other was saying with their mute messages back and forth between bodies, she was bound to be surprised to find this was not necessarily so.

Jamie was just a few months past two, already a runner, already subject to nightmares, when Isla got pregnant again. James was busy with schemes to expand into a small chain, then a large one. Both his ventures and hers for sure had their perilous, gambling aspects, but she hadn't imagined he would think his was threatened by hers. "For God's sake, what were you thinking? Jamie's barely under control, never mind another one," he said when she told him. He was angry, and looked for the moment quite unlike the tender man who'd been so delighted, swamped by sentiment, when she'd told him she was pregnant with what turned out to be Jamie. "You know what a dicey time this is anyway." He used the word *sabotage*.

She leapt from disappointment to injury, then directly to fury. "You know what causes pregnancy, I suppose? People have known all about it for quite a few years now, although I understand there was a time—Neanderthal, maybe?—before the connection was made. Turns out it's a mutual sort of thing. One act, two people, you know the drill." He looked at her as if he found her unpleasant, even barely tolerable. She couldn't imagine how she was looking at him.

He turned away first, moved to the drinks cabinet, poured a Scotch. "Sorry," he said, with no heart in the words.

"Me too." She didn't imagine either of them was apologizing, only expressing regret at an unpleasant exchange. Maybe also they were speaking of sadness, that between them they'd just damaged and diminished something they'd counted on.

With Alix, Isla was in labour much longer than she had been with Jamie, fifteen hours, which was unexpected and the wrong way around, she thought, in these matters. James stayed at hand, although a few times he looked too weary to go on, and during moments when she had her wits together, she was able to think that was natural: she was fully occupied, while he was just waiting, which could also get very tiring. By the time Alix appeared, they were both collapsing, although they revived briefly, cheerfully, on seeing her. The crumply red skin, the frail curls of red hair! The plump little fingers and toes! The scrunched-shut eyes, the tiny, devouring mouth! "She's gorgeous," James said.

"Perfect," Isla nodded, and promptly fell stone-tired asleep.

Having more than one child makes all the difference in the world, she concluded a few months later. With one, life still seemed optional, as if not every choice and decision were already made, and a range of possibilities might still be open. With two children a gate closed and locked.

Which was fine; it was only that certain choices had been irretrievably made.

Jamie, it turned out, was not entirely pleased with his sister. This sort of thing was expected, although Isla felt she'd gone to some lengths to prepare him, then to reassure him. Nevertheless she had to watch, when he began by playing with Alix's little fingers and toes, that he didn't go on to slap her small cheeks, or lock his own little fingers around her delicate throat. "I hate her," he said bluntly a couple of times, and Isla gave him points for honesty, at least. Also he was mesmerized, could stare at Alix for ages as if she'd appeared by magic and he was waiting to see how this trick was done. And also he could touch her with enormous, grave tenderness.

He had, Isla supposed, like any growing human being, increasing reserves of ambivalence. He could feel two or three contradictory things very strongly, or he could feel two or three contradictory things in a muddled, unsure sort of way, but he could at least feel two or three contradictory things, which seemed to her an achievement.

James was the big surprise. "My baby angel," he crooned. "My little sweetheart." Who would not lap up such tenderness? Isla would have lapped it up herself; certainly Alix did.

His stores expanded: to three, to five, to eight in cities spread over the country. He was often away for days at a time. Isla found, slightly to her surprise, that she wasn't lonely. She made friends and had family. She liked, for the most part, being in the company of Jamie and Alix. Alix picked up speech very early, perhaps from her brother because her early sentences, among more pleasant ones, included "I hate you."

Isla was also glad enough to see James when he came home, bringing fresh air into a space that sometimes felt too enclosed. She remembered her father did much the same thing, bounding with his outside-world stories into her life with her mother. She hoped Jamie and Alix wouldn't see her, as she was afraid she had sometimes seen Madeleine, as slightly pathetic.

When he came home, James read stories to Alix, and to Jamie if he was around but Jamie was growing out of toddlerhood into boyhood and had his own friends. Alix rode on James's shoulders, and roared as he pushed her high on the swing set or caught her at the bottom of the slide. He carted home reams of paper from the head office store and coloured pencils and crayons from the now-separate school supplies outlet. Both children had all the paper, pencils, and crayons they could dream of, which Isla thought might make them take those things too lightly. James watched them draw, and tried to play tic-tac-toe with Alix. Upstairs in his home office they played elementary games on the computer. At night Alix lay loose as a rag doll, splayed on her back, legs and arms tumbled, mouth open, breathing hard in the deepest, most worn-out, safest, and most contented of nightmare-free sleeps.

Sometimes James went on at length about inventories, expansions, new products, hopeful contracts. Isla sympathized with how swiftly things changed, how quickly the importance of words like *ergonomics* and *virus* had to be absorbed, acknowledged, and dealt with. Other times he didn't have much to say. She could understand that, too. He was tired, and anyway there would be many aspects of his daily life she could know nothing about, and which wouldn't be interesting, and would be wearying to set out to explain. Same went for her: too many exhausting, small details.

Sometimes he asked people important to his business to dinner. When Jamie was six, Alix three, one of those people was Martin Amery. "You'll have things in common," James said, introducing them. "Martin's been working in advertising and now he's going out on his own. We're thinking our businesses might help each other to grow." To Martin he explained, "My wife's always been interested in advertising. She used to talk about it back when we were first dating."

Had she? And did he expect anything to come of this? No. He'd only intended to create a little dinner-time conversation between them, hadn't of course foreseen more. But she liked Martin, who struck her as a serious, energetic man with serious, energetic ambitions, not unlike James himself, although since Martin was short and pudgy and blond the resemblance wasn't at all physical. Moreover, he took her seriously. He phoned the following week and suggested they meet. "If you're interested," he said, "I have an opening you might want to take a look at."

And so she did. That closed gate—it now seemed to her that it only really meant she had secured herself a base from which she could begin to operate outwards.

Madeleine said Isla was lucky to have opportunity handed her "on a platter," and she was right. Who said no to serendipities that fell right into the lap?

James, for one. "You want to do what?" he asked, sitting up sharply. The kids were in bed, he and Isla were alone in the living room, she on the deep, soft, flowery-pastelly sofa, he in the matching chair across the coffee table from her. "When did you dream this up?"

"Over lunch. It may not work out, I may be no good at it, or we may not get along, or I may decide I was wrong to think I'd be interested, but I want to do something and this sounds good to me at the moment."

"There'd be nobody home with the kids."

"The kids are going to be home less and less themselves. We'll just have to organize care for when they are and you and I aren't." She thought it might be useful for him to hear he could have more opportunities himself to do more than play with them. She thought that might be a good thing for all of them, not least James. This hint flew right by him. Or he ignored it.

"But if you were working for Martin, and I've given him all my business, it doesn't look good. It *isn't* good. I don't want him thinking I won't dump him if he doesn't work out. I don't want him thinking he has some kind of edge. Have you thought about why he's really interested in you? It's not as if you have any experience."

"Yes, I've thought about that. We've discussed it." She hadn't, though, thought of how unhappy James would be, or how far he would stoop. "Obviously it's a way to get some experience. Then I may or may not move on, or get out altogether, who knows? Or his business may fail. I don't think either of us imagines any edge with you. He's just setting out to sink or swim, and so am I, and we seem to get along all right so we thought we might sink or swim in the same boat."

That sentence didn't go well, but she expected James would know what she meant.

"You didn't think we should talk about this?"

"We are talking about it."

"But no matter what, you assumed you're just going to do it?"

"Well, I don't know about 'no matter what.' Things might come up, I suppose." She didn't want to feel angry, or hurt. She didn't want James to feel those things, either. She reached across the coffee table, touched his knee with her hand. "Here's the thing. I have to do something or one of these days neither of us is going to like me very much."

"There's volunteer work. There's going back to school. There's other ad agencies, even."

"Yes, there are," she agreed.

He sighed. "I see you're planning to do whatever you want, never mind anyone else. So I wish you luck, but don't come crying to me when it blows up in your face."

"I won't."

She was fairly proud of herself, felt she'd demonstrated in this exchange some of the professional skills she would need. Naturally she was disappointed in James; not only because he was so opposed, but because he was so objectionable, not to mention transparent, about it. When he began touching her breasts in bed that night, they wound up making love with unusual, forceful, nearly angry and equal passion. It felt very good.

So did the work. Starting off writing bits of ad copy, she found an unexpected talent for adjectives: words like *vital* and *discerning*. She developed a gift for verbs, too, although verbs turned out to be of less consequence in advertisements, at least in print, and might even be absent altogether. She told James, "It feels as if I'm exercising a part of my brain I didn't even know was there. I mean really exercising, like jogging or lifting weights."

James was not Martin's only client. Nor was he his biggest one. When Martin set out on his own, he drew some clients of his former agency with him, and worked hard to get more. Isla watched him and imagined this helped her understand better how James's very busy days went. Martin scrutinized Isla's work and often told her she would have to start over. Every Friday, over a long lunch, they talked about clients, bounced slogans and presentation ideas off each other. It was very satisfying when sales charts sparked upwards as a result, presumably, of certain campaigns. Two heads did work better than one. Martin, the artist, covered napkins with little drawings, showing her shapes and plots and how words might fit into and around them. He said clients found her easy to talk to, and clever, and quick, but with a comforting appeal. "Will you be mad if I say maternal?"

She did not, of course, attend any meetings between Martin and James. It seemed to her that James was now not unhappy that she was occupied in ways that interested her, and that she came home as lively and as tired as he did, and with stories to tell, entertaining information to offer—was, in short, not a drain or a particular strain on him. There was money in it to boot, which might not matter to him but somewhat to her surprise did matter to her. Nor did the kids seem to mind. She'd read somewhere that the successful raising of children amounted to gracefully encouraging a long succession of farewells. At first she had found the idea inexpressibly sad, saw herself having her heart perpetually torn, waving an endless bye-bye.

Madeleine said, "Your father would have adored these children, it would have made him so happy, how well you've all done." How had Madeleine borne losing her husband? Isla sometimes looked at James as he watched the late TV news, or as he lay sleeping, and wondered how she would feel if he vanished. She thought she would miss his boldness and determination and impatience. Certain habits. A warmth in the bed. The knowledge there was something, someone, to fall back on if need be.

Between Bert and her job, Madeleine was too busy, but James's parents would have taken over Jamie and Alix's spare-time care, if Isla had considered that wise. "Why have a babysitter when you have us?" James's mother asked, and there was no good, kind answer. Isla said, "I know, and it's very generous of you to offer, but we want them to have a place nearby to go to after school, and anyway Mavis has a houseful of kids and that's good for them." Mavis, who lived down the street, was large and red-faced and ate a great many chocolates, which as an addiction was preferable to most other things, a sort of jolly attachment to sweetness. Isla thought Mavis looked like someone who enjoyed kids, embraced them, but wouldn't hurt or ruin them. There were no such guarantees with James's parents who had, after all, raised James, who had turned around and pushed his father aside.

Isla saw that she no longer regarded this as admirable, or inevitable. She supposed she saw these matters now as a parent might, not as a child; as someone vulnerable, not as natural victor.

Nevertheless, ten-year-old Jamie was in Mavis's care the late afternoon he and a bunch of kids were tearing around Mavis's back yard and he tripped. Mavis called Isla from the hospital emergency department. "He'll be okay but it was close. You'll want to come."

Martin just said, "Go."

She thought she would try to reach James from the hospital, saving time.

Mavis was holding a restless, upset seven-year-old Alix, and trying also to keep a grip on her own eight-year-old Tim when Isla raced into the waiting room. "I told them not to run with sticks in their hands," Mavis said, "but they did anyway, I guess. He tripped. He's got a pretty bad gash on his forehead, but it missed his eye as far as I could tell. I think they're just putting in stitches right now. I'm sorry, Isla. I told them not to run with those sticks. They were pretending they were guns."

Isla's mistake. She wouldn't let him have a toy gun, felt those awful computer games were bad enough, and stupidly hadn't foreseen that Jamie would then just conjure make-believe weapons. "Not your fault," she told Mavis, because although it was, it also could as easily have happened in her own yard. "Settle down, Alix, please, you're not helping."

Jamie had eighteen stitches. His entire forehead was a swollen, discoloured, angry-looking wound. This all came as a big surprise to James when he got home, since in the hospital panic she'd forgotten, after all, to call him; a difficult omission to account for. "Jesus, Isla," he said, and to Jamie, "That'll teach you not to be careless and do what you're told. There's a reason for rules. Maybe you'll pay better attention next time." He folded Alix into his lap. "You won't be so silly, will you?" he asked, and she shook her head solemnly. Gratified, Isla thought. A little creepy.

"I think we've all learned things today," she said, and took the desolate Jamie into her own arms. "It was a hard one, wasn't it, honey?"

At work the next day Martin asked, "Everything turn out okay?" and Isla nodded. He had four kids of his own, and said, "Shit happens, doesn't it? It's fucking scary, not being able to keep them out of harm's way all the time." That about summed it up.

Jamie and Alix kept on changing. This, it seemed, was how a parent learned to keep saying farewell, waving goodbye. One year, one season, one day, Jamie was loud and clumsy, so that every time he moved it seemed something toppled off a table or fell from a wall, and the next moment he was quiet, precise in his movements, his body held tight into itself even when he was running. He got a pimple on his chin, his voice cracked and changed, he was clumsy again, but quiet again also, speaking in short and often sullen bursts. There was a rhythm to this, Isla supposed. The main thing to know about this rhythm was that nothing lasted forever.

Alix was confident, flying high on her father's shoulders, then for a while unsure and timid. She had a large and loud array of best friends, giggling helplessly in the basement, screaming in small-girl hysterical pleasure, and then she could spend whole glum weekends on the sofa, sunk in private sorrows she wouldn't discuss.

Each of them, although never in any coordinated way, ricocheted off joy, swivelled into sadness, plunged into mute irritability, bounced up again into joy. There wasn't much to assume about either of them, not a lot to hold onto. Isla thought Jamie might be more consistently thoughtful and possibly even more kind and responsible. Alix she took to be turning into someone fairly tender-hearted but also indulged into assuming that whatever she desired would triumph. In their different ways, she thought they would finally be people she'd be happy to know, by and large.

So much hope, so much investment, so much love—she would die before she would let anything bad happen to either of them. Jamie had the faint but discernible white permanent scar on his forehead to prove how close disaster could come in a moment of recklessness, heedlessness. "We're lucky," James said sometimes, and she would reach out to touch wood, and wish he'd keep quiet.

She wondered if he ever contemplated his children looking at him and saying something like "Old man. Get out of the way." She supposed not. If he did, he would surely be wary of them, and suspicious.

His own father had been taken quite by surprise.

James had ten stores, and now and then there was a ripple as he cruised close to the edge of going too far. Even if he hadn't talked about what was happening, she thought she knew when one of those times was at hand. His jaw muscles clenched harder and more often, and he got impatient not only with her, and sometimes Jamie, but even with Alix. When he was very snappish, she understood they might be on the verge of losing everything.

Except they couldn't lose everything, because there was her work, as well. With savings and a relatively small loan she bought into a partnership with Martin. They hired more staff. Like James, they were flying, although comparatively low to the ground. She and Martin mainly saw each other only at work. They each had other concerns, other demands on them, but she thought they liked and trusted each other and certainly they worked well together. It probably helped that otherwise they didn't appeal to each other. And that there was no slowing down. And that they had to keep learning, and also making things, campaigns and ideas, where nothing had existed before. They were successful, and that created its own adrenalin, a precious excitement. Isla felt blessed and indulged by all this that had fallen, really, into her lap: Madeleine's word, *serendipitous*.

It didn't always look as if James had much fun. That strokeable jaw of his grew heavier, his long thighs thicker. He would never be fat, but he did have a belly he didn't always hold in. The nice way of seeing this was that he had the appearance of a man of substance.

She was changing too, had a pudgy ease to her own belly unless she was careful, and definite lines around her eyes and the sides of her mouth. She was getting the occasional grey hair amidst the mainly dark red, but didn't plan to do anything about that unless it began coming in streaky and strange. She joined a fitness club and got up a half hour earlier to make time for a quick workout. Two childbirths had broadened her hips somewhat, but that was like a badge, or a medal, she thought, and not unattractive.

She began to imagine, a decade or so into the future, both kids grown and gone, herself and James left mainly to their own devices. She thought that would not be a particularly passionate or dramatic or freshly involving stage, but would likely be perfectly tolerable. It would then be a matter of whether tolerable was enough, and she suspected that when the time came, she would decide it was not. They quarrelled, sometimes as nastily as when he'd objected to her starting work, but mainly about the normal gratings of regular life: what dates suited them both for vacations, who would attend parents' night at the school. She figured they were partners, not unlike she and Martin although less scrupulous and polite, and in a far different sort of enterprise.

When the kids were grown and gone, she would turn her attention to other possibilities. Meanwhile she and James still now and then turned to each other in bed, and each said on these occasions, "I love you," which on her part was no longer true, at least not in the old, loyal, reliant, encompassing way. He was there. That was one of the virtues of her theory of the gate, being gated: they were both simply there.

Martin began an affair with one of their clients. Because it involved a client, although also maybe because he couldn't keep such exciting news to himself, he told Isla. She said, "Be careful," meaning not only because it could hurt their company if it went badly, but because Martin liked his family and was not the sort of man who would enjoy discomfort over any long haul. Discomfort, of course, being quite different from excitement. Isla considered whether having an affair might add a vivid subplot to her own life. His romance was making Martin quite sparky and youthful. But she couldn't think who to have an affair with who wouldn't be more effort than he was worth, or more dangerous. Not to mention, when could she fit such a momentous thing into her schedule?

Anyway, disloyalty didn't interest her, even if Martin's pink, electric rejuvenation was an illuminating sort of advertisement for its benefits.

Sex, thoughts of sex—maybe, on good days, of love—must have been particularly in the atmosphere, a congestion of hormones, budding and renewed, troubling the vision, distorting the air, creating waves of heat, causing hallucinations of oasis on the horizon. All that sort of steaminess, breathlessness. Not just Martin. Not merely Isla's own speculations, which anyway were nothing near real desires. Whatever Jamie was pursuing at fifteen, perhaps only hopes, he was pursuing for the most part out of the house, tremulously and tentatively in love for the first time, with a wiry, thin-chested, sharp-eyed, and soft-tongued girl named Bethany, who joined them for dinner sometimes, or to do homework at the dining room table with Jamie, but who did not often meet Isla's eyes. It was difficult, and unwise, to imagine her little running boy having sex, but she had to suppose that even if he and Bethany were not, he would be wanting to, trying to. There was a sharp sort of reek to him, some alteration of his chemistries which he couldn't seem to camouflage or control.

Alix, at twelve, was getting ideas of her own. Isla hadn't put them there. The requisite discussion of biology, attraction, affection, had of course provided Alix with no new informa-tion. How could it? Isla would have liked to make clearer to her that there was more to it than strokeable jaws and long thighs, but heard her own voice soften and thought she was not entirely credible on the subject. "I know that," Alix said with weary tol-erance. Maybe she did. She did not, however, know enough to follow Jamie's example out of the house.

James was home. Dinner was over. Jamie was out some-where with Bethany. Alix was in the basement with Tim, Mavis's boy, with whom she had played more or less since the day Isla went off to work. They'd played house, computer games, and soccer together, had had spats and tussles and giggling secrets together. "That's the way to grow up," Isla had thought, watch-ing them. "So there's nothing so mysterious you lose your head for no good reason." Between being friends with Tim and shar-ing a bathroom with Jamie, she didn't think Alix could have too many odd or unrealistic notions about the attractions of males.

Evidently she was wrong.

She heard a roar from under her feet. By the time she'd reached the bottom of the basement stairs James was hauling narrow, pale Tim out from under the pool table with such ferocity, gripping his poor thin arm, that Tim's head cracked on the underside of the table. Alix was still under there. "What's going on?" Isla called, although she could see what was going on, and only intended to break the moment, break James's grip.

For a moment longer, while the boy steadied himself on his feet, James held on. When he let go, it was so that he had both hands free to start swatting at Tim, open-handed blows to Tim's dancing, dodging head. Tim, looking unfamiliar in this dimly lit drama, was hampered by loosened, unfastened pants. He ducked under one of James's flailing hands, gripped the material at his waist, made a run for it. Panicked and solely intent on escape, he brushed past Isla and pounded up the stairs, out the front door, away.

Alix was unfolding herself from under the pool table in far more leisurely fashion. James was panting. Alix regarded her father calmly, her red hair standing out in the light like a fiery angel's. Her little green plaid shirt, her worn favourite, was untucked and hung partly open. She didn't even have breasts yet! What, if Tim were groping her, had he been groping?

James was trembling. When he yelled, all his words ran together in Isla's ears. They may have done likewise with Alix, who watched him gravely, steadily, not moving or speaking, until he wound down. Then she nodded, stepped around him, stepped around Isla, climbed the stairs, went silently to her room. Isla, who couldn't think of a word to say, also turned and went back upstairs. She listened to James, still in the basement, pounding his fists on this and that, and pacing. She was astonished by his heat, by his rage, but she was far more amazed by Alix.

Later, in bed, still in a fury, James said, "Do something. And keep that kid out of this house."

"Oh no, I don't think so. They've been friends a long time. That wouldn't work."

"Well, make something work. Did you see what they were doing?"

She sighed. "They're exploring. We do have to speak with her, but you know, this is just the beginning. There's a lot of hormones ahead. And you could talk to her too, I mean without yelling and getting upset. It's not just my job."

Truthfully, she didn't know what she could say to Alix. What unnerved her was not Alix's lust but that gentle, remote expression as she regarded her father. She had looked as unfamiliar as a stranger right then. She'd looked untouchable.

If Tim could touch her, good luck to him, Isla thought, which made her giggle, so that James turned in bed to look at her. "There's nothing funny about it," he snapped.

She guessed there probably wasn't. "I'm just trying to remember what it was like to be twelve. Pretty confusing, as I recall. You feel caught in the middle then. Between one thing and another."

"They did not look confused to me."

Well, his daughter hadn't. Poor Tim, though. "I expect he was terrorized enough to keep his hands to himself for some time. And everything else, too." She heard herself giggle again, and again James looked at her sharply. "But Alix wasn't exactly cowering, was she? That was an unusual kind of look she was giving you." Isla heard in her voice a tinge of satisfaction, and what was that about? "I guess it is something to try to sort out, but James, you can't just tell me to deal with it."

He shifted unhappily. "I only thought, you're both female, you'd know how to talk to her about that sort of thing."

"About sex? Lust? What? I *have* done that. Maybe what she hasn't heard is a man. What Tim might have had in mind, and what she needs to look out for in the future. Maybe she needs that little chat."

But then all their lives turned over, and whatever Isla had thought Alix might have needed to look out for in the future became something quite different. As it did for herself, for Jamie and, not least by any means, for James.

How had he managed? Had his brain not felt explosive? Filled to bursting with his composted, degraded little privacies?

What a masterpiece of will, to carry on his regular life, expanding his business, fretting over its large and small matters, eating their dinners, occasionally taking their children to movies, occasionally supervising their homework, occasionally turning to Isla in their bed, giving no signs, no hints at all.

He said, eventually, that it was a separate, and small, part of his life. Perhaps so, to him, although that he could see it that way was in itself what? Very ill.

Besides being a separate and small part of his life, it was criminal. That wasn't even to mention that it was wicked, immoral—all those words that didn't too often come up in their household, or in most households in general as far as she knew. He must have known that, would have had to be monstrously stupid not to.

That was the third time in her life she had anything to do with the cops.

And this is what she means about how stupid seventeen-year-olds are.

They're so stupid they get hankerings, cravings, for men who wind up, years later, like James.

Other seventeen-year-olds are so stupid that to blot out fathers like James, they absorb terrible shit into their bodies, or begin undetectable journeys towards some ridiculous, unfathomable faith.

Or they're so stupid they shoot people without actually, necessarily, meaning to.

They're so stupid, she thinks, it's almost necessary to feel sorry for them. They are defenceless in their stupidity, and arrogant in it, too. They know nothing about being thirty-nine-year-old mothers doing their best to get accustomed to humiliation and horror, or forty-nine-year-old women getting accustomed to joy, and they care nothing, either.

They are damaged and dangerous.

They need embracing, they need to be held tight and restrained. They need to be kept out of harm's way until the danger is past. They are haphazard and foolish and need looking after. Isla obviously failed to accomplish this duty. Other people, strangers to her, have obviously failed also, and now here she is, after another encounter with cops, knowing precisely the full and desperate results of these failures.

Pretty Good Punishment

RODDY'D HAVE THOUGHT BEING IN JAIL would be mainly sitting around without much to do but watch his back, but not so. It's abrupt and startling and loud, but it sure isn't slack. It also isn't a jail, exactly, but a detention centre. As Ed Conrad, the lawyer his dad found, explains it, some people serve short sentences here, the ones convicted of fairly minor, relatively harmless crimes like break and enter; not like attempted murder, armed robbery. But others are like Roddy, being held for court appearances on charges they haven't been found guilty of, at least not yet. Either they can't get bail or they don't have enough money for it. Roddy's probably in both boats: bail's been denied, but even if it wasn't, Ed Conrad said it could be something like ten thousand dollars, or even more, maybe twenty, or fifty, and there's no way his grandmother or his dad could come up with so much. If they would; and maybe they wouldn't.

This is his third day. There's a system here for organizing the day and also for organizing the future, even if nobody knows yet what or how long the next part of his future will be. It's amazing, how an act that's extraordinary to Roddy gets absorbed like it's normal into a process that's already worked out. Like he's one car on an assembly line, getting put together like every other car with just a few individual options.

The only time something doesn't seem to be happening is at night and even then it's not totally quiet, and lights are left burning. He has nightmares. Every morning so far he's wakened up shaken and scared; like in a movie where somebody's doing something like going up a dark staircase and you know there's something awful just waiting and you want to yell out, "No! Don't! Be careful! Turn back!" but the person keeps going up anyway, and something bad happens. That sort of nightmare.

But even waking up shaken, he isn't confused. Since the very first morning here, he's known right off where he is. Well, it'd be hard to get confused in a small bare grey room with a metal cot, a little sink, and a lidless crapper; totally different from his ceiling-sloped room at home, with its pictures pinned to the walls and his own deep bed where he should be, with a bag of money tucked away underneath. That other, parallel life he had in mind.

Things happen in sleep, he guesses. Like moving overnight from one world to another. Life from before is already so much a memory it's like it's somebody else's memory. The present is unstable and the future for sure is unknown, but the past—it's some other place and person altogether. Which is so weird it makes him light-headed.

There's more to it, though, this knowing right away, before he even has his eyes open. Maybe it's air, maybe sound, maybe light. Or maybe it's believing deep down that where he is, is where he belongs.

How can Mike stand being out there, free, knowing he must be in the wrong place? But maybe Mike doesn't know that. He likely has other things on his mind.

He wasn't in court when Roddy was. That was the first morning. Other people showed up, Roddy's grandmother and his dad, Ed Conrad of course, but not Mike.

Roddy got driven there in a van with a few other guys and a couple of guards; cops, he guessed. There wasn't much talking. He didn't know anybody. The courthouse, where he'd never been before, is next to the regional government building and looks like a regular office except up on the second floor, where he got taken, it's separated into two big courtrooms plus a bunch of smaller rooms. He saw his lawyer in one of them with some other guys and a couple of women, laughing.

Big gloomy portraits, probably dead judges, hung on the walls. All men. Roddy wondered if he'd do better with a woman judge, somebody who looked like his grandmother, say. But a woman judge would most likely look like the woman in the doorway of Goldie's. She wouldn't like him at all. A man might understand more how something can go accidentally wrong in just a couple of seconds. At least how something can happen that wasn't ever intended.

And that he was sorry. Which ought to count?

Anyway, nothing counted and there wasn't even a judge, just some guy who's a justice of the peace, and it wasn't a totally real court, just one for remands and, for some people, bail. His dad and his grandmother were in the second row, staring at him. They looked like they'd been up all night, kind of loose and grey in the skin. Maybe they sat in the kitchen wondering over and over where they went wrong. Roddy would have liked to be able to tell them they didn't go wrong, but also that everything did. "What the fuck," he and Mike used to say, meaning, what did it matter what they did, good or bad or anything in between? In a huge world with too many possibilities and in a little place with hardly any, *What the fuck* made them potentially invisible, insubstantial, and free.

They were wrong, and it has come down to Roddy, and *what the fuck* doesn't apply.

Everything in court went really fast, case after case, guy after guy, boom-boom, break-and-enter, assault, driving drunk. When it was Roddy's turn a clerk or somebody read the charges—*attempted murder, armed robbery*—and his lawyer sighed and said, "We understand these are serious allegations, but my client has never been in trouble before with the law. He's only seventeen, and his family is willing to guarantee his next court appearance and his good behaviour in the meantime, with whatever stipulations the court cares to apply, if bail were granted."

For an instant, Roddy wanted to add his own voice. He wanted to promise he would honest to God never even leave his own room again, if he could just go home now. Nobody would have to worry about him going outside, never mind going wrong. But of course he didn't speak up. Of course he couldn't go home. He didn't belong there.

"Bail denied," the justice of the peace said crisply, and set the next court date for a week away. So that was that. Just as well. He did want to tell his grandmother and his dad something, though. All he could think of to do from across the room was wink at them, which was stupid, probably looked like he didn't know what he'd done. He guessed he was somebody who did important things wrong. He wondered if maybe everybody wished he was dead, that he never was born, that that wouldn't have been any great loss.

Maybe one of the kids of that woman he shot, Ed Conrad said she has two, both grown up, will shoot him down in the courtroom next time. People sometimes do that sort of thing, he's seen it on TV. It'd be fast and unexpected, and he'd be out of all this without hardly noticing.

It took all Roddy's courage to ask Ed Conrad, "The woman?" All he knew, really, was that she was alive; because of the attempted murder, not murder, charge.

The lawyer sighed. He sighs a lot, in Roddy's brief experience of him. "She'll be in hospital a while, that's for sure. Did you know she's paralyzed? Pretty unlucky shot, if you ask me, for a guy who says he doesn't know how to use a gun." Paralyzed. Shit. The information almost drowned out the contempt in Ed Conrad's tone. Even his own lawyer was disgusted by him. Imagine her family.

Imagine his own.

He did that? Having never done anything big or important before in his life, he caused that? Lots of times when he was young, he used to imagine being somebody else, or at least doing things that didn't crop up in the life of somebody like him. He'd pictured circumstances, like Mike or maybe some littler kid drowning, where he would be a hero, jumping into the water—raging, rocky—and hauling the person to shore. He would be a picture-in-the-paper sort of hero, somebody who'd done something memorable, notable, large. Now he is somebody else. He has done something memorable, notable, large. His photograph has maybe even been in the newspaper, he doesn't know how that sort of thing works. This isn't what he intended, never what he meant.

The day here starts with a loud wake-up buzzer that scratches through speakers in the corridor ceilings. So far, Roddy's already been awake, all three mornings. There's lots of shouting, swearing, a racket of guys getting up. Everybody's supposed to make their own beds and get dressed and more or less tidied up. Everybody wears brown jumpsuits. Roddy's not built for jumpsuits. Some guys fill them out, and look tough, but his hangs off his bones.

They have about twenty minutes to do all that after the buzzer goes. Then the cell doors unlock and they form a line in the corridor and get herded, at least that's what it feels like, down to the cafeteria, where they line up for cereal or scrambled egg lumps, toast, milk, and juice. Like school, only without choices. That's a thing about being here: not having choices, hardly any at all.

What Roddy thinks the people who run the place should do at the start of the day if they really want to make guys feel bad about the trouble they're in, is make them stay in bed for a while after the buzzer goes. Everybody'd have to lie there looking at the bleak, stupid hours ahead, and it would make at least some of them feel bleak and stupid themselves. Which would be pretty good punishment. But maybe whoever organizes the schedule figures the night hours are better for that, and that's true, too: every night so far Roddy's lain awake for a long time turning and thrashing as if a new position could magically alter events. If one kind of pain could kill another kind, he would slam his head into walls.

So he's not surprised when other people take to violence. Nothing real big, not so far as he's seen, anyway, because there's always guards around, but little flashes: a couple of guys sort of stumbling hard into somebody else; the occasional jostling of pool cues in the rec hall; muttered threats in the shower stalls. The chemicals of anger are breathable, smellable. Being here must be how it is for a wild animal: wary, hyper-alert to small shiftings of grass and scents. Rabbits he's flushed. Moles and groundhogs tunnelling for shelter underfoot. Toads and insects blending cautiously into the background. Out there it's not anger, though, not rage turned inside out, it's survival.

It's survival here, too, probably, in a different way. Still, Roddy may not be burly, but he has words to back him up: *attempted murder, armed robbery*. Even here, those are major words. He tries to keep in mind Sean Penn, somebody like that, some small guy playing a prisoner. A certain swagger is called for, although not so much he looks like a challenge. He has also renamed himself Rod. This is no place for some kid called Roddy. It seems like a Rod really could be an attempted murderer, an armed robber. Rod might, actually, be who Roddy now is, or at least who he's becoming.

After that quick court appearance the first day—it couldn't have taken more than five minutes, although the travelling and waiting took a lot longer—he got brought back here to the detention centre. Then a guard told him he had an appointment with some guy called a counsellor, and took him off to one of the offices at the front. The guy had a file in front of him and a stack of printed papers and forms. He looked up and said, "Hi Roddy, I'm Stan Snell, we'll be working together to figure some things out for you, make some plans."

"Rod," he corrected, for the first time.

"Okay, whatever." Older guy, mid-thirties maybe, how big a deal could he be, a shit job, working here? Not that it mattered what he was like, except for being a stranger with Roddy's life in his hands.

This guy wanted them to make plans? The idea of plans hadn't crossed Roddy's mind. He hadn't thought of *doing* anything in particular, just of being someplace: here, then someplace else.

"You've been remanded a week, I see." News, Roddy saw, travelled fast. "I've already got some of your school records, so we can see where you're at, since you'll be taking classes wherever you go from here." He could get Roddy's school records? And wasn't this summer holidays? "And we'll want to talk about any particular interests or skills you have, because there's also possibilities like woodworking, mechanics, computers, cooking, that sort of thing. Because," and he leaned forward, looking earnest and boring right down to his short sandy hair and the dark blue tie knotted tight against the light blue shirt collar, "you obviously need a goal, or you wouldn't have wound up here. You need to want to be something. That's how you stay out of trouble. It's drifting around, no real focus, that got you here, I figure."

Roddy couldn't say what got him here. A disaster, mainly.

"So is there anything in particular you want to be? Some ambition? A wish, or a hope?"

Besides not being in jail, or an armed robber, an attempted murderer, Roddy guessed he meant. "I don't know," he said. He really didn't know. It'd seemed there were years and years before he had to think about being something, even though of course he also knew there were not. By seventeen, his dad already had a full-time job.

The idea of wanting something, and then actually being it, was strange. As far as he could tell, his mother was the only one in the family who had a big achievable goal and, tipping herself off a bridge, got what she intended.

"Because now's the time," Stan Snell went on. "I know it probably doesn't feel like it, but this can actually be a good opportunity to get on the right track." He opened a file. "I see you were suspended a couple of times and missed a lot of classes the past couple of years. Otherwise you weren't doing too badly; not failing anything, anyway. So obviously you're not stupid." For some reason Roddy was pleased to hear that. "So why were you skipping?"

To go wandering. To go shoplifting. To hang out. Roddy shrugged.

"Because it seemed easier than doing the work, right?"

"Not so boring." Stan Snell leaned forward.

"Well, I don't know about boring, but here's how it works here and wherever you go from here. Assuming you're found guilty. If you don't mind, we'll just assume that for our own planning purposes." Found? Roddy *was* guilty. He didn't see much way around that.

"So as you already know it's up at six. Breakfast. Exercise. Then you'll be starting classes or maybe job-training sessions for three or four hours a day. Including weekends. Eventually you'll also take a turn at some of the jobs around the place, like in the kitchen, whatever, another three or four hours a day. There'll be counselling sessions, therapy, whatever you want to call it, but I don't know how regular or soon that'll be, or whether it'll be just you and a counsellor of some sort and how much will be group work, that depends on a lot of things. Dinner, then you get maybe a couple of hours to watch TV, play pool, whatever. By eight-thirty you're back in the cell. You're supposed to spend the time till the eleven o'clock shutdown doing homework and studying. The idea, you understand, is that you need hard work and routine and discipline. Given what happened," and he looked down again at the file, "you might be around for a while. But that'll give you the chance to figure out what you want to do when you get out, so hopefully you don't wind up back in."

Oh. Roddy hadn't thought of that. The possibility of committing further crimes. He hadn't got that far into the future. It's not like he's got some desire to hurt people. He couldn't imagine actually wanting to do something like what he did, actually setting out to do it. Or setting out to do something and having that happen and not caring one way or another. He couldn't imagine that.

But it probably happens to people. They get hard. They don't care. In real jail, there'd be more real tough guys, probably, more guys hunkered down into true crimes.

Like attempted murder, armed robbery? He was forgetting again.

"These," and Stan Snell stacked up handfuls of paper, pushed them into an enormous brown envelope, "are aptitude and intelligence and personality tests. You can fill them out over the next week. Give us some idea what you're like, what you might be good at. They're to be returned to me before your next court appearance. Ask any guard for a pen. You'll have to give it back, and only use it under supervision." So that it wouldn't become a weapon, Roddy supposed, against himself or anyone else. "And watch your step. There's no screwing around here. Step out of line, there are penalties. If you do step out of line, you'll find out what the penalties are. Any questions?"

Not that Roddy could think of, not right that second.

"Jack?" Stan looked up at the guard in the doorway. "You can take the young man back to the rec hall now. Show him what's what down there."

Roddy could guess. It would be like starting school: when he was seven and just moved to town, except then he already knew Mike, which was enough to begin with. His grandmother said the first day, "You'd be wise to watch for a while, see what people are like, not be too eager right off the bat. You'll make better friends in the long run." Being tough and sort of angry-looking wasn't what she meant, but the point was to be what she called *standoffish*. "You might look standoffish," she advised, "but that's all right, too."

So what should a standoffish Rod do, in the doorway of a rec hall with a couple of TVs at different ends of the room, big but mounted high up, out of reach and with mesh guards built out around the screens, and a pool table, and shuffleboard, and a whole bunch of wood tables and chairs with magazines and cards and a big battered-looking bookcase thing with some paperbacks and videos, and a couple of sofas and a few easy chairs and two guards and a bunch of guys more or less his own age?

A standoffish Rod would lean casually against a wall. He'd survey, narrow-eyed, what everybody was doing. He'd have his arms folded over his chest. He wouldn't show by even a flicker that he was worried about accidentally sitting in somebody's place, or getting in somebody's way, or drawing the wrong somebody's attention. It's the first moments that count.

He wouldn't plan to make any friends; maybe not ever. The idea of Mike, pictures of the two of them hanging out, Mike standing on a sidewalk, head back and laughing and laughing with that full big roar he got after his voice changed—a moment from a whole long time of knowing each other. Funny how what should be a lot of flowing and particular memories came down to a few pictures; that kept giving Roddy a kind of electric shock in his head every time.

People disappear, that's all. They just go. Pictures didn't mean shit, people just go.

There was only so long he could stay leaning, standoffish Rod, against a wall, arms folded, looking around the room narrow-eyed, assessing, with any luck, menacing. He felt dizzy, that first time, pushing off from the wall. Like he was seeing the room up close and far away at the same time, like it was real and sharp as a razor, and also all flattened onto a screen.

Was he crazy?

That might account for that moment in Goldie's. Maybe only a crazy guy would let everything get so far out of hand, not on purpose, totally unintended, but there it was, that undoable moment.

He rolled slightly on his feet, swaggering somewhat, he hoped, trying for an impression of being ready to spring. It was hard to tell if anybody was noticing. He expected they were. It's automatic, pretty much, sizing up a stranger coming into a group. Something like smell, there were signals. His ought to be dangerous but not quite cocky. Someone prepared to be cool, but not necessarily.

As long as he didn't look like some asshole who'd left himself glued too long to a wall.

Guards in this place don't generally look very interested or alert, although he has decided they probably are, and that bored, faraway expression is probably as cultivated as his own swagger. The guards here wear navy blue pants and shirts, and wide black belts with different things hanging off them, like flashlights, that don't make much sense unless they're more for hitting people than throwing light. The guards look, for the most part, not only uninterested but like people called in to fix particular things, like the plumbing. People with narrow interests, in keeping the peace, more or less; a goal not unimportant to Roddy as well.

When he launched himself into the rec hall the first time, there were two guards, one to the right of the doorway, the other over by the high-up meshed windows across the room. Between them: three guys shooting pool, a couple of others at one of the tables shooting the shit, a couple watching junk afternoon TV, four playing cards, looked like poker. One sitting in an easy chair with a pad of lined paper on his lap, writing. Recounting some crime, a confession, making notes for his trial? For all Roddy knew, the guy was writing a poem about sunsets or something; because you just couldn't tell by looking at people what they were likely to do.

There was one pacer, a guy walking the room, half the room, back and forth, frowning. Big eyebrows. Big all over, but mainly what Roddy noticed was thick eyebrows hanging heavy over little blue eyes. He looked too stupid, with those tiny eyes, dense eyebrows, for planned cruelties or organized meanness, but ready for random ones.

Roddy set out to cross the room, making for the window side, so that he could tell himself that he'd made that start, had become a registered presence and could go on, slowly, from there. The big-eyebrowed guy had other ideas. He shifted in the midst of his back-and-forth, sidestepped to put himself in Roddy's path, no way around without chickening out, or so Roddy saw it. "Larry," the guy said, his name, Roddy supposed. "Gimme your smokes."

Okay, Roddy understood the moment. "No." Larry crowded so close they were almost touching chests. "Back off, asshole," Roddy felt he must add. He kept his eyes narrowed and his feet planted wide, tried to keep Sean Penn in his mind's eye like a map.

The guy, Larry, nodded slowly. He looked like he was trying to think. When he opened his mouth, Roddy thought he could as easily have been going to say, "You're dead meat," instead of what he did say, which was "You hadn't better be holding out on me." The point was, he backed off. He sidestepped away again, back to his pacing. This was good, and a relief, but also shook Roddy's confidence about whether he had any talent at all for assessing what someone might do.

"Rod," he said to Larry's back, and wondered if that sounded uncool or in any way fucked up and desperate.

That was three days ago, when he actually was uncool, fucked up and desperate. Now he has his footing, more or less. He can be herded into this rec hall and go to the pool table and pick up a cue and look around questioningly, and somebody will join him. He can slump in a chair and watch a dumb talk show for an hour without being disturbed, or he can say, or nod as somebody else says, "What shit, eh?" Easy moments, if not friendly ones. All he wants is to survive. Any particular attention, he hopes, will go elsewhere, be somebody else's bad luck.

Mike maybe feels something like that. If Mike's even close to being the person Roddy imagined, he'll be suffering too, in his different way. Still, people can get used to things awfully fast; like Roddy himself, getting used to this place, that it has requirements and rhythms and customs and in that way is like outside life, only tighter and more enclosed. There are things that get done in certain orders and ways, and it's kind of relaxing that there are some assumptions, it's sort of a comfort.

So he is startled by an unexpected tap on the shoulder, whips around fast in his chair, jumping slightly, ready for—what? Not ready, only startled. So he's not as relaxed as he thought.

It's a guard standing behind him, saying, "Follow me," and when Roddy stands, taking his arm. "Let's go."

"Where?" As if there's a choice; as if this was an invitation he could decline if where they were going didn't appeal. Anyway, there's no answer. The guards, mainly, aren't so much unfriendly as not interested, at least the ones on the day shifts, who are older than the night staff and so are more accustomed to bad boys and sad stories. This one steers him down the long corridor towards the front of the building, where the offices are, but he's not going to see Stan Snell this time, but is suddenly turned towards the right and into a small room where, already sitting beside each other, with a desk between them and the doorway, are his grandmother and his father.

There should be some kind of warning.

For sure he figured they'd come whenever they were allowed to, but he thought he'd have notice. He also figured he wouldn't have to see them so close and directly, because they'd be getting together in a big busy room, full of the buzz of families, and might even be separated by metal and glass, like in movies. Not that they'd be just across a little room, just them, and no place to look and only their own sounds to hear.

He keeps standing. They're both looking up him, but sort of flatly. Hard to read. His dad's wearing a suit, like he's going to church. Roddy's grandmother is also dressed up, in a plain navy dress she hardly ever wears and a white necklace and white clip-on earrings. Roddy feels exposed in his jumpsuit, and as if he's made a mistake about the formality of the occasion.

He's surprised how fat his grandmother is, sort of pathetic in this fluorescent light. It's like she's somebody new, a stranger, and her bulk kind of falls over the sides of the chair, but she's empty-looking at the same time. "Well, son," his dad begins. He never calls Roddy *son*, not for ages. Otherwise his tone's as flat as his expression. "Quite a mess."

Roddy has nothing to add to that. His grandmother does, though. "Why?" she says. Her plump hands are set flat on the table, fingers like hot dogs, or sausages. The two of them, really, her and his dad, they look lost here: the pair of them swamped and bowled over by life.

Oh, Roddy is angry. He looks away from them, off towards the corner, so they don't see his rage. Everything in this place is grey-painted, or green. Colours supposed to douse flames, maybe.

This is what he was trying to get away from. Exactly this. Away, he could have made himself up without contagion from best dark suit, best navy dress, rippling flesh, disappointment. All that. Look what they've done. "Get that look off your face," his dad says. Now his dad has an expression, and it's anger, too. His voice is shaking with it. "Don't you dare go glaring like that. After what you've done. What the hell did you think you were doing?"

"Getting away," Roddy blurts. It just comes out, and then what he didn't mean to say comes out, too: "From you." His grandmother's face goes crumbly, like pastry.

"What did we do so wrong? What didn't we do for you?" she asks, so softly and sadly it's hard to hear, even in this small room. "What did you want we didn't give you?" But those are such loser questions. He can't answer questions like that. He won't.

"Speak up," says his dad. "What the hell got into you? Do you have any idea what you've done? And I don't mean just to your-self, which is bad enough, you've ruined your life, you know, stupid kid."

"Frank," his grandmother murmurs. "We don't want to spend our conversation this way, do you think?" Still, it's a lot of words, from his dad. A little late, and unhappy and angry, but a lot of words, anyway.

Roddy narrows his eyes. Of course he fucking knows he's ruined his life.

"You'll be lucky if you ever get out of here," his dad's going on. "You and your friend Mike—he had something to do with this, didn't he? You can't tell me you could think up something this bad all on your own." Roddy won't tell him anything, including that. "And if that woman doesn't get better, well, Ed Conrad says everything just gets that much worse. No bail, for sure." He throws his hands up off his lap: in despair, in disgust? Or bewilderment. "I just don't understand how you could do this. It's not how you were raised. Was it drugs? Were you on something?"

No. Not drugs. Hope. Possibility. Blindness to downsides. But his father doesn't seem to think Roddy contains any possibilities of his own, figured out for himself, carried out by himself. He must believe Roddy is aimless and just lets himself be led astray lightly. He doesn't even give Roddy that much respect.

"You know she's paralyzed, right? What did you think, it's like on TV, you shoot somebody and they get right back up? It doesn't count, nothing real happens?" Honestly? Kind of. "Anyway, Ed says there's no way to get you out on bail unless she's in better shape. Not that we have the money anyway. A lawyer's expensive enough, and we have to fork out for him because we can't qualify for legal aid. And how could your grandmother and I guarantee your behaviour, if you're capable of something like this?" All of a sudden his dad's full of words. Where have they been? Has he been storing them up for the right occasion, along with a lifetime's worth of bitterness? Like he's the one who's betrayed?

"He's also saying you might as well get it over with, just plead guilty and take your medicine. Well, he says you've pretty much confessed anyway. The only way to get a break now is if the woman gets better real fast, or to give your friend Mike part of it. Not the shooting, everybody knows he didn't do that, but the robbery. That it was a set-up between the two of you. Jesus Christ, Roddy!" This time his father slams his hands on the table.

"No wonder," Roddy hears himself saying, "my mother jumped off a bridge."

His grandmother gasps and says, "No."

His father, though, his father completely changes colour, grey to red. He stands up fast. He's a big man. Roddy takes half a step back, even though he's on the other side of the table. His dad's mouth opens, but then closes again. He shakes his head. He looks down at Roddy's grandmother and says, "We're getting out of here. We're leaving him to it."

She looks from Roddy to his dad, who is already walking around the table, walking, not looking, past Roddy, walking past the guard and out the door. She stands. She has tears in her eyes. She has trouble getting her bulk around the table, between it and the wall. She pauses in front of Roddy and puts a hand on his arm. "Oh dear," she says. Away in there behind the fat and trembling lips and sorrowful eyes, she's all by herself. When he was younger, he had some idea her flesh was a place to hide in, where he'd be safe. Now he thinks if he tried to hide in there, he'd never get out.

Still, this is nearly as bad as what he did to that woman. He almost reaches out to his grandmother, except his dad, out in the corridor, says, "Let's go," and she turns and follows her son.

Loyalties, Roddy supposes.

What just happened? Once again, nothing he meant, not what he intended. The guard takes his arm. "Back we go, then. Man, you are one dumb peckerhead." Like it's his business.

There's a tap on the door frame: his grandmother again. She puts a hand on Roddy's arm, although the guard doesn't like it and frowns. "Roddy dear. I know you didn't mean what you said. You've always been a smart boy with a good heart, and I won't believe that's changed. Please dear, don't let one mistake spoil it. All right?" She squeezes her plump hand on his arm again, and is gone. Shit. He wants to run after her, he wants to fly weeping into her lap like a kid. He does have a good heart. He wouldn't even hurt a toad, or shoot a groundhog, so how come he has taken to hurting actual people? If he has a good heart, where in his soul does so much awfulness spring from?

His grandmother wears a perfume that's like a combination of flowers, heavy on lilacs. He's given her bottles and bottles of it for her birthdays, Christmases. The scent still hangs in the doorway, the corridor, as the guard starts taking him back to his new life; to the rec hall where guys are still playing pool and cards, watching TV. His new, strange, foreign territory: rooms like this one.

He has a memory of a few lovely dark moments out in that field, looking up into the sky, feeling purely contented and happy. He cannot get over the distance between now and just a few days ago. Probably the woman in the tight, wrinkled blue suit can't get over it either. He hopes she's not a nice woman. He hopes she maybe even deserves what has happened, so that maybe this isn't so much to do with him, but with her being punished for something, and he just got picked for no particular reason to punish her.

It could all be her fault. Would that help?

The Short Book of James

P ERHAPS IT WAS UNUSUAL EVEN for a peaceable woman like Isla to reach the age of thirty-nine with only two encounters with cops, for speeding and for not quite coming to a halt at a stop sign. James came home pale one March evening, about to make up for that.

"We have to talk," he said immediately. Naturally she was alarmed, and naturally thought something had gone wrong with the business. He was going to tell her he'd blown it and they were poor, or as poor as they could be, given that her own work was thriving. "Are the kids out of the way?" Jamie was upstairs doing homework, Alix in the basement, alone, watching TV. Isla would have thought them old enough to join any discussion of financial disaster, but didn't argue. He sank into his chair in the living room without taking his overcoat off. He leaned forward, looked down into the oval hooked scatter rug she'd picked up three years before, a souvenir of a holiday which took them through Amish country. He was just opening his mouth to speak when the doorbell rang. James, already leaning forward, simply opened his mouth and threw up on the rug. Isla's own mouth opened. He was shivering, looked fluish. Something was bad when she could look at him and hope he just had pneumonia, something like that.

There were two officers, one male, one female, both cold in the dark late-winter evening. They asked for James. Isla nodded towards the living room. "In there," she said, hearing in her voice a distinct recognition that some new experience was cropping up in their lives. Alix came upstairs, Jamie down. James reached the doorway between the living room and the hallway, stood holding the frame, as if he might fall.

The woman cop spoke his name, his occupation, his place of business. "You understand why we're here," she said. All her words were statements, although in tone they came out as questions. The male cop faced James to the wall, patted him down, took out plastic handcuffs and fastened them to his wrists. It seemed to Isla that James put his hands behind himself, ready to be bound, without being told. She thought of all the programs they'd watched on TV in which this very scene had occurred. Although not usually in silence. On TV, people usually had plenty of loud questions, lots of high-volume denials. Bystanders also contributed, which she realized she, Jamie, and Alix were failing to do.

The male cop, moving slightly behind James and holding an elbow, shifted him efficiently to the front door. The woman hung back. "You know what this is about, too, I expect," she said. Isla shook her head. If she'd spoken, she would have had to say, "No, what is it?" and she wanted as much time as there could possibly be not to hear the answer to that. This felt like a last, turning moment between an ordinary way of going on, a reasonably predictable, fairly comfortable existence, and a pit she was about to fall into.

She heard James say from the doorway a faint, breathless "I'm sorry." Not "I'm innocent," or "I swear it's not true," or "This is an outrage." He did manage "Get my lawyer" and was gone. Isla could see headlights reflected off the open front door; the cruiser, she guessed, although without flashing lights. Well, no emergency here, no one running away or defending them-selves, no one creating a threat or a disturbance. Just another unhealthy, unbreakable silence.

Finally Jamie said, "Mum?" He was fifteen, his voice was deep, but he sounded like a child; her scared little boy. James's, also. And over there Alix, James's *little sweetheart*, his *angel*, as well as his antagonist in a mute recent moment, now standing at the top of the basement stairs with her eyes wide and a finger in her mouth, chewing. A habit from childhood.

"It's okay," Isla said, but heard the voice of someone talking to toddlers. "Well no, it's obviously not okay. But whatever it is, we'll take care of it. I need to speak to the officer for a few minutes and then we'll sit down and talk, the three of us. Why don't you wait in the kitchen?"

"You might," the constable warned her, "want to go down to the station. You might not have time."

What, to talk to her children? "James can wait. Whatever he needs at the moment, he can just wait."

Because here was the thing: if he'd been falsely accused of anything at all, he'd have been furious. He would have shouted, punched walls, railed. He would not have looked abject, guilty, defeated, whipped. He would not have thrown up. He would not have been silent or pale. He would never have said only, "I'm sorry," and then, "Get my lawyer."

She knew that much about him. She understood she was about to learn more. "Excuse the mess, I'll just get rid of the rug," and she rolled it, its faint knotted pinks and purples and blues shrinking up in her hands, and carried it to the kitchen where her children were sitting across the table from each other, doing nothing at all, not even speaking. "I'll just be a few minutes. Don't worry, it's probably only some stupid misunderstanding to do with his work." She got a garbage bag from under the sink, stuffed the rug into it, twisted it shut, gave it to Jamie. "Could you put this out in the garage? And Alix, while he's doing that, you know how to brew coffee, don't you? Would you mind? That's for me. You guys have whatever you feel like."

"Dad said to call a lawyer." This from Jamie.

"Yes, I know. We'll get to that, but first we have to find out what this is about. In the meantime your dad'll be fine. There are procedures. It's not like TV." As if she knew.

Back in the living room she sat carefully on the edge of the sofa while the cop, looking not very at ease and occupying James's usual chair, introduced herself as Constable Donnelly, "Sylvia, if you like." She seemed to be trying to keep her expression flat. Perhaps that's always how cops tried to look. "Now," she began.

She took a breath and locked eyes with Isla. "What's happening is that your husband's being charged with three counts of sexual assault, including one on a minor. Basically. Those are the main charges so far. There may be more. Probably will be, actually. And there are other charges, kind of under the umbrella of the assault ones. *Included* is what they're called, some of them."

Having begun, these words, these sorts of words, went on for some time. It occurred to Isla in the part of her brain that was observing this moment that the constable, Sylvia, was prepared to continue, word after word after word, until she could see that Isla had caught her breath and caught up. She was offering time. She was also observing Isla for shock.

Because, she would think, could anyone not know, truly, if her husband contained these possibilities? Would it be possible to share any kind of life at all with someone and not know? *Yes*, Isla could say, *yes, that is possible. I guess it is.*

She couldn't tell what shapes her features might have fallen into. The rest of her body was frozen too, but at least she knew where it was. Her feet and knees were together, her hands clasped on her lap, a serious pose for hearing serious news. Sitting this way, she had managed to give herself the gift of stillness; an ability to absorb blows without falling or folding. She saw she had unfamiliar freckles on the backs of her hands.

"The charges," Sylvia was going on, and on, "have to do with three girls from two of your husband's stores. That's one reason I say there may be more, the investigations are continuing and more may come forward on their own once they hear. I'm telling you that so you understand, I'm sorry, but this may be just the beginning, not the end." Certainly the end of other things, though.

"The youngest complainant is fifteen, the other two are eighteen, although I understand there are some questions about how old at least one of them was when the offences occurred. Allegedly occurred, sorry." That was nice of her; a kindness, that she was sorry.

Fifteen? Jamie's age. Not much older than Alix.

"Now of course what we mean by sexual assault can be all sorts of things, and as far as I know, in this case it's not rape. The charges at this point mainly have to do with aggressive touching, kissing, fondling, that sort of thing. Although rather forceful. These are part-time employees in your husband's stores, did I mention that? After-school jobs, weekends."

Like Isla. Who had watched James stride languid and liquid, in his bone-draping suits, through his father's store two decades earlier, and had wanted him.

"It was the youngest girl, her parents, who made the first complaint. Allegation. The older two came forward after they heard about this other problem. They're in university, both of them. They say they were trying to handle the situation on their own because they need their jobs to pay their way through. They work in different stores and apparently didn't know each other, so the chances of collusion are fairly slim."

How long had James known he was in trouble? Quite some time, surely. Days, anyway.

Was one of those girls, young women, even just one of them, attracted to James? Had she been deliberately seductive, alluring, brushing against him, wearing a special, radiant smile when he came into the store where she worked?

Would anything be better if she had?

"What they're mainly saying he did was corner them in private places—an office, a storeroom—and force himself up against them. Manhandled their breasts and fondled them elsewhere with his hands. One of the three, so far, says he exposed himself and pushed her hand onto him. We've interviewed them extensively and taken statements. They're quite detailed."

All these words struck like hailstones. Each one made a dent. The trouble was seeing. The trouble was watching James in her mind.

Because she could see him. She wouldn't have imagined such a thing, but now, yes, she saw James groping, forcing himself into the hands of young women. How could this be? She saw slim bodies bent backwards, or shrinking. She saw him demanding, overpowering, overcome by a mere desire—no necessity, just a desire—his features distorted into an expression she had not herself seen but did not, suddenly find out of the question.

He had betrayed her in ways she couldn't start to distinguish or begin to count, but here was this part: that she could see it. Which was also a fatal betrayal. She thought, "Well, that's that."

Some very cold part of her brain began to take over. This was useful. It helped grief start to settle itself into place. It helped displace shock. It got some necessary things done. Isla stood. She would have shaken the constable's hand, if she'd been confident the constable would want to shake hers. Was it possible some people would think she collaborated with James, cooperated, encouraged his forays into young flesh? Perhaps. These things happened, and it could well be a direction in which police minds would turn. Others would blame her for other reasons.

If she were going to blame herself, it would be for inattentiveness; for not dreaming of anything very bad, much less this.

"Will you want someone to come and be with you?" This was like a death in the family. Did Constable Sylvia Donnelly think loved ones and acquaintances would come running with comfort and casseroles?

"No, thank you. Not now. I'll have to talk to my children."

"Would you like me to do that with you?"

"That's very kind. It might even be a good idea, but I think not. I think we need to be on our own. So that I can tell them," the first bitterness poking through skin like a broken bone, "that their lives are turned inside out. They were watching TV and doing homework an hour ago, you know. They were kids. We had an ordinary life an hour ago. Nothing special, just normal, a bit dull." Her voice broke. She would not weep. "But I guess it's special now, isn't it?"

"I'm afraid so," Constable Donnelly said softly. She touched Isla's arm. So it seemed she didn't feel too contaminated. "Do you want to know what will be happening to your husband tonight? The process?"

"Not especially. His lawyer will know, I expect."

"All right. But one thing you should be aware of is that once he's formally charged, some basic information becomes publicly available. Name, address, charges. His first court appearance will be tomorrow as well. Just brief, I expect. A formality. But there's no telling whether someone will pick up on it. Reporters. It depends. But you might want to prepare yourself and your children for that. Maybe cancel the papers if you get them, leave the TV turned off."

Oh James. Bad enough, what he could apparently feel able to do to those girls, those young women, but even if they worked in his stores, they had to be more or less strangers to him. Look, though, what he'd done to his own children! "Thank you," she said, "for the warning."

At the front door Constable Donnelly pulled a card from a uniform pocket. "Your lawyer will want our names and extension numbers. You might, too."

"Yes. Thank you." She closed the door firmly; but it did not seem, looking around, as if the inside of the house were now any safer than the outside. It was all polluted, all unprotected.

Alix and Jamie appeared from the kitchen, Alix holding carefully in both small, long-fingered hands Isla's favourite blue pottery coffee mug. "Here, Mum. I think it's how you like it." She presented it with slow ceremony, as if she were giving a presentation, or a gift. Probably she felt, Jamie too, much as Isla had: needing to know, but still warding off knowledge with small, hopeless gestures.

Isla put an arm around each of their shoulders. "We'll go to the living room, shall we?" She had a notion that the kitchen, communal and packed with family history, should not be spoiled for them. They rarely used the living room, so it would be no great loss if they found they couldn't enter it again after this. The living room was where Isla and James read, watched videos and TV, sometimes shared late-night junk food, even sometimes held hands. The living room was already ruined for her. She thought how carefully and warily from now on she would be approaching and choosing parts of the house that might survive some of this. The least contaminated corners, these were what they would have to squeeze themselves into.

Wherever was she going to sleep? Not in that bedroom.

She sat, deliberately, in James's chair, still warm from Constable Donnelly, for whom it had probably been warm from James. If Jamie and Alix, near the edge of the sofa, had any pictures of James in this chair, it was time to start erasing them. She wondered at how clearly she was understanding these small, acute matters, and how she had previously managed to miss much larger ones.

Under this ice, such a bonfire blazing! "Let me tell you," she began, "basically what's going on."

Quite soon, Alix began crying. Jamie turned stony. Isla abandoned the chair and moved between them, cradling Alix with one arm, holding the other across Jamie's back, gripping his shoulder. It didn't take long to tell what she knew. She could feel things snapping, giving way, collapsing in on them. "Did he do it?" Jamie asked finally. Alix looked up, blotched and tragic.

"I think maybe," said Isla. Should she not give them more room for hope? Lies made the air in the house thick tonight, repellent and musty, but he was their father. They had their own attachments to him. "But of course we don't know, and sometimes the police make awful mistakes." Alix brightened slightly, Jamie did not. Isla took a deep breath and felt the ice expand in her chest.

"What we have to do is stick together and just work things out one thing at a time. So now, you two can decide whether you'd like to take tomorrow off school, while I call your dad's lawyer. How's that?" Small tasks, she thought, little steps, would be bearable. Any leaps and bounds and they'd go crashing right through the starred, flimsy glass under their feet. At least that was how she felt about it. She certainly didn't want her children cut by any more flying glass.

Although they would be. There was no stopping that now.

She wished she knew the right thing to do. She wished the right thing to do had crossed James's mind before he lunged at little girls in storerooms and offices.

"I need to call Bethany first," Jamie said abruptly. Isla was surprised; she couldn't even call Madeleine yet, or Martin, certainly not James's parents, could barely contemplate reciting all this to James's lawyer who, she realized, would have to hand the case on to one of his partners more adept at criminal law. "I won't be long. I don't want to talk to her, I just want to know if he did anything to her."

Oh.

"Not Daddy, he wouldn't do that!" Alix cried. "That's gross!" It was like a mutation of Alice in Wonderland: Alix shrinking back into little girlhood, Jamie growing old. Isla wondered what she was becoming. Something not nice. But hanging on with icicle fingers.

"Go ahead, then," she told Jamie. "The lawyer can wait." She held Alix, stroked her flamboyant hair, feeling it spring up against her hand. "It'll be all right, sweetie, don't worry, we'll take care of it, it's all right to be upset, but of course it'll work out." She had no idea what she was talking about, except that she was lying.

Jamie knew, too. "Bullshit," he said, and left the room to call Bethany.

Well, what was Isla supposed to tell a weeping child, a broken-hearted little girl? Was she supposed to be wise?

At least she was supposed to be something. At least performing acts of motherhood gave her something to do. "How's Bethany?" she asked Jamie when he returned to the living room.

"Fine." Which she supposed answered the question.

She didn't have the strength to prevent him retreating blackly and silently to his room. She spoke, briefly, to James's lawyer, gave him the skeletal facts, and the phone numbers of the cops. Alix was whimpering on the sofa, that child who once lay sprawled in her dreams, exhausted by joy. Isla covered her with a blanket and sat down to watch, and found herself waking, cramped and stiff in the chair, with the first dartings of light. Amazed they'd all slept; but sleep has its purposes: anaesthetic, forgetful.

Had James slept? Under what circumstances?

Alix and Jamie did not go to school. Alix, looking like a fawn, a puppy, something young and vulnerable to the bullet, the boot, refused breakfast. Jamie had orange juice, Isla dry toast. "Your father," she said cautiously, opening the wound because it had to be done, "will be in court today, I think. If you want to see him, either of you, we can probably make arrangements."

"No," Jamie said. "Not me."

Alix was watching her brother. "Me neither," she said sturdily.

When Isla called Martin to tell him she wouldn't be at work and, briefly, why, he said, "Jesus, I don't believe it." He was a better person than she, then. Except it was just an expression. He could as easily have said, "You're kidding," although she clearly was not.

She said, so he wouldn't have to, "You should start considering what this is going to mean to us. How public it gets, for one thing. It's not going to be very useful, having a partner who's married to someone accused of serial sexual assault. On kids. If you can imagine. Not exactly a plus in the minds of most of our clients."

He was good enough to say sharply, "Don't even think like that, Isla. Just deal with what you have to deal with, we're not going anywhere without you. Could you use a drink later, if I came by?"

She thought she might. "You're a pal." He might be an unfaithful husband, Martin, but he was no molester. That, today, ranked him high on her list of virtuous men.

She called Madeleine, who gasped of course and said, "Oh, my God. Oh, my dear. That's incredible. Tragic. I'll be there as soon as I can manage, can you hold on?"

"Of course. Thanks. I might ask you to stay with the kids for a couple of hours, would that be okay? They're not in school, and I expect I'll have to be out for a while."

"Anything. Anything I can do. That son of a bitch."

"Yes."

He wasn't a son of a bitch, though, he was the son of two fragile parents who had to be told. Was this her job, too? Plunk plunk plunk through the day, one dreary horror after another?

James's lawyer phoned. Not the one she'd called last night, who handled his business affairs, but an expert in criminal matters. He introduced himself as Stephen Godwin. He said, "I'd like to see you in my office as soon as we can. I'll be speaking with your husband at some length today, and he'll be making a court appearance this afternoon. I want to raise the matter of bail then, so I'll need to know how far you can go with that, and also a few things about him. That he has a home, solid member of the community, no history, faith of his family, that sort of thing. Later on we'll need to talk more in-depth. More personally. His tendencies, for example, that you may have noticed. I know this must be a difficult time for you, but the earlier we get going the better, I think. Eleven? Eleven-thirty?"

What an invigorating conversationalist, this Stephen Godwin. *Tendencies?*

"Actually," she said, "no. Let me see, how can I put this?" She was pacing the hall with the portable phone, up and down, up and down, click-clicking to the beat of her words and a quite refreshing anger. "Let's see. He no longer has a home, there's not a penny headed his way for bail, and it also turns out I have no idea what his *tendencies* might be." The kids had stayed in the kitchen, but were probably listening. There was a limit to the number of things she could care about, or prevent.

His voice became soothing, as if she were a dangerously skittish large animal. "Now, I know how you must feel." Really? "This is a terrible time for you and of course you're upset, anyone would be. Believe me when I tell you, though, because you know I have a lot of experience in these matters, that later you'd regret not swinging into action today. You and your husband have been together a long time. And there are your children to think about. These things are more apt to get out of hand if they're not dealt with promptly. The best defence is a good offence, that's what I'm talking about."

"I do not," she said frigidly, "need instructions about giving some thought to my children. I made arrangements to hire you, and that's as far as I go. Oh, and I also need to know if the media's going to be interested. The police mentioned that possibility."

"I see. Yes. Well, they may be. All I can say is, it depends on what else is going on. But very likely at some point. Respected businessman, young employees, all that. It would be very unwise to speak to the media, though, I should warn you."

"I believe I'm aware of that. In any case, I'd have nothing to say."

"Please, let me repeat, don't let your anger, natural as it is, get in the way. If you don't mind me saying, it rather sounds as if you're assuming he's guilty. Is there any particular reason for that?"

"No particular reason, no." She could hardly say she had found she could picture James being guilty. Or that he had admitted it in his own disgusting way when the doorbell rang. She imagined Stephen Godwin shaking his head when he hung up, thinking no wonder James bent hard over more flexible women.

"Daddy can't come home?" Alix asked back in the kitchen. So they were listening.

"Do you want him to?" Not a fair question. What was the kid supposed to say? She didn't have time to say anything, because Jamie spoke up in a new growling, sort of menacing voice.

"He'd better not."

Oh dear. Isla pulled out a chair at the table. It happened to be James's usual chair. She was doing it again, she saw: already replacing his image with hers. Sunlight was making the maple tabletop glow golden; how could this terrible day be so painfully sunny? "Look," she said, "I'm not sure what to tell you. I don't really know how to help. You two are sad and angry and confused, and so am I. But I'll tell you this, we are not going to let each other down here. Inside this house we can cry or yell or swear or whatever, and we will also take care of each other. I won't tell you this isn't bad, because it is, and I can't tell you what's going to happen, because I don't know. But we will get through. And we'll have to think of other people, as well. Your grandparents—your father's their son, and I'm going to have to tell them, and that's hard. The main thing is, we have to stick together and look after each other, and we'll be okay." It wasn't much of a pep talk, but they wound up sitting taller.

Madeleine arrived then, opened her arms, and Isla, walking into them, finally felt herself at risk of breaking down into individual, collapsing atoms and molecules. She could have disintegrated entirely within her mother's tight arms; but wouldn't, of course. She had children, too. In a moment she straightened, said, just, "Thank you."

Madeleine nodded, stroked Isla's arm. "I know," she said, and Isla thought maybe she did.

She left Madeleine with Alix and Jamie, the three of them playing an absent-minded game of Scrabble, with the TV on in the background. "No news, though," Isla whispered to her mother.

It was awful, standing in James's parents' familiar living room, telling them. "Oh my God," his father said, turning pale.

He went, suddenly, from aging to old. Isla understood that he, too, had pictures. His mother was like Alix, features folding, face bending into her hands.

They weren't bad people. He was the only son, the only child, they had. This was a life's work collapsing in on them.

Except abruptly his mother changed, grew fierce and stern and powerfully determined. Her mind, only momentarily uncertain, was now clear, but in quite a different way from Isla's clarity. "Now then," she said, "what do we do? This is ridiculous. It's atrocious. We have to take care of it right now. Get rid of it." Whatever that meant.

His father, roused and rallied, maybe also bullied and blinded, found words, too, and anger. "What foolishness," he said. "A man's name ruined, and for what?" Of course it was his name, too. He'd be sensitive on the subject of what became of it.

Isla couldn't help, explain, account for, or comfort. She could barely save herself. She left them then to the task of erecting whatever walls they could manage. It was what parents did; unlike wives who leapt to conclusions. She also left them Stephen Godwin's name and telephone number. For all she knew they would try to bail James out. For all she cared they would succeed. "How can we keep the children from finding out?" James's mother asked at the door; a rather belated nod, in Isla's opinion, towards her grandchildren's well-being.

"They already know most of what I just told you. Well, for one thing, they were there when he was arrested." His mother shuddered at the word, her picture of what "arrested" entailed, and Isla touched her hand. "They'll be all right. They stayed home from school, of course. But oh, I forgot to mention it might wind up in the news, I'm afraid. You'll need to be ready for that."

James's mother looked stricken. "Oh no." His father had his hands on her shoulders. He looked stricken, too. Well, wasn't everyone?

"What do these girls want?" he asked. "What is their purpose in this?" He must have forgotten his son's ruthlessness, the way, when James wanted something, he set out to get it.

Back home, time felt suspended, vacant. There was nothing to do, and everything. Alix drifted wanly and aimlessly around the house; Jamie was in the basement, arms folded, watching TV furiously. In the kitchen, Madeleine was making egg salad. "I thought we'd have sandwiches," she said. She looked at Isla helplessly. "I don't know what to do. I don't know how to help."

"Just being here. Thank you. Except, do you know how I made such a mistake? Could you tell what he was like?"

"Oh, honey, no. How could anyone tell? Don't beat yourself up. Whatever's wrong is in his heart, not yours. And you know, one thing I've learned very well is that you can never see all the way into anyone else's heart. If someone's determined enough to keep something hidden, there's no real way to know what's in there." How did Madeleine learn that? From what experience was she speaking? Isla couldn't ask. She didn't think there was room in her head for more information, much less revelation.

"At least, I suppose," Madeleine was continuing thoughtfully, "we can be grateful it wasn't boys. That would have been even more of a shock."

They stared at each other. Isla saw her mother begin to struggle with her expression, and felt something unfamiliar bubbling up in herself. She heard herself snort. Then they were laughing, howling, tears ran from their eyes. "Oh my God yes," Isla gasped. "It could always be worse." It was irresistible. They couldn't stop.

"Mum! Grandma!" Jamie sobered them instantly. He looked like thunder.

Madeleine caught her breath first. "Don't be cross," she said, "we were just letting off steam. Everybody has to let off steam, you know."

"I'm going out." He turned. The front door slammed behind him.

"Shit," Isla said.

Alix drifted into the kitchen. "Were you guys laughing?" She sounded as if she were willing to disbelieve her own ears if need be. "Where'd Jamie go?"

"He needed a walk," Madeleine said. "Are you hungry? I've made egg salad for sandwiches. Your mother and I were just talking. We probably got a bit loud and carried away."

Isla wasn't sure she could keep anything down, but the sandwiches were good: a childhood sort of taste, an ordinary, mother-made sort of lunch. Alix picked at hers. "Are you going to see Daddy? Because maybe he could say. You know." That he'd done nothing, Isla supposed; Alix must mean he could say that. Or that the misunderstanding, misinterpretation, just plain evil, lay elsewhere. Or that, magic daddy, he could rewind events and restore them all to the relative bliss, the general beautifully, magnificently dull assumptions of twenty-four hours ago.

"Maybe," Isla said, not committing herself to whether that meant he could maybe explain, or that she might go and see him and ask.

Poor Jamie, out there trying to run faster than the pictures, and faster than his mother's and grandmother's idiotic, necessary laughter. Isla understood the impulse. If she didn't have him and Alix, if she weren't responsible, she would jump in the car and drive off, foot to the floor, across the country, to some other continent, anywhere she'd arrive before the pictures could catch up with her. But she did have Jamie and Alix, she was responsible. All her options, just like the pictures in her head, were narrow. They were also governed by James and what he had done. Salt in the wounds indeed. She laughed again, this time sharply and to herself. Alix and Madeleine both looked startled.

What were James's options, as he currently saw them? Until recently they must have looked enormous, expansive, an all-he-could-greedily-eat buffet of delights. She found herself standing. "I'm going to court," and like Jamie, was gone from the house.

It was urgent, suddenly, to get a good look at James. Scrutinize him for any connection at all between what she had thought and what she now knew. She wished there were a way to pin him down the way thoughtless collectors pinned down butterflies: in order to discern the elements of their beauty in that case, the elements of James's elusive, sly wickedness in his. A matter of camouflage. A matter of creatures creating shapes and colourings in order to escape being noticed. To be able to carry on their intentions unhindered—that now sounded like James, all right, although also somewhat insane.

The woman at the courthouse information desk was helpful in directing Isla to the right courtroom. It was a more straight-forward system than she'd expected: one large, busy space dedicated to first-appearance remands, the woman explained. Would expressions like "first-appearance remands" come to roll as trippingly off Isla's tongue? She thought not.

She slipped into a row near the back. Other people were also coming and going. She could see where the lawyers sat, and the bench where prisoners from the jail were rotated through as their cases were heard. Other people accused of crimes arrived, with or without lawyers, from the outside world, through the same door Isla had used. There weren't as many spectators as she would have thought, no great crowds of distraught families, for instance. The room itself was unceremonial, functional. No especially glossy, expensive woods here, no scales-of-justice carvings, only a large, spare, grey-painted room with benches and tables. She discerned a sort of assembly-line system: a name called, a man, usually a man, identified, charges read, arguments made for or against bail, occasional huddlings between lawyers and judge, frequent agreements without the need of huddlings, bored, accustomed voices following familiar scripts. To Isla it was amazing and foreign: all this life, all these plots for robberies, drug deals, quiet evenings at home gone awry, off the rails. What violent spectacle, what vicious drama! And all done so quietly!

And oh look, there was James; one of the few prisoners wearing a suit, although of course it was yesterday's suit. All things considered, he didn't look too bad. She understood she'd been hoping for black eyes, cut lip, some vicarious vengeance like that. She also would have preferred him to look more slumped and shifty-eyed but there he was, sitting straight, tall and, nearly, proud. Well no, surely not proud. He was just, with the aid of a tailored suit, still camouflaging himself. What nerve, though. And what energy even to try pulling that off.

Stephen Godwin turned out to be a sleek and silvery fellow who hustled in for the few seconds it took to remand James, without bail. The lawyers made some hurried, mumbled agreement, and that was it. The world of crime was humming, Isla assumed, and James would be among its smaller, if creepier, potatoes.

She, however, was no further ahead. Shocked she might be, despise him she might, but she nevertheless needed now, like hunger, like breath, to see him and hear what he had to say. Again, the system worked in surprisingly straightforward ways. She was directed to the relevant jail, some kilometres from the courthouse. Who knew these things? Off she drove.

At the jail there were formalities to do with identification and handing over possessions and stepping through an apparatus similar to an airport metal detector. There was no patting-down search, and the visitors' room was an actual room, not one of those grilled, glass-boothed things from the movies, but another plain space, this one with straight chairs and a guard.

James, appearing through a doorway, said, "Isla! Thank God." In other circumstances those words could have been nearly touching. And he should have stopped there. "I hope you brought a change of clothes, and my shaving stuff. I can't believe I'm not out on bail yet, but as long as I have a few things from home, I guess I can stick it out for a couple more days."

Such resilience, such bounce-back capabilities.

He really was extraordinary.

He was a good-looking man, although looser of chin and more sternly lined than he used to be, but she thought he was not a nice-looking man. Had he ever been? Was there some moment of transformation she'd missed?

"Look," he said, in a more subdued tone, nodding towards the guard, "I can't talk properly here. But I'm sorry. Truly, I never wanted to upset you, and anyway, this is all stupid. Not true, any of it, a complete over-reaction. And nothing to do with you, nothing to do with my feelings for you, honestly." Honestly! As if she'd be too stupid to notice that even denying, he was confessing. Or as if she could have any idea what might have previously been his feelings for her, or what they were now. Except that he wouldn't want her to think badly of him. He didn't in general like to be ill-thought-of, but must have some particular pride when it came to her.

Something, among so many other things, he might have considered beforehand.

"It was just something small and separate. But I swear, nothing to account for all this, believe me. I'm sorry there wasn't time to talk about it last night. Warn you better. I'll tell you everything when I get home, okay? It's not all what it sounds like, okay?"

She was staring; shook her head finally, not to say no, but to clear it. "You're an amazing man, James. Really quite impressive in your way." He started to speak, then decided, perhaps gauging her expression, against it. "Now, while you're being amazing, do you have any advice about how I can help your son and daughter understand that their father's a child molester?"

He looked horrified. "For God's sake, Isla, I'm not a child molester. Jesus! How could you say that?"

"I guess because I heard the charges. So far. I gather there may be more. How would you put it?" She was curious. They might just have had a long-term translation problem.

"Not children," he insisted. He seemed to imagine he had some right to insist. "How could you think such a thing? We *have* kids. You know better than that."

"So," she said mildly, "you'd understand if some middle-aged guy hired Alix in, oh, three years or so, and then jumped her? That'd be fine with you, quite understandable and not child-molesting?" Her voice hardened. "Since you ask, she and Jamie are kind of upset and confused. A little off-kilter. So I have to get back to them." She looked at her watch. It was the silver-banded one he gave her, engraved with her initials, for Christmas a couple of years back. She saw that she was beginning the inventory of things she would need to throw out. Too bad. She liked that watch.

"Isla," he said in a pleading sort of tone. Beseeching her for mercy, empathy, something soft like that? Apparently he could make his voice do anything he thought might be useful. Or else her name was the last familiar thing he had to hold onto. That could be sad.

"I have to go. There's just a couple of things I need to tell you. One is, if you get bail, which won't be from me, you're not coming home. Another is, I'm not your valet, so if you need underwear and after-shave, you'll have to find some other way of getting them. And third," she leaned forward, looked hard at him, last hopeless chance for seeing into whatever that dark space was behind his eyes, "what the hell did you think you were doing? What possessed you? What made you dream you had a right to risk your children this way, never mind me? And which part of your brain told you it was all right to throw yourself at young girls? What the hell did you think you were doing? Who did you think you were?"

She ran out of breath.

His eyes narrowed. He too leaned forward, astonishing man, looked ready to leap. The guard made a small reminding sound. They were staring hard at each other. Nothing was familiar. Some long history was erased.

"You should be careful," he said slowly, flatly, the cold sound of true anger, "about asking questions you don't really want answers to." It was by no means the first time she'd heard him say this, something like this; but it was going to be the very last time.

Standing, turning, leaving, she paused in the doorway, turned briefly back. She smiled brilliantly. She waited just long enough to see his hopes start to rise, his eyes to begin lighting up with relief, and for affection, real or manufactured, to begin softening the edges of his mouth.

Smiling brilliantly, then, got her safely, thank God, all the way home.

Like a Secret

THE QUESTIONS, WHICH SEEM BOTH hard and mainly pointless, at least have given Roddy something to do here at night. Form after form, page after page, they help him tune out the racket, the shouting and swearing back and forth that goes on, the kind of flying threats for tomorrow that float and dive-bomb along the corridor from one mad guy to another.

Worse: occasional whimperings, or loud sorrows.

He can't imagine anyone's so interested in him, his desires, inclinations, and gifts, that much will come of all this. Probably everything's just fed into a computer, which spits out some bare and simple plan of action that, however many questions there are, doesn't truly take him into account. Well, because how could it? Like at school, the questions are mainly multiple choice. Like at school, they're trickier than they look; and when they seem most innocent, he is most suspicious that that's when they're possibly trickiest, so that he has to circle and circle around them, like a dog tramping a patch of floor to lie down on.

Most of the answers aren't right no matter how careful he is, because the questions don't take shadings into account. Like, "Would you rather a) play hockey, b) swim, c) watch TV?" The way he would answer that is, he'd rather watch hockey on TV, like he used to do some nights with his dad, the two of them mostly silent except if there was a good goal or a bad fight, but connected, too. Another one comes closer: "When you watch TV, do you like programs about a) sports, b) nature, c) drama?"

Still, much is left out. He feels squeezed into choices he wouldn't otherwise make.

The intelligence tests have lots of questions about patterns and shapes: which word does not belong in this series of words, how would this shape look if it was turned inside-out and sideways? Trains and airplanes hurtle towards one another at varying speeds: when will the moment of collision occur? He's good at patterns of words. He can transform shapes in his head and see how they would be, inside-out and sideways. Speeding objects are harder to calculate. The only sure thing is, they will collide. Which would be the point, if these things mattered at all.

At least the intelligence tests, if devious or confusing or just plain hard, must have plain answers, too. Questions on some of the other tests, the ones about what sort of person he is, he'd like to either skip or have room to explain. "When you are angry, are you more likely to a) yell, b) hit something, c) hit somebody?" There's no place for "none of the above," no space for saying that mostly he goes off to his room, or out, alone or with Mike, either downtown or into the country, depending. Getting his head clear, working the anger off, dulling the edges. But hitting something, that would be pointless, and feel kind of made up; and he's hardly ever hit a person out of anger. More out of something like treading water: holding a place for himself, not getting pushed over, or around, or drowned.

Some people do yell when they get mad. Mike, for one, he's seen Mike dance around with his arms waving, raging up at the sky, even about nothing much, like a flattened bike tire, some small thing gone wrong. Roddy's vocal cords don't work that way, nor do his arms feel capable of grand gestures. Yelling is caring too much. It's too naked.

The aptitude tests are weird, too. "Would you rather work with a) numbers, b) words, c) hands?"—that's an easy one. But what about "When you think of a dangerous animal, is it more likely to be a) a dog, b) a leopard, c) a skunk?" What could that have to do with anything? Unless that Stan Snell, the counsellor or therapist or whatever he is, can steer him towards being a circus-trainer or a zoo-keeper, what difference does it make what he thinks a dangerous animal is?

The woman works with words, he guesses, if she's in advertising. She's probably rich, and for a job like that she also probably has to be smart. It'd be unbelievably hard to be smart and have to lie absolutely still, not feeling anything. Maybe he and the woman are both in the same kind of trouble that way, their heads going around and not being able to actually do anything about any of it. He imagines the hospital bed is about the size of the cot in his cell. Even if Roddy lies very still, there's still the hardness of the mattress beneath him, the rough blanket above, his heart beating, little digestive rumbles down below in his belly. Where his heels rest and how his eyelids quiver when he concentrates— she can't feel any of that? And if she itches, she can't move to scratch? Oh, but then, she probably can't itch, either.

For being so fucking stupid in the particular way that caused all this, Roddy, with his cot, his grey walls, his lidless crapper, is in totally the right place. He has to belong in this world of the dimwitted, the dense, the furiously hard-done-by. Not bad, necessarily—he himself is not bad, and he can't be the only one—but sort of mutated, sort of twisted, sort of bleached-out somehow. There are guys here that are like dried-up snakes flattened out by a truck. A few are even freakish like, oh, albino squirrels.

The sounds, the unrelenting din of voices rising and falling and boots clumping and cutlery clattering and pool balls dropping into pockets and TVs blaring and even just pages turning, are one thing. The smells are another. The place stinks of disinfectant and containment: the mad fragrance of frustration, which brings them all to rage of one sort or another. In the middle of the night guys cry out, awake or asleep there's round-the-clock grief. Roddy supposes he could do that too, if he chose, if he wanted, if he didn't mind other people knowing what goes on in his head.

If he imagined they cared.

He knows more now about how things work. Stan Snell and Ed Conrad have both explained that after he's sentenced, a couple of weeks from now probably, he'll be moved on from detention centre to reformatory. That should be a good word, *reformatory*, promising hope and life-changing, happy improvement, but obviously it is not.

There's no question about pleading guilty, which he'll be doing today. Because he is guilty; and because of course that first night, he confessed, just blabbed away to the cops about the whole thing, right down to what he and his dad and his grandmother had for supper. Everything except Mike. No wonder Ed Conrad sighs a lot. Roddy would, if he could, look for the mercy of understanding, an official, judging comprehension of one small, shattering, mistaken event. "You can hope, I suppose," Ed Conrad says, "but I sure wouldn't count on it."

Roddy was under the impression justice moves very slowly, but the lawyer has explained otherwise. "Pleading guilty speeds things. It's going to trial that takes forever." What Ed Conrad has done for Roddy is make a deal, a trade. He's proud of himself for pulling this off. "You plead guilty to the armed robbery, the attempted murder gets dropped. It's a good deal, you know, sawing off the attempted murder. I told them if they held on to it we'd be going to trial because you wouldn't plead guilty, and there's a good chance you'd skate on it. But if they dropped it, you'd plead to the armed robbery and the whole thing's off the books. Everybody saves money and time, you get points for not dragging the thing through the system, which means not dragging some witnesses through the system, either, like that woman, and you're better off all the way round, and so's everyone else." He grinned. "Except me. For me it'd be better to rack up big bills on your dad's tab, trying to defend you somehow."

Nice.

He's probably right, though, he spends enough time defending guys who've done what they're accused of doing, so all he can do is get them through the best he knows how. Maybe it's not his fault his heart isn't much in it, as long as he does what he's supposed to. Probably this is pretty good, good enough. Roddy's glad he won't have to testify and doesn't have to see anybody else testify, either. Not so much the paralyzed woman, and anyway how could she, but other people, like his dad, maybe, because of it being his gun. And like Mike. Either way, it'd be hard to hear whatever Mike had to say.

This way Ed Conrad said the charge'll get read out, the cops will have something to say, just the facts, basically, "no big deal." One thing he said might happen is if the woman or people in her family want to make some kind of statements before Roddy's sentenced. "You should be thinking about something to say to the court, too, make it clear what a good fellow you are, and a very sorry one."

Ed Conrad gets a rusty-metal tone sometimes in his voice. Is it just Roddy, or does he not like any of his clients very much?

"Write something down," he said. "At least make a start," and Roddy has tried. Except he may be good at spotting what word doesn't belong in a series of words, but he's stuck when it comes to whole thoughts about something important. He's written, "I'm sorry," but then—what else is there to say? That he'd change everything if he could? That he never meant it to happen? Words don't change anything, they don't fix, they're nowhere near big enough for real life.

Maybe that's why there's so much yelling here, and those other worse, suffering sounds: because words don't do the trick. Given time, Roddy, too, may lose more and more of them, be reduced, finally, to pointing or grunting.

This morning when the wake-up buzzer goes off in the corridor, Roddy's routine is instantly different. A guard comes for him, so Roddy doesn't join the usual lineup for the cafeteria. He and three other guys get taken right to the showers, and when they're finished there, instead of putting the brown jumpsuits back on, they're handed real clothes. His grandmother, or his dad, must have dropped off his stuff. His only pair of dress pants, dark grey, which he's never worn since his grandmother picked them up last year, a bargain, "because there'll be occasions in your life now, you know."

So there are.

Also there's a white shirt he hasn't seen before. New. Specially bought? And who wears white shirts?

People accused of big crimes, he supposes.

And in fact he thinks he doesn't look too bad. His body's better suited to dress pants and white shirts than to flailing around inside brown jumpsuits.

One of the other guys has nothing to put on except the jumpsuit. That's pathetic; to have nobody who even cares enough to bring clothes. "Fuck you," the guy says, "what're you looking at?"

"Settle down," warns a guard.

They're loaded into a van, going back to the courthouse. It's like a drug, smelling for a few seconds the hot, free air, inhaling deep, like a flashback of a week ago, two weeks ago, a whole seventeen years when this sort of air was normal, breathable, taken for granted. Also, just for the moment between the front door and the van, heat bearing down on the top of his head. A country kind of day. A swimming pool and toke and beer and ice cream kind of day.

Not ice cream.

He and the other guys and the guards get to the courtroom by elevator from the parking garage in the basement, no moment outside at this end of the journey. They file in through a side door, and get lined up side by side on a bench. Birds on a wire. Roddy's grandmother and dad are sitting together in the second row in the part where the audience, or whatever it's called in a courtroom, watches from. There's a lot of strangers sitting out there. They could be here for one of the other guys, or just out of curiosity, to watch any case at all, suck up other people's bad luck. Like his; he, for one, feels pretty doomed.

Or Jesus, some of them might be related to the woman. He doesn't know if he'd recognize the husband if he saw him again. In the doorway of Goldie's, he was just a figure, not a person whose features, in the middle of Roddy's own catastrophe, get remembered. Also she's got those two kids Ed Conrad mentioned, older than him. So maybe one or two or three or twenty of the people out there are from her family. He had that stray picture of one of them standing up in the courtroom, pulling out a gun, popping him one. This still doesn't seem impossible, although also, it does. He doesn't want to die. Just breathing is something. Does the woman feel that way, too? Not likely. She probably thinks just breathing isn't much at all.

Is anybody keeping a close eye on these people?

His dad and grandmother look at him and his grandmother smiles and nods, but then their eyes bounce away. They came up with these clothes, they're paying the lawyer, but maybe they haven't forgiven him. Or his dad hasn't forgiven him, and his grandmother has settled on one certain loyalty.

People make big mistakes to be loyal. It can get them into all kinds of trouble. Look at him: when it came down to the day, he got cold feet about Goldie's, but he didn't back out. He thought that'd be letting Mike down.

That's not totally true. He didn't back out because he didn't want Mike to think less of him; which is not quite the same thing as loyalty.

Once again, Mike isn't here. Roddy looks away, down towards his knees, his lap, his thin unbound wrists. A real no-hoper, one sad, bad case, that's how he figures it looks.

This time there's a real judge, black robe, the full deal. When he comes in, and everybody's stood up and then sat down again, his eyes take a run around the room, taking in Roddy and the others but not pausing especially. Maybe for him it's just another day at work. Like Roddy's dad getting up every day, maybe this is only a job he does because he has responsibilities, he has other people he has to look after. He doesn't look all that interested in the people in this room, anyway, although it's hard to read either kindness or cruelty into a fat sort of face and a little bit of grey hair. The black robe is mainly the point anyway. It looks totally serious.

When Roddy's case is called, it's like going on stage. He's moved away from the others, off the bench at the side and into a chair beside Ed Conrad's, behind one of the desks out in front of the judge. At another big desk there's a woman, and one of the two cops that busted him. The bigger, older one; the nicer one, although not somebody, obviously, on Roddy's side.

Now here is Roddy in another way he wouldn't have dreamed: standing up beside Ed Conrad admitting armed robbery. "Guilty," he hears himself say when the judge asks for his plea. Ed Conrad said he should speak clearly in court, so he does, and then the word "guilty" ricochets and reverberates around the room like he's proud of it.

Everything sounds bad. The woman, the lawyer on the other side, sitting at the other table with the cop, says some of what happened. Then the cop takes it from there, the facts of the thing, including all the stuff Roddy told them himself, which was everything except Mike.

The cop also reads bits from other people's statements: the woman's husband, describing being outside in his truck, hearing the shot, running in, seeing Roddy. Seeing Roddy throw up, too, and hand the gun over to Mike, and run out. Embarrassing, the throwing up part, and the running.

"We have been unable to determine that the defendant did not act alone." It takes a second to unravel that sentence. It means, Roddy guesses, they tried to rope in somebody else, Mike, and couldn't, but they're leaving it open. Mike's maybe not out of the woods yet. Maybe that's why he's not here. Even so.

Ed Conrad leans over with a friendly expression like he's just going to ask his client about something or other, and whispers, "Sit up. Uncross your arms. Get that look off your face." If he means Roddy should stop squinting, he can't do that. It's bad enough everybody knows he threw up. It'd be way worse if he cried.

The cop says, "The victim remains in hospital, with an undetermined prognosis as to her full or limited recovery." Which means Roddy isn't the only one who isn't exactly sure what he's done. It's so weird there's this woman, somebody he probably wouldn't recognize on the street unless she was wearing that blue suit again, and both their lives are suddenly completely different because of each other. Roddy shakes his head, because it won't come clear. Ed Conrad clears his throat and shifts in his chair and frowns.

The cop says this and that about Doreen: that she was away from Goldie's for a few days visiting her sister; that robbers might have expected her to do the same as she did last year, which was let cash pile up in Goldie's until she got back, only this time she changed her mind. The cop says, "The timing indicates forethought and foreknowledge. Deliberate planning targeting Goldie's, not a random choice." Ed Conrad objects. He says that's an unprovable assumption, not one of the facts of the case the cop's supposed to be giving. The judge agrees. Ed nods to himself like he's done something smart.

When it's his turn to ask questions, about all Ed Conrad does, though, is raise the subject of how Roddy's dad stored the shotgun and ammunition. "My client is only seventeen, after all," he says. "The adults in his life have some responsibility to protect him, even from himself."

"Was that a question?" the judge asks.

"Oh," Ed says. "No," and sits down.

If this wasn't about Roddy himself, it'd be kind of funny. Ed Conrad has nerve, though. Considering who's paying him, it was kind of brave to suggest some of this could be Roddy's dad's fault. Or he's stupid. Whatever.

And that's about it, except for both lawyers, Ed Conrad and the one against Roddy, wrapping things up. The one against him goes on about vicious crime, youthful violence, brutal, reckless behaviour, innocent victim, the need for harsh penalties to set an example. It sounds to Roddy sort of general; like it's not really directed at him.

Ed Conrad is different. For one thing, he talks slowly and softly about Roddy's mother, and what does he know about her? He talks about a boy wrenched from one place and set of people to another due to family tragedy. A hard-working but difficult family situation, loving grandmother and father doing their best, a good sturdy outlook for someone with that kind of support. A reckless, immature, tragic act, he says, by a boy still with promise, who might be destroyed by harsh punishment. "He did a terrible thing," Ed Conrad says. "But he is not a terrible boy. One out-of-character act should not destroy so much potential."

What does he think he knows about Roddy's character? Roddy has no good idea of it himself. Nor about potential. He doesn't want to think about that word at all. It means a future that's lost. What he could have done, whatever that might have been if he'd ever worked out such a thing.

What Ed Conrad really has no business doing, though, is bringing up Roddy's mother. If he'd known the lawyer was going to get personal, for sure he'd have told him to leave her out of it. She had enough trouble, without getting dragged into this. Blamed in a way, although Ed Conrad doesn't exactly say that. "My mother was great, we had fun, I trusted my mother." He would like to stand up and interrupt Ed Conrad and say that. He glares, narrowing his eyes as best he can. Ed Conrad frowns back, quickly, a warning.

The judge says, "I'll set sentencing for one week today, ten o'clock, this courtroom." Ed Conrad thought it would be a couple of weeks, but the judge probably doesn't figure he has much to think about. Maybe he'd sentence Roddy right now, except that would look too fast. "I'll hear victim impact statements now, along with any statement the defendant cares to make." The judge sounds sort of bored. Like whatever's getting said, he's heard it before. He probably has. None of this is probably new to anybody except Roddy.

He hears Ed Conrad sigh, and sees a tall older guy in a suit, not a suit like Roddy's dad's but smoother, and dark grey and three-piece instead of black and two-piece, walking from behind Roddy to the front of the room. He doesn't look upset or nervous, but he does look real serious. He's familiar, or his shape is: last seen outlined in the doorway of Goldie's. The judge says, "Please identify yourself to the court," and he says his name and where he lives. That he's the husband. Also a lawyer. He gives some long-named company, and his own is one of the names. For sure he looks a whole lot smarter, and more expensive, than Ed Conrad.

"I'll be brief," he says, "because I don't think this young man," nodding in Roddy's direction but not looking at him, "is worth much of the court's time. My wife, however, does deserve some attention." That hurts, even though it makes sense the guy has to be bitter. "So I want to tell you just a little about her, so you'll understand the person who's been hurt by all this, through no fault or act of her own." Well, that's true. She did nothing except show up at the very wrong moment.

"She and I have been married for just over six years. Her first marriage ended very badly, and it was hard for her to make a happy life for herself in its aftermath. But we did. We have." Hurray for them. Ed Conrad frowns at Roddy again in his quick sidewards way.

"She has two children, both now young adults, whom she worked hard to help through the very difficult years after the end of that first marriage. I'm not here to invade her privacy, but I do want to say that all her adult life she has been a dedicated mother, as well as a creative and talented businesswoman as partner and vice-president of a major advertising agency. A productive and energetic member of society. But of course what's most important to me," and the guy's smooth voice drops low and goes bumpy and rough, "is that she is my partner. We've each made a second chance for ourselves, which is a considerable triumph at this stage of our lives."

You'd think he'd know something about second chances, then. You'd think he'd consider sparing one for somebody else. But Roddy supposes that'd be quite a lot to ask of this man. "We enjoy our life. My wife is a person who knows the value of celebration, and that's what we were setting out to do—celebrate a happy moment with ice cream. That's all she was doing: going for ice cream." His voice breaks slightly there. If Roddy's heart feels clogged up with sentiment, what about everyone else's?

"And now because of this one kid here, she's in a hospital bed where she can't move or feel. She is paralyzed. Even in the best of medical hands, even the best possible outcome would mean months, maybe years of recovery. This boy," and suddenly he is looking at Roddy, right into Roddy's eyes, a hot stare that welds Roddy's eyes, too, so he can't look away, "this boy blew up her life, he exploded our hopes, he did something more terrible than he can imagine."

How does he know what Roddy can imagine?

But he's right.

"There's no way to redress this. There's no sentence that fixes it. There's no possible justice. I just want to ask you, your honour, to keep in mind, when you're deliberating, a loving, hardworking woman who was finally happy." Shit. Happy. Loved.

Going back to his seat, the guy walks stiffly, kind of jerking, and doesn't glance Roddy's way. Roddy feels tiny, stepped-on, like an insect, one of the ones nobody but him sees any beauty in.

Now he can hear somebody else moving behind him, coming up beside him, soft short-stepping sounds. A girl. A young woman, right beside him, almost in reach if he leaned over slightly and stretched out his arm. And as if she is inclined to lean over slightly and stretch out her arm and touch him, she pauses in her journey to the front of the room. She is looking at him in a really strange way.

She's got the wildest red hair, flaming out unbound and amazing. The dress she's wearing doesn't look like it belongs on somebody with that hair; it's long and brownish and he can see through it to the shape of her legs, all the way up. She's real thin. She looks—weak's not the right word, but something like his grandmother's glass animal figurines that she keeps in the china cabinet. She looks like she could break. Or be blown over.

Her skin, it's pale and pure and like he can see right through it, like her dress.

Mainly it's her eyes: really intent, staring right into him. Not like she's angry or any second could pull out a gun, more that she's trying to see right inside his head. He almost nods at her, just as gravely, a way of saying, *Come right in, you're welcome, feel free, look around. Save me.*

Something is happening here that's light-headed and also terrible in a way: he is being washed over, his whole self, top to toe, with warm, sincere, perfect love of this girl.

When she turns away and continues to the front of the courtroom he feels released, freed, relieved, although at the same time adrift and more lost than he already was.

Her voice is high and clear. She says she is the daughter and her name is Starglow. The judge says, "Your legal, birth name, please," and she sighs and says, Alix.

She's looking at Roddy again with those serious eyes. She says she doesn't hate him. If not hate, what? Love? No, that's him. Pity's not quite right either.

She says she only wants to say that her mother is someone with a good soul. "She is paralyzed in her body," this girl says slowly, talking to Roddy like she's touching him, so his skin feels like it's rising right off the rest of him, "but only in body, never in spirit. My mother has the promise of serenity, she can be a revelation of peace of the spirit. It's very hard, but something so great can't ever be easy. I just want to say this is a promise. It encompasses everyone who's willing." Her eyes still hold Roddy's. Oh, he's willing. He even thinks he can glimpse what she means by *something so great* and *peace of the spirit*. But it's like a dream, what she means that he understands, it's not quite graspable, and slips away.

His head swims, he feels faint, like he could go falling right over, as she slips past him, back to her seat. Everybody's kind of frowning, rustling, resettling, including the judge. In this whole room, it's like Roddy's the only one who got any of what she was saying. For a few seconds there, he almost had hold of something.

"Thank you," the judge says finally, in a what-the-hell-was-that sort of voice. Roddy is offended on her behalf; although probably that's small-minded of him. Whereas she is large-minded, huge-hearted, enormous of spirit, and wouldn't care. "Now then." The judge turns to Ed Conrad. "Does your client have anything to say before we adjourn?" Ed looks at Roddy. Who finds himself standing. This is like Goldie's: something he's doing without deciding or thinking.

Now what?

Now here he is, standing up in his dress pants and new shirt, looking at a man in a black robe who's waiting for him to speak, but the point is the girl. She told him something important, even if he can't quite hang on to its meaning, and he needs to tell her something back. A message between the two of them. "I'm sorry" is what comes out. "I'm really, really sorry. I didn't mean it. I'd do anything if it hadn't happened. I don't know how it happened. I'm just sorry."

Ah no, he has blown it. That was exactly what he already decided was useless, and it's also not even close to anything he wants to tell her. How come there aren't words for what he truly means, the scope of his regret, his sorrow, his sudden weird love?

His gratitude, too. "And," he says, turning slightly so he can just glimpse her, "thank you."

That's better. That's closer.

Everybody stands up. A cop appears to lead Roddy away again. Roddy, looking back at the emptying courtroom, sees his grandmother and dad regarding him helplessly, the exact expressions that would be unbearable if they were the people he was looking for, but he's watching the girl. She's following her mother's husband, her stepfather, he supposes. She doesn't look back, but surely the way she moves, the certainty of her spine, the firmness of her feet, the transparency and sway of her dress, even, tell him that maybe after all, she heard, not so much his words but his intentions. The way he's the only one, he figures, who had a clue about hers.

He'd be okay, if he could keep looking at her. No need to talk, although he'd like it if she did because her words mean something. *Starglow*, he says to himself, then adds *Alix*, but out loud so the cop says, "What?" and he feels sort of like a fool, but not really.

It's not that any of what just happened makes sense; more that it doesn't. Riding back in the van, he feels, not happy, but nearly peaceful. He keeps his eyes closed, to concentrate on how she looked to him, standing beside him, holding him hard with her eyes. That hair, that thin body, those words she spoke that he cannot remember, except for knowing that while they were being said, he felt strong, and almost sure of something. And how his skin felt like it was lifting right off his body.

Catapults and Boiling Oil

"**Y**OU AWAKE, MUM?**"** Well no, she was not. But because this is Jamie's voice, and because this is exactly what he used to do, creeping to her side of the bed some mornings when he was little, she rouses herself. This is like swimming through peanut butter. "Hi," he says. "How you feeling?"

She feels helpless, that's how. She feels dependent and doomed and despairing and tethered to heaven knows what apparatus and incapacities. She feels rage flaring hotter and faster than any goddamn internal flame Alix could dream of. That's how she feels, what does he think? "Okay," she says. "Tired."

"I thought you'd want to know Grandma and Bert are on their way back. Or will be soon." They are? She thought they'd agreed to leave Madeleine and Bert in happy ignorance as long as possible, off on their much-planned, much-anticipated month-long holiday on one of those tiny and obscure Caribbean islands that are particularly hard to get to. Once there, also difficult to get away from, especially if you're old, and have a dicky heart, as Bert does, and are on an organized, inflexible charter, as they are. Why get them upset when they're far away and when there's nothing they can do? That's what Isla believes she, Lyle, Jamie, and Alix decided. So what's changed, and why?

Although it's true, it would be awfully nice to have a mother right now.

Madeleine is seventy-four, Bert seventy-six, so the worry before they left was that some emergency would crop up with one of them and they'd be stuck without convenient or adequate help. "Stop fussing," Madeleine said. "We'll be fine, and if we're not, look what a beautiful place it is for a funeral." Madeleine has become vastly light-hearted in recent years, an advertisement for a certain kind of old age.

She deserves better than this. Of course, so does Isla.

Madeleine and Bert have been together far longer than Madeleine and Isla's father were married. When Isla married James, while James's mother and Madeleine wept, it was Bert who gave her away. He's a nice man. Kind. He is small, plump and has been balding slowly, slowly, for several decades. Isla assumes that her mother, if she has hankerings and cravings, must have quite different ones from her own. This is not something they've particularly discussed, although they've smiled together about Bert's fondness for stripes, and his pale stubby legs when he wears shorts, and the way his eyes crinkle closed when someone else sneezes, an endearing, odd habit. When Madeleine says, "He's a good man," Isla understands this has a very large, encompassing meaning. In the absence of pieces of paper and formal vows, Madeleine and he seem to jog along happily together, affectionately. They still touch each other often, randomly, on the shoulder, the knee, elsewhere. Bert appears to regard Isla and her difficult children and her unfortunate history as a set of awkward luggage that travels with Madeleine and has to be taken into account in the larger interests of devotion.

If they quarrel or have confusions, any chaos, they keep it to themselves. Since they've both retired, they've been on journeys through parts of Europe and much of North America. These days they tend to go on organized tours, although since Madeleine has also learned to do things like scuba dive, safety doesn't seem one of her most compelling concerns. Bert, too, has become more adventurous, or at least willingly follows Madeleine into the sea, despite his jittery heart. Apparently everyone was wrong to worry about something bad happening to one of them on their journey. Also there appears to be no point at which mothers get to retire. However old they get, however far beyond reach they travel, they're always vulnerable to the call, to being hauled back.

Jamie must see something to this effect in Isla's face. "Well, we decided she had to know, Mum. We couldn't hold off any longer, she'd kill us." Does Isla not have a voice any more? But oh, to see Madeleine suddenly appear at her bedside, the way people do appear suddenly—there are tears in her eyes again. Heavens, she's sentimental. At any rate, moody.

When Jamie and Alix were little, Isla would have run into fire or traffic for them. Well, she still would, although now she'd be wondering why they didn't know better than to get themselves caught in a fire or traffic. This is the trickle-down effect of maternity: that Isla wouldn't dream of saving herself at the expense of Jamie or Alix; that Madeleine would trade places with Isla in a heartbeat.

Those are hypothetical choices, obviously. In some families, that would be a good thing; not every parent is steadfast.

Isla would trade places with some other mother's son, though, she'd change places in a second with that little asshole who shot her.

Oh, now she remembers what she was going to ask Jamie: about the drugs. How he truly and deep-down managed to kick the desire for that deep slide into creamy darkness. His other universe.

"How are they getting here?"

"Lyle says they're floating home on a big raft of money. But really, a little private plane"—poor Bert—"and then some kind of boat, and a plane to Miami, but there's a layover, anyway it's going to take forever and it's pretty complicated, but they should be on their way soon. Lyle worked it out." Madeleine will be desperate.

Back when Jamie was fifteen, and in the process of growing tall as well as lean, he still could be caught with the open, sometimes clumsy, sometimes yearning expressions of child-hood on his face. He'd said once he might like to teach, but it was hard to imagine him as a teacher; a man of authority; any man. "There's time," Isla had told him, because she'd thought that there was. "You can do anything you decide you want to do." She should have rephrased that. She meant it in happy ways, as in a world of good possibilities open to him. She didn't consider the awful ones.

His father thought he, too, could do whatever he decided he wanted to do. She hadn't considered that, either, although soon after that conversation with Jamie, was compelled to. Now, standing over her hospital bed, Jamie has that expression again, that open, clumsy, yearning one. Only now he is a man. Some things are not retrievable.

Here is this other strange thing: that she longs to put her arms around him, but is already forgetting how it is to feel her feet on the ground, or shake her head, or put her arms around anyone. She is forgetting air and motion and solidity. How odd, surely, to lose track so quickly; at the same time, to want so ferociously what's been lost track of.

She wants her mother. Madeleine can't fix this; nobody can ever fix anything for somebody else, really, that's one of the hard lessons of being a grown-up, not a child. But she can be a fiercely sturdy, dependable presence.

The police and James's lawyer were right: his crimes were of interest, not huge interest but quite enough, to the newspapers. There was his name, the name of his business, its many loca-tions. He had a wife, it was noted, and two adolescent children, who of course were not named. Not being named did them lit-tle good. Everyone who knew them knew who they were.

Mavis brought cheeses and cold meats to the door. A few other neighbours and friends dropped by or phoned. Isla felt pathetically grateful; but what on earth could anyone say? "I'm sorry" covered a great deal of ground: sorry for, sorry about, sorry altogether. Then what?

For the first few, worst weeks, Madeleine took leave from her job and moved in. She cooked and played cards and handled the phone, screening messages, some of them very ugly. In this way she was able to tell them James was staying, as a condition of bail, with his parents. Isla tried, although not very hard, to imagine what it was like in that household, the shamed, ruined son back in the nest.

She also wondered if James tried to imagine what it was like in the home where she and Jamie and Alix still had to live; but of course he did. He telephoned too, a few times. When Madeleine asked if anyone wanted to speak with him, no one would. Alix looked at Jamie, then followed his suit. Isla thought Alix looked as if she wanted to talk with her father, and wondered if she should intervene, but did not.

Sometimes, passing Jamie's bedroom door, she heard his voice in long phone conversations with Bethany. Isla, still struck nearly dumb herself, wondered what he had to say, what he confided. She had new admiration for Bethany, who must listen so well. She wondered about Bethany's parents' views.

Madeleine arranged for Jamie and Alix to switch schools. She said, meaning well, "No one will know you. You'll have a fresh start."

Did James not consider that sort of upheaval before hurling himself on the young bosoms of his employees? Two more came forward. More charges were laid. The list became too complicated to keep track of, and anyway at a certain point, the specifics were hardly what mattered. He would plead not guilty, Madeleine said, having talked to his mother. Stephen Godwin would argue that in the case of the younger girls nothing had happened, and that with the older ones anything that had happened was voluntary, even welcomed. "Consensual" was the word he intended to rely on, evidently. "The idea seems to be," Madeleine reported, "that they'll withdraw rather than go through a trial." His mother, she said, had arrived at the firm view that James was innocent of everything except, maybe, impure thoughts. That being so, she was very angry at Isla: for weakness, for faithlessness. "So I told her," Madeleine said, "that I didn't care to hear that sort of nonsense and if that was all she had to talk about, she shouldn't call back. I'm sorry if that was the wrong thing to do. But it's bad enough the woman's delusional, I won't have her insulting you while she's at it."

A couple of times, very late at night, the phone rang and without thinking Isla picked up her bedside extension. "Isla, don't hang up. I need to talk to you." She was tempted. She thought she had a great deal to say, but once started, where would she stop? And it sounded as if he intended her only to listen. And he failed to say, "Please."

Mainly she decided words weren't big enough, or complicated enough, or maybe years in advertising had simplified her vocabulary so it wasn't adequate now for anything as complex as her feelings. *Betrayed* didn't come close, nor did *rage*, really. Wounded to the point of staggering, flailing unspeakability? Something like that. She couldn't get warm, and also could barely make herself move, spent hours curled in her bed, under blankets. She supposed this was grief. She hadn't imagined anything so painfully heart-stopping was possible.

So it wasn't so much that she had nothing to say to him, or too much, but that she couldn't begin to say what she meant; and so she hung up without speaking.

In time, though, something else became noticeable. It was that, when she did manage to pull herself out of bed, it felt as if she'd lost a good deal of weight. It took a while to know what this was: that some part of her, a tiny corner of her heart, was lightened, was almost grateful for the clarity of his crimes.

Because what he had done was so pure, so decisive, it spared her a more grinding departure, the one she'd vaguely foreseen a few years down the road when she would want to leave him, for no good or obvious reason. Now pinned, nailed, guilty, he had relieved her of her own hard decisions. The upheaval of common habits, the absence of certain sounds, those were disorienting sorrows; but waking up one morning she found herself smiling, and then again, on another morning. This said nothing good about her. It said much that was unpleasant to learn. She supposed it meant that while their betrayals, their general heedlessness of each other, were different in detail, they were equivalent in scope. A difficult conclusion, but there it was, true anyway.

None of this meant the shock didn't still nearly knock her flat every electric time she pictured him in storerooms and offices, bending over young girls. Of course there were questions: like, why? And whether there are prescriptions for love, and acting out love, and fatal symptoms of the endings of love and all the gnarled and convoluted ways of reaching the endings of love. Also, does love matter? If so, why? These questions counted both enormously and not at all, which she would not previously have thought reasonable or possible, but which was both.

Madeleine slept, without difficulty, in Isla and James's old room. Isla had moved across the hall into what had been James's home office. She remembered when she'd thought of the house as a fortress of sorts, and had considered that a good thing. Now it really was a fortress, it really did contain them all. They might as well have kept pots of boiling oil on the windowsills, catapults at the doors.

Bert came around often to see Madeleine. Martin came also, a special kindness since it meant neglecting both wife and lover. He brought along work discussions and decisions, and if Isla didn't want to get out of bed, he went upstairs and hauled her down. They went over contracts and campaigns, spreading papers out on the coffee table. He said, "Whenever you're ready, come back."

Jamie was often out, and at home stayed unnervingly adamant in his silence. Not unlike Isla herself. She touched him, tried to touch him, but could not feel that she reached him. She saw the wariness in his light footsteps, and possibly furtiveness. She said, "Talk to me," and also "Listen to me," but he would do neither; or could not. She imagined that like her, he was quietly, internally, absorbing various blows. Assessing trustworthiness, too. He was taking care of himself in his own way, and it wasn't so different from hers, after all. Alix, on the other hand, took to hanging around in the living room. Suddenly younger, more like a nine- than a twelve-year-old, she sat on the sofa in pink flannel pyjamas with Bert and Madeleine, watching TV while Isla and Martin worked haphazardly nearby with their campaigns and contracts. Sometimes it was possible to look around and see all this as a cozy scene. Not entirely a family scene, but an awfully cozy one.

Except Isla could no longer believe what she saw. If James could surprise her, and if she could then even startle herself, surely anything could rear up shockingly out of anyone. Bert might be any damn psychopath beneath those striped shirts. That she knew Martin had serious secrets meant he knew how to be clever with lies. Obviously her judgement was skewed. What she thought she saw wasn't necessarily close to what was right in front of her face. This felt insane. Just thinking the word *insane* felt slightly insane, daringly and dangerously real.

What had walked handcuffed with James out the door, she decided, was not, obviously, her life, but what she'd understood of her life. Life being not merely circumstances, but decades of putting together puzzles, information, clues, pieces of knowledge and observation, sensations, tones of voice, smells and colours, everything, into something that added up to what could be relied on, what was true, if not for everyone, at least, at very least, for herself. "How could he?" she cried to Madeleine, and didn't mean how he could press himself on young girls, but how he could not just tell lies, wicked enough, but actually, himself, be a lie.

Madeleine got very angry then, voice pitched low, a sure sign. Her mouth was tight, her darkened red hair, much like Isla's but dyed now, looked dishevelled, as if earlier she had been running her fingers through it. Her hands were flat on the kitchen table and she was standing, leaning into them hard.

"Isla. You listen to me. People like us can't recognize people like him and we shouldn't be able to. It doesn't mean we're stupid or foolish, it means we're hopeful and good. You hold onto that, and don't ever doubt it. You will not let him ruin that. You will not." She was pretty magnificent. And she made being trusting and hopeful sound like virtues, not stupidities, without entertaining the third possibility, that they were both.

She was a mother, of course. And look at James's mother, her defence of her misunderstood, betrayed, mistreated boy. "Maybe," Isla said. "In the long run. I just don't see a long run at the moment."

"Well, I do. Now go have a shower. You look like hell. The kids'll be home soon, and I want you cleaned up and dressed. Then get organized to go back to work. Martin's been saying to get back when you're ready, but at this rate you're making yourself less ready, not more. You're right if you think some people won't know how to look at you, or what to say, but any longer and you'll be making everything worse. Including yourself." This was harsh, and unmaternally abrupt. In her alarm, Isla turned sulky. Evidently it showed. "You're not a teenager," Madeleine said, "so don't stick that lip out at me." Oh God, she was! She was frowning at her mother and sticking out her bottom lip! Which began to quiver. When the kids came through the door, she and Madeleine were still laughing.

At dinner, Madeleine had her own announcement. "You know, I do like being around every day. Besides being my family, which means you're excellent by definition, I'd think you were all fine, admirable people if I didn't know you from Adam." The kids had stopped eating, Isla noticed. They were looking at their grandmother warily, as if waiting for the disagreeable shoe to drop. They too, Isla saw, no longer took their own goodness for granted, nor perhaps anyone else's.

"It's tempting to stay, but I think I'd be wiser to hold that for my dotage when I have to ask one of you to look after me." They all smiled. "For now, though, we'd each do better to get on with our own lives. You two," looking at Jamie and Alix, "are settled in school, and your mother's about to go back to work, and I'm missing my own job and my house. Now Alix," because she'd spotted the uprush of tears, "I know it's hard, but you're going to be fine now." She'd brought tears to her own eyes. Isla touched her arm. "Now, that's enough from me. Think how chatty I'm going to be by the time one of you has to take me in."

"You can come live with me, Grandma." Tender Alix. "I'd always look after you."

"I'm sure you would, honey. Let's just hope for your sake it doesn't come to that any time soon."

Jamie was silent, as usual. As usual, he went out as soon as they rose from the table. "You'll have to keep an eye on him," Madeleine told Isla as they loaded the dishwasher.

"I think he talks to Bethany. I hear him on the phone some-times. But you're right, of course, I'm keeping an eye."

That didn't go so well, did it, that business of keeping an eye?

Because here, hovering above her, is what has become of that boy. Ten years on he is a man, although still a young man, with grave depths in his own dark eyes. Somewhere in there is a world of lost possibilities. There is also knowledge he shouldn't need to have of terrible acts, some done by him, some to him.

For a while, when she thought he was going out most evenings to meet Bethany, he was. Then he wasn't. It was some time, though, before Isla knew he was finding places, under-passes and alleys, strange rooms and apartments, where it was possible to find substances that could make him feel better. Or feel nothing. Feel, anyway, as he much later described it, as if he were flying through some other universe, a bright and kaleido-scopic and painless one. It was difficult to stay there, though, and he had to try harder and harder to get to where the colours were rich and the action was fast and there were no troubles of any kind, none at all.

It didn't take long for this to happen. Apparently it doesn't take long, if a person's determined enough. Also if a person's determined enough—like James, too, she supposed—it's possible to keep certain flaws, vices, deficits, private for quite a while.

Of course Jamie was troubled, she knew that. So was Alix, so was she. Being troubled was normal, as far as Isla could see, and if Jamie's marks plunged, it was hardly surprising. Although Alix's didn't, Alix's shot higher, and she bent with great focus over her homework and projects. Isla herself had difficulty concentrating at work, and wasn't amazed when Jamie had a similar problem. The one who amazed her was Alix.

"I'd like to move," Isla told them one night over dinner. "What would you think of getting another place altogether? Rent something, till we sort ourselves out?" She tried to sound casual, as if they were really deciding, but her own heart, frankly, was set. There weren't many unhaunted spaces left for her in that house—a chair here, a corner there—and they were tiny and kept getting tinier. She felt that was perhaps melodramatic, but on the other hand, what exactly, at that point, was not melodramatic?

Jamie said, "Yeah, sure, whatever. I don't care." Alix looked confused and on the verge of protest, but said only, "Would we have to change schools again?"

"Not if you don't want to."

Alix sighed. "Then okay, I guess."

A lot of losses; but when she moved the three of them into a rented duplex, a shiny and compact, renovated, surely temporary place close to downtown, she was thinking it would be better for them, too, a neighbourhood where no one had seen anyone taken away in handcuffs, placed in the back seat of a cruiser, vanishing from view but not from a community of curious minds.

Still, those were the months, weeks, days, and long evenings when she must have failed them, each of them; the hinge period when, if she'd been wiser, or slightly more sane, she could, possibly, have tilted them one better way or another. When they were very little, hurtling boisterously, screeching and laughing down slides, she was a good mother who stood at the bottom and caught them; but when they were truly sliding, she missed, they slipped right through her hands.

The therapist—well, that was one obvious thing to do—the therapist told Isla it was hard to extract information from either Alix or Jamie. "They seem withdrawn," she said, "although it's very important they open up, especially with regard to their father. This sort of event could be permanently damaging." Well, no shit. But Isla didn't want to talk about James, either. Her sympathies were with her children. Jamie finally dug in his heels and refused more appointments, and Alix, as usual by then, followed his lead.

He did not, however, allow Alix to follow him out on his evenings. Isla asked where he was going, what he was doing, who he was meeting since it was no longer Bethany; a loss that must have given him much more to mourn, although he refused to say what happened, just shrugged and insisted, "No big deal," even though it had to be. "It's private," he said. "My own business." It was, Isla thought, as if he blamed her, not his father, for all the chaos and sorrow. Well, she was on hand, present and blameable.

"Guys from school," he said he was meeting. "New buddies. We hang out." He was restless and irritable, but why would he not be?

Each of them had a birthday. Two birthdays. Two Christmases. James telephoned on each occasion from wherever he was, which was only briefly in jail. His sentence, the legal part of it anyway, was scarcely harsh, although he seemed to feel that losing his family had been excessive. The second year, Jamie and Alix each spoke with him briefly, came away angry in Jamie's case, sad in Alix's. If it was a rule that one parent should never speak ill of the other, Isla was lost for words, but she tried. "He loves you, you know. That never changes." She wasn't sure that was true. Who could speak for someone like James? She said, "Everybody does stupid things in their lives, some are just stu-

pider than others. And you know, people change, people learn."
Certainly she had, if not in notably benign ways.

"Would you see him?" Jamie asked.

"Good God, no, but it's different for you, he's your father."

Jamie turned away. "Thanks for reminding me."

He was seventeen, that hard age, although he seemed hard
in blank, opaque ways she couldn't see through, even though
like staring at glass brick, she could now and then make out his
shadow, his shape. "I can't tell," she said to Madeleine, "how
much is a stage and how much I should be really worried
about. And then what I could do in any case, when he hardly
speaks; and he's nearly a grown-up, he has to be his own person.
Whatever that is." In all ways he bore less and less resemblance
to the glinting little Jamie, her formerly familiar boy.

"I don't know either. You weren't easy at that age yourself."
Really? Isla didn't recall being difficult. That seemed reassuring. "I never dreamed," Madeleine said later. "I never once
dreamed it was more than it seemed. Extreme, maybe, but basically ordinary, given the circumstances. I'm so sorry."

If nothing else, Jamie was fortunate that Lyle came into the
picture. That awful night Alix caught Jamie shooting up in the
bathroom and Lyle found a rehab centre and drove Jamie away,
into the night, to be helped, although that time only briefly—
what a blessing Lyle was.

If there are awful, unintended surprises, bolts of sheet light-
ning striking innocent living rooms, there are miracles, too.
Salvation, redemption, whatever the words are for these things,
take various forms. Isla and Lyle ran into each other, literally ran
into each other, at the revolving door of a downtown hotel
restaurant. A cliché, an encounter out of a silly movie, him waving back towards someone at the desk, her rummaging, head
down, in her purse for her car keys, each of them leaving separate lunches with separate clients where they'd been discussing
separate kinds of business. What would she have done, how
would events have unfolded, if that moment had not occurred?

For one thing, she wouldn't be lying here paralyzed.

"Oh, sorry," and he'd grabbed her elbow, unnecessarily steadying her. She was at the same time saying, "Oh, sorry," to him. They'd smiled, then both laughed. Two years after James, helplessly worried about Jamie and his vague but apparent troubles, stupidly oblivious to the dangers of Alix, still struggling to keep her mind on her work, Isla was not in a mood for much laughter. She was smiling mainly out of aesthetic pleasure: his ranginess, jutting bones, deep eyes. Not handsome, exactly, but someone who looked as if he had a real life. It was raining quite hard, and neither of them had a coat or umbrella. Lyle said, "Want to wait this out in the bar?" and she said, "Okay, let me just make one call," and there the afternoon went.

It went, though, fairly impersonally. He talked about cases, and she thanked God he wasn't a lawyer who specialized in gross and grubby crimes, such as employee-molesting. She chatted about slogans and ways to bring, say, a brand of disposable diapers onto the market. "A rather saturated market, at that," she said, and he found that funnier than maybe it warranted.

"You could use that," he said, "in a loopy sort of campaign," and she thought, yes, she could, and wrote it down, and did use it and some other light-hearted lines and eventually the campaign won her and Martin an award for its off-key, bad-joke approach to disposable diapers. "It must be fun," Lyle said, "to be able to play with words. I don't get to do that. There's not much playfulness in a courtroom."

She knew that, but had no intention of mentioning how she knew.

When the rain stopped, they both looked at their watches. Outside, they shook hands. Isla realized she was walking away in sprightlier fashion than she was used to. "That was nice," was what she thought.

A couple of days later, he called her at work. "I know it's not raining, but I've been trying to think of some other reason you might like another drink with me and I couldn't come up with any good one except I'd like to, would you?"

That time they talked about children, his far more than hers. Teenaged daughter and son, tough ages, that's pretty much all she had to say right then about Jamie and Alix. Lyle was happy talking about William and Robert, a few years older than her two, and already in university. Imagine that, she thought, fairly bitterly.

Certainly they didn't talk about marriage, their marriages. Just his, "Widowed," her, "Divorced," his "Sandy," her "James," his "cancer," her silent shrug.

They went to a couple of movies, had drinks afterwards, discussed plots and characters. She saw no reason to invite him to her home, that rented duplex. In fact it was rather pleasing to keep him to herself: a private sort of treat, as unaffected and untouched by her real life as her real life was unaffected and untouched by him. He said, "You don't talk about yourself much, do you?" but he didn't seem to require an answer, or a reason. It was restful to be in the company of a man who made an observation, not, apparently, a judgement.

They toasted his legal triumphs. When he won a case in which he had defended a drug company and its officers who'd been charged with deliberately permitting, encouraging, gaining from the massive overseas distribution of medications long past their expiry dates, she was slightly taken aback. She herself was obviously capable of misleading, with catchy lines and one-minute plots, but still—she wanted to think of Lyle as someone to admire, and to be glad to know. "What sort of case wouldn't you take?" she asked. "Who would you refuse to defend?" presuming an existence of lines, just inquiring where they might lie.

"Hitler," he sidestepped, grinning at her. "You?"

"Stalin. Pol Pot."

"Well then," and he'd lifted his glass, "at least we know we have standards." And made it into a joke, perhaps just as well.

He said, after a few weeks of these easy dinners, movies, drinks, conversations, "You know, I'd like you to see my place. I think you'd enjoy it. Why don't you come out for a weekend, just hang around eating and drinking and staring at nice stuff that isn't made of cement?"

Well, why not? She thought he was attractive and clever and good, easy company. She also thought that if it wouldn't get too much in the way of life itself, she wouldn't at all mind seeing his thighs, touching his ribs. Things build up. Trust and even affection don't always have much to do with desire. "If you think we'd come back still friends," she said, "I'd like that."

Somewhat cryptic, she supposed. How was he expected to know what she meant? He laughed and said, "Why wouldn't we?"

Alix and, at least theoretically, Jamie went to spend the weekend with Madeleine. Isla went off with Lyle to fall in love, at the turn at the top of the lane, with his home. He put her bag in the guest bedroom, which she thought was unusual, even possibly strange, but he said, "We can just take it easy, okay?"

He led her outside, back to the porch and its deep chairs, him with a beer and in bare feet (high arch, long toes, she noticed) up on the railing, her with white wine, bare feet (flattish, stubby-toed) beside his. "Over there," he was pointing, "there's a creek. Pretty aggressive this time of year, but not even close on its best days to being a river. Out there's the shed, the old barn was falling down so I saved as much of the wood as I could and put up something a lot smaller. The main part of the land is twenty acres, just from the road in, and this around here. The other fifty, back up behind that little hill, I rent out to a neighbour. I'm no farmer, but I didn't want it going to waste. Bad enough, I figure, people like me buy up these places, without letting them go to waste."

"Why is it bad? What do you mean, people like you?" There were daffodils blooming around the base of the porch, tulips in bud, tiny blue flowers running wild in the grass. This man beside her maybe planted those bulbs and blooms, crouched down, fingers digging into the earth, hoping for future beauty, planning for it.

"Guys who wouldn't know a real day's work if it rose up and bit their ass. Guys like me, from the neighbours' point of view. I figure it's a reasonable enough attitude. It takes a while to get comfortable here, though, or at least get other people comfortable enough they don't resent you too much. But a latecomer never really belongs. Which is okay. I never intended to. Wouldn't know how, and I don't have the time. Still, people like it, I think, that I've shown some respect for the place, made it better, shaped it up. So it's obviously not just a hobby, it's my home. I'm not romantic about it, either, it's not some stupid goat-farming, back-to-the-land dream, people around here have been through that and it really pisses them off. And I'm not a weekend gent, verandah cocktail parties, that sort of crap. There's a few of those around, too. This is where I live, and it's something I've hammered out for myself." He suddenly grinned. "Every. Fucking. Nail."

There was a breeze. The air smelled odd to her, and sounded odd, too. "Not everyone likes it out here," he said. "Being in the middle of nowhere isn't to everyone's taste. Too quiet, some say, too out of it." Who were these *everyones* and these *somes*? Not a question she could ask.

"Quiet," she said instead, "in this racket?" Rampageous birds, mainly, ducks and crows but also smaller bold black ones Lyle said were grackles, bright jays and cardinals, a few robins, red-winged blackbirds, whole clouds of other, duller, brown flocks sweeping and clattering and soaring over them and away. He identified a raw sweet chorus, which unlike the birds would continue far into the night, as frogs. "Jesus," she said, "how many frogs?"

"Thousands," he smiled. "Millions, maybe."

It's possible that without him, all this could have felt creepy; but without him, she'd have had no reason to be there herself. She was accustomed to cars, trucks, ambulances, taxis, screaming brakes and sirens, all those urban bells and whistles, the great human racket, most of it, if occasionally dangerous, at least somewhat predictable. Hordes of birds, "millions" of frogs—in their masses, she couldn't see much reason they mightn't gang up on human intruders, dive, swoop, hop, and crawl through the air and the grass, onto porches, under doors, through window screens, tormenting and pursuing and driving them out.

"No," he said seriously. "That's more what humans would do. Animals, and I include birds and frogs, are more generous."

His mistrust of humans reassured her. She thought she might be able to lean, just a little, on his wariness; although it was too early to tell.

He was still working on the interior, he said: repairing floors and doors, sanding them down to the original oak, gradually finding colours, one room at a time being papered and painted. "When I see things, I know them," he said. "So I wait till I see something right." Nothing he said sounded random to her, or insignificant.

"Also, I like my comforts. It meant updating all the wiring and plumbing, but I'm not into inconvenience or hardship. I keep an office here, too, so I'm wired to the world. I couldn't do it, otherwise." He liked wood, it seemed, glowing true oak panels in that office, for instance, and nothing cheap, or cheaply done. Also she'd seen nothing fluttery in any part of the house as they'd passed through, no flowery wallpaper patterns, not much in the way of pastels. The kitchen and its cupboards were downright stark, contrasting black and white against hard maple floors, the living room painted a deep burgundy with high ivory ceiling, the bold yellow sofa and matching wing chairs reeking of ease. She could see why a tall, narrow-built man without much spare flesh might go looking for excess comfort, furniture he could sink into without bone hitting structure.

Perhaps for a similar reason her own plusher body, not unlike his furniture, would appeal to him, who could say?

"It was pretty neglected when I bought it," he said. "An old couple left it to their kids, they couldn't agree what to do with it, so it sat empty a while. Property goes wild fast, grows up out of control, and inside, things start to collapse. Mice, squirrels, things like that you kind of take for granted. Other things, well, I opened the door of the second bathroom when I was still just thinking of buying, and there were huge bells of fungus growing out of the walls. Giant pinkish ones, not even little mushroomy things." He shook his head. "I'm prepared to see beauty in a lot of unexpected places, but that wasn't one of them. I almost threw up. Did close the door fast, tried to put it out of my mind for a while. It was the most disgusting thing I had to do, fixing that bathroom. Knocked a few grand off the price, though."

"How long have you owned it?"

"Three years now. After everything."

After his wife, Sandra, died, of course. "Tough times," he said. "She was home, mostly. It was hard, but also in a lot of ways good."

Either he was a man lacking words to describe large experience, or he had faith Isla was sufficiently wise to fill in the gaps. She could not be sure which it was, but hoped for the latter. Certainly he'd been through events foreign to her—she might have wished James dead, but that was just bitterness, and anyway, he didn't die. She thought it might be possible to seriously admire Lyle, a man who emerged from horror with hard-won, hard-thought-through grace. If that turned out to be what he was.

"The dining room's last on my list, and a few more touches in the bedrooms and bathrooms. Then it'll probably be time to start over again. Do one thing, something else immediately starts falling apart." Well, yes. "I used to figure if I could get things how I wanted them, they'd stay that way, that was the deal. Also that I'd go on wanting more or less the same things. Not true, either one. I should have known better, but we have to find things out for ourselves, don't we?"

Evidently. She'd nodded. "Funny," she offered, because in some way this followed, "how sorrow always seems more powerful than joy. Joy just kind of jogs along, but grief, that really throws a person off the track, onto a new one."

He thought for a moment. "It's how it looks, all right. I'm not sure, though. Maybe what comes from joy just doesn't leap out, there's nothing sore-thumb about it. But grief's nothing but pain. It makes the lessons learned more noticeable, for sure, but I don't want to think they're bigger than what we get from a good run of pleasure." Looked at that way—well, she saw she could stand to rethink a few things. It was nice, what he said, a nice way of seeing.

"But on the other hand, such a rage I fell into when Sandy got ill, I can't tell you." No, and did Isla especially want to hear? "I wasn't much help to her for a while, when she could have used something better from me, but that anger, it took me over, like I'd gone blind. Just staggering, nothing-else-mattered blind. I actually put my fist through a wall. And it felt good. Everything I'd planned and assumed, you see: good family, good career, a good life ahead as far as I could see, and then. The end of everything." Isla found herself nodding. She couldn't have put it better herself.

"The worst thing—for me, I mean, not for Sandy—was growing apart for a little while. She was on a journey I wasn't going on, but it still disrupted every part of my life, small to large. I probably blamed her for that. I don't know if she knew or not. I imagine some people come closer in a situation like that, but we fell apart for a time. As if we could find less and less in common to talk about, that could be spoken out loud. I knew I was failing her badly, which made me even angrier, but I couldn't seem to find a way to do better. Be better.

"Then, it sounds strange, but we got past all that when what was going to happen finally became obvious and inevitable. I guess we were both exhausted from trying to be brave or whatever, and we both just gave up, broke down. It was," he said, looking away, far from Isla, seeing pictures she couldn't and didn't particularly want to imagine, "a strange time. Strangely good, in its way."

"And then?" Stupid; she'd just wanted him to haul himself out of history, away from old pain.

"Then she died," he said flatly. Back indeed. "We all knew it would happen, but even so, when it did, the boys needed a whole lot of help and that got me through the worst. In a funny way Sandy did, too. She died with as much grace as she could muster, and it would have been shabby to let her down. But you don't want to hear all this."

Not really; but also yes, of course. This was the early stage of their acquaintance, when much information had to be exchanged swiftly, facts of various levels and sorts flying back and forth, establishing a scale of compatibility, possibility. Her turn would come and what would she say, exactly how would she recount her own history? As flatly and sufficiently as Lyle, or in some more incoherent or jumbled or dramatic fashion? And if style reflected content, did it mean Lyle was a flat and sufficient man?

"Of course," she said, and touched his hand.

The trouble, one trouble, with middle age was that while there were prospects for the future, there was also a good deal of past. An awful lot to catch up with, imagine, try to picture and fail to picture. The entire scent and sensation of someone's life, perfectly familiar to him and maybe even to a very few others, had to be strange, foreign, irretrievable territory to anyone recently met.

That this worked both ways was not exactly a comfort.

So was one supposed to try to fill in all those blanks, sketch word-pictures of all the multiple joys of half a lifetime, as well as the griefs, the greatest of which he was now recounting in his spare way? Or should one better just recite the facts, the chronology of events, leaving emotion where it perhaps ought to be for people like them: all in the future, in their own hands?

Naturally it was important that she know how he'd cared for and about his dead wife. Because that was a whole large lost part of his life, and also because if he hadn't, what would that say about him? She wouldn't have wanted to find herself in the country for an isolated weekend with a man with a cold, easy-come, easy-go heart.

At least they were just into their forties, not their seventies or sixties or even their fifties. That much less to have to out-line, describe, explain. God knew what people did who met up in nursing homes, although perhaps they had an unusual amount of patience and spare time for recounting.

She rearranged her features along, she hoped, the lines of solemn attentiveness. What did Lyle see in her face as he spoke of his dying, dead wife, his two grieving sons whom Isla hadn't yet met, as he hadn't yet met Jamie and Alix, the ups and final down of his own personal, particular crisis? Warmth, she tried to adjust for. Empathy. Sympathy. All that was real enough, per-fectly genuine, but having to attend to a display of reality, she noticed, rather took the silky edge off true sentiments.

"One thing about death," he went on, popping open another beer, "it really hauls you up short." Isla imagined it would, for sure, although death was by no means the only event that could do that. "I didn't think I was in the wrong life, exactly, I like being a lawyer a lot, and I love my boys, and I was proud how they got through everything, even those tough years when teenagers can go off the rails in the best situation, which we were not in, the three of us, anyway, obviously I wasn't going to give up any of that. At the same time, the boys would be leaving and moving into their own lives. Sandy and I'd had a sort of picture of a future when that happened, and it wasn't that it didn't suit me, too, as long as she was going to be the other part of it, but once she was-n't, it was out of the question. It wasn't me, just on my own."

He paused. So Isla had to say, "What was it that turned out not to be you? What had your plans been?" Honestly, she was happy to ask. These were clues, as well as distant lost dreams.

"Oh, we'd figured that as soon as the boys were settled in university, we'd both take a year off from work and hit the road.

We talked about places we'd travelled to and wanted to see again, like, I don't know, Paris for me, and some awful little hotel in some awful little country in Africa for Sandy, and places neither of us had ever been but wanted to go to, like maybe India, China. We were going to take a year and a whack of our money doing that, and then we figured we could do it again every few years.

"But you know, to be honest I'd have liked travelling with Sandy, I think, because she was pretty adventurous and curious and damn near fearless as well, so it would have been a new way of seeing for me, I figured, even the places I'd already been. But without her, I'd only have been thinking about how much better it'd have been with her, and I'd have been miserable for a whole lot of reasons, not least that I'm not, myself, a happy traveller."

This surprised Isla. For some reason she'd assumed that a man who looked like her picture of a cowboy, at least at that moment, which was to say a lanky sort of fellow in blue jeans, might have cowboy-like qualities. A range-traveller, a roamer, and perhaps, just to complete the picture, even a laconic one. It was also disorienting that his dead wife was coming to life in ways that did not reflect her notion of someone named Sandy, someone safely unmysterious, which Isla had maybe mistaken for safely unremarkable.

Imagine being a person of whom it was said that she died with all the grace she could muster. Isla imagined desperate resistance, a distinct and helpless shortage of anything remotely like grace.

At the late end of that first day, warming up in the living room from the chill of the evening, Lyle stroked Isla's neck, her arms, her throat. Her fingers were tentatively on the bones of his stranger's spine. She was the one who said, "Let's go to bed," and he nodded.

What she remembers most vividly from those earliest days is her surprised, startling pleasure. She thought then it had to be rooted in the freedom of knowing nothing depended on this, because nothing was required or would come of it. Some weeks later, though, she realized if that were ever true, it no longer was. Familiarity was breeding delights she had not previously imagined herself capable of. Playfulness, the notion of letting go, romping. Simple enjoyment, it turned out, was serious business.

When he said, finally, very quietly, "Tell me about your husband," they were in bed. Her bed this time, the kids once again with Madeleine. He'd waited a long time to ask this. Perhaps the thought of her former husband had entered his head now because he supposed he was lying between sheets she had previously shared with James. This was not the case, of course. All that bedding was long gone; into the trash, not to the poor, because she'd felt strongly at the time that no one so poor they needed charity sheets deserved the additional corrosion of James's presence in them, however faint. His impression remained; like the Shroud of Turin, only not.

"It's not a nice story."

"That's okay. At our ages, we have lots of not-nice stories."

Not like that one. She had her hand on his chest, and felt his breathing and heartbeat speed up, then slow, then speed and then slow. It was a good story to tell lying down in dim light and not looking at him. "I see," he said at last. "That's pretty bad. Now it makes more sense why you don't trust me. It'd be strange if you did trust me, after all that."

At which point, of course, and after all that, she began trusting him.

He seemed, extraordinary man, to adapt himself to her history. He has made a point of being a man who phones if he's going to be late, who doesn't make plans he won't keep, who as far as she can see takes care not to tell lies; who is cautious about any possible interpretations of betrayal, except for that one time: sitting in the truck, waiting for her outside Goldie's.

Who rescues her son, as best he can, and would no doubt rescue her daughter, too, if anyone could figure out how to do that.

Jamie, released from six terrible weeks of very expensive rehabilitation, hung around more, and sometimes had conversations, serious-looking ones, with Lyle, the two of them sitting stretched out on lawn chairs, Isla's side-by-side men, a beer each between them. She didn't ask what they talked about; Lyle didn't say. Another demonstration of rectitude.

But Jamie slipped away. Began going out more and more often, came in late, grew grey-skinned again. "He's using," she said to Lyle, not as a question.

"I expect so."

"I'm not going back into rehab," Jamie said flatly when she confronted him. "I'm fine, honest. I learned a good lesson, believe me. I'm not using, I swear." Little liar, pants on fire. She was investigating other programs and possibilities, seeking more expert advice when the phone rang and when she answered it was Jamie, with the smallest of voices. Charged with trafficking. Asking for help.

The funny thing is, he wound up spending more time in jail than his father did. James was only actually in for six months when all was said and done. Of course, he also lost the business, although for financial reasons, not on the face of it for strictly legal or moral ones. Whereas Jamie spent more than a year behind bars, and according to Lyle was lucky, at that. It was very bad: selling, not just absorbing into his own body, drugs named crack, Ecstasy, and cocaine; with hints, too, of heroin. Isla's boy, skulking through a decayed underworld of needles and spoons, trembling and vomit, filthy rooms, dangerous alleys, this time peddling his baggies of costly pleasures, his parallel universes of cravings, longings, desires. His quest for relief, if not joy, gone entirely sour.

"Did you know he was dealing?" she asked Alix.

"No, just using again. But you knew that, too."

Isla still can't remember much about Alix from then, except that she was unobtrusive and worked hard and did well. That must have been when her transparency was developing, that eerie knack she has for vanishing so that other people look right through her. It's in her skin now, that transparency. In those wide, fervent eyes.

Who would believe so much misfortune?

Mrs. Lot, probably. Mrs. Job.

Lyle found Jamie the most experienced, best lawyer he could; sat sturdily in the courtroom with Isla as she listened to the grim information of her son's secret life; let her grip his hand hard as she watched Jamie's body ripple with fear, hearing a two-year sentence, to be followed by three years' probation; allowed her to weep in his arms for something that had nothing to do with him, was neither his fault nor his problem. That good man. Who said, "Stop beating yourself up, I don't think there was a damn thing more you could have done to stop him, or help him. That's not how it works." Isla could not believe him, of course; but she did believe in his dogged kindness. His loyalty.

In prison, much happened for which Jamie was ill-prepared. Sometimes she heard of these things at the time, sometimes not until later. There will be some matters, she supposes, she has never heard, never will hear. But in the course of the fourteen months he actually served, he beat and was beaten, he was bruised, cut, broken and God knows what unspeakable else. He also, she was told by his jailers, his captors, hammered his own head into walls, sweated into sheets, vomited across floors. He spent a number of days in the infirmary for one reason and another, including fevers and chills. She was told that in the early days he sometimes thrashed so violently he had to be bundled into restraints. She saw him, when she visited, when he was capable of her visits, becoming paler and more gaunt, and sometimes he was damaged in obvious ways: a cut lip, a bruised eye.

Then he began filling out again. His eyes cleared, a pinkness budded in his skin. "I'm working out," he told her proudly. "I'm clean," he whispered shyly. "You can believe me this time." It seemed true, looked true. Who did this for him? Someone; not her.

Again because of Lyle's efforts, and because of a particular employment program for promising former offenders, Jamie works—his first and only actual job! At his age!—for a florist. In this most gentle of pursuits, he handles orders and shipping and some of the paperwork. He does not arrange or care for the flowers and plants, since that requires particular talents and knowledge. He says the smells can get overwhelmingly sweet, even nauseating, but he has learned some things about flowers, some of their names, for example. He likes the people he works with, he says, and also the regularity of the money, although not the amount. "I tell you," he says, "this business of going straight is really hard on the wallet." Which is a joke, but also true.

This is the sort of job a twenty-year-old might be doing part-time to cover tuition, or rent, not a twenty-five-year-old grown-up. He has some vague notion of someday working with people in trouble; addicts, most likely. When he first mentioned this, Isla asked, stupidly, "Isn't that dangerous?"

"You mean, being around druggies?" They laughed, but yes, that's what she meant. Temptations are tricky, redemption hard to be sure of.

She says now, out of nowhere, to the worried-looking young man leaning over her, trying to smile with his bent-up, little-boy mouth, "I am so proud of you." A simple, true, hard thing, and she is astonished when his eyes rise up, spill over, with tears. Oh.

People do get restored.

She might, too.

"Where are Alix and Lyle?"

Now he looks uncomfortable. "In court. The guy who, you know, shot you is up again today. Pleading guilty, I think."

Well, so he should. So he must.

All this may be quite a shock for him, too. Although not necessarily. He could be just evil.

"How about Martin?" Because wouldn't he want to see her?

"He tried, but they won't let anybody in yet but family." But Martin *is* family: a sturdy, benevolent brother. He was loyal to her when some clients at first shied away, as she'd expected. She herself saw James as a sort of Chernobyl of moral contamination; or, maybe, some clients saw what he did as unremarkable, his misfortune lying only in being caught, in which case they would be dodging the contamination of misfortune. "Fuck 'em," said Martin, that man of few but useful words.

He'd helped her pack too, when she moved herself and Jamie and Alix into the duplex. He hugged her close, bought her a drink, when she finally confided the existence of Lyle; and although she couldn't quite sympathize, she was as loyal to him when his life blew up. His wife learned about his lover; his lover learned his wife was pregnant. "Christ, Isla, they've both left me! My kids, too, she's taken the kids." This was real anguish, and for that she did sympathize. She wasn't sure what he'd expected to happen, though; she supposed he'd somehow expected nothing to happen, couldn't picture anything happening. It was a point of view she had learned a good deal about. She fed him, gave him drinks, listened. That's what he'd done for her, which made it, not exactly a debt to repay, but something with a value she understood.

Recently Martin's been hinting he wouldn't mind selling the agency, or the large part of it that's his to sell. "I'd kind of like to take the money and run. Do some travelling, reward myself before it's too late. I get tired, you know, trying to keep up. So many changes." She hadn't figured out what she thought about this, but now needs to tell him to yes, sell, run off, indulge himself, do anything his good heart desires. Because this is not a matter of snip-snap and she's striding as if nothing has happened back into her life.

Her fiercest desire right now is to run screaming out of her own skin, her own life.

She can't even kill herself. She can't even lift a finger to do that much. Who would help her?

Jamie says, "But if you want to see Martin, we'll try to figure out a way, don't worry." How assured, how confident this young man sounds. Her cleaned-up, capable son. Maybe Alix, too, can be saved. Not, of course, through Serenity Corps, not as someone named Starglow. Alix has something, though. She knows something about faith, even if it's blind, dumb, stupid faith, and where did that come from? In the aftermath of her father, not to mention her brother, not to mention, maybe, even her mother, how was it she could come, so quietly, so surreptitiously, to believe anything at all?

A self-satisfied, self-assured stranger must have looked good to her. A Master Ambrose, preaching serenity, what could be more appealing? Who, choosing between the tender, broken-hearted story of an Alix and the peaceful, floating, weightless, and transparent possibilities of a Starglow, would not choose to be Starglow? Ditching a whole sorry past. Opting for a whole unknown, silvery future.

Now she and Lyle have gone off to court together. That's nice, although they're probably not exactly having a meeting of minds. And Madeleine's someplace on water, in air. Everyone's gathering in some new formation, for some new purpose.

Her son is silently holding her hand, or at least that's what he appears to be doing, and is staring rather bleakly off into space; or out a window for all she can tell.

She hears a sound from herself like a laugh, and Jamie looks down at her sharply. She's remembering, though, that in those first dreadful weeks after James, she longed, wished, desired desperately, not to be able to feel. And then something similar, again, after Jamie himself. And now she has achieved her longing, her wish, her desire; except of course what she meant was, she wanted not to be able to feel her feelings. That had nothing to do with her body. This is fulfilment not only far too late, but also twisted in the extreme.

She should have paid better attention not only to this hospital's many fundraising campaigns for its various medical miracles, but also to stories of grief in general. It's not as if there's any shortage of those, it's not as if a hundred of them don't land on the doorstep every day. It's entirely possible that some victims of torture, say, actually pray for nerves that can no longer flicker or twitch or respond, can no longer be touched by the electric impulse, the wire, the brand. She should know if there are people somewhere, in some circumstance, who would consider her blessed. She should also know if there are people who would rise to this circumstance, and how they would do that. She is, in the scheme of things, too ordinary for this. Extraordinary events regularly occur to ordinary people, and what are they supposed to do then? How do they learn, on the fly, what to do?

She is too small in spirit for this one. She is exhausted. She is insufficient to the task. Lyle and Alix are just coming through the door, looming up beside Jamie, as she says, "Help me."

She has almost never heard herself say that before. Isn't that odd. What kind of person is it, who hardly ever says "Help me"? They look startled, too.

Well, how do they imagine she feels? Dependent, surely, and doomed and despairing. Terrified, really. "Help me," she says again, but even she has no idea how they might do that. She would like to feel sorry and tender towards their bewilderment, all that concern on their loved and individual faces, their no doubt genuine desire to do as she asks and help her, really help her, but how can they? Moreover, any one of them can turn around, walk away. They have that choice, and she couldn't stop them.

She has to close her eyes because it would be really bad, too cruel, if they could see how much, right this minute, she hates her beautiful, reliable Lyle, her tough, weak-willed Jamie, her soft-hearted, soft-headed, gossamer Alix. There's a goddamn internal flame, if anybody's looking for one.

Still. "Help me," she cries, her eyes flying open again, trying to demand, hoping to insist, but willing, right this moment, to beg.

A Clear, Steady Gaze

SHE'S HERE AGAIN, ON THIS DAY of his sentencing. Coming through that courtroom side door with four other young, anxious prisoners, Roddy scans the room and yes, finds her, third row back. Looking just the way she did a week ago. Same dress, even.

His terror subsides, although does not vanish. The suspense of her presence, or absence, that caused his hands to tremble, is relieved, but there is still the suspense of his future, as it will be defined by the judge. None of this is in his control. But then, look what he did before, when he did have control; or believed that he did.

His grandmother and his dad are out there, too, watching him come in with the others, looking nervous and sad, even though he's caused so much grief, and shamed his grandmother, and made his dad angry. He nods to them, and smiles, as best he can. His grandmother smiles back, his dad nods. But after that, and he knows this is weird as well as amazing, his eyes need to swerve back to the girl.

The picture he's tried to hold of her in his mind's eye this past week is perfectly true.

There were moments of doubt. He was afraid, a little, that he'd made too much of her, had made her, for one thing, too beautiful; but no, here's that pale, pale skin, like she's not even really from earth. Grave eyes that see right into him, through him.

Maybe it would be too thrilling to be any closer, some kind of shock; but if he could touch her skin, put just his fingertips on her breasts, if she would let him do that, and if she would take his head between her hands and lay it to rest on her lap and look down at him with those steady eyes while he looked back up into them—maybe that would be everything. He feels it could happen. Everything has already shifted, it's all unpredictable, so how can he know what's possible and what is not? Look at her, looking at him. What does she see?

It sounds almost crazy, even inside his own head, but it's still true: he has fallen, toppled, plunged into some kind of love.

He doesn't think this can be what people mean when they talk about love. If other people felt this, the whole world would be lit, the air everywhere would be radiant.

He can get through this.

Oh. He hadn't realized he wasn't sure about that.

He sits very straight on the bench, much straighter than the four others. He isn't tall, he isn't large, but he can take up space here, he can be significant. Although in her eyes he'd be significant, love or not. He forgets.

In the brief, long week between pleading guilty and today, he has learned some things for sure:

That he cannot count on mercy, because even though what he did was so quick, only a few seconds, it was also large, with awful results. He can't imagine a length of time that's right for balancing out those two things;

That even when a place is very busy and noisy and possibly dangerous, and contains a multitude of questions that are supposed to be answered and many hours are totally filled, there are spaces of unavoidable time when pictures rear up. Too often, but not always, it's the moment in Goldie's, those seconds that won't be undone no matter how many times he has to see them unfold. Or sometimes the pictures are of his grandmother's house, the stone walkway in from the street to its grey-stuccoed homeliness, and going through the aluminum front door and up the mottled yellowy-browny carpeted stairs to his own room, with his own muddled colours and his own pictures of intricate, transformable creatures pinned to the walls, and his own life that isn't his any more, like he's dead now, or gone off to be reincarnated a new way;

That going to sleep isn't safe. Sleep can easily be more troubling than being awake. Because he's been having dreams, awful ones about his mother, as bad as when he was a kid, after he and his dad moved. This week, even the dreams that start out good, with his mother playing with him maybe, or hugging him, the two of them happy, and young too, turn bad, so that when he wakes up he's scared he hasn't been just crying out in the dream, but for real. Last night, his mother was paralyzed. She couldn't even speak. And where she was paralyzed was on the top railing, crouched there, of what looked like a bridge, although he couldn't make out anything besides the railing, no expressway or railroad or river below. She was wearing something glittery, a gown, or maybe it was her skin under moonlight. She looked at him. She was asking him with her eyes to do something, asking him to help her. He couldn't tell, and she couldn't say, whether she wanted him to lift her down or push her off. He would have to decide, because he had to do something, it was night, and cold and she couldn't help herself so he had to. He thought, in the dream, "My mother." She was familiar and helpless and frightened, strange and, mainly, sad. He was trying in the dream to understand what he should do: push or pull. What he did was reach out in the gentlest of ways and give her the gentlest of pushes so that down, down she went, vanishing soundlessly into the darkness.

Jesus. He woke weeping. And cold. And hoping that in his sleep, he'd made as little sound as his mother had in the dream. He wiped tears from his eyes, from his cheeks.

Then he set out to restore, in the dream's place, the details, each feature and shape, shift and shade, of the steadying, salvaging figure he saw, who saw him, for the first time a week ago. And now he can see that that vision is real and true because here it is, in this room, a few feet away: that one bright thing to hang onto, that one lighted face.

What does she see with those pure eyes resting on him? Ordinarily he doesn't like being stared at. Well, he's not all that attractive. This is different, though. Her eyes don't stop at his skin, or even his bones.

If he could hear her speak again in that airy voice, what might she say? Since matters of guilt or anger don't seem to concern her, he doesn't think she would say, "I forgive you." Those would be words to do with the past. She sounded before like someone more interested in the future.

Well, there could be romantic and loving words. Those would be nice, but possibly too large a miracle, too unlikely for words.

Something simpler, then, and more possible. "I like you, Rod." Or "It's my belief you're a good person."

She's on her own today, no lean stepfather, contemptuous lawyer, loving husband, bearing his unbearable details into this high-ceilinged room. Could she be here on his behalf, on behalf of the whole family of that woman, her mother, the whirling lady in the wrinkled blue suit? Or is it how it seems, that she's here to look at Roddy with her own thoughtfulness? The room doesn't feel real, it's like he's in another dream but this time somebody else's. Like he could just float right away. All of this, every part of it, his light-headedness and the powers of her clear, steady gaze, would sound crazy, he knows that. But that just makes it more like what she said last week when he was in court, that it didn't look like anybody understood, except him.

When his name finally gets called, just like last time he has to go sit beside Ed Conrad, stand up for the judge, sit down, try to listen. She's there behind him, though. He doesn't know what name to call her even in his thoughts. *Starglow* feels sort of right, *Alix* more real.

Like Roddy and Rod, maybe. The judge uses *Rod*. He says, "This was a most unfortunate, reckless event. Through no fault of her own, a woman lies paralyzed, because of a young man's careless, criminal act. For which he can give no good reason. I will tell you, young man," and he stares down at Roddy in a way that's quite different from hers, angry, even though if anybody here was going to be angry it ought to be her, "I am very, very tired of dealing with people like you who think they can just take whatever they want, no matter who gets hurt in the process. You boys who feel you're entitled to anything you feel like, without working for it, or deserving it, and with no heed for anyone who gets in your way."

But that's not right! Roddy wants to rise up and protest. It does matter that someone got hurt. He would have heeded, if he'd considered beforehand the possibility that heed would be required. He doesn't feel entitled to anything he feels like. Only, it looked easy, that's all. And it had to do with being Mike's friend: not so much doing it, not the robbery, but the weeks of planning, all those conversations, all those rehearsals. Something they did together, the way they always did things together, only this time aimed at a spare white and chrome high-rise future, and freedom.

"I would like to make an example of you, to be frank. So that anyone else like you out there would learn loud and clear that no one's entitled to violence, or to take something without having earned it. But I'm restrained somewhat by the fact that you have no previous record and despite some family difficulties, you do have the support of those nearest you. And so in trying to balance the seriousness of your crime against your prospects for rehabilitation, I am sentencing you to eighteen months of closed custody, to be followed by two years' probation. It's my hope and my intention that during this period, you will receive the counselling and educational help that will steer you onto a more productive path. You have much to atone for, young man. And you have an opportunity here which I hope you'll take advantage of, and learn to appreciate."

What Roddy hears is, *Eighteen months.*

Eighteen months is forever. As everyone stands again, Roddy turns, desperately seeking her eyes. Which are on him. They steady him. How will he survive eighteen months?

Ed Conrad leans close and tells him, "It'll work out to maybe twelve months, you know. Even ten if you do all right. You're lucky, it could've been a lot worse. This judge, he can be a real bugger. You got off lighter than I thought you could hope for. Anyway, use the time well, you'll be okay." These are the kindest words, or the kindest tone, anyway, Ed Conrad's used with him.

Roddy's lucky? Even twelve months is one-seventeenth of his whole vanished life. A huge long time.

A cop takes his arm. "Come on then, you got places to go." Roddy has just the briefest, tiniest of impulses to shake off that grip and leap and grab her hand and run with her and hurtle over the benches and past all the people, including his grandmother, who is crying, and his dad, who has an arm around her shoulders, out the door, down the halls, into the sunshine, into the town and then into the country, to run and run, on and on. He could do that with her. She'd be like a shield, something like that.

He did that before, didn't he? Bolted from Goldie's, ran and ran, although alone. Wound up lying, for just a few precious moments, in the darkness under the stars, totally content and at peace.

Already, she has vanished. By the time he's been hauled back to that side door of the courtroom, and has turned one last time for one final look, she has taken that skin, that flying, flaming hair, that thin straight spine and those perfectly knowing eyes out the other set of courtroom doors, the one used by free, innocent people.

He has a moment of doubt. Does she not know?

Of course she does. Only, she's a lot older than him, and she knows what is necessary and what is not, and a last look would have been possible but must not be necessary. She must believe he is ready, something like that. He straightens his shoulders, as if he's not scared and not guilty, even though of course he is guilty, and is so scared of what's next he could fall, bones collapsing, to the efficient tiled floor.

Here he goes, instead, off into the future that's supposed to pay off the guilt, punish the sin, but it can't save him. Nobody would believe what he believes can save him; but who could he tell anyway? Only her, a closed, two-person circle of knowledge, but she's gone, and handcuffed, he's being marched away to the van that'll take him on to the next place: no looking back, also no need for goodbyes.

A Great Deal of Coming and Going

EVERYBODY SAYS HER CARE HERE is the best there can be, but Isla's in the strange position of having no particular way to know that. She understands that among Northern's medical luxuries is the very mattress she lies on, the latest thing in somehow keeping her skin almost aloft, minimizing abrasions and sores. She gets scanned by brilliant machines, which continue to show the bullet fragment still wedged into its crevice of spine. She has seen pictures. It's the tiniest of tiny dark darts.

Dr. Grant drops by often, sometimes to supervise or assess one unfelt test or another, other times just to ask her own view of how she is doing. Her own view is plain and strictly vertical; and scared, of course, that, too.

He is only a few years older than Jamie, and not dissimilar in appearance, and could be her son, Jamie's wiser, sensible brother. He is confident, not unpleasantly, of his skills and also believes there will be great leaps, "as it were," in spine-injury treatments in the foreseeable future. She likes that "as it were," its deliberate comic alertness. She also likes that he seems to share her awe, showing her the scans, at the damage that can be caused by something that's barely visible.

As far as she can tell all the people on staff, day and night, not just Charlie, Charles, Dr. Grant, are careful and gentle and competent, but of course she can't really know that; can't even feel what they're doing, never mind how their hands touch her. She sees them only from the hips up, and then only if they're bending at an accessible angle. It's strange, only seeing people from a single perspective. Strange how much, in normal life, must be judgeable from motion: tilt of shoulders and hips, length of stride, state of speed, or of grace. She depends on lines beside mouths, depths of eyes, brightness of smiles, and whether smiles travel between lips and eyes.

She likes the young day nurse, Janet, who's mainly assigned to her, who is unfailingly lipsticked and highlighted and eyeshadowed even after eight or ten hours on duty, which surely implies an equivalent attentiveness to her patients, most relevantly to Isla herself.

As well, nothing that happens with Isla's body, whatever mysterious processes have to go on, cause Janet to blink or flinch. Olga, Isla's main nurse on most night shifts, is older and therefore should be more experienced, and therefore more hardened, but she does sometimes sigh, leaning over one or another of Isla's extremities. Which seems truthful, and more reliable in its way. Isla imagines Olga has stumpy legs and thick hips. Her husband has stomach cancer and her two children live far away. Olga's voice brightens when she shows pictures of them and her grandchildren, holding them up to Isla's narrow line of vision. Isla admires how Olga must work beyond her own tiredness. Maybe out the other side of exhaustion, even.

Perhaps everyone does, all the specialists in this and that, and nurses, and interns and orderlies and aides of one sort and another, the cleaners who come around with their large floor-cleaning machines, and who empty wastebaskets and wipe sinks—an entire ward-sized beehive, a thriving anthill of care.

She has to suppose they know what they're doing; even if it seemed slipshod, wrong, even amateur that when she asked, "Help me," Lyle went to get a nurse and returned with plump-faced, trim-bearded, soft-handed Ben, who said, "I know it's not easy but you have to try not to get agitated," and with his handy syringe, sent her off.

They do this now and then. Sedatives may on occasion drip into her veins, but for fast action they use the needle. Which doesn't matter, it's not as if any number of needles can hurt. Even Jamie, who knows a few things about bodies and has some skills with veins and syringes, could do it easily, if he were allowed. Only, that one time—being put under was not what she meant by "help me." Did they all misunderstand? Did Lyle, for one, decide the demand was too great, did he believe everybody was already giving her more help than anyone could reasonably hope for?

True enough. She is very lucky that way.

Still, there is a good aspect of going under, something lovely about it, and that is the gentle process of coming to again, rising up. This is when everything's misty and mainly grey, muzzy with tinges of rosiness softening horizons and edges: like being in a rowboat tied to a dock, a gentle rising and lapsing sensation, a stirring and falling back, restful and sweet.

Each rising up becomes brighter and higher, every lapse slighter. All of it is rhythmic and comforting; like being rocked, or like being held. That's the part where everything's still safe, and unknown.

Time begins to resume. Formlessness takes on shape and boundary. Clarity creeps in. Rhythm missteps.

Then comes the unbearably lonely moment: when she remembers no one can help, no one can reach her.

Oh, come soon, please, Madeleine.

At the moment she's alone in the room. The air is different when nobody's here, not even a hidden presence sitting off to one side where she can't see. It's less clogged not only with breathing, but by emotion. That's how she can tell.

Everyone has their lives. Lyle has to sustain his career and Jamie his job; who knows about Alix? But in a way, it's a relief for Isla, too, from the hovering, the concern. The love. Gratitude is far easier when it's owed to people paid to take care, who have actual functions, who don't just stand over her, bravely or mournfully. Those are strenuous connections, wife, mother; daughter too, when Madeleine gets here. Lyle, Jamie, Alix—they intend to show strength and support, but may not realize they ask the same great things from her, and that this isn't easy, or even possible.

They may love her, but how they must resent her, as well. That's how she expects she'd feel in their place: love and dislike both. Some combination either ambiguous or radically ambivalent.

She thinks she can feel her face contorting with grief. That happens sometimes, when there's no one to hide from.

Later, when this is over, she will be profligate with her courage, beneficent with her empathy. Just, not at the moment. At the moment, family can be just one more bloody thing.

This is more or less the nerve ward here, the bone yard, and the woman in the next room, who has a new hip and a new knee and possibly no loving family, loyal or otherwise, presses (lucky her) the bedside buzzer again and again, demanding small attentions. A dangerous practice, Isla imagines. Assuming the woman only wants a fresh magazine, or her pillows adjusted again, nurses complain among themselves and no longer respond fast, if at all. Sometime that woman may really need them, and then where will they be?

Perhaps attending to Isla who, however complicated her care, causes them no extra trouble. Although she might, if she could.

Naturally she can't summon help with a buzzer. The equipment she's attached to, however, the unseen monitors and regulators and providers of air and nourishment and alertness, or unconsciousness, so much machinery humming and whoofing and ticking—its vital information about the state of her body is also transmitted, as she understands it, to the nursing station just outside her door, a continuous data flow.

Sometimes she listens to them talking out there. Deliberately eavesdrops. Now she can match faces and voices and stories, by sight or sound, unless someone's called in from another ward to cover an absence, a day off, a vacation. There's one doctor, a man she's never seen, who sounds curt and presumptuous, a serious fellow who discusses only the care of his patients and doesn't join in the personal: kids, engagements, jokes, parties, who said what to whom yesterday. Isla is glad she isn't one of his patients. She imagines his manner might have an effect, small, unintended, but an effect nonetheless, on how his patients are treated by other staff. Nothing may be personal, but she knows herself that also, everything is personal when people are together so much. He ought to know better. She'd like to tell him to change his tone, lighten up, talk to them about just one thing from his own life, or theirs.

Isla can hear Rachel's voice out there this morning. She's an aide, some title like that, a skinny dyed-straw-blonde a decade younger than Isla, whom Olga describes as "peppy." And peppy she is, despite two difficult teenagers and an ex-husband who "just buggered off, vanished, poof," a few years ago. Difficult offspring are familiar to Isla, an ex-husband of mysterious destiny sounds positively appealing, but she has never, herself, had to scrape a living the way Rachel does: among other things, sponge-bathing Isla's body; washing her face; other unspeakable chores. Now Rachel covers the space between doorway and Isla's bedside with "Hello there, I heard you were on your own, want to get pretty?"

A diverting idea, although what are the odds? Even the most optimistic aide can accomplish only so much. "I hear Dr. Grant will be coming through in a while. Thought you might like to get spruced up a bit beforehand, if you want. As long as you're on your own anyway."

Isla wonders if her visitors get on staff nerves; how Rachel knows Dr. Grant is planning a visit, when Isla did not, and if that means anything; what even an aide may know about her, and her prospects, that she never hears. She only knows what she can overhear, or what's brought to her deliberately, or what's delivered randomly, like dogs dropping bones at her feet.

Rachel says, "We'll start with a depilatory, shall we? I've told you, haven't I, that your legs are totally excellent?" So they are. Or were; limbs that go unused wither quickly. She may already be shrivelling. Dr. Grant, so young he could be her son, might well look at her and wonder what possible reason she could have to desire sensation, what possible point there could be in his efforts.

"Shall I do your hair, too?"

"Please. That would be great. And makeup? Do you have time?" How swiftly meek the disabled become; how acutely thoughtful of others.

Also, there being no choice, how willingly dependent, how deliberately, entirely, immodest.

"No problem. Say, was your hair as bright as your daughter's when you were her age? Hers is really something."

"Not quite, but yes, my mother had it too, more or less, although it dulls down with age. Alix just has a livelier version. Do your kids look like you?"

"Sean does, my son. He's got my eyes and my nose. Janie takes more after her dad. It's all the wrong way round in our family. In," Rachel grins, "more ways than one."

"I know. They're tough years."

"Aren't they, though? Some days I'm glad for the long shifts. Often enough it's easier to be here than at home."

Isla, if she could nod, would nod pretty vigorously. "You know, though, they'll be fine in the end."

"I hope so." Rachel doesn't sound very sure. Then again, for a number of years Isla wouldn't have sounded sure, either. And there's still Alix. With any luck, her future remains up in the air. Which is to say, there is hope.

"Your skin is so soft." Rachel, applying foundation, gently massages skin upwards, not downwards, kindly implying there is still some point to uplift. "Honestly, you'd never know you're anywhere near fifty." She even knows Isla's age? What else? "You want greeny-blue eyeshadow, or the browny-grey?"

"Browny-grey, please. Do you mind doing this sort of thing?"

"Gosh, no, I enjoy it. I used to think I'd like to go to cosmetic school or whatever they call it. Even when I was little, the best part of having dolls was making them look different from how they were when I got them. Some weird results, so you'll be glad to know I've gotten a lot better at it." She's just chattering, she means well, she would never intend to compare Isla to a doll: stiff, lifeless, and vulnerable to any playful desire. "There." Rachel stands back. "Want to see?"

No. Yes. Oh dear.

Well, there it is: startlingly large eyes now, due to flesh falling back from the bones, cheeks highlighted but nicely, not garishly. And Rachel's right, she does have soft-looking skin; although is it verging on crepey? Still, an enormous improvement over her first view of herself in this hospital light.

There's something wrong with the eyes, though. Or different. They belong to someone frightened and unfamiliar and wild. She sees them widen with this further wild fear of being observed, found out, examined. Are these the eyes Lyle and Jamie and Alix have been looking into day after day? "That's enough," and she hears her voice come out rough. "That's great. Thanks." It's possible James was right: there are some things it's better not to look at, inquire into, too closely.

This is a shocking way to live. It is shocking to be able to see Rachel's arms, although not her hands, shifting briskly back and forth, presumably moving skin cream up and down Isla's arms, and feel nothing. The gap between knowing and not feeling is electric. All this must be monstrous. And perhaps makes her a monster.

Nearly suitable for late-night TV.

But often enough people do grow accustomed to the most monstrous knowledge, she knows that. She listens to the rhythmic swish-rasp of Rachel's clothes as she massages whatever limb she is touching, the slight damp sputters of skin cream rolling from tube into palms. The tiny clicking sound of

Rachel's spine straightening, the tiny whirl of cap being replaced onto tube, tiny shuffling of supplies into the case Rachel carries. Rachel's smile above her again. "You look terrific. I'm good at this, aren't I?"

"The best, absolutely."

"Now you'll feel good about yourself when Dr. Grant pops by, won't you?"

But why should she, especially? Now she's wary. She's reminded of what she already knows: if she drops her guard, she's not exactly in a position to reach down and pick it up again.

She hears herself snort; but what a busy day, what a great deal of coming and going! Because now she also hears, speak of the devil, Dr. Grant's familiar rat-a-tat on the door frame, there's his young man's throat being cleared. Here's his serious face bending over her, with the particular look of a man with something particular on his mind. Now what?

She is, in an odd way, the hostess here, and the art of the hostess, setting a guest at ease, feels called for. Well, that art is really not aimed at guests, but at the hostess's desire that an event go smoothly and with a maximum of goodwill. So she says, "Why don't you pull over a chair and get comfortable? You must get tired of being on your feet all the time." In the circumstances, this seems the best she can do.

He sets himself tight beside her bed, arms crossed on the chrome bed railing, chin poked forward and resting there like a curious child's. This takes a few moments of shifting and settling. The lines at the corners of his eyes and mouth are faint, the furrows in his forehead slight. He is marked by absence, by all the experiences he hasn't had, or which have failed to seriously mark him.

"So," he begins. "Here's the deal. You'll have realized by now that that bit of bullet hasn't done what we'd hoped. It was a gamble, that it'd work itself out, but now we've decided"—who is this *we*?—"it wouldn't be wise to wait too much longer. And one of the right ORs came free unexpectedly. So how does the

227

day after tomorrow sound to you for the surgery? First thing Thursday morning."

Jesus. "That soon?"

"Well, yes. We can't leave it much longer or we'll be running into other problems. I know you're surprised, but really, it's only quite this soon because of the OR cancellation. Which I, for one, take as a good sign. So try not to worry. Because when it comes down to it, the body rallies itself in some bold and beautiful ways, you know."

She ponders *rallies* and *bold*, and sees he is a man of poetic and optimistic inclinations.

She reminds herself to breathe. The inhalation comes with a slight whistle, and with that louder whuffing sound off to her left.

"Of course what we're looking at, nipping out that little sucker, is a little bit complicated. Or delicate, rather. But still you know, in a way you were fortunate you got hit where you did." Yes, yes, she's heard this, too often. "And then sometimes there's a ricochet factor to complicate matters." Which he already said are, as things stand, "a little bit complicated." Also "delicate."

"And then?"

"Well," and he pauses, "then I guess we'll see. The flat fact is, we don't know. Getting that fragment out may finally be, pardon the expression, the magic bullet. Or, frankly, we may find there's extraneous damage. It depends. We won't know for sure till we get in there. And of course out again."

She guesses she knew all this; just hadn't applied it to the day after tomorrow. When everything will be transformed, once again, in a matter of moments. One way or another.

"For sure you couldn't be in a better place." Yes, she could. She could be on the porch, eating ice cream from the basement freezer with Lyle. There was ice cream there, aging but still good, and there were cones in the cupboard over the microwave. They didn't need to go out, not for anything, even for ice cream. "But I expect you have a few questions, right?"

Don't ask anything you don't want the answer to. James's true words. How much information is askable, bearable?

"Odds?"

He frowns again slightly; those small lines in his forehead will get much deeper, she imagines, in the next very few years. "Well, that's hard to say." Of course it is. "I guess we're pretty sure of getting the fragment out, it's not the most complex thing we've ever done."

"But."

"But what happens from there, the odds, I honestly can't calculate. I'm sorry. But here's what I do think, and I know it doesn't sound very scientific, but the best thing you can do to help is, you should focus on strong, positive thoughts, keep in mind all the people who care for you, and beyond that, trust us to be very good at what we do. Which we are. I honestly believe faith in good outcomes can make a difference." Does that mean that previously, before all this, what she had, unbeknownst to her and with the occasional exception, was an aberrant faith in negative outcomes?

"Beyond that, just put yourself in our hands."

They both look at his hands. They are such young and human hands; whereas she would now prefer them to be certainly older, and maybe also supernatural, even extraterrestrial, at any rate spectacularly and obviously and unhumanly gifted.

Imagine going into a line of work in which real, true lives are in the balance! Many years ago and in an optimistic frame of mind, Isla contemplated volunteering for one of those crisis hotlines. People would phone her with their terrible troubles—bad marriages, dying parents, their own illnesses and burdens, the dark weight of their loneliness—and she would talk them generously, compassionately, helpfully through the night. This, she had supposed, would lighten her own heart. It also struck her as a way of crossing her fingers against misfortune. And to be truthful, a way of making her own life more interesting and various.

Which it then became, all by itself.

But on second thought: what exactly, specifically, would she do with a caller holding a razor blade to the wrist? With an incoherent voice confessing a desire for pills, for death, or for that matter, for murder?

What if she failed? What if somebody died?

She found she lacked the stomach for failure, or for death. For tipping, with the nudge of a word or a misplaced breath, a life one way or the other.

This young doctor does that every day. How can he sleep? How can he get up in the morning? How can his hands not tremble? What does he imagine the word *trust* means, to be able to say it so easily, as if it could be gained or given so easily?

He lays the back of his hand against her cheek; in other circumstances, a lover's caress. "Just hang in with us a little bit longer. You're a tough cookie, you can do it. Everybody's impressed by how well you've handled this so far."

Really? Then they haven't been paying very good attention, have they?

He unwraps his arms from the bedrails, stands to his not-very-tall full height. "Try not to worry or brood, okay? Keep yourself tuned to good outcomes."

Yes, well. What sort of moron would not brood about life in the balance? Still, *brood, brooding*—those are beautiful, euphonious words, suggesting a seductive, dark, and luxurious intensity.

She wouldn't mind clinging to him right now. She wouldn't mind folding herself right into his young, stalwart body. Or, if she could feel it, she would like it if he held her hand. She would like a sense of his hands. "Thank you," she says.

He grins, a boyish, light-hearted grin. "I promise to get a good night's sleep beforehand, I'll be perfectly rested and raring to go." Then abruptly he grows solemn and touches her, probably on the arm. "Honest to God, I won't let anything bad happen to you."

Doctors aren't supposed to say things like that. And Lyle said something like that, pledging to be, if nothing else, no James, but a very bad thing happened anyway, which Lyle didn't prevent. He meant what he said, and he would have prevented it, but he did not. These aren't smart promises. They aren't keepable.

"Help me," Isla would like to say again; but look what happened last time she did that. And anyway, he is gone.

Christ. Thursday.

Alertness to death, or its possibility, or the possibility of any imminent disaster, is supposed to sharpen the thoughts pretty pointedly. Certainly any of that would have sharpened hers, entering Goldie's. But who is so perpetually and piercingly conscious? Well, she might be now; from now on; given a chance.

And who is so tidy? Who doesn't have a thousand loose ends trailing behind at the end of each day?

Day after tomorrow: only a few hours; far too little time, and far too much. She is nowhere near ready, and also wishes to God it was over with, done and known: thumbs up, or thumbs down?

Because what if it fails?

Also, what if it works?

A Few Good Words

"**G**UESS WHO I'VE BROUGHT?" If Alix were a nurse, or a kind aide like Rachel, she might spontaneously appear above Isla like an unnerving angel. She does glow, in her way; *luminous*, in fact, would be the word. As nurse to patient, this might be comforting. As daughter to mother, it's eerie. Also startling. "Oh sorry, were you asleep?"

"Just resting my eyes." True, actually, but also a mild family joke, since it's what Bert always says when he's caught napping, flustered at being witnessed in an unprepared, innocent moment.

"Good, because look who's here!"

"Sweetheart," says Madeleine, stepping forward. "Oh, sweetie."

Alix claps her hands, delighted as a child. "I just picked up Grandma and Bert at the airport. Are you surprised?"

Oh, she is, she is. She beams, she thinks she beams, upwards. "God, yes. I am so glad you're here." She would leap into her mother's saving arms, if she could.

She would bury her face in her hands, to hide from the shock on Madeleine's face, if she could.

"Me too. But I'm so angry!"

"Me too."

Madeleine looks, although tanned from her holiday, not only shocked but exhausted, and also old in a way she wasn't before. As with Lyle, Isla can see more distinctly and differently from this angle the crumplings and failings, the sheer skin-thinness of age. Madeleine's flesh looks nearly worn through, as if there's not much holding her together right now.

When did all this happen?

Gradually, Isla guesses, in a sneaking-up, day-to-day sort of way; and some of it suddenly, recently.

Madeleine's hands are down where forgetful people's hands tend to go, somewhere around where Isla's hands must be. It's hard for those accustomed to touching her to remember everything she can't feel. For all she knows, Madeleine's holding on hard. It would be like her to be trying to squeeze strength and life into her daughter, one more time.

"I wish I'd known right away. And even then, it took so long to get here. What a journey! I was never so glad to see anyone in my life as Alix at the airport."

"Where's Bert?"

"Coming along with our car. Alix took us to our place to drop off our things, but of course I wanted to get right here to see you, so he was going to take a few minutes to get squared away and then come pick me up. Oh, sweetie, why didn't you get in touch instantly? I hate not having been here. Then it made me crazy, being so far away."

"I'm sorry. We weren't sure what to do. We didn't want to upset you, so it was hard to find the right time."

Madeleine raises her eyebrows. "The *right* time? Precisely when did you think that would be?" Oh, they are alike, she and Isla. She is injured, and from pain, anger swiftly proceeds. This used to seem to Isla a useful progression, but perhaps has outworn its virtues.

"I know, you're right, I'm sorry. But now you're here, and thank God. I was really missing my mum." Isla is trying to lighten the moment, but she means that exactly: she has been missing her mother, who is now here. Another *good sign*, would Dr. Grant say?

"And you're in time." Barely. "The doctor was in a while ago, and they've scheduled surgery for first thing day after tomorrow. Kind of a surprise, but I guess it's a good thing it's going ahead."

"Oh wow." That's Alix, of course, stepping forward from behind her grandmother. "Thursday?"

"At least I didn't miss that. I couldn't have stood it, if I'd been gone for that." Madeleine's eyes well up. Isla hasn't known her mother to cry since those nights after her father died, when she could be wakened by desolate, heart-broken sounds.

She also hasn't expected to need a stiff upper lip with her mother. "Please, don't cry, it's all right. Everybody says this is the best place in the country to be, and the doctor is hopeful. He was only holding off because they wanted to see if the scrap of bullet would work itself free, but it hasn't. It's the tiniest thing. I've seen pictures. You should see it. Amazing." Madeleine strokes and strokes Isla's forehead. Isla closes her eyes. Madeleine's trembling tenderness: nearly what she hoped for.

Although after a little while it starts to feel morbid; as if Madeleine is grieving over a corpse. Isla opens her eyes fast. "So how was your trip back? Pretty complicated, I hear."

"Let's say it was quite an adventure. Lyle was very clever to set it all up, finding a little boat here and a little plane there, a couple of quite odd hotels. Mind you, Bert says he won't be flying in a four-seater again, although in my opinion we hit worse turbulence in the bigger planes."

"Poor Bert."

"Yes, and he'll be arriving by now. Oh, Isla, I'll be back as soon as I can, but I should go, just for a little while. I was dying to see you the first minute I could." She stops; not knowing, Isla imagines, where to go from the word *dying*.

"I'm happy just knowing you're in reach. But I bet you're worn out, so why not get caught up at home instead of coming right back? Do whatever needs doing and have a good sleep, and we'll see each other tomorrow. Because I expect we'll all need our strength."

"There's so much to catch up on, though."

"Well, you know, there's a lot but really only a little. Tons of details, but only a few major facts. You know the big stuff. Honestly, I'm not lying, as long as I know you're back, I'm happy."

This is nearly true. Near enough.

"Oh dear. I expect you're right. I'm a bit worried about Bert, so maybe it is best if I get him tucked up at home. I'll see about later on, but otherwise, I'll be here first thing tomorrow. Oh, Isla." She makes her way through the apparatus to touch Isla's forehead with crimsoned lips. "Take very good care."

A little late for taking care. "I will, Mum. You too."

Alix is still sparkling. Whatever happened to serenity? "Wasn't that great, seeing Grandma? I almost didn't make it, I had to absolutely race to the airport after court. Oh."

Obviously that came out wrong.

"Court?" Isla has Madeleine's gift for raised eyebrows.

"Well, yeah." Alix looks away briefly, then back. "I wanted to talk to you about that, but maybe not now. I didn't know about the surgery being so soon."

"No better time, then, is there?" Because there may be no other time—is that cruel? Perhaps not. Perhaps it flies right over Alix's head.

"Well, okay. I wondered if you'd mind hearing about it, and that boy—would it be all right? Because I think it's sort of important."

Look at her: under the wispiness, the transparency, this has always been a child, girl, young woman, who can, if she wants, make harsh decisions. They aren't always astute decisions, but they can certainly be severe. There is an echo right here of Alix at twelve, rising slowly after the scrambling Tim from under the pool table, shirt askew, staring her father down in a quite unnerving way. More recently her decisions have been made in the interests of faith, desire, belief; maybe false faith, foolish desire, misguided belief, but she seems to know something about means, if not ends. Tender-hearted to start with, and lately intent on achieving equanimity, which she has perhaps mistaken for peace.

235

Look at her skin, look at those eyes, that glorious hair. Regard her longings. Are they not Isla's as well? "Okay," Isla says cautiously.

"His name's Rod. You probably know that. I heard his grand-mother and his dad out in the hall calling him Roddy, and in court he was Roderick in the documents, you know, the charges, but the lawyers and the judge called him Rod."

A little too much on the subject of names, that. Isla has been avoiding his name when she could, and now he's got three. Perhaps it's a subject that interests Alix because she also goes through the world with at least one name too many.

"I don't know how much you remember about what he looks like." Weedy. Unappealing. Moving fast and stupidly. That's about it. "He's kind of thin. His grandmother's totally fat and his dad's big, but Rod doesn't look like either of them." Probably, then, he resembles his mother, and where is she in all this? Isla knows very well that whatever a son does, a mother attends to him. There she was herself a few years ago, sitting two rows behind Jamie in court, listening to his offences, hear-ing his contrition, bearing his punishment.

"And I don't know how you feel about him." Really? Time for raised eyebrows again.

"How long did he get?" That's how Isla feels, a bit more than a day before surgery that's her interest in him: the extent and degree of his punishment.

"Oh. Eighteen months. And two years' probation." Alix's tone does not suggest whether she considers that too much or too little. Doesn't even suggest an interest; as if punishment isn't the point. Well, it is to Isla. Eighteen months! The little shit will still be barely old enough to vote when he gets out.

God knows where she will be.

Of course he's very young to be facing a ruined life. If it's ruined. He certainly has many more years than she does. Her time is compressed, possibly even down to a day, whereas his, at seventeen, is extensive, expansive. Like Jamie: he could start over. Damaged and too-experienced, Jamie nevertheless had that chance. There was time. As there is for this boy; not so much for her. "I see," she says.

"The thing about him, Mother," Alix says, with more courage, Isla thinks, than she is necessarily aware of, "is, he has this look about him." Indeed he does: panic, shock, inevitability. "It's like, he looks lost. Like he doesn't understand who he is or what's happened. Like he's all up in the air, know what I mean?"

If she means the boy is stumped by events, rolled over by regrets, baffled by his own whereabouts, bewildered by unexpected outcomes, then yes, Isla knows.

"Did Lyle tell you about when we went to court together before?"

"A little." That the boy pleaded guilty, had in fact confessed fulsomely and instantly to the police, evidently. And that Lyle and Alix both made statements to the court. In Lyle's recounting, his own statement sounded far too close to a eulogy. Of Alix's he said, "I'm sorry, but I couldn't make head nor tail of it. I'm afraid it was beyond me."

"Lyle said what he was supposed to, but I screwed up. I was going to talk about what a good mother you are and how you stick by us no matter what and all that, and then I was walking past him, Rod, and I looked over at him and it was really weird. I just stopped. There was something about him, and I kept looking, I guess I wanted to see what there was to him, and you know what?"

No, Isla does not know what. She does know there's only so long she'll tolerate Alix babbling about that reckless little asshole. As if he was interesting. As if there'd be any point. As if she has time.

"We just stared at each other. Like for a few seconds nobody else was there. And he was all, you know, empty and lost-looking? And all of a sudden I realized I'd had this awful attachment to anger. Like, I'd really hated him, and it was such a horrible feeling, like he was huge, because he'd done this huge thing and here you were and, oh, you know, everything was wrecked. But then when I saw him, he's not huge at all, he's just kind of pitiful, and then as soon as I realized that, I could feel the anger and hatred going away, like, lifting right off me. I mean, we were totally still, just staring at each other and it was like he'd been empty and was filling up in some way. Oh," and she waves her arm, "I don't know how to describe it right." Of course she doesn't. Obviously. "But anyway, I did finally say some stuff, I think sort of about how brave you are, and this is a challenge but your spirit makes you whole, kind of redeemed no matter what. Don't worry," and Alix smiles slightly, slyly, "I didn't say it was a blessing you had this challenge, or you're lucky to have it."

A joke! Alix has actually made a feeble, but darkish, joke!

"So then I thought and thought about what happened, and you know, sometimes when you think about something too much it gets kind of fuzzy and maybe wrong. The memory, I mean. So I had to go back today. I guess partly to hear the sentence, but mainly, honestly, to look at him again. See if I saw him the same way, and how it felt."

"And?" And what does she want Isla to feel? Sorry for him? She had quite a full and enjoyable and entirely earned and deserved life going on, until this empty person decided to mess with it. Pity is not quite in her repertoire.

"And the thing is, I did. See him the same way, I mean. So what I wanted to tell you, or maybe ask you, I don't know, is," small frown, deep worried breath, "that I want to see him again. I want to know what you'd think if I go see him in jail."

If Isla could feel anything, she imagines it would be in the category of gut-punched.

Is there something about her that attracts the people she cares for towards notions of betrayal?

"It's just, there's something I think I could learn that's important. I mean, to me. And he looks so, I don't know, full of *need*. I've been thinking about how he'd ever get used to knowing the horrible thing he did, and how he could live with it. He doesn't look like there's really anybody to help him, either."

Isla hasn't had in mind that he should ever get used to knowing the horrible thing he has done. She's thought his swift, stupid act should go right on haunting him. That and some hellish prison for a very long time would have suited her fine. "Well," she begins carefully, "but you said he has family. Grandmother, father, whatever. Helping him would be their job, don't you suppose?" Although evidently they have already helped him, somehow, straight into crime, directly to punishment. "And where's his mother?"

"Oh, that's sad, too. Somebody said she killed herself, jumped off a bridge or something when he was a kid."

He's still a kid. But that is sad.

"He and his father'd already moved back in with his dad's mother before that happened. They've been there ever since."

So: blame the mother, what else? If his mother hadn't screwed up, Isla wouldn't be here. Everything would be different. And who would have known what they'd escaped? Not Isla, for sure.

"I didn't mean he's alone in the world, exactly, more that he looks alone. Like there's nothing *true* in his life, you know what I mean?"

Oh. Now Isla does suddenly know. She sees Alix has just told her something, but not about the boy: that Alix perceives aloneness and emptiness in him because those things are recognizable and familiar to her.

What a disastrously self-absorbed mother she has been: grateful, glad even, that at least during their worst times, Alix was more steady than Jamie, worked hard, did well, caused no real trouble.

Quietly waited her turn. Bided her time. Cultivated, as she waited and bided, her desires and longings. Her *yearnings*.

"Yes," Isla says slowly, "I think I do see something of what you mean."

"Then you wouldn't mind too much? I don't want to make it harder for you, but I have to ask. You know those moments when you *know* something's right?" Not really. Those seem to be moments that occur to other people. Like Lyle finding the place he belongs: some kind of magic.

Now she gets to give an opinion on whether her daughter should form an attachment, never mind what kind, to a kid who shoots people. Who shoots Alix's mother, one person only.

Imagine if Alix ever stumbled onto some normal, unworrying, probably not very interesting middle ground; but looking up into her daughter's intent, unwavering gaze, Isla sees this isn't likely. And really, there do have to be people on earth, surely, with intent, unwavering gazes. "Well, it's upsetting, of course, you'd know I was lying if I said otherwise. But I take your word that you know what needs doing. For yourself, I mean. I really can't give a damn about him. Let me just ask you, though, please, to be careful. I only saw him once, and just for a moment, but it wasn't the sort of moment that would make me think he has any good prospects."

Imagine Alix visiting him wherever he has, thank God, been sent, although for far too short a time. Imagine her listening to him explain and explain, making attempts on her compassion and pity.

"Here's something that'll make you happier, though, Mum. The other thing I wanted to tell you is, I think I've decided I'm not going back to Serenity."

What? Isla feels pistol-whipped: smacked hard one way, then the other. Could she have misheard?

"I'm sad, because besides everything else, most of those people have been my truest friends," a quick smile when Alix adds, "which I guess means I wasn't as detached as I was supposed to be—but I've thought about it a lot, and I'm pretty sure I've decided."

"Why?" By which Isla means, *What miracle is this, at last?*

"Well, because even Master Ambrose says he can show us some of the ways, but he can't actually carry us anywhere, we still have to carry ourselves. So that's all I think, really: that maybe this is a good time to carry myself." She pauses, frowns a little, makes another vague sweep of her arm above Isla. "Because what's happened changes so much, doesn't it? It means thinking about everything sort of differently. That things really do happen, it isn't only detachment."

Hard to have to be shot in order for a daughter to have the odd life-saving epiphany.

But hallelujah anyway. Goodbye Master Ambrose, farewell brown dresses, au revoir dumb obedience? Oh yes, hurray. "You're right," Isla says far more mildly than she feels, "that is good news, it makes me much happier. It feels like a good sign." From too much ill luck, does she now court having too much good fortune? She wouldn't care for her quota to run out before Thursday. "But what, really, were you looking for there? Can you tell me now?" That great puzzle.

Alix looks surprised. "Just what it says: serenity. I mean, I heard 'Serenity Corps' and I thought, 'Bingo. That's it.' Not so mysterious. Kind of disciplined but peaceful. The *courage* to be serene."

Well. Isla does see the appeal. The appetite and the desire.

It also feels as if somewhere in this conversation, Alix has offered, not an answer, not salvation, not even any credible variation on faith, belief, or desire. But a parable of some kind. A useful story buried in there. "I'm very glad, Alix," she says again. "I can't tell you." And really, she can't.

Everyone is on the edge of one drastic sentiment or another these days—really quite exhilarating, and strange. Life on a scale she hasn't particularly noticed before: microscopic, and close to the ground. The narrowed, focused perspective of stillness, of infinitesimal swayings this way and that, and tiny steps, crucial totterings, small, delicate, perilous, optimistic advancements.

Perhaps.

Alix will visit that boy, she wants to help fill him up.

Alix wants to save herself. She is not in favour of harbouring hatred.

She is leaning down over Isla. How rare this is recently, an embrace from Alix.

In jail, there can be no embracing of prisoners. There's that rule to rely on.

But skin is a hard, hard loss. "I wish you joy," Isla says, by which she means, although Alix will have no way of knowing this, that she hopes for Alix the blessing of unburdened embraces. Absolute attachment.

It sounds like a benediction, *I wish you joy*. Benevolent, in fact. Now she has just a day to find some other good words. Not happy words, necessarily, but good ones.

Not Too Much Buddy-Buddy

ALL THAT TALK ABOUT CLASSES, studying, counselling, chores in the kitchen and laundry, tough discipline, hard schedule—but nobody mentioned Roddy'd have a room-mate. Cellmate. Nobody said he wouldn't have a little space and time of his own.

Like everything else recently, this is totally new to him.

Even he and Mike in their high glossy shared apartment were going to have separate bedrooms. They counted on that much from Goldie's for sure. They checked out advertisements. They knew what sort of rent to expect. "We'll need our own rooms," Mike said with his usual confidence, "especially for bringing back babes."

That was going to be some glamorous change, some high-quality transformation, that parallel-universe life.

So what a surprise, another shock among many, to be driven away north in the van to this huge four-winged grey-walled place, which has guards outside as well as inside, who stopped the van and checked what they called the "cargo," one name at a time. And to be led inside and told to stand still while being hummed over by metal detectors, and stripped naked and inspected and showered, no dignity to this, no idea any of the four of them arriving together might be a particular human, and then—exhausted and heartsore, literally by then Roddy's heart hurt, to be steered to a cell, to watch the guard keycard the lock, to feel grateful that he'd now get to be by himself, quiet finally, even just for a little while, a few solitary minutes to catch his breath, close his eyes, retrieve the necessary visions and begin learning how to hold on to them. And then to see a guy on a cot looking up from his magazine, already a resident of Roddy's new home.

Shit. Oh, not fair to get nothing, nothing at all that he wants.

The metal door locked behind him. The guy sat up, nodded neutrally, not even apparently bothering, as Roddy was, to try to assess raw danger, bare kindness. He said, just, "Darryl. Called Dare."

Roddy said, "Rod." Added, since that seemed insufficient, "Hi." The guy didn't look much bigger than him, and his nearly-shorn hair looked to be the uniform of the place, not a statement of fashion, like Roddy's, or of outlook, necessarily. Major muscles, though, in his arms, and little dark eyes Roddy took to contain potential for meanness, although maybe that's only what people imagine about little dark eyes; and anyway maybe he was only squinting to give the impression of menace, the way Roddy himself hoped to do.

Darryl gestured. "That'll be your bed, that one."

"Yeah, I guess." Darryl had pictures taped up on the wall on his side of the cell, so Roddy supposed he'd sort of made that part his home. Naked women pictures, huge, gargantuan breasts, the kind Roddy's never even dreamed of, so spectacularly impossible for somebody like him. He couldn't imagine it'd be a good idea to put pictures of tiny multi-legged creatures on his side of the room. Too weird, never mind that they belonged in some other, earlier, innocent time. Darryl's pictures say he's a normal guy, whatever that is, and moreover one who calls himself *Dare*. Roddy's pictures wouldn't exactly give a similar message.

The same kind of lidless crapper as the other place, the same tiny sink. Two desks, though, and two chairs, all bolted into the floor, and a couple of shelves each, bolted into the walls. Roddy's had two towels on them, and some sheets and a pillow, but they might also be intended for books; the business of taking classes. Darryl's did: a few texts and a couple of notebooks.

He watched Roddy taking this in. "You been here before? You know how it works?"

"No. Not really." Dare's not as big as Mike, and darker-skinned and while muscled, not as sort of bulked up. As an enemy, he might be more like Roddy himself, someone who goes in low, fast, hard, and mean. A bad enemy, especially with just the two of them in a small cell, or a good ally, especially outside the cell. Or maybe neither one.

"First thing, you could make your bed up. You probably got about fifteen minutes before a guard comes around and checks everybody. Last guy in here got out yesterday. He jerked off about six times a night so you probably want to turn over the mattress while you're at it."

Oh yeah. Gross. Somebody else's mattress. Guy after guy had slept, or not slept, on that nasty grey thing. Not that Dare offered to help Roddy turn it over. Not that, on the other side, it was much less repulsive.

If he thought the detention centre had reeked of something backed up and leaking out, not water systems or even cleaning chemicals but something more to do with contained bodies, it was nothing to this place. Danger is as serious here as desire, and adds its own smell.

Everybody's under eighteen, that's what the whole place is for. Roddy's among the oldest ones here, but he feels practically virginal, almost innocent. Sure he can say "armed robbery," but there's rapists, and guys who've run in gangs since they were little kids. There's guys to stay well away from, and sometimes that's obvious just from looking at them. Others go around looking nervous, which is about the worst thing to do because even with guards around, there's ways to get hurt. There's lots of low-voiced threats, and hidden weapons like sharp lengths of metal stripped from the bottom of beds, there's pool cues poked hard into a belly or back.

Dare's here because he stabbed a guy late at night outside a bar. "Stupid fucker died." He told Roddy this their first night of cell-sharing. It was his biggest crime, for sure, but not his only one. Seemed like he'd earned his name. "Armed robbery?" he said. "Me too, a couple of variety stores but I never got busted for those. I used a knife, though, not a gun. I've never used a gun."

He sounded impressed.

Roddy remains impressed the other way round. Knives. Maybe the results could be just as accidental, but sticking somebody—you'd get blood all over you, you'd touch actual flesh, it'd be completely personal, close-up, and real. There'd be particular in-your-face smells, and certain sounds. It didn't seem possible. But a lot of things don't seem possible and they happen anyway, including to him.

"Guy was where he didn't belong," Dare explained as if this would sound reasonable, even obvious once pointed out. "Bunch of preppy kids slumming. Thought they were cool. Fuckin' pissed me off, lording it around like tourists or something, like they were kings of the world. So this frat boy, I mean it turns out he really was a frat boy, he's going on about how any of them could fuck our sisters and girlfriends and probably would, and like how they had these big-deal futures and too bad about us losers, real snotty shit, and I finally say, like, 'Shut up and fuck off or I'll give you a future,' and he goes all, 'Yeah, you'd like that,' and back and forth and so on and then fuck, I finally just say fuck it and pull out the blade and then he starts backing off, he says, like, 'Whoa, dude,' and I say, 'Way too late, asshole,' and I stick him. Three times. He goes down, just folds on the sidewalk.

"Everybody goes to split, me too, a lot of yelling and running around, his friends go totally out of their minds, but you know, like, he *was* an asshole. Big mess of blood all over the sidewalk. Weird." Dare shook his head; but he didn't sound sorry, exactly; more, still, sort of surprised, but not entirely amazed. Didn't he scare himself? And if not that, didn't what happened scare him, the result? Well, he wasn't likely to say, was he? Any more than Roddy would. "His buddies won't be going to that part of town again any time soon, I bet. They can take their futures and shove them right up my hairy white ass. But hey," and he turned on his side to look at Roddy, lying carefully on his fresh-sheeted bed, "you shot a broad?"

"Yeah," Roddy said. "Wrong time, wrong place."

"She die?"

"No. Still in the hospital, though." He didn't want to say *paralyzed*. It would make her sound too much a victim, himself too much someone who only really defeated the helpless. "My lawyer got the attempt murder charge dropped." He tried to sound as casual as Dare. Word gets around.

Darryl likes to talk, but he could be a worse cellmate. At least he doesn't go on and on about nothing. It's not completely impossible, when they're in the cell together, at the end of days that already feel endless when there's months and months more to come, for Roddy to slip behind closed eyelids into the visions he needs to hold on to. He can still, if he tries hard, make out a flare of bright hair, the skin he could almost see through, most of all the eyes that saw right into him. The days are hard, and the nights, too. Not much silence. There's so much yelling and other noise, practically round the clock, it's kind of insane. Everybody seems angry, prisoners and guards, too, and not just about small day-to-day matters. Roddy's kind of angry himself, but keeps in mind that quiet menace is the weapon he has, if he has any at all, if he needs one. It's not so much that bad things happen here, although they do, but that everybody goes around as if they could happen, any second and for any reason, or for that matter for no reason. There is not a moment's rest from knowing that.

He still has the dreams that wake him up, but even in sleep, he's learned not to wake up upset in any obvious way. He's trained himself already towards desolation—there's a word he comes upon in English class and likes the sound of—and silence. The dreams of his mother come the same every time, but they're still a surprise every time. He wakes up to the idea that, never mind what he thinks he remembers, he mustn't have been very lovable. He must have had something about him that turned his mother's heart away and took her to the railing of that bridge off which, night after night, he continues, sometimes gently, sometimes not, to finally push her.

Later in the day, occupied and fully awake, he can think, so what. Shit happens. To hell with it.

Only, not first thing in the morning.

Anyway, there's better dreams to have.

He has some of those, too.

But you can't count on dreams. The counsellor here, or therapist, or whatever she is, that he got dragged off to see once, more to come, asked him stuff like that: is he sleeping well here, does he have dreams, what are they. Like he'd tell her. Like he'd say anything about trying to hold a vision when he's awake, and in his sleep having a completely different one. How in a dream he puts his fingertips onto the perfect round nipples of that Alix, that Starglow, and is wakened, those much happier times, by something like electricity.

Like some woman maybe in her forties should hear that? So she could tell him this and that about it that wouldn't be right at all? No way.

She looks okay, but that's likely her job, to look okay to guys here. He saw her his first full day here, but not since then, in a little grey office down a mile of long grey corridors. She stood up from behind a grey metal desk and stuck out her hand and said, "I'm Mrs. Shaw. Hello, Rod," which was a good start. "I'll be in charge of your counselling and education program. I mean setting you up in courses, not teaching them myself. I do personal and group counselling, though, so we'll be spending a fair amount of time together, one way and another."

He shrugged. She had one of those business-type leather briefcases that she slapped down on the table and opened with a sharp double click. It was jammed full, and messy. She was kind of jammed full and messy, too, but with a low voice and friendly eyes. People probably found it easy to tell her things, he figured, although he wouldn't be one of them.

She said, "I'd say from those tests you did, and from your school records, that you have a lot of potential. That's not as rare here as you might think, but it's a very good start. It gives us something productive to work with. Hope that when you leave, you'll be better off than you probably feel you are today." He had nothing to say to that; although hope would be nice. Also he liked knowing that, same as Stan at the detention centre, she realized he wasn't hopeless.

"And I have a copy of your pre-sentence report here. Comments from your family, some of your teachers and friends, a couple of people you worked for."

He was startled into saying, "You talked to people?"

"Well, no, Rod, I didn't, but other people did. A PSR goes to the judge before someone is sentenced, to help the judge figure out the best thing to do." So people had conversations about him. Felt free to talk, give details, tell stories, maybe true, maybe not. Is just anybody allowed to start demanding this and that about his life now?

Would Mike have been asked questions about him? Could Mike talk about Roddy without faltering, without showing anything? Roddy was desperate to ask this Mrs. Shaw, "What did Mike say?" Also, "What's he doing, does he still work at Goldie's? Did anybody notice if he looks like he's keeping a secret? Was he uncomfortable talking about me? Or sad? Or did he keep his mouth shut?"

Is Mike haunted? Does he feel guilty? Does he wonder how Roddy is doing, does he wonder at Roddy setting out to protect him?

Does he think about the woman at all?

There are no answers from Mike, who hasn't called or written or visited, as far as Roddy knows. Maybe he tried. Maybe nothing gets through.

He must wonder, though. Except Roddy can't be sure of that, not any more. They've gone off in totally different directions, him and Mike. One moment in Goldie's.

"It looks to me," Mrs. Shaw said, "as if you have a nice family. Your grandmother and your dad speak very highly of you." They do? Even his dad? His dad spoke at all? "You and your father moved in with your grandmother when you were what, seven?" He nodded. "Can you tell me your first memory before then? What you recall from when you were very small? Where you lived, your home then?" She looked inviting; there was something shrewd about those blue eyes, though, something about how she widened them that didn't look natural.

There was nothing to say. His mother laughing and playing, making up dramas and games, and days when she didn't get dressed. "I don't remember much. We lived in a house, it seemed big but I was only a kid, so I don't know. Then we moved."

"After your mother got sick."

He shook his head sharply, felt his lips tighten. He had no words for this woman on that subject, none at all. At least she noticed. Or at least she didn't push at him. "How did you feel about moving?" she asked instead.

Violently. He felt violently enough to scream and kick and resist the whole way. "Okay, I guess. My grandmother's okay."

"Yes, she sounds it. And your father?"

"Yeah, him too."

She waited a few seconds. "Still, it must have been a big change for you, moving to a different house in a different place, without your mother. Did you find it very difficult?"

Not after he and Mike started hanging out, which was practically right away. Then it wasn't so bad. "Not really."

And so on: about school, about friends, about hobbies and habits, all questions he did his best not to answer. "Where did you get the idea for the robbery?"

He shrugged. "I don't know. TV, maybe."

Finally she smiled slightly and looked at her watch and said, "I expect that's enough for the time being. I'll tell you what I think we'll do next, and that's assign you shortly to one of the groups that meet every week. Everybody takes turns discussing their questions and problems, things that have come up in their lives. Most people find it quite useful, although I bet you don't think much of the idea right now. You'd be surprised, though, how often people learn they have a good deal in common, and how helpful it is to exchange points of view and experiences. So I'll organize that for you, and we'll see how it goes. I really do think you'll find it interesting. And of course it helps you get to know some of the others better, too."

Oh no, that wouldn't be happening. Exchange points of view and experiences? He didn't think so. He's not the kind of person, it turns out, who gets second chances. He sure can't have guys knowing he has dreams, or for sure that he's cried. He'd be really fucked then. Sit around in a circle of guys talking about backgrounds and crimes, motivations and hopes? Their *feelings*, like they should have any here?

Bad idea.

Still, maybe she meant well, maybe she truly had hopes.

More likely she figured he's just an asshole. One among many.

"Now," and she leaned forward, passing a sheet of paper over the desk to him, white paper grid-lined in day-blocks along the top, time-blocks down the side, "here's your class schedule. Our goal, I think, will be to get you the high school credits you need to graduate by the end of your time here. That should be doable, if you buckle down. You'll begin tomorrow. What do you think?"

It hardly seemed to matter what he thought, did it, if it was done, decided, and starting tomorrow? "Okay."

"Good. You'll get your books and other supplies when you turn up for class. I expect you'll do fine. It may sound strange, but in many ways it's easier here. Not the courses, but the learning."

That did sound strange, but it turns out she's right. He's taking math, history, and English, and one thing that's different is that there's no way to skip, there isn't any kind of decision to make about that. Also that there's only guys, and that every classroom has a guard as well as a teacher. The teachers come from outside. They probably like it that there's no skipping, and that mostly the classes are pretty quiet, because of the guards. They maybe don't like it that a lot of the guys are either really stupid or let on like they are, pretending they're sleeping, some of them, or staring up at the ceiling, or just sitting there not lifting a pencil. Also different is that the desks and chairs are bolted down.

Classes take up a little over three hours a day. Some of the stuff he already knows from before. Sometimes he has to put an effort into not looking too smart. He doesn't think that's one of the good ways to get attention around here.

Everybody also gets assigned chores, really massive ones, not like weeding or trimming a hedge or vacuuming. He's in the kitchen this week, next week the laundry. In the kitchen he peels bag after bag of potatoes, pile after pile of carrots. It's stinking hot, there's always a racket of pots slamming around, and mainly it's mindless and his fingers hurt and he's aware of how closely he's watched, due to having knives in his hands. He has no idea why this work gets done here by prisoners, "clients," they're called, instead of getting shipped in from outside. Maybe it's supposed to be discipline, or training, or punishment.

He doubts the laundry will be easier, or more interesting, and Darryl says it's even hotter and steamier.

He and Dare aren't assigned to the same jobs at the same time. "They like to keep everybody mixed up and moving around," Dare says. "So there's not too much buddy-buddy." Dare reckons he can be out of here, himself, in eleven more months; just before Roddy, if Roddy also keeps his nose clean. That's Dare's goal, "keeping my nose clean, keeping them happy," and he's been here for a couple of years already, so he should know how that works. Roddy almost immediately figured out that Dare must have been only fourteen, maybe fifteen, when he stabbed the frat guy. Hard to know how different he's gotten in here, but it's pretty freaky, thinking of a kid that age out on the street in the middle of the night, so bad off he'd kill somebody. A kid who has grown older and stronger and is now Roddy's cellmate.

He's okay so far with Roddy, though, at least has been willing to point out the most basic customs and rules.

But the third night, something creepy happened that made Roddy think if Darryl got into a better state of mind here, it'd be some kind of miracle. Same thing happened the next night, then there was a break for a while until again last night, around midnight, one of the guards came and unlocked the cell door and gestured to Dare to get up and get out. Dare came back bleeding from the nose the first time, limping and bent over the second, and last night he vomited, mainly into the crapper.

No wonder Roddy sleeps lightly, dreams uneasily.

"What happened?" he asked the first time, and could have bitten his tongue, such a stupid, maybe dangerous, question. Still, how could he have avoided asking, "Can I do something?" thinking at least of stopping the blood that sprayed the cell when Dare shook his head.

Well, it's not what Roddy figured at first, what he most feared, what everybody's most scared of in jails. It's more of a game, as Darryl finally explained it, but probably not one that's going to bear down on Roddy "unless they decide to use you for bait. You know, like training fight dogs with puppies, shit like that."

Okay, that was insulting, but being insulted is better than some of the things that can happen here.

Dare talked about it like it's just something he does, just another thing to put up with, but what it is, is a middle-of-the-night boxing club, organized by bored, maybe greedy guards. They roust out their favourite inmates, and their unfavourites. They set them up inside a ring of tables and chairs in one of the rec halls. They place bets, and then the guys fight. "No rules," Dare explained. "Except, don't get killed, or kill anybody, because that'd be too hard to explain."

It's like street fighting, he said; wild wrestling, no gloves or timed rounds or real regulations. "It's complicated, though.

Like if you're the betting favourite, but you lose, you're in all kinds of shit. Not right then, but later. Or I guess if you win when you're not supposed to, but that hasn't happened to me."

"Doesn't anybody notice the next day when you're all smashed up?"

"Oh shit, everybody knows, except maybe the top brass, those kind of people. And you know, people fall down. They trip over stuff or bang into things, who's to know? They can think all they want, but they're not going to know."

It would be dumb to even wonder why guys who are tough and have real serious records—like Darryl, for one—go along with this. It's because this place is all about power. Who has it, who doesn't. At the high end there's the guards, who are up close, with immediate or invisible powers. Administrators, those "top brass," don't count. Sure as shit therapists don't. It's useful to see power stripped down, no camouflage or extra flesh, so he sees how it really works.

"I'm good," Dare said, like even if it wasn't his choice, he was still proud of himself. "I don't hardly get beat." Quick grin through battered lips. "At least not when I'm not supposed to get beat."

"So you were supposed to this time?"

"Shit no, why'd you think that? You should see the other guy." All this confirms Roddy's belief that going unnoticed is best. He also has a feeling that because Darryl was chosen, Roddy doesn't need to be; like he's somehow hiding, or hidden, behind Dare's in-demand fists. The idea of just-one-from-a-cell doesn't make sense and is not likely true, but it seems like it might be. He feels a little bad about that, but safer.

Besides classes and chores, there's workshops in this and that. It's amazing how many sharp tools get into the hands of guys who might want to use them. Not just the kitchen, with its knives; Roddy signed up for woodworking, and is learning about chisels and lathes. So far he's made a salad bowl set, one big one, four small, all a bit tipsy and rough, but still real-looking and useful, although the wood is donated and is obviously not the best grain. It's kind of cool, feeling it turn and shape in his hands and become something.

He gave the bowls to his grandmother to take home with her. She's been once, on her own because his dad was working. She caught a bus north, and said she'd try to make the journey at least once a month, maybe twice. It wouldn't be easy for her to do that. For one thing she's so big, it has to be really uncomfortable on a bus. She took the bowls and said, "Oh, Roddy, these are lovely. You do have an eye. I'll take very good care of them." He knows she will; she's sentimental that way.

She also said, "Will you be all right here? Do you feel safe?"

"Sure, it's not as bad as it looks, honest."

She was nervous; out of place and unfamiliar, of course, with the customs. She chatted on for a while about people in town, little events, keeping the air filled, as best she could. It wasn't very interesting. He didn't know the people she spoke of, her acquaintances or his dad's, very well. A minor accident involving one of her friends and a transport going through town was as good as it got. Roddy understands that of course the most interesting of the town's news is bad, and so falls too uncomfortably close to his own bad news. Which will have been a huge deal, and humiliating for her and his dad, no need to say it out loud.

Just before she left, she got tears in her eyes, and started shaking her head back and forth. She looked even sadder right then than his mother, in his dreams, up on the bridge. "Oh, Roddy," she said, "I'm so sorry all this has happened. I never dreamed such a thing, never once."

Well, he could have said, but did not, you can't count on dreams anyway. Dreams don't mean shit.

What he did say was "You don't have to come visit, Grandma, I'm fine. It's a long way on a bus and it's not for a whole lot more months. I'm okay."

"Of course you need visitors, Roddy, and I don't mind a bit. I miss you, I want to see you. Anyway, most times your dad will be driving, it's just, this time he couldn't. And you know, the bus is quite interesting. Lots of interesting people."

Yes, he imagined: others coming this way.

"So by bus or by car, dear, I'll be back very soon. You won't be forgotten, believe me. You're very precious to me."

What do you say to being called *precious*? Someone of value. He flushed and looked down.

Now he wishes he'd had the gumption, or the courage, or the cruelty, or the compassion, to order her not to come back. His dad, either. It's hard enough figuring out how to be here, without being reminded and jerked back by tenderness. He can't afford to let down his guard, he feels this very strongly. But—*precious*. That nearly cracked him, honest to God.

The Useful Mother

THEY KNOCK HER OUT OVERNIGHT, then when she wakes up they sedate her, they do this and that busy, unseen thing with her body, adjusting here, prodding there, an anaesthetist comes by to tell her about procedures, question her about allergies—they don't seem to know anything about what's important: that time is short. They have their priorities, their necessities, and in the end, which this may be, they don't care about hers. It's as if none of them has become acquainted with her. They've gone back to the efficient bare bones of her body.

So it's unexpectedly late in the day when Lyle, Madeleine, Jamie, and Alix are allowed to come back. By then, Isla has quite a number of things on her mind.

She is missing acutely, for one thing, her lost ability to make lists, to write down everything she needs to remember. Today this strikes her as a great loss even among much greater ones, as beyond her as throwing herself into Madeleine's arms, or embracing her children, or wrapping her legs around Lyle.

The kinds of things people choose: as their houses burn they grab photo albums rather than jewellery; in an invasion they hike up their skirts and their children and run. What has come first to Isla's mind, besides hope and its unshakeable partner dread, is the extent of her abandoned possessions: right down to her underwear, aged panties, the slack-elasticked bras she wears, if at all, for gardening or lawn-mowing—there it all lies in a bedroom bureau drawer, alongside the nice stuff, right where she innocently, carelessly left it, not dreaming that stepping off that porch could finally come to mean someone else's hands rummaging, sorting one thing from another.

"If things go badly," she tells Madeleine, "I want you to just tip my whole underwear drawer into a garbage bag, never mind sorting or saving. But everything in my closet is in good shape, I think all those clothes can be bundled up and given to some charity, whichever you like. Do you suppose anybody'd want used shoes? If they do, that's okay, too. A clean sweep, though. Everything out. It shouldn't take long, do you mind?"

Of course Madeleine minds. "Please, don't even think about that kind of thing. You're going to be fine. Just concentrate on how well tomorrow's going to go, and getting better, don't worry about little things." Little? Madeleine's never been stupid before. Perhaps she sees this herself. She sighs, which is too bad, but says, "All right. If need be, you can be sure I'll do whatever you want."

Love is hard. It makes a person too vulnerable to the well-being of others. That's how grief happens.

Also joy.

"Thanks. I'll feel better if I know it's all taken care of." She turns her attention to Lyle. "We've never talked about funerals. I want any useful organs—do you suppose there are any?—donated, then cremation. And no open casket, nobody staring." As long as she's talking, she doesn't have to wonder whose eyes these might be in a very few hours, what they might see from someone else's more flexible, entirely different perspective.

If she paused, she'd be scared rigid.

When she laughs, everyone frowns. Never satisfied, these people.

The machinery off to the side, where she can't see, starts to whuff and clatter at a new quickened pace. Lyle's long fingers reach out, touch, linger over, her forehead; but just for an instant, seeing his hand coming, she thought he was striking her, and her eyes flinched closed.

Which is crazy. In a million years Lyle wouldn't hit her, so where did that come from? Could he have seen fear before her eyes snapped shut? Did he glimpse doubt? "No doubt," she says, or intends to.

Except he has already broken a promise. In her mind's eye, her own right arm rises, swings back, swings forward straight, hard and fast into Lyle's jaw, snapping his head back. Which might be why she would dodge his hand: a fear, a knowledge, that he too is furious. Specifically, as well as generally.

If it were possible, she would protect him, even from herself, but that's no more possible than it was for him to protect her from the unguessable vagaries of an innocent step off the porch, a guileless walk into Goldie's.

There's grief here: for skin, that singular good thing, and everything it comes to mean. Head-to-toe touch. Bones and flesh. All that *meeting*. All that gone.

She has a memory, although it's not her own memory, of him in another hospital, with another wife in terrible trouble. In this memory Lyle and Sandra, Sandy, are sitting up straight beside each other, holding hands tightly, both their faces taut and drawn as that famous painting of the farmer standing with pitchfork and his solemn, pinched, shoulder-to-shoulder wife.

For all Isla knows, this is an old routine for Lyle.

"I don't know if you've already made burial arrangements for yourself?" He shakes his head; looks struck dumb. "I don't suppose it really matters where we each land up. You'll have to do what you think best, I guess." Tricky etiquette, deciding which wife to be buried with. If his arteries had exploded, where would she have put him?

Not with Sandy. Although his sons would have had something to say. And why would it matter? Dead is dead. "You should discuss it with Jamie and Alix, though. But of course you all know that. And you know my will is in the top left-hand drawer of the rosewood desk in the spare bedroom, right? It shouldn't be out of date, except maybe to do with the business.

It doesn't take into account that I think Martin wants to sell now. It says he should be offered my share of the agency, and the money should go into trusts for Jamie and Alix. That's probably okay, more or less, but if he's into selling rather than buying, I'd like you to go along with whatever he wants."

"Please, Isla, don't worry. I'll do the right thing, trust me, I promise." Well, he does look trustworthy. "It's not going to go wrong, you know. You're going to come out of this right as rain."

A curiously old-fashioned expression, is it not, right as rain? And rain is not always right, is it? Sometimes it floods, sometimes it drowns. "I expect so. But bear with me, I need to know I've thought of everything. I'm sure in a few days, we'll be laughing." But she isn't sure at all, and having said the words out loud, has frightened herself again. Promises and big predictions are bad luck, they invite random shock.

"It's just that it's kind of morbid, Mum," Jamie offers. "Depressing."

"Not to me. And surely to God it's my turn to be depressing."

That was sharper than she intended. It silences them all, until Lyle says, "I know it's hard, Isla. But you can count on us to do whatever you need, whatever we can. You know any of us would go to the ends of the earth for you."

That's nice. "I'm afraid you'd probably have to. Since I can't seem to do that myself." Well, she thinks it's funny. "Hey, work with me, all right? I'm dying down here."

"Should I get somebody?" Madeleine asks Lyle anxiously.

"No!" Isla cries; then more calmly, and cruelly, "I'm sure everything's easier if I'm knocked out, but it doesn't do much for me." Having said that, though, again she isn't sure. It almost seems as if something goes on when she's out of reach of the world, although she can't put her finger on what it is, or where it takes her.

She is forty-nine years old, and may, or may not, soon be fifty. She once had red hair, which has darkened and greyed and grown coarser. She had excellent legs and strong arms, but all their skin and muscles are shrivelling. She was a fool for lanky and lean, but some foolishness is a curse, some a blessing. She has been very good at her work, and likes to make lists, and has been known to race after running children with the object of rescue.

She is smart enough, but seems to have pulled up, puzzled, at the line drawn by wisdom.

She has patience, but not this much.

Now this is what it comes to: these people, this mass of dismay and affection are her only real grip on the planet. The only ones she can think of right now, anyway, and they seem both too much, and also not nearly enough.

"There's one other thing I want to be clear about. If I get through surgery but there's some other difficulty, I want you all to understand I do not want to be kept plugged in to anything that just keeps me breathing. We all know these things happen, so in case there's any doubt or discussion, if it happens to me, just let me go. Do you promise?"

Lyle's mouth is working strangely, lips tugging at each other, although not with laughter, not his usual way. Perhaps this, too, he has lived through before. "All right," he says finally. "We understand. Don't we?" and looks to the others.

Brave words; his and hers both. And if she is unsure she meant her words, and she is, can she be certain of his? She can feel in her throat some clotted protest rising up, a terrible desire to stay on this earth. To merely keep breathing, if that's all it comes to.

But to be kept merely breathing is as unknown, dark, and solitary as death. And you have to be brave about something, she has to mean what she says. Only, she doubts, too. She hopes she can trust Lyle not to doubt.

Madeleine places a thin, firm hand on Isla's forehead: driving in reassurance. Testing. Something like that. As when Isla was young and got sick and Madeleine was assessing her temperature and willing her well while she was at it. "There's nothing to be worried about. I hope you know that." Even lying, Madeleine's voice is as firm as her hand.

Is it strange that the details of tomorrow's full-tilt run at a dark, solid wall are, if nothing else, simpler than considering the—well, complexities is the easiest word—of staying alive? And even so, there's only so far a person can take that train of thought before it dead-ends. Grief and panic come to their own conclusions at the exact moment life does, which is not precisely comforting, but certainly puts a limit on things.

Tomorrow. Maybe tomorrow. How is that possible? But it is.

Being mourned and missed would be good. Being a burden, their pet cripple, would not.

Being healed would be fine.

Her options are too broad, too radically disparate.

Alix steps forward, light catching her halo of hair. "Do you have anything in particular you want me to do, Mum?" Well, no, come to think of it, the kids get off scot-free here, task-wise; as if they really were kids. "Because if you don't, here's my plan, if it sounds okay." She sounds firm, practical, and—could it be?—normal. "I'm going to go shopping. So the next time you see me, I'll have all new clothes. Then I think I should write a letter or two. For luck, in a way."

If no one else knows what she's talking about, Isla does. The perfect gift, too, no more goddamn brown dresses. One letter, no doubt, to Master Ambrose. The other, well, the other doesn't bear thinking about. But maybe yes, for luck, in a way.

"Get something gorgeous, then. And really bright, okay?"

"I will." Alix's jaw is strangely set, descending over Isla, brushing lips to forehead. "I'll see you, for sure." She stares down for one last, long moment. Then she's gone.

Well. It's a hard way to win, but triumph is triumph. Take that, Master Ambrose.

In the strained, puzzled silence left by Alix, Madeleine places a hand on Jamie's much higher shoulder; is she shrinking? Leaning? Hard to tell, from this angle. She does look more rested today, and also much stronger. "I wonder," she says to Jamie, "if you and Lyle would mind leaving your mother and me alone, just for a few minutes. Do you feel like a coffee?" When Lyle nods, she looks at him fondly, and when he and Jamie have gone, and she has settled herself in that well-used chair beside Isla, she smiles and says, "Haven't we been lucky, the two of us, really: my Bert, your Lyle. So fortunate in our second choices." Second chances.

"But." Madeleine takes a deep breath. "Here's what I wanted to say, and it may sound odd to you, but for some reason it's got stuck in my mind: I've been wondering if you've missed being brought up in some faith, if you wish you had that sort of comfort right now." She's right, this is startling; ominous, even. "If so, I guess I'm sorry, but I just couldn't do it. The stories, yes, I know we told those, but not the kind of religion people go to church for, or say they feel. So I'm sorry if you've ever felt that was missing. And I guess in a way I wish now I knew how to pray."

Oh dear. "You do? That doesn't exactly charge up my optimism, you know." Isla would like to get Madeleine smiling. She'd like to feel there's some faint reason to laugh. A faint smile is what she gets, a mere flicker. "But no, I can't see that religion would make much difference to this. Not to me. It hasn't particularly crossed my mind." Belief has, trust has, hope has, even some of the stories have, but not what Madeleine's talking about.

"Good. Well then, my actual point is, I may not know how to pray, but I'm with you, I don't believe any of it makes a damn bit of difference." Doesn't she look angry now!

"Anyway, you know, Mum, if I were going to pray, or even wish very hard, at the moment I'm not sure I'd know exactly what for. Know what I mean?"

Madeleine's blue eyes may be more opaque than they used to be, but they can also turn sharp. "I think so. Yes. You must have thought I was stupid, telling you not to worry, and you'd know I was a liar if I said I'm not worried, so I won't waste more time on phony business like that. I am worried, and you must be as well, and that's all there is to it. But I do want you to know that we may not be able to pray, but I'm aiming every ounce of strength and will I have in your direction. And you know, I believe that counts for something."

As does Dr. Grant. "So do I." So she does: Madeleine's own formidably honed, undiluted and disciplined will—nothing to mess with, a powerful weapon on Isla's side.

"And afterwards, I'll be here to help. You'll have some work to do then, and I'll do anything at all that I can." Her little teeth are gritted, her faded eyes glitter. "I've wished a hundred times I could trade places with you, but after a while that's just self-indulgent, and a waste of energy. So since we can't do that, I'll do anything else. Whatever gets you back on your feet."

Ignited, this is a fierce energy, Madeleine's. She sparks and radiates, her little body looms huge in its silvery, goldeny, deep-bluey will. Those colours cannot be visible; Isla sees them anyway. Bert once called Madeleine a "hot little number," which Isla found peculiar and possibly disrespectful and which put a small dent in her affection for him. This might be what he meant, though, what he was seeing.

"Thank you. I've been so lucky you're my mother."

"Hardly. But we all do our best, don't we?"

Some do, some don't.

"And this will go by. It won't be easy, but you'll do it." Madeleine is saying reassuring words, but her real and hard, true meaning is in her eyes, which are saying, *You shape up, you get through this.* "Now I'm going, but I will see you very soon. And you will be fine." Each word is separate and distinct and determined; no mere "catch you later," but a promise, and a demand. One more time she places her palm hard and firm on Isla's forehead, and when she leaves Isla is under the impression that she has been scorched by her mother's hot touch, and her magnified gaze.

Could she really, truly, be seeing these people for the last time? She can't take this in. She knows, but the information dazes, it blinds, it is impossible; although possible.

"Mum?" she hears from the doorway; Jamie's voice, naturally. They have organized these moments of privacy, they must have: a chart regulating potential last words. The luxury of careless, or even carefree, conversation has vanished, and so—what words does Jamie bring? Her children are unnerving, they require gearing up for. Look at Alix and her desire to spend time, perfectly good, precious time, with the insignificant-in-the-world author of this small, barely remarkable, hardly noticeable-to-the-world personal tragedy. Also Alix's leap into freedom, that announcement as well. Isla's children, her tilted, aslant offspring, are prone to springing surprises. Like kids on tiptoe trying to slip out of a sleeping household, knowing perfectly well the need for alertness and caution, they trip, stumble, knock over lamps. They are often clumsy; or just inattentive.

Jamie settles into that bedside chair, and like Dr. Grant leans into the railing, hovering close. The resemblance, this near, is a good deal less marked. "You know," he begins. "how grateful I am you stuck by me, and I'm sorry about causing so much trouble." He's said that often enough before, it hardly needs repeating now.

"The whole mess took a big chunk out of my life, though"— hers too, she would say, not to mention Lyle's, but anyway—"so I'm running behind most people my age. I knew I didn't want to spend my life at a flower shop, but I guess I was taking a while to figure out how to make a change. But now it feels like I better get moving. I mean, all this," and he waves his arm overhead in a wide gesture so much like Alix's he might have caught it, like measles, from her, "it makes you think." Think what, that life is short, or uncertain? That shit happens? Awful shit, good shit, what?

"So I thought you'd like to know that Lyle says he'll help me find out what courses I still need, or if I can just write high school equivalency exams, and then I think I'm going to apply to university. I don't figure," and he suddenly grins so brilliantly she can almost see her little boy again, the one with no lines, no shadows, no sorrows yet and no crimes, "all that experience should go to waste. It should be worth something. So I think I'd like working with people in trouble. Addicts, maybe. Stuff I've talked about but I never got off my ass before. I figure I better. It's time."

A clean sweep, evidently, a full hundred per cent of her children achieving epiphanies from, it seems, just standing around looking at her. She may not have been an entirely good or wise mother, but she certainly seems to have turned, lately, into a useful one.

As with Alix abandoning Serenity, if not serenity, she says, "That's very good news." And "I'll help you any way I can." The opportunity may, after all, arise. And, once again, "I'm very proud of you, Jamie."

"Thanks. I wanted you to know, anyway." Just in case. "And I'm proud of you, too, Mum. I can't even imagine how hard this is, but you hang in real good. Kind of an example, if that doesn't sound stupid."

"Not to me. I don't mind at all."

He frowns. "Can you stand a little bit more news?"

Oh dear. Maybe not.

"Because I don't know if you want to hear this, but Dad asked me to tell you he's thinking of you."

Dad. Jesus Christ. Why wait for surgery when the heart can slam closed any moment, when your own child will first lull it, then take a hammer to it?

"Well," he goes on apologetically—she must be staring with quite a noticeable ferocity—"he asked me to tell you. I promised I would. Anyway, I thought I should."

Yes, what a shame, if she'd slipped off into her death-or-life-or-paralyzed-or-crippled-or-totally-healed tomorrow, without thinking of James. What an omission.

Then again—what exactly is shocking? Only, maybe, that this comes out of the blue. That Jamie is in touch with his father, for one thing. Then that he calls him *Dad*, as if he could just as easily toss him a beer, put a hand on his shoulder, give him a tie or barbecue tongs for father's day, talk about prospects and women and jobs.

Like a normal son, with a normal father.

Other than that, his words sink slowly in and she finds her heart, having briefly leaped and thudded and banged—not her real heart, she has no idea what it's doing, but the heart in her head, the one susceptible to shock—rising slowly to meet them, settling finally into a kind of wonder: James. That doesn't feel so bad. The name doesn't hurt that much.

Well, her concerns at the moment are rather larger than one long-lost, well-lost husband. Also it's been a decade, for heaven's sake, ten whole years of intervening events. Still, it seems as if there is as well some larger sort of release. Something similar to the way Alix described events in the courtroom, looking at that boy and feeling hatred and anger and vengeance lifting right out of her, through her skin, off her shoulders, drifting away.

Relief.

Jamie looks very anxious; no doubt afraid he's made a godawful blunder.

"You talk to him?" That does amaze her, that they might be in touch; after everything, so much harm.

"Not really. Not very often. But, you know, he phones Grandma and Grandpa, and one day a few years ago I was over there when he called. Grandma just handed me the phone and there he was. So yeah, we said a few words then." Isla's ex-in-laws, yes, still holding out, as best they can, for their son's essential innocence.

As Isla has held out for Jamie's essential innocence.

"How are they? His parents?" What a swift and thorough amputation that long side of life underwent, once disaster started its roll. How brutally unsentimental she must have been.

Although they would not have welcomed her.

"Grandpa's pretty deaf and his arthritis slows him down, but what's really sad is his mind. He doesn't even know who I am a lot of times any more. Grandma's cool, though, except it's hard for her to look after him. I go there sometimes to help out. Mow the lawn, have a coffee, keep her company for a little while. Try to cheer her up."

Isla probably knew that. She often forgets her children have these other private lives and tasks, and larger attachments, bigger families, their own different loyalties. Alix's Serenity Corps doesn't count in the scheme of these things, and Jamie's various crimes didn't, either. Those have been her children's addictions, but their loyalties and attachments have been more enduring.

"It would have been rude not to take the phone when she handed it over," Jamie goes on explaining. "It's not like I called him, or wanted to talk to him."

"It's all right. I know. How is he? What's he doing?"

"I guess he's okay. He sounds all right. I don't know, how much do you want to hear?"

"Oh, some medium amount, I expect." She tries smiling. "Enough for the basics, not so much it takes more time than I can spare."

"Thanks, that really helps." But he smiles back. "But if you're sure—he's living in a little town out in the Rockies now. He has a computer store, nothing like before, but he says he makes a living. He sounds, I don't know, kind of settled in. Old. Remember how he always used to be so intense about the business, flying all over the place? Not like that any more.

"And then," he pauses, "I don't know if you want to hear this, either, or maybe you already know, but he got married again."

Whoof, there goes that heart again. Although not banging so high or hard this time, and just for a moment. "No, I didn't know. When did he do that?" As if *when* matters. Like *where*, it's hardly one of a person's key questions.

"A few years ago. Five, maybe."

Five years ago, remarried Isla was still learning relaxation and trust in Lyle's arms, Jamie was still tangled in his swamp of troubles, and Alix was soon to embark on her quest for serenity. Or Serenity. "Did you know?"

"Yeah. I'm sorry. I didn't think you wanted to hear anything about him. Grandma even wanted me and Alix to go out west with them to the wedding, but we didn't."

What a family for secrets, what a family for lies. An inherited gift, perhaps, or only a need handed down, like heirloom silverware and the best furniture. "Alix knew, too?"

"Yeah. I didn't give a particular shit, but she did for some reason." Perhaps James's newish wife was only Alix's age? Since those were his tastes, after all: young, untried, budding flesh.

"Do they have children?"

"Gosh, no, she already has grown-up kids." And so Isla sees that some part of her was hoping James was prey right to his bones of his own foolish desires. And she sees that some part of herself is disappointed, and strangely, stupidly hurt, that this is not the case.

It makes what happened to them more personal, she supposes; more to do with her, or the two of them together, than she has come to believe.

Neither her fault nor her responsibility, but still personal.

Also that her children have been so terrorized by her and her fury that they have kept every morsel of news about him all this time to themselves. And that even now, even at this last minute, Alix still does.

"How did he hear about me?"

"Grandma read about it in the papers, and then I told her, anyway. And she told him, I guess. He called Lyle's, I talked to him there. And he said to say hi, and he's thinking of you and wishes you well, and," Jamie shrugs, "that's about it."

Sure is.

"Did I upset you? Should I have kept quiet about him?"

"No. No, I don't think so. You did the right thing. When you're talking to him again, tell him hello for me."

"Really?" Jamie looks astonished, as well he might.

"Really. You might tell him I'm thinking now that at least we both had a run at second chances. Sometimes it must get too late for that, but it wasn't for either of us." And she can hope the girls he assaulted feel as benevolently about the opportunities he offered them. Thrust upon them. This is all very well and detached and long-viewed for her—learning serenity at this late date, is she?—but he's the one who did something terrible. "Is he sorry, do you think?"

"I don't know. We haven't talked much about any of that. It's hard, on the phone. But you'd think he'd have to be, wouldn't you?"

Yes, you would. "Perhaps you could ask. You can say things, you know, you have a right to ask questions."

Don't ask anything you don't want the answer to. There's that about it, too.

"Maybe, but I'm not real interested. He really fucked up, and I don't think I'm much into forgiveness."

"Me neither, probably." And this is also more or less true. A successful lift-off of anger, packed, formed, and real, hurtling up through the atmosphere to explode far enough away it can cause no more great harm here below—that's not the same thing at all as forgiveness. Like hatred, forgiveness requires investment, it needs constant tending.

Even indifference sounds easy and light, insignificant, but it is not.

Sighing seems the appropriate gesture, the right sound for indifference. Jamie naturally misunderstands. He frowns. "You tired, Mum? I don't mean to wear you out. I know you're supposed to be keeping your strength up."

"No, I'm fine. I'm happy you're here."

"Should I have told you before?"

"Probably not. This was a good time. I'm more in the mood now than I might have been."

That blank dark wall comes closer by the second, and what happens in the event of collision? Alix packs up her Serenity dresses and attends jail visiting hours, Isla supposes, and Jamie heads off to school. Madeleine clings to Bert, Lyle mourns and moves on. More weathered, perhaps, and certainly wearier, but he's done it before.

While James leans back in his Rocky-mountain recliner and nips at his Scotch and says, "That's too bad. That's a shame." And maybe thinks, "She should have believed, she should have been loyal, she should have stood by me, no matter what."

If she had, everything would be different. For one thing, she wouldn't have been buying ice cream with Lyle, and her sighs would have had a much different quality, not to mention intent. She could have become quite a martyr to contempt and loathing by now.

Instead she has had another life: caressing and arguing with Lyle, picking up and putting down books, flowers, towels, doing laundries and dishes, cooking meals and eating them across the kitchen table from each other, curling on sofas and beds and in front of the fireplace, apart or together, weeding gardens, mowing lawns, bringing in wood, taking out trash, all of that, on and on.

And then she stepped lightly, unwarned, off that porch. She was even laughing, so was Lyle, as she climbed into the truck. Why didn't they consider what a treat it would be to sit on their own sweeping porch, feet propped side by side on their own spindled railing, looking out over their own shadowed land, eating their own ice cream in the dusk and congratulating themselves on being able to hope for much the same for the next thirty years?

That's the moment that needs rewinding, right there. Not an earlier one.

"Thank you," she tells Jamie, so emphatically that he looks slightly puzzled by the cause for large gratitude.

"I'm kind of relieved it's okay."

"I know. But it is."

"Then," and he stands, "I'm going to take off too now. Maybe by the next time I see you, I'll have some courses lined up. Or exams. Something figured out, anyway." He bends, like Madeleine, like Alix, presses his lips briefly to her forehead. Eyes closed, she tries to memorize the impression. "It's going to go fine, Mum. You be well, and don't worry." And he is gone.

People bring their own gifts. Like a birthday: big surprises, and a few bright things of value.

Not least of them, hope that her children's lives have been saved. They will fail now and then, their hearts may get broken by one thing or another, but they should be immunized against their own worst, deepest illnesses. Having gotten the most dangerous out of the way, they can now be more alert than most people to the true, bone-deep confusions and threshings they're capable of. No small knowledge, that.

If, if, if she gets her body back, that possibility which is too dazzling to dwell on, so bright she can't open her eyes to it, but if—she must try to remember this sharpness, compression, vitality of impression. Like Alix's lips, Jamie's lips, Madeleine's hand. Because it's easy to forget; in much the way she forgets how a floor felt under her feet, or how her wrists could turn in the simple, taken-for-granted moment of writing a list, pulling a weed from the garden, touching a hand, or a thigh—all of that vague and theoretical now.

Also remarkable. Imagine being able to do those things!

Imagine skin. The state of organs, bones, muscles, nerves, may be more perilous and probably should be more worrisome, but it's skin that seems to her most miraculous, and therefore most lost. What can she do if she cannot touch and cannot be touched?

Now here is Lyle's skin, rough and stubbled and anxious, here are his palms and fingertips on her hair, tender comfort, there is that narrow mouth, and also behind it the hidden, solacing tongue. But she cannot remember exactly his skin. She has lost and forgotten the nerve-ends and deep ragged breaths of desire.

"Hi," he says. "Pretty soon, huh? You scared?"

The others come with their various answers, assurances, pledges, assessments, promises; Lyle brings the question. This is part of his skin, knowing that this good question has to be put into the air.

Scared? Oh yes: fireworks of terror, landmines of fear, chaotic suspense. Is *suspense* too mild, does it apply only to bad thrillers and pulse-racing flicks? No, suspense is the pure dry ice of not knowing. Heart-stopping. "I am terrified. And I don't even know what to hope for."

"Oh, but that's obvious, don't you think? Because we can work with life. As long as you're alive, we can always figure out ways to do that."

Not only the good question, the good answer, as well. Is he not frightened now of vast promises, though?

"How about you?"

"Am I scared? Jesus yes, I've been petrified since the second I heard that shot. I don't think there's been a moment since then I haven't been scared. Even in my sleep. Even my dreams are scary." They've had so little time to themselves, just the two of them, and perhaps too much of it has been spent being more brave than honest. He is a man whose inclination is to act, to fix, to do something or other that changes any impossible circumstance. "Also, very fucking angry. You?"

"I was. I may be again, but right now it seems dangerous. More likely to harm me than anyone else."

"You talked to Alix."

"Yes. She startled me."

"What did you think?"

"Of her plans? I couldn't be happier she's leaving that wretched cult. I don't know how to feel about what she thinks she sees in that boy. Except I guess," and she grins up at Lyle, "one of us should be researching forgiveness, and she's certainly the most promising candidate." He smiles too, and reaches out to stroke her hair again. No flinch this time. "What do you dream?" she asks. She has not been dreaming, herself, as far as she knows; although it's possible that with the drugs, she may have hallucinated now and again.

"You really want to know? A lot of times I dream about being paralyzed. Is that tasteless? Does it offend you? I dream about trying to move, run, fight, escape, all that. Then I wake up drenched. I think that's because of the helplessness. And then I wonder how you can bear it."

"I can't."

She could not, she thinks, have said just that to anyone else.

"Not much longer. Hang in a little bit longer."

Yes. But then what? "You know, if you didn't hang in yourself, I wouldn't blame you. If it all got too hard."

How startling, shocking, the sudden sound of full, head-back laughter, a great gorgeous, joyous Lyle-whoop she hasn't heard for quite a while now. "What, you mean if I did a bolt, you wouldn't blame me? Oh, Isla, that is such bullshit. You shouldn't even try to bullshit me that way."

She laughs, too; at least makes her small gaspy sound of amusement.

"Okay, no bullshit: eight blessed years. Thank you."

"Me, too. But also nicely flawed, those years, don't you think? We don't want rosy glows."

"Certainly not. No rosy glows."

"So no bullshit, no rosy glows, I want to tell you, I want you to know, I can't imagine my life without you. I'm so goddamn glad I met you. Just that. And I didn't expect it, so it's even more of a miracle."

Exactly. Her, too. That stupid, careless kid. Taking potshots at miracles, blowing holes right through love.

"So now you know I'm not bolting, you know what I'd like?"

"What?"

"I'd like to stay here. Just talk through the night. Maybe fall asleep in the chair. Hold your hand—I know, I know, you can't feel it, but I can—and just talk. And not talk. Till the cows come home."

"Or the orderlies come."

"Same thing."

"A last night together?"

"No, just a night. I don't know about you, but I don't want my dreams, and I don't feel like one of those godawful wide-awake dark nights of the soul. I just want to hang out with you. But if you want to be on your own, just tell me, no bullshit."

Well, he's right, she might have wanted to be alone, to get her own house in order; but it's unlikely there's any tidy packing up and neat preparing for the unimaginable and ungovernable.

Who knew it would come down to hours, then minutes, then—what?

"I'd like that." She looks up into his wounded, anxious, kind eyes. "I don't know what would have become of me without you, and I can't think of a better companion for any night, but this night in particular."

She thinks it's possible their shared, large and small, brutal and beautiful and ordinary events, put into words and stories offered up to the darkness, could grow by morning into a sturdy, protecting, safe shelter. That whatever happens then, tonight they can make something from all their eight years of bits and pieces, discarded, forgotten or cherished or only dreamed of, or still hoped for. Each word a brick. "Do you remember rain?" she begins. Because rain takes them back to the start.

Salvation, like anything else, mainly comes, she imagines, in small measures like this. She also imagines he's holding her hand, which she expects is a fine thing to be doing, and would feel astonishing.

Belles Lettres

NOT A WHOLE LOT OF MAIL comes to people in jail, but some of what does come is juicy. Darryl gets letters from some girl in his old neighbourhood and at night in their cell, reads them out loud to Roddy. "Man," he says, "you know, she's only fourteen? Like, she was maybe eleven, she didn't even have tits or anything last time I saw her, and listen to this." He rhymes off a couple of paragraphs that have to do with different things she and Dare could do with her breasts. "Christ, they gotta be huge," Dare says. Roddy gets hard just listening to how she imagines Dare could put himself between them and come. He also remembers, though, on his first night, Dare talking about the previous cellmate who jerked off six times a night. Except he hears Dare himself jerking off later, when they're supposed to be sleeping.

Sex is weird in here. Some other kind of stuff goes on, he guesses it's bound to, but otherwise it's mainly guys blowing off steam, like Dare, or Roddy for that matter, in the middle of the night, or getting all glaze-eyed in the steam of the showers, soaping themselves up and off right in front of everybody, and then everybody whoops and makes jokes, because there's no room for privacy anyway.

Well, Roddy too. There's a kind of getting used to things. Also there's no stopping it, or himself.

If everything hadn't gone wrong, if Goldie's had worked, if they'd taken off finally, him and Mike, and found that glassy two-bedroom place in a city high-rise, and gone prowling like they talked about, it could have been happening for real: real breasts, real thighs, real skin, real other, glorious, foreign places. He'd be unstoppable. He is unstoppable. He's seventeen, for Christ's sake.

At least Darryl used to know, or has at least met, that one girl who writes him. He and some other guys get letters from total strangers, too, sexy invitations, but also with questions, and often promises. The funny thing is, the ones who get letters from girls they don't know are the ones who've done the worst crimes: murder, rape, 'way worse than Roddy. If it wasn't for Dare, he probably wouldn't even know that. Most of those guys are tough, or appear to be, and they don't talk much except to each other, and they're watched pretty carefully anyway, and a few of them spend a lot of time completely alone, because they're either dangerous or plain bad, hard to say.

It's just that Dare's been here a while, and he's one of them in a way, and he does tell Roddy things sometimes. If they weren't in the same cell, he probably wouldn't have anything to do with Roddy. Armed robbery isn't a big deal here. Although actually shooting somebody counts for something. Roddy's in a strange kind of position, sort of in the middle of things but cautiously, as much as he can manage, also off to one side.

He's for sure not a rapist, and he's not a murderer even if he came close, and he can't figure out why anybody'd write to somebody who was, especially if they didn't know them. Dare shrugs. "Takes all kinds. Some of them, you know, they'll come in handy later on."

When guys get out, he means. Roddy gathers that some of these girls are offering everything. "They sound kind of dumb," he ventures.

"Well, yeah." Dare speaks as if Roddy's stupid himself.

Then there are volunteers, who aren't stupid, most of them, but—who goes into a jail on purpose? Some of them are hard to put up with because they're all filled up with virtue and want to pass it on, it feels like, to the wicked. Well, maybe that's not fair, but it's how it feels when they sit down in the rec hall without being asked and interrupt TV or whatever to talk about courses, or careers, or some self-improvement program or religion they've got a bug about, or to give different kinds of advice, or ask really rude questions, like about guys' families and crimes and "How do you *feel* about this," or "How did it *feel* when you did that?" The other kind of volunteers may say the same sorts of things, but they've got a different look in their eyes. Like they want something back besides virtue.

They're almost always women, not men, and what's that about? The guards don't like the two days a week the volunteers come in, they get all tensed up, which Roddy guesses makes sense considering what could happen if one of the volunteers, or one of the guys, made a wrong move. What the volunteers, who get some training and are screened before they're allowed in, are supposed to do is talk about futures, and give some kind of idea of normal life in a normal world, and maybe help out with schoolwork. Mainly they don't, as far as Roddy can see. Mostly they're not very pretty, either, or very young.

They can't possibly know that after they leave, the guards are angrier and more impatient than other days, and the guys laugh and make jokes. Like Dare says, if you can zero in on the right kind of volunteer, just like the right kind of letter-writer, and feed her the right kind of line, life's suddenly easier because there's gifts coming in like money or clothing or food, although not in some underhand way, everything's supposed to get approved before it's passed on. "You gotta do it," Dare encourages, "you gotta be able to, like, trade shit and have something to offer. And anyway."

And anyway, it's something to do, like a game. In return for various promises, and besides real and useful things in their hands, guys pick women to write letters to, and win plenty of promises back: offers of jobs for when they get out, or of places to stay, or of protection or safe-keeping, or even of love.

"What a joke," Dare says.

He also says, "Get in there, make a move. It's easy. Just make like you've had a lot of bad times and you want to change everything from now on, and watch what happens. They all want to save somebody. You should be a good guy, give them a chance. Shit, at least then you'd get mail." Because of course nothing comes to Roddy, not even magazines. He guesses he could subscribe to something. And he could do what Dare says, get hooked up with somebody outside. He knows Dare's right, that it's easy. That doesn't mean he knows how to do it.

Then he does get mail. One slim envelope for him among three for Darryl, dropped off in their cell at the end of a day, as mail is regularly delivered, a high point for Dare, anyway, often enough a prelude to his semi-private night-time delights.

Roddy doesn't recognize the handwriting on his, so maybe it's starting to happen: some strange woman writing.

But "Dear son," it begins. Well, no reason he'd recognize his dad's handwriting, why would he? Nobody he knows of writes letters. This one's real short, all scrawled on one page. "Dear son, I'll be driving up to see you with your grandmother one of these days pretty soon, but thought I'd drop you a line. Guess we've had a few wrong turns along the way, I don't know, but I'm sorry about everything, anyhow. When you get out, maybe we could go someplace the two of us for a few days. You could think about where. I'm sorry how things worked out, hope you're doing okay where you are. You're a smart kid, and not bad, just made a bad mistake. Anyhow, I'll be seeing you soon, but think about plans. Just wanted to send a line or two along to say, Good wishes and all best to you, Dad."

Not exactly a big outpouring of sentiment.

But also, it really is. For his dad to write a letter at all is amazing. Roddy reads it over and over, looking for clues, hunting for meaning or tenderness or some clear intention even between lines, before he tucks it inside the front of his math text. It's like every sentence says something different. One doesn't totally lead to another. Never mind. The point is, his dad meant to say something, a shock all by itself.

Would Roddy want to go someplace with his dad? Imagine the silences, and what would they do with so many hours? He doesn't think his dad really means it anyway, or wouldn't if the time ever came. He's just, like, putting his hand out, kind of offering to shake.

When his dad comes to visit, maybe they'll talk about it; although more likely not.

"Got a chick going there?" Dare asks, raising his eyes from a page of one of his own letters.

"My dad."

"Bummer. Listen to this, it's from Kitty. 'I can come on a dime, so anything you want, it'll be fine with me. I remember how you always went looking so cool. So anything, I mean it. Use your imagination.' Jesus Christ." Dare looks up. "Fourteen's illegal, isn't it?"

"Doesn't sound like she cares."

"Yeah, but I might. No, I wouldn't. Fourteen sounds prime."

But if she's so prime, how come she writes hot letters to a guy in jail for knifing somebody to death? Even if, before, she was a little kid with a crush, now wouldn't she look at Dare's hands on her and wonder at what they've done? Even Roddy can look at them and picture them thrusting, blood-splashed, and he's sure not planning to have them anywhere on his body.

Of course he can look at his own hands and wonder at them, too.

What people, parts of people, can do: be loyal to a friend, for instance, and kind to a dog, and wide open to the beauties of bugs and wildlife and air, and deadly, near-deadly, with a knife or a gun. Cut off the small bad parts, like a bruised apple, and what's left is just ordinary, not remarkable, mainly good.

Darryl is here for a bad hand, Roddy for one faulty finger. Not fair. Not the whole story.

Another day, same hour and way, after breakfast, after classes, after lunch, after kitchen duty, after shower, after wood-working, after dinner (meat patties, peas, potatoes peeled and cut by his very own hands), after an hour in rec hall watching a game show, the kind that tests the desire to get the answer first and sometimes works out that way, after getting herded with the others back to the cells for, supposed to be, an hour or two of homework and studying or whatever—then the mail comes, with another letter for Roddy.

Something more from his dad? No, it's a different handwriting on the plain white envelope, which has no return address. Not his grandmother's, either, he knows hers from shopping lists, notes for school, notes left on the kitchen table telling him where she is, reminding him about this and that. Maybe Mike. That'd be amazing. What would he have to say? He's sorry? He's got plans to bust Roddy out? He's grateful, and hopes Roddy will still be his friend?

Roddy's nervous about opening it, excited as well.

"Dear Rod," he finds inside, on a sheet of plain white paper like the envelope, but typed, not like the envelope. It doesn't look personal. And it isn't from Mike.

"I hope you remember me. I was in court with my stepfather when you pleaded guilty, and then by myself when you were sentenced. You may remember I spoke. I don't know what's a fair sentence, but I hope you are doing well with what you were given.

"Anyway, I thought both times when I saw you in court that I would like to meet you. Don't worry that I want to yell at you or be angry or anything. I don't. I just thought we might find some good things to talk about. So I would like to visit you. Are you surprised? I thought I could come Sunday the 18th, what do you think? I hope you will think it's all right, but I'll understand if you don't. It might seem like a strange idea, but I've thought about it and I don't think it's so strange, and I hope if you think about it, you'll decide it's all right. If I don't hear from you, I will come during visitors' hours on that day. If you don't want me to, please let me know, you can call collect, here's my number."

It's signed, "All my best, Alix," then in brackets afterwards, "Starglow."

He stares and stares at the thing. Is it real? Is she?

Her words look to him, like her eyes, calm, cool, and deep. He doesn't know what good things they could talk about. What did she see in him? What does she want?

Is it anything like what he could want?

Probably not.

He reads and reads this letter, sitting on the edge of his bed, hunched, scrutinizing, oblivious to Darryl a few feet away on his own bed, with his own mail. Roddy tries to see into each word, tries to put her gentle, absorbing tones from the courtroom to the tune of the few paragraphs in his hands.

He likes that she calls him Rod. He wonders what the *Starglow* is about.

He wonders what he could possibly say to her; besides *I'm sorry*, which he has already said, and doesn't change anything, and couldn't possibly be her purpose for coming here anyway. She says she isn't angry and does not want to yell. Perhaps she'll do all the talking and he can just listen, just look, just fall back into her eyes.

What is she expecting to see? What if she takes all that trouble and time to come all the way up here, and go through the hassles of visiting, the search, the metal detectors, the guards' eyes that are somehow both wary and bored, and finally sits down across from him and looks at him and thinks, "Oh no, this was a mistake. This was a waste of my time. This isn't what I thought I remembered."

There was something, though. He believed it, and if she saw it too, it has to be true.

Imagine not saying anything about her mother, imagine seeing past that! Maybe she can see past anything, then.

Sunday the eighteenth. From nothing, from just getting by, to one plain white sheet of paper, to a real girl, woman, coming to see him—this is no one to make fun of and nothing to laugh about. Or to use. He won't be talking about her with Darryl, for sure, or anyone else. This is like magic. Nobody'd believe it. They'd look for the joke, or the trick.

Is there one? No, couldn't be. She isn't like that, and neither is he. She saw him in court the same way he saw her: as if they should know each other. Like there was something between them that could make all the difference.

For the longest time, nothing good happens to him and then, suddenly, something good does.

Various Monstrosities

L YLE IS MOWING THE LAWN, back and forth, back and forth. He's wearing blue jeans but some time ago took off his shirt, so that the golden summery tinge of his chest and back has begun shading to red. He keeps his eyes focused downwards as if mowing the lawn were the most demanding of tasks, requiring his entire attentiveness.

Still, now and then in the process of turning and heading back in the direction he's come from, he looks up to smile, or to make a small friendly gesture.

In advance of today's gathering, Lyle gets to spruce up the grounds and Isla gets to soak up the day's warmth and its many manifestations and shadings of green. The sweet scent of newly cut grass combined with gasoline fumes has to be one of the world's finer smells. Too, the fumes create a hovery, hazy effect in the heat as Lyle and the mower make their patient, slow, thorough way back and forth, back and forth.

The smell of gasoline means movement to her, going someplace.

Well, here she is. That's going someplace. To be sitting again on this porch off which, more than a year ago she light-heartedly, mistakenly stepped, that's a very long journey.

If a circular one.

She has been waiting for this very scene. Her picture of this sunshine, this greenery, this prospect and perspective, as it now finally appears on this August afternoon, has been her private reward, her lure, her temptation, her desire, for months. And now, here she is. She hadn't pictured some of the details exactly, like the old shades-of-blue woolly afghan tucked around her knees, keeping her legs from the sunburn they wouldn't be able to feel any more than they can feel the warmth of the wool. She hadn't taken that sort of thing into account. But looking out and away from herself, the view is precisely what she held in her mind's eye.

Finally she has one thing she wanted and, moreover, deserves.

She is settled in here again. She has learned that the mind often likes to have its thoughts reflected by the body; so when it says *settle in*, it intends the body to show, with a certain shifting of hips, how that's done.

When, long ago, she rose up out of warm dreaming drugs and into, again, a vision of anxious, kind faces, it was, as she muzzily saw it, another moment out of a very old movie: melodrama or horror, it wasn't clear which. In this movie a new face—it's always a face—is being unwrapped, a new person in some way emerging. There has been surgery, performed out of vanity (in which case it goes badly) or to repair some mutilation (in which case it most likely goes well), but the main thing is the moment when everyone gathers to see the results.

The head is wrapped in layers and layers of white gauze. Slowly, slowly the long winding bandage is unfolded, unwound. The camera moves from the watched to the watchers, recording their stunned, wordless response, giving nothing away. Finally, in a mirror, the camera seeing now through the eyes of the patient, the new face is revealed. Lips widen in rapturous smile. Eyes widen in shock. Whichever. It's a big moment.

Those old movies didn't generally venture too far into the aftermath. Isla quite sees their point.

Dr. Grant appeared overhead, but by then she already knew.

She could feel her shoulders on the sheet, her spine rippling down the mattress, her arms, her curled fingers. Some of those fingers were curled into a hand. Long fingers, strong grip, slightly roughened skin, therefore Lyle's. Madeleine, on the other side, was stroking her forearm. This was altogether a miracle. To feel!

Therefore to move; although not yet.

There were her lungs, pumping; her heart, beating; her blood, she could almost feel the blood slipping warm through her arms to her fingertips, and along the multitude of small venous trails winding in complicated ways around her ribs' sturdy, flexible structure. All those nearly lost places.

But. Thereafter, the no weight, no sensation of all parts below. It was oddly difficult to distinguish the precise endpoint. Somewhere around her hips, as near as she could tell. She looked up into Dr. Grant's face and thought that like half her body, he was erasing sensation, expression. Watching hers, though, assessing it.

"So you see," he began. "Good news and bad news."

"Yes, I do see," she agreed.

A half measure, then. One of fate's, or God's, or mere chance's little compromises. She had thought, mainly, death or life, kill or cure. She hadn't very closely examined half-life, partial result, semi-cure. Just one goddamn time, and this would have been a good one—oh, anger flared up, she could feel anger quite well—she would like a total, complete, one-hundred-per-cent measure of something. Something good, of course, was what she meant; total disaster being strangely common in the world. Look at people fleeing starvation, rape, war, who have lost everything—there's total disaster on both large and personal levels. So obviously that's possible. Why not total joy?

Now what? "Now what?" she asked. To feel Lyle's fingers holding hers was a magic thing, to understand Madeleine's fingers stroking her arm also was, and to know that with some effort she could embrace Jamie and Alix, both of them hanging back, both of them watchful, undecided. But she was not, right at that moment, grateful. "Now what?" was an accusation, and intended to be.

"Now you have a lot of work to do, and a lot of good things to look forward to. Now you're far, far better off than you were a few days ago. Although I do realize it's not everything you hoped."

No shit.

Work, yes. Weeks and weeks, month upon month of it. *Rehabilitation*, that sterile, unfreighted word that amounted, mainly, to anguished learning of new tricks, compensating ways of hauling herself up, down, and along. Boring *and* painful, an especially unfortunate combination. Praise for finally pulling herself upright with a tight grip on parallel bars, and dragging herself along them a very short way purely with the new rippling, tensing, surprising powers of her arms, the happy applause from her trainers and dear Martin who was there at the time, was distressingly gratifying. She was, in truth, flushed with accomplishment. Later she wondered if that was just pitiful; but decided it wasn't, quite.

Very annoying, those legs, though. Eventually she could have whipped along fairly perkily without their dead weight.

Brave, daring Lyle had the tiny, trouble-making fragment of bullet set in a silver ring. "A souvenir of the wars," he called it as she opened the small velvety box, and looked relieved when she first laughed, and then smiled, and then placed the ring, gleaming dully, on her middle finger, right hand.

He has an odd, good touch with the celebratory and sentimental.

It's good, too, to be able to think of him again in terms of light touches; but what will he do, what has he been doing, for more adamant, ardent touches? That golden body out there mowing the lawn, back and forth, back and forth, is not one that goes unused easily. He told her long ago that in the several years between Sandy's death and meeting Isla, there was no one important to him but his sons. He didn't say, and he's a lawyer and speaks carefully about delicate matters, that there was no one in his bed, or his life, just not in his heart.

The rules of love, even if there are such things, alter. She has been the shocked survivor of this hard fact before.

He went to the hospital just about every day except when he was out of town for something to do with one case or another. Same when she was shifted to the rehab centre at the same hospital. Madeleine went almost every day, too, except for a few-week stretch when Bert got the flu and then she got it, too. Both she and Lyle learned the exercises Isla had to do, they were both taught how to help her.

Isla hasn't minded Madeleine raising and lowering her legs, bending and turning them; although Madeleine is obviously uneasy, scared of doing harm she can't predict or understand. Isla imagines it must be a lot like having a new infant in the house: constant assessments and cautious gaugings, as well as small triumphs. She hates to think of herself that way, but all this must surely seem somewhat familiar to a mother. At any rate, it doesn't seem totally unfitting to be helped and touched and manoeuvred by Madeleine.

Not by Lyle, though, and not by her children. Lyle should never even see her legs, or lift her, or wheel her or ever have to take her capacities and incapacities into account, although he has to, and does. To have as well her withering calves and thighs under his manipulating hands—no. Above all else she does not want to be his helpless child, his burden, his very own personal cripple.

Although she is all of that. He is attentive and has the wisdom also to just let her be; but he can't help it, neither can she, that balances have shifted.

That the unexpected word for this is *shame*.

It's different from being embarrassed. That has to vanish, or be bitten down on, or otherwise put out of mind, and she learned fast in the hospital, and again in rehab, that dependency is by definition immodest. Need instantly, flatly, overwhelms preference.

But *shame*—that's what swamped her in the moment, finally, of driving up the laneway, rounding that curve, seeing the place in full bloom, coming home just like that very first time with Lyle, years ago, except this time the kids had strung a huge red and white "Welcome home" banner between two porch pillars—in that moment of utter familiarity and absolute strangeness she glimpsed herself here again and felt shame: for no longer being the woman who marched capably around here on her own two feet, that woman who needed her loved ones only for love.

Now her needs are capacious. A physiotherapist is to come three days a week, for a while, to run her through her meagre paces, although many of the exercises Isla can now do on her own. She is committed, as in the rehab centre, to four half-hour sessions each day, raising and lowering herself from a bar, curling her arms, hands grasping weights, carefully shifting her head, up and down, back and forth.

Now her arms are taut and hard as metal, muscled and brown. They get stronger and more capable every day. In terrible contrast, her legs are shocking, remain shocking, become more shocking all the time, poor pale and skin-shrivelled hopeless things. She thinks if she were a sea creature, something sensibly designed along those lines, her useless legs would simply drop off. Humans are not so efficiently constructed, and so her legs, too, have to be exercised, the aim to sustain blood circulation, to stretch irrelevant muscles. So that, strangely enough, her legs don't have to be carved away somewhere down the line, atrophied and, moreover, diseased.

Also as Dr. Grant likes to say, you never know, fresh possibilities are always emerging. It's not, he insists, out of the question that these legs of hers will be of some use again someday.

One fine use would be wrapping them around Lyle's lean hips.

Now that she can feel his skin, she remembers desire, if in small, flickering ways. They seem to edge towards it now and again, but Lyle is careful, careful. Or tactful. Or unwilling.

The day before he brought her home, he said to her, as he did years ago in a quite different context, "Let's just relax and see how things go." He was leaning forward in his chair, knees touching her wheelchair, holding her hands, looking into her eyes with an expression she thought contained too much kindness, which she saw as forbearance. "We'll find our own ways, don't worry."

It was generous, what he said, and even probably true. But that still doesn't make it possible.

She also doesn't believe Dr. Grant. Or she has decided that what he said about hope has nothing in particular to do with her. She can't waste scarce hope on faint possibilities. It has taken months for her to retrain and redirect hope, so that it's becoming as taut, hard, metallic and muscled as her arms.

Diminished resources become monstrously precious.

She has been busy for months examining various monstrosities.

Now there are new ones, of a different sort, right in front of her, no avoiding them. A ramp, wooden and unweathered, swoops from the porch to the ground. Inside, Lyle has widened doorways to make way for her zoomy new wheelchair, what he calls "the sportscar model" for its lightness, manoeuvrability, and speed. He has refitted, carefully and capaciously, the bathroom downstairs so that it is now the very model of a spartan, gleaming washroom for the handicapped. She loathes the sight of it. He said he made a choice between converting a room downstairs into a bedroom or installing one of those chair-lifts on which she can ride up and down stairs, and decided on the latter. He custom-ordered it to blend with the house itself, with wooden arms and iron fretwork at the sides and a paisley cushion, but it is an ugly thing nevertheless, a blot on his wide, graceful staircase.

Those are the most obvious changes. Thanks to her practised, muscular arms, with concentration and care she can pull herself out of the wheelchair onto the sofa, or into bed. They can share a bedroom again. She can touch his skin in the night, and he can fold his arms around her. They cannot any more, though, fling themselves lavishly and fervently around one another, and there are things—*things* is how she thinks of them—that protrude from her body and perform various functions—*functions* is how she thinks of what they do—that cause her, and perhaps him as well, to do what is necessary to keep lower bodies apart.

It's early days. They are still circling new customs, devising new habits.

"It's a triumph for all of us, you know," Dr. Grant said, "that you can go home." Because if his surgery hadn't worked, if he hadn't restored some capacities, this would have been nearly impossible. Also if she hadn't worked so desperately, herself, all this would have been nearly impossible. She longed so hard for the picture that's in front of her now, so amazingly, vividly, perfectly real that it seems in some way unreal: the porch and its spindled railings, the gardens, the looming trees, the expanse of lawn Lyle, shirtless and golden, is methodically mowing.

Yes, she worked very hard for this. Yes, it was worth it. No, she would not want to be anywhere else.

Only, there is *shame*.

She tips her face up towards the sun. At this time of day, sunshine beams into the porch, lights it and heats it, and this moment, this very sensation, is what she longed for, precisely. She wanted air, she wanted colour, she wanted, to the extent that it's possible, to be free.

A year ago, if Lyle were mowing the lawn she'd be out crouched in the garden picking tomatoes or flowers or weeds. Or in the kitchen pouring beers for the two of them. Or taking a turn herself with the mower. The lawn is huge, but Lyle hasn't ever wanted one of those riding mowers because he says this one gives him needed exercise. Also contemplation time, since it's a dull job that needs to be done but leaves the mind open.

So what is he contemplating today, going back and forth under the sun?

In the old days they came home from their different, interesting careers, and outdoors they painted and trimmed greenery together, made gardens and repaired eavestroughs and sheds, and indoors they cooked, cleaned, played together. Without kids, household chores had a different quality than they used to, which was that they didn't feel so much like chores. They went for walks, too, down the lane, across the fields, just small outings, nothing strenuous, but also nothing she can contemplate now.

Oh. Something else. Sometimes on their walks, they have lain in the tall grains of one or another of their rented-out fields and made airy, cool love.

These stabbings of loss sneak up.

Well, they are bound to. She knew that. She just didn't realize how they'd keep startling her.

She is hardly seductive now, or desirable, with her limp limbs and various attachments, unwieldy, repellent. She is watching a man of considerable beauty mowing a lawn, and has a desire to stand and go to him and lean into his back, wrap her arms around his ribs, his chest, his whole miraculous self.

Except that it's a theoretical sort of desire, reclaimed from memory.

Anyway, making love is many things, many ways. Many feelings as well, of course.

When he shuts down the mower, the silence is abruptly immense. He pulls his shirt off a fence post and wipes off his sweat-shiny chest. He looks across green and blue space at her, smiles. She smiles back. Before, she might have gone with him indoors, upstairs, into the shower. They would have roughly, gently, scrubbed each other's apparent and hidden surfaces. They would have laughed, embraced this way and that, and maybe made their damp way to bed, bodies linked top to toe, happy impulse.

Today, going by her he pauses, touches her shoulder, says, "You okay?" and when she nods, continues indoors.

She's cried several times since she got home; quiet weeping, like now. Not wanting him to know the extent of her grief. How scared she is.

She saw this moment, on the porch in sunshine, but as a photograph, a still life, an achievement. Which it is, but it is also a narrow, hard-to-discern opening to something else.

Snap out of it.

This is a glorious day. And among the changes, those details Lyle has known to take care of, as opposed to the details they each have yet to discover, is a smooth poured-cement walkway at the bottom of the ramp, a fresh trail across the lawn to the lane and the new moss-green van, with its handicapped parking sticker, which she may hate but which of course comes in handy. Practical, competent, thoughtful, foresightful Lyle: simply doing these things, taking care of them in her absence.

The smooth concrete beckons. She's become a damn good wheelchair driver, deft on the corners and a devil on the downhill, actually found herself enjoying the rehab centre parking lot, wheeling about, testing manoeuvres. For the moment, she's on her own. In a moment she has tucked the afghan tight and turned the chair, so lightweight and sturdy, and hurtled pellmell down the ramp, flipping the switch for the motor, buzzing down, full-tilt, to the lane. Whirling at the end, buzzing full-tilt back. She is making her own breeze! This is fun. She'd like to travel a hell of a lot farther and faster, and one of these days she might learn to pop wheelies if that's possible in this thing, but meanwhile this is her on her own, having a whim.

Back and forth she goes, like Lyle with the lawn-mower, at each end of the walkway reversing and turning.

It begins to seem as if the laneway could be manageable. A small journey, not the whole way, but just a jaunt through a short distance of hard earth and gravel. Given patience and time and a decent surface, a person can go almost anywhere in a good wheelchair. She could go to town. She could travel deeper into the country. She supposes it's illegal to putter along the shoulders of expressways; otherwise she could really take off.

Just to do it; not to escape.

Okay, it's bumpy, and she has to go slowly, and keep her eyes on the ground to foresee ruts and large stones. Steering is certainly trickier on a rough surface, and probably a heavier wheelchair wouldn't bounce so capriciously. But how exhilarating, to be able to do this! To know she can get away, although she doesn't want to get away, just finds she very much likes knowing she can.

And can go back, too, when she wants. At the curve of the laneway she turns more slowly, cautiously, wary of the tilt of the land here, and stops. Here again is that first vision. Mutilated by ramp and walkway, yes, but that sturdy brick house, that embracing porch, those looming, sheltering trees. Well, home.

And Lyle now stepping out onto the porch, dressed up in khakis and blue shirt, hair plastered down from the shower, looking around, looking this way, starting to laugh when he catches sight of her, starting to wave.

She waves back.

This can work.

She throws herself into gear and hurtles cautiously forward. He steps off the porch. They meet on the new concrete path. She feels flushed and nearly triumphant. He looks, she thinks, impressed. It's interesting to feel impressive. She must have been used to that before, out in the wider world, but it's all new again to her now.

"Hey," he says, "making a run for it?"

It's also nice that they've pretty much given up worrying about any painful qualities attached to verbs. Like *run*. That was hard work, too, all that censoring, the flushing over some blunder or other. Observing embarrassment, not to mention observing her own sensitivities soaring a little too high. "Yup," she says. "Trying to figure out how far this puppy would go on one charge." Every night, once she's in bed, the chair gets recharged. This one's her starter model, with a second on order. She and Lyle are, as he says, very fortunate not to be poor. Well, she is fortunate, it's her money, that exceedingly comfortable sum she and Martin got from selling the agency, that's paying for home care, physio, wheelchairs. Lyle financed the house renovations. The loathsome bathroom alone cost a small fortune.

"I was thinking about getting all the way to the road, so I could really zoom. And learning to pop wheelies, do you know how that's done?"

"Not a clue. On a motorcycle, yes, that's how I fell off once when I was a kid, doing a wheelie and the bike and I both went flying. Mind you, that was accidental. I was actually trying to go straight and flat, and the thing just reared up on me."

"Were you hurt?" She's pleased there are still new moments of history to learn, that they're not running out.

"Nah, I was too startled to be hurt." Yes, that shock of things happening: a useful, momentary anaesthetic. She knows.

"But listen, you want to get yourself up here and start getting ready? They'll be coming along one of these hours."

To celebrate her coming home. Martin, and Lyle's sons, as well as Jamie and Alix, Madeleine and Bert. Lyle mowed the lawns, and hired a cleaning person to whip the inside into shape, and a caterer is bringing food, although there should only be nine or ten people, depending on whether Lyle's boys bring companions along. No doubt there will come a time when Isla will have figured out how to whip around the house, the kitchen, so competently and smoothly that with her and Lyle working together like the old days, a meal for ten will be a minor effort. Probably her only difficulty cleaning the house will become dusting the higher shelves. She will learn to trim low-slung shrubs, pick long-stemmed flowers. She and Lyle will find new rhythms for working and playing around here together.

But not today.

She likes that he doesn't offer to push her chair up the ramp. He doesn't *hover* like someone assuming she's gone either stupid or incompetent. To be honest, Madeleine hovers a little too much. Maybe it's finally age catching up. Maybe it's that Isla's her daughter. Still, she is coming early to help Isla get dressed.

Isla will, of course, be wearing a long, camouflaging, summery dress, one of the new ones that now mainly make up her wardrobe, this one beige with a pattern of small blue and yellow flowers, more elegant than some of the others. It's a style that comes close to Alix's old Serenity Corps outfits. Too bad Alix got rid of them, they might have been useful.

Jamie is supposed to be giving Alix a ride today, since she is far too poor to have a car. He has become so reliable that he risks sliding into a solidity that is almost alarming. Her children, Isla thinks, are not good at half measures, although since she has found she so much resents half measures herself, she can hardly be critical.

Alix is another story. Naturally. She appears to have flown from serenity straight into chaos. This is not exactly true, of course. Where she has gone is from the Serenity Corps into two-rooms-plus-bath in the depths of the city; from fresh air to grime; from a loopy spiritual quest to a loopy social one. But there again, that is just Isla's frivolous take on the subject. Her real and serious one is more respectful, if also leery.

Her children have taken up solemn pursuits. Jamie is studying, for the next three or four years, psychology, sociology, and various workings of the actual physical brain. No more flowers for him. He is pursuing his notion of working with drug addicts, but it now seems unlikely he would relapse, even in very bad company. And Alix, wispy Alix no longer wears transparent dresses, and has redirected her attentions from old criminals to young ones. Which is to say, from the nasty Master Ambrose to the nasty kid who shot Isla.

And those like him.

Isla tries to avoid thinking along the lines of frying pans, fires. Too easy, for one thing. Probably wrong, for another. Alix has found a voice and it turns out to be quite a determined, even loud one. As when it rang out one night on the TV news, in front of the government buildings, loudly protesting, along with an exceptionally scruffy-looking bunch of supporters, the closing of a particular service for law-challenged youth. "Look at that," Lyle said, leaning forward in Isla's rehab centre room. "Isn't that Alix?" So it was.

She visited that boy, Rod, every other weekend. "I'm trying to understand him," she explained; which Isla thought, but did not say, would have to be quite a project, understanding the young man who had shot her mother. "I know it sounds awful to say, but he's really kind of sweet in a way. He doesn't know *anything*." As if those were the same things. Naturally she met other people in the course of visiting him: families of young criminals, their girlfriends, some of the young criminals themselves, Rod's pals, presumably. "I want to know how these things happen," she said. And became shrewd, in her transparent way: "Because it's terrible, what happened to you. We should find ways to keep it from happening to anyone else."

Well, it didn't just happen, did it? Alix's sweet Roddy pulled a trigger, hardly a passive event. But yes, it would be a good thing if other sweet boys didn't pull further triggers on anyone else.

Alix earns a small living working in a youth job centre, finding training and work for the troubled. She also volunteers at a drop-in centre for street kids, although as Isla understands it, the boy who shot her was very far from being a street kid, was as close as damnit to being a bumpkin. She gives speeches in high schools and, for that matter, on street corners and in front of government buildings. She has become passionate on the subject of nipping crime in the bud.

"Because," she says, "if you're young, it can all look so *bleak*. Not enough jobs, too many stupid jobs, not much of a future. They need *dreams*. They need to want something for themselves, and a lot of times nobody really helps them find it. They need *hope*."

Yes. Well. In that, they would not be alone.

Is it significant that Isla's children have not, either of them, directed themselves towards the problems of the crippled, the paralyzed, those on the receiving ends of addicted or dream-deprived bullets?

It's alarming, even unnerving, how radically and swiftly Alix can shift her attentions. She didn't even return to the Serenity Corps farm to pack up the rest of her things, just because, she said, "there's nothing there that's important now."

"Is your Master Ambrose angry?" Isla asked. She rather hoped that he was. But Alix seemed puzzled.

"He doesn't get angry." Oh, really. "He'll know I've found my serenity my own way. And I know I wouldn't have been able to do it without him. He understands working through to the end of attachment."

Isla doubted it. She doubted abandonment was what Master Ambrose had in mind. "Good for you," she said drily. "Good for him." Alix, poor dumb bunny, looked pleased.

But she's not a poor dumb bunny at all, she's just stuck with a large, still-flailing heart. Isla worries about both Alix and Jamie, out there with dangerous, desperate people. They may not know quite how dangerous it is, neither of them having had a moment like Isla's in Goldie's; that delicate pas de deux of violence she danced with Roddy, Alix's young friend, her project, her cause.

Today's gathering was Jamie and Alix's idea: a celebration of their mother's various triumphs. Isla remembers a time when it was possible for celebrations to be unambiguous, but she has been so much the centre of attention the past year, unhappy attention, that its charms are now slight. The gesture itself, though, this business of a number of people making plans and arrangements so that they can be together in the same place at the same time on her behalf—that's really quite touching. Even Martin, who did go travelling after they sold the agency, and only got back from India a couple of days ago, will be here. Everyone will have stories to tell, it won't be a gathering dedicated entirely to congratulating and cosseting Isla.

She has another picture in mind. Many hours from now, she expects to look around the table, when everybody's leaning back in their chairs and there's a clutter of dirty dishes and spills, and dusk has descended and all the faces are shaded and shadowed, replete and relaxed, and be happy for this event. That it contains most of what's counted so far in her life.

Except for James, of course, and she can certainly live with his absence.

Otherwise, everyone who counts will be here. It'll be another memory-keeper sort of picture; like the one she had of sitting on this porch in the heat and light of the day, also come true.

How remarkable it is, looking forward to certain moments, anticipating with some hope certain events. She smiles at Lyle. "You're right, it's time. I'll just roll in and start getting ready. Mother should be here soon."

She can wheel right into the shower in the new downstairs bathroom, lift herself onto the shower seat, push the chair out although careful to keep it in reach, work the taps, shampoo her own hair; and she can do all this in private, with only the power of her own arms, a luxury she wouldn't even have noticed a year ago.

This is the sort of thing she needs to hold sharp in her mind. Not gratitude; but a respectful nod to partial blessings.

She hears the phone ring while she's in the shower. It remains odd to feel hot water pouring over half of her body, but only see it pouring over the rest. As if the rest of her belongs to somebody else.

Lyle comes to the door when she turns off the shower. "That was Alix. She'd like you to call her." His face is grim and displeased.

"Isn't she coming?" Instantly Isla sees a hole in the dinner-table picture she's made. Things falling apart.

"No, I expect she'll be here. But she does need to talk to you. And I'll just say right now, I'm not happy about it, but it's up to you." Whatever it is. When Lyle doesn't pass on messages, it generally means he doesn't want to be in the middle of something. He punches out Alix's number and hands the phone over.

"Mum," Alix says, and it turns out she also has a picture in mind, but one that's radically different from Isla's.

Only Alix would dream up such a breathtaking notion. Literally, for a moment or two, Isla can't breathe. "I know it'd be hard, Mum, but you're good at doing hard things. And I think you're good at doing good things, too." As transparent as her Serenity dresses—how foolhardy Alix is, what strange expectations she has, what hopelessly unrealistic demands. A couple of Christians strolling stupidly, ignorantly, into a coliseum of lions.

Which has its appeals.

She takes the deepest breath she can manage, given that her chest still rattles ominously and is not what it once was. "I think, actually, that saying it'd be *hard* doesn't quite capture it. And I think you vastly overrate my *goodness*." Perhaps Alix is still, optimistic child, in search of the ideal, perfect mother. Which she is obviously not going to get; and which anyway she's too old for. "You do seem," Isla says slowly, "to be expecting a great deal from me."

"Not expecting. I wish you could bring yourself to do it, but it's completely up to you, I understand that, and sure, you can totally disagree. You're the one who knows how you feel, all I have are impressions and an idea or two. I wouldn't ask if I didn't think it was important. For everybody, I mean, not just you."

Lyle has gone quietly away. Isla can hear him in the kitchen, taking plates from the cupboards. She can help set the table, if he will just put plates and cutlery, a few at a time, into her lap. She can wheel around and around the dining room table, setting out knives, forks, spoons, wine glasses, napkins.

Sandra, he said long ago, died with as much grace as she could manage. Isla remembers that; and she remembers believing that would be beyond her. That she would struggle, and cause damage. That if dying with grace meant being reconciled, she would fall sadly short.

Has Lyle found it hard to live with a woman who doesn't manage her own heart in ungrudging ways? He's held Isla while she wept, and he has wept as well; he has listened gravely to her rage and has joined her in it. He has been remarkably restrained about how devastatingly his own hopes, plans, and pictures have been ruined. This is not at all the life he had in mind, a clumsy ramp cluttering his porch, a wife who can no more be his partner than she could be Martin's. Except Martin could fly away.

So could Lyle. He hasn't, but he could.

Oh. She hadn't quite realized the extent of her doubt.

"But surely," she says to Alix, "he's already said no?"

"Leave that to me. It's you I'm interested in. I mean, wanting the best for you."

Isla sighs. This will not be the day she expected. The picture she had in mind is going to turn out differently than the one she was longing for. On the other hand, she does realize that of all people, she should not be surprised by this.

Her at the Wheels

R ODDY IS FUSSING WITH HIS TIE, which he can't seem to get knotted right. His fingers have gone kind of spastic, and since he's never had much to do with ties anyway, he keeps screwing up, undoing it, starting all over.

Before he began messing with it, it was a very nice dark blue silky-but-not-silk tie with tiny white flying things, like seagulls. Alix got it for him because she says he'll feel better if he looks right. "I know it sounds stupid, but clothes really can make a person feel stronger inside," which is one of the things she says she learned from the dresses she and the other girl members of the Serenity Corps used to wear. "I could look around and see I belonged, wherever we were, out on the streets or at the farm. Like, I wasn't alone. We were all in it together."

Different, then, from a jail uniform. Everybody dressing the same there didn't mean everybody belonged, or felt together with each other. "But," Alix says, "it's about whether it's your choice or not. For me it was." Whatever. The Serenity Corps sounds weird to him, but he supposes she's right, it must have been her own choice. And it must have had something to do with making her into who she is: strong, clear, generous and, well, *sweet* is the word he thinks of, but not in some phony, sickening way. Sweet like honestly good.

He owes Alix. He owes Alix everything. There she was, every other Sunday, waiting in the visitors' room with her wide-open expression, her eyes willing to absorb anything that came her way. She saved him. Not because she said anything in particular that made some big difference, but that she kept turning up, looking willing to hear whatever he had to say. Who could deny somebody like that? Somebody who so obviously could be hurt, being open-eyed and willing, but who didn't expect to be hurt, but who would not be especially surprised to be hurt.

For the first while, he didn't know how to talk, what he should say, what she wanted to hear. So she talked, instead. She told him true stories. She told him about her father, which was the worst one. Well, the worst except for her mother, but she didn't need to tell him that one. She told him also about her brother, who had trouble with drugs for a while. "He was in jail, too," she said. "But I wasn't allowed to visit him. I was too young."

The strange and also best thing was that she didn't really say how any of this made her feel, she just recounted events. Even forgiveness didn't come into it. That was another part of her sitting across from him: that forgiveness didn't come into it.

In counselling and the group therapy sessions, everybody was supposed to go on about how stuff made them feel, and as things went along, also whether they were sorry. The stories some guys had! The kind of things somebody like him never ran into, like fathers who beat them, not like his dad just moving silently through the house; like mothers who locked them out of their apartments while they had sex with strange men for money, and who didn't, like his, just throw themselves in the dead of night off a high bridge.

He stayed quiet as much as he could during those sessions not, as he'd supposed, out of an ambition to keep himself to himself and therefore safe. More from embarrassment at the paltriness of his story, shame at his crime's small foolish motives.

Some people really do suffer. Now Alix, hauling him into both her life and her work, isn't going to let him forget.

When she visited, she talked about the Serenity Corps, and how she met Master Ambrose and a whole group of them downtown here one day, just a few blocks from where her place is now, as a matter of fact, and how their faces appeared to her, and the ways they moved. "They looked so peaceful and certain. As if they knew. Or as if they knew how to go about knowing. It was very powerful to see them together. And him in the centre. He looked wise, you know? Not loving, because that's not really part of serenity. More as if he understood the depths of contentment. Being in place. Well, it's hard to explain."

Then she'd left them, the guy she called Master Ambrose, the whole thing. "You learn," she said easily. "Then I thought maybe it was necessary to move on. Not just because of my mother, but because when something changes like that, other things do, too. I thought, the Serenity Corps teaches the ways of attachment and detachment, but maybe there was another circle to it: that I'd gotten too attached to it, so if I wanted ideal detachment, I'd have to leave." That made sense, in a roundabout sort of way. Everything made sense while she was talking and Roddy was listening and watching her so attentively it felt like he hardly was breathing. "I figure Master Ambrose understands. Since he's the teacher." Roddy wondered about that later, though: if her Master Ambrose really would understand.

"Do you like being called Starglow?" He was curious about that. He liked the way she called him Rod, but that was different, that was still his real name.

"Oh, yes, I'm keeping that. Because you know how stars are so far away, and there's so many of them, and on a clear night you can look up into the sky and feel so small that you think that truly, nothing much counts? Everything that happens is tiny, it's just a speck, less than a speck, in the universe, and either that makes you feel kind of bad because obviously you don't matter at all, or you're relieved because every speck counts but you're not the whole thing, you're not what everything spins around? Like that, anyway. I thought Starglow was so cool and far off, it had light, but distance, too. So yes, I like being Starglow. It reminds me. Makes me mindful."

Mindful is a word Alix likes.

You might think that feeling like a speck in the cosmos, even a good speck, would make someone watch things happen in a remote sort of way. He has learned this is not the case. Alix takes her speck very seriously. When she wants something, like today, it doesn't look like much is allowed to get in the way.

She's getting dressed right now, too. She'll be wearing a long, light cotton dress, not so different from the Serenity Corps dress he first saw her in, long ago on that amazing court day, except it's a pale blue with a pattern of tiny white flowers, sort of like the seagulls or whatever they are on his tie. She's got jeans now, and T-shirts, regular clothes, but for good, she still mostly wears drifty long dresses.

This day is already causing extra trouble. She was supposed to be getting a ride with her brother, but when he heard what she had in mind he said no way. Actually what he said, which Roddy could hear because he was yelling on the phone, was, "Jesus Christ, Alix, you can't do that, are you insane?"

It's a real small place, Alix's. You can hear practically everything from everywhere in it. Roddy heard her brother's phone slamming down. "Well, that's it," she said brightly. "We'll have to rent a car, then." She is so careful with the little bits of money she has. It's a sign of how important this is to her, that she's willing to spring for a rental car for a day.

Roddy said no, too. No way. But here he is, struggling with the tie Alix got him. He's also wearing beige cotton pants and a blue shirt. "Casual," according to Alix, "but also respectful." He's not sure what she means by *respectful*. That he cares enough to be clean and normal-looking, he guesses. It's strange to him that he does actually look normal. It's sure not how he feels. He wants so bad to run away; except then he couldn't come back. Not that Alix has said so. He just wouldn't be able to face her.

He doesn't have any idea how he's going to handle this, but he can't see any way out. He was kind of counting on Alix's mother to say it was impossible and out of the question. He wouldn't even have minded much if she'd said it was disloyal and disgusting. He isn't sure himself that it isn't disloyal and disgusting, but here it is, happening anyway. No wonder he's yanking the tie again, starting over. The possibilities for disaster are huge. He thinks about this sort of thing now, he takes possibilities for disaster into account. Today he has entire movies' worth of outcomes unfolding in his head; none of them good, none of them happy prospects.

Alix isn't innocent, whatever she looks like. She said, "I'm not raising it with them till the last minute. Then whatever they decide, nobody can change their minds." She raised it with him days and days ago. She has different methods for different people; which means she figures and calculates. She maybe understood that if she'd sprung it on him, he most likely would've bolted without thinking what that would mean. Instead she has coaxed and discussed and sort of wheedled and finally challenged him: "You have to know what it's all about. Otherwise it'll keep haunting you, and you'll never be able to rise above it. You'd always know you weren't big enough to do what needs to be done. That's an awful thing to live with, I imagine." Oh, his angel can be harsh.

But serene in her certainty. Nothing harsh in her tone. Not like a counsellor, suddenly snapping, or appearing to snap, yelling at some poor sullen goof, "Think, think, think! Is this what you want your life to be like? Can't you get it through your head that if you do this, that happens? Do you intend to be a fuck-up forever?" They were always switching gears, the counsellors: sometimes quiet and understanding, sometimes tough and even cruel. Not cruel like some of the guards, but in their own ways.

Alix makes many things possible. Or, like today, unavoidable. Jesus, it was easier to face down guys inside, less frightening to get beat up, as he was twice for no special reason except being in the wrong place when somebody got in a bad frame of mind. One night, one crazy guy set a mattress on fire. Who knew where he got matches, but smoke filled the corridors, guards were running around yelling, alarms were going off, all sorts of shit happening. Not even that was this scary.

Alix, the vision of Alix, carried him through every day of those months. Not the counsellors, or the classes, or the work, or any of the guys, not even Dare, but knowing Alix would be coming. That she was willing to make that journey again and again, and looked every time as involved and intent and as pleased and interested to see him as she was the very first time.

He owes her everything.

Because she told him her own stories on visiting days in that nearly flat way that left out all the feelings, she finally made it possible for him, too, just to recount events. He entered this process cautiously, though, talking about his grandmother, his father, and moving from city to town. "Why was that?" she asked.

He told her about his mother: so much gaiety he remembered, and the sadness. The first vanishing, and the last one. Alix's big eyes blinked, but she only nodded and said, "I see" as if she actually did see. Maybe even saw his mother climbing the bridge, perching on its edge, toppling over, down and down onto the unforgiving expressway; the infinite whir of tires on concrete, the eternal glitter of headlights.

He told her about Mike, too; although not everything. He talked about Mike and his mother coming to Roddy's grandmother's door, the ways their friendship began and then flourished. Their explorings, their adventures, even the shoplifting, and the beer and the dope, he told her about; but he stopped well short of their big plans, and their dreams. Dangerous territory, for Alix as well as for him.

When he was coming to the end of his sentence, Mrs. Shaw, the head counsellor, had him into her office and said, "You've done quite well, I see, in your courses. We thought you would, and I'm glad you've achieved something while you've been with us." *With us*, like they'd invited him and he'd accepted. "I could wish you'd been more forthcoming in group, but sometimes people gain more than they're aware of from those sessions.

You may find that, as well. Now, what are your plans for when you leave? Do you have something firm in mind? Because that's very important for getting off on the right foot, and if you don't, we can try to help get you set up and settled."

But he wasn't like some of the others. He did have a home to go to. His dad and his grandmother were picking him up. He didn't know how being with them would be any more, after all this. "It's okay," he told Mrs. Shaw. "It's taken care of."

He was more grown and changed than they knew. Not hard, exactly, but grown. His dad, looking much older, said, "Hey son. Good you're coming back." That was it. He didn't mention any father-son trips in their future. At home Roddy's grandmother kept touching him, his arms, his shoulders, his back, his hands, and peering at him. Like she had questions she was scared to ask.

When she called upstairs, "Dinner's ready, Roddy," he told her at the table that his name was now Rod.

Although it wasn't, really. Much closer, but it still didn't quite fit.

He couldn't sleep for the silence at first. Also, he was strangely lonesome. He missed Dare, in a way. His room was a kid's room, with its kid quilt on the bed and those insect pho- tographs all over the walls. What a geek he must have been, he thought; but then felt disloyal. He felt kind of protective towards the previous Roddy: somebody headed for trouble, who didn't know anything.

For the first few days, he pretty much stayed in the house. If he went out, people would stare and he would know they'd be thinking ugly things about him. And what if he ran into the woman? Alix's mother? And there were places he couldn't go now, like Goldie's. Like a lot of places.

But at home there wasn't anything to do, except feel more and more trapped; worse than jail, in a way, since now there was a choice about going out, and choice always makes everything harder. His grandmother kept trying to feed him, and she kept smiling at him, but she seemed shy of him now, and didn't have much to say except the same kind of rambling gossip she talked about when she went to see him in jail. When she went out, she said, "Will you be all right, Roddy? Rod, sorry." Like if she was away for a couple of hours, he'd go rob a store, maybe shoot somebody? Maybe that's not exactly what she meant, but it was how it sounded.

By the fifth day he had to get out, no matter what. He thought around suppertime there wouldn't be too many people around, and a lot of the stores downtown would be closed and he might have the streets more or less to himself. And mainly he was right, and it was nice kicking along, looking in store windows, breathing free air, wondering at everything being the same when he was so different. Like he'd had a whole life while everything else stayed still, like some old "Twilight Zone" episode.

Then, turning a corner, there was Mike.

Maybe they both went red; Mike did, anyway, and Roddy felt his own skin turning some colour or other. He wasn't going to speak first. Anyway he didn't know what to say. He should have known this would happen, he should have been ready. "Hey," Mike said finally. "Hey. Good to see you."

"Yeah?"

This wouldn't be like him. Waiting, giving no ground—he could see how Mike would be confused and thrown off and uneasy. "When'd you get back?" *Back*, Roddy noticed, like he'd been on a holiday.

"Few days ago. I didn't figure you'd still be in town. Couldn't you get your hands on enough money to leave?" Maybe it was strange that now, actually seeing Mike, Roddy was angrier than he'd been when he was arrested or in court or in jail. He wanted to punish Mike, make him suffer, make him feel even a little of Roddy's abandonment. Here was Mike strolling around town like he was innocent, like nothing had happened to him or Roddy or anyone else, just like he'd never crapped out on a friend, not even a thanks, just going on with his regular life the whole time. Well, piss on that. Roddy's fingers curled into fists.

Mike looked down. "No, well, no, I didn't." He looked back up. "That whole thing scared the shit out of me. I mean, how'd it happen? That was never supposed to happen. I mean, Christ!" So he'd washed his hands of it; declared his own innocence. Probably he'd have to do something like that, just to get through the day.

Good question, though, how'd it all happen.

"So yeah," Mike continued, "it pulled me up short. So I'm finishing school this year and then I'll get out of here. I don't have a job, though. Everybody figured I was in on the Goldie's thing. I know I owe you for keeping me out of it, but everybody knows we were tight and nobody figures I didn't know. So I can't get a job here. Look, you want to go someplace, grab a beer or something? Like, I know I owe you for not taking me down, too."

"I don't think so," Roddy said coolly. About going someplace together, he meant. A beer! "So how come you weren't around?"

"To see you? My folks said no way. Honest to God, I'm sorry about that, too, but they said it'd be asking for trouble."

"Guess it would have been."

Mike shifted back on his heels and sideways a little. "Was it bad?"

What kind of stupid question was that? "Could have been worse. And I got my Grade 12. Nothing much else to do. I got by. Met some guys. Hung out. I made it, anyhow."

"What're you going to do, stay here?"

"I don't know yet. I've only been out a few days."

He had almost nothing to say any more to this guy who'd been his best friend, his buddy, since his first day in this town. "I got to go. I got a lot of stuff to do, catching up now I'm out." As soon as he turned away and wasn't looking at Mike any more, he felt nothing at all. Mike was as remote as the town. He heard Mike behind him say, "Roddy," but he didn't turn around and no words followed that one. He guessed people don't necessarily disconnect at the same time, or turn remote on each other. He guessed he might have felt worse about it if he hadn't had so long to get used to the idea of not being Mike's friend any more.

Alix called to see how he was doing back home, and to ask if they could visit like usual, and she rented a car, which is what she does when she absolutely has to, and drove to his grandmother's. She sat on a Sunday afternoon talking nicely with his grandmother, and politely greeted his dad, who passed through the kitchen as if even Alix couldn't hold his attention. Roddy's grandmother was welcoming enough, but very uneasy, knowing who Alix was. Alix said finally, "You want to go outside, Rod? Aren't you dying to be out there after being inside so long?" His grandmother flinched, like Alix was being tactless, but it was just a fact, only true.

Even sitting beside Alix on the front steps, not going anywhere, was a relief, the first time since he got out that he felt comfortable, like he belonged. That was with Alix, nothing to do with the place or whether he was indoors or outdoors or whatever. She said, "You're not very happy here, are you?" *Happy* was a funny word. He doubted he was supposed to be.

"Not really."

"Have you had time to make any plans, or have you just been getting used to being home?"

"No plans yet." Plans stumped him. He didn't have much confidence in them anyway, the only real, detailed plan he'd made having gone so horribly wrong. "I guess I'm still getting used to the idea of being able to. Or having to. Having a choice, I mean."

"Well then, I have one. Or not a plan, just an idea." When she looked at him, he fell right back into her eyes. Her skin was amazing; like it was lit from the inside. Her idea was amazing, too.

"What I figured was, whatever you do, you probably can't do it here. I bet it's not easy, right?" She knew everything. "So this could just be for a while, till you get on your feet and figure things out, but there's my place. It's really tiny, but it's central to everything you could be interested in, and also you could help me. I do these talks about crime, and you know about the volunteer stuff with the drop-in place, and I figure you could help, if you wanted. Because you've been there. Kids would listen to you. And my job, it's about finding jobs for people, so I don't see why I couldn't find one for you. So anyway, that's my idea: move into my place for a little while until you get fixed up yourself, and help me and I'll help you." She must have known his stunned longing. "I only mean that, though, just sharing the place. It's two rooms. We could figure out a way we could each mostly have one. Plus there's a bathroom, of course."

She had it worked out. She'd thought about it, about him, and come up with this plan. She made it sound like a kind of trade, each of them doing something for the other. "Why?" he asked. She was offering this huge thing, way bigger than Sunday visits, and she had to have reasons that didn't totally have to do with him, so what were they?

Of course she understood. She understands everything, even if like today she doesn't always let understanding something make her soft and merciful about it. She said, "Because we need to carry it through. None of it's any good otherwise. I'm not sure how it should work, but I have this feeling about how to get there."

He wasn't clear at all what she was talking about. What she meant by *through*, or *it* or *there*. "Okay," he said. "Yes."

Alix, who has learned a whole lot about the justice system, took care of most of the details, like making sure moving was okay with the probation office and how he'd be reporting to them. She talked to his grandmother and his dad, too, so persuasively and compellingly that although they said no to begin with, they said yes in the end.

Roddy felt *swept up*. He felt *overwhelmed*, and *compelled*.

But that was okay.

"You be careful." His grandmother was still very worried as he carried his two suitcases out the door the next weekend. She had tears in her eyes. She'd probably had whole different pictures. But maybe she was relieved, too. Anyway, she hugged him. "You come visit, you hear? You're always welcome. And be sure to phone. And you come back anytime you need to, all right?"

His dad said, "Be good, son." The two of them stood out on the lawn waving as Alix drove Roddy away. It was another case of saying goodbye to a life. He guessed it would be that way for them, too, except they had to get used to something different that wasn't their choice, while he was heading off to adventure. Which wasn't altogether his choice, either, but still a wild turn of events.

It seemed whenever he saw Alix, his life kept turning over.

He felt bad, how easily and light-heartedly he was leaving them, especially knowing the care they'd taken, especially compared with what happened to a whole lot of other people; but he couldn't feel bad for the actual doing of it. He was young, they were old, things happen, that was the only way to look at it. They probably saw it that way too, and just had to get used to it. He had big things to get used to, too. He couldn't wait.

Alix said in the car, "I've got a bunch of stuff about different colleges and universities you can look at when you get settled. And I can tell you about what jobs are out there. But," she glanced at him and smiled that perfectly comprehending smile, "don't worry, I'm not planning to pressure you. The right way will come clear, I know that."

She has a funny sort of faith in things coming clear. He likes that, although doesn't, himself, have the same kind of confidence. She knows more than him about that sort of thing, though: faith, hope, all that. She's actually paid attention to it, studied up on it, in her way, if that Serenity group means studying up.

Her place is over a variety store. Two rooms, as she said, plus tiny kitchen, and bathroom. The bathroom has no outside windows, and so is very dark. The main rooms have a big front window each, facing the street, which is busy and took some getting used to, with the sounds of traffic and loud conversations floating upwards from the sidewalk, and sirens. On the outside, the windows are real dirty. Inside, Alix keeps the place neat as a pin, as his grandmother would say, and they do the actual cleaning together and take care of their own dishes and so forth; but it's still shabby. In her bedroom Alix has a single bed and a dresser and some shelves. Where Roddy sleeps used to be her living room, and still sort of is, and has a couple of wooden chairs at a plastic-topped table, an old soft green nubbly chair and an old soft green nubbly pull-out couch, which is where Roddy sleeps. It's kind of a pain, having to fold it up every morning and unfold it each night, but in this sort of space, there isn't a choice.

It's not exactly the sort of place he and Mike had in mind. Instead of riding an elevator home, as he and Mike had imagined, he climbs up dark stairs. Instead of looking out over the whole glittering night-time city, that brightly lit panorama of life being lived, the view is of brick and concrete and grit.

A year ago, everything in his head and his life was different.

Same goes for her, he supposes.

And for sure same goes for her mother, and everybody else in her family. "You ready?" she asks, coming up behind him. "You look good. Just right. Don't look so grim, you'll live through it, you know." She smiles as if she's made a joke, but come to think of it, it seems possible he might not live through it. Depending on people's inclinations and moods. He can't hope to get through unscathed, anyway. It's a good thing he trusts her. He means, trusts the power of her presence.

And she really does look powerful. Not in some suit-and-briefcase way, but in the firm way her mouth is set, and how her eyes are so clear and untroubled it's like there's nothing worrying at all about what they're setting out on.

Is her family used to this? Do they have ways not to look at her directly so they're not dazzled? Roddy remains raw to it. After a couple of weeks here, he is still constantly astonished. Every time she comes through the door, or he does, and he sees her again, it's almost like the first time, being captured. Being lured, although not in some bad way. He doesn't know what it is. She *appeals*, he guesses: to his desire to be whatever he can, for her more than for him. "Be careful," his grandmother said. And his father, "Be good." Well, he would, if he could tell what *careful* and *good* mean in this new world, on this spectacular, unexpected, terrifying occasion.

So far Alix hasn't really asked much of him; except for today. What she said at the start was "You should explore, take your time," and that's what he has done: getting up first in the morning, to be out of the bathroom before she needs it, setting out cereal and juice for them both and then, when she goes to work, he leaves too. He walks her to the bus and then, every day, even in rain, goes exploring. So many different kinds of lives being lived by so many shapes and colours of people! Even different kinds of food, fruits for instance that he isn't even certain are fruits, and whether they're supposed to be peeled or chopped up or cooked or just held like an apple and eaten. "It's wild," he tells Alix. "I can't get over it."

"I thought you'd like it." She sounds happy for him.

Now she says, "Let's go," and he can look at her as pleadingly as he wants but she pays no attention and so, yes, they're off. She locks the door behind them. He's been slightly surprised that she is very conscious of security, and insists that he always lock up as well, whether he's going out or staying in. "Because," she explains, "I know what I know." He imagines she means about young criminals, although he can't imagine young criminals being tempted to climb those dark stairs to a couple of unpromising rooms. He would like an opportunity to protect her, actually to show her what he could do on her behalf. This isn't likely to happen, though.

The car is old and rattly, but she insists it's safe enough, because rental companies have to maintain some standards. Since the company she uses is called Rent-A-Clunker, he isn't sure about that, although he bets she gets the best one they've got. They would look at her and know it would be something like sacrilege to put her in danger.

They putter through the city to the expressway, along the expressway, cautiously in the right-hand lane, to the cut-off that's the road that becomes the main street of the town where he mainly grew up. All the way he is wishing for something to go wrong: something small, not life-endangering, nothing that would send them into oncoming traffic or into an abutment, but just something that would bring them quietly and definitely to a halt.

Naturally this doesn't happen. It wouldn't be likely to, with her at the wheel.

She's a driver who pays total attention to the traffic and road. Even so she tells him who he can expect, although of course not what, that's beyond even her. "My brother Jamie. I know he sounds scary, but he's been in trouble himself. I think he'll be okay once you're real and not just an idea to him.

"Lyle's sons. They're older than me and Jamie, really smart guys, but we never got to know them very well. Like they were grown up by the time Lyle and my mother got married, and Jamie and I were kind of going in our own directions so we've never hung out. But they're nice. One's a scientist, the other one just got a job with one of those companies that does polling, you know? Politics, different products, I don't know. Anyway, they're not hard to talk to. I mean, I've never talked to them about anything real, but that's okay, they're nice. And then Martin, he's my mother's old partner in the ad agency. They sold it and made pots of money so he retired. Cool guy. He's just back from India, so I can't wait to hear about that.

"My grandma, she's great, and her friend Bert, he's a pet. They've been together forever, although they never got married. Of course they're incredibly old now. My grandma doesn't have as much energy as she used to, but she's still tough as nails. We've always been able to count on her, and Bert just kind of comes along and does nice things for everybody."

Even the old people are "tough as nails." Doesn't she see, these people could hurt him?

They live way out in the country. They could kill him and bury him and who'd know?

Well, that's stupid and creepy. Even so he looks nervously at Alix, who concentrates on the road. She wouldn't take him into a trap.

Tough as nails. Jesus.

In town they drive past Goldie's. He keeps staring forward, and so does Alix. He wonders if she notices Goldie's in particular.

Then off to the left there's the street that leads to his own grandmother's street. "We'll go see your grandma and dad again soon, shall we?" Alix asks. So she remembers, she does notice these things.

Also she is assuming a future.

Then they're past the strip malls and the service stations and doughnut shops and back in the country, familiar territory to him. He sees himself as a little boy pedalling his bike along here, not so long ago, wading in ditches, climbing fences, lying in the grain, under the sun, watching rabbits and anthills. Back in that other life. Alix is pressing the brake, switching on the right-hand turn signal, turning into a hidden laneway that's sort of familiar. Like, he's been up here partway on his bike, not the whole way, though. He never wanted to get caught by anybody who owned land he was prowling.

He's caught now, he guesses.

The car rattles and rumbles on the rough, pitted surface. It's too late for something important to fall off. If anything went wrong now, they'd be stuck here. Now he's hoping the car holds up, holds on, so they can get out of here when the time comes, or if they suddenly need to.

There's a curve at the top of the lane, and then, "See?" Alix says. "Isn't it perfect?"

Yes. It is. It's like a perfect picture, a photograph; except for the people.

"I guess we're late," she says. "Looks like everyone's here."

A couple of guys are playing horseshoes at the side of the house, and an old woman and an old man are standing over at a garden, looking at flowers. There's a young guy and an older one sitting on the porch railing facing each other, their legs dangling down. There's another older guy on a big wicker chair. Everybody's holding some kind of drink. There's a woman on the porch, beside the guy in the wicker chair. She's in a wheelchair. Not one of these people is moving now. Their heads are all turned in the direction of Alix's car. Just staring. Nobody's talking, either.

Alix touches his arm. "Come on, pal, let's go. It's showtime." She gets out her side and yells, "Hi, everybody, we made it." Slowly, Roddy opens his own door. Sets his feet on this foreign ground. They're all watching. He can't read a single face. Alix is at the front of the car, waiting, her hand stretching towards him. He's never held her hand, and would like to.

She pulls him forward. "Let me introduce everybody," she calls out. She sounds strange, too high-pitched. Her tone must also strike them as false and discordant. He sees a flinch here, a thinning of lips there, and picks up, as if he were a bat, a gasp or two, and a sigh. Alix stops. "Sorry, I guess I'm nervous." She's nervous! "I didn't mean to start off that way. I know this is hard, but here we are, and everyone, this is Rod. So let's all try to be kind, okay?"

Necessary Sensation

T'S A SLIM FIGURE THAT STEPS from the passenger side of Alix's car. No one large at all. Over the clattering sounds of horseshoes, of careful, self-conscious conversations, of Bach preludes and fugues, chosen for calm and civility, drifting through the open windows from indoors, they have all heard the car coming up the lane, another of Alix's rented rattletraps, and each one of them has paused, and then cautiously, tentatively resumed their various activities; so as not, Isla supposes, to make too big a deal of this; so as not to frighten or upset her further than each must suppose she is already frightened and upset.

This is considered a very poor idea by everyone except, obviously, Alix. The response was unanimous, although expressed differently from one to another. "Oh, that wretched child," Madeleine said. "How could she think of such a thing?"

"Fucking idiot," said Jamie, who'd refused to drive them here himself. "She should have stayed in the Serenity Corps if this is the sort of stunt she's going to pull when she's out."

Lyle said, "It is too bad. But it was up to Isla to say yes or no." Any concern Isla ever had that he would over-protect her from outside circumstances, or even from herself, was misplaced. What he seems to have decided is that he has done what he can, and will do what he must, but she gets no further particular breaks for being half-paralyzed in a wheelchair. By and large this is a good outlook, but she wouldn't have minded too much if he'd said definitely, fiercely, "No way. I won't have it." Instead he looked furious but said only, "Oh, Isla. Why did you do that?" and then, "This wasn't just Alix's deal, you know. Everybody's involved in today, and it was supposed to be a celebration. For you, but for everybody else, too. I'm not clear why Alix gets to change rules that affect everyone."

Isla isn't clear either, but it seems Alix does. Because Alix has larger and more compelling desires than anyone else? That having made her way from Master Ambrose, that large and liberating leap, she demands and deserves every encouragement and reward?

To be truthful, though? Curiosity. The fact is, there is no better time. As Alix put it: on Isla's own ground, with her own people.

Also a yearning for judgement; also a desire, within Isla's own desperate stillness, for havoc.

Now here he is, a slim figure, no one large at all.

Alix has reached for his hand and is drawing him towards the porch. At the same time, Lyle's boys are moving from the rough horseshoe pitch beside the house, Madeleine and Bert leave the garden, Jamie and Martin get up from the porch railing where they've been sitting. They're like sentries, all of them gathering closer. Or maybe a mob.

Only Lyle doesn't move. He keeps his seat beside Isla, resting a beer on one knee as if this is so casual an occasion and acquaintance he doesn't need to stand for new guests.

And of course she doesn't move, either.

Closer, the boy is, well, a boy. Alix, having called out a too-boisterous greeting, looks abashed, even timid, even afraid. Finally understanding she may have made an awful mistake?

So she should.

Closer, Isla recognizes the shape. Last seen with a gun in its hand, and turning, rising up on the balls of its feet, settling back down flat on them. Look, there's the finger. She stares at that finger, the one that altered everything, caused grief and pain that that slim shape has no notion of. There it is.

His left hand clutches Alix's like a scared little boy's.

Isla is avoiding his face, doesn't want to look into his eyes. The last time she did, they were locked together, so briefly, his gaze and hers, in awful inevitability. Here it comes again.

"And," Alix is saying, "this is my mother. Isla. Mother, this is Rod." Then even Alix is lost for words. The silence is long. Isla can't even hear anyone breathing, except for the sound of her own shallow breaths.

She looks at his right hand and puts out her own. She wants to feel that hand, that finger of his. "I believe," she says drily, "we've met." She would have expected that to come out more cold than dry, but evidently not. She feels his hand tremble and weaken in hers. She looks up finally, and sees that his eyes are desperate. His greatest desire must be to tear free and run. She tightens her grip, her newly strong hands put to good use. Not that he would run. He's far too frightened, a poor thing in a trap.

Why did he come, then?

Well, Alix, of course. Alix has some hold on him, far beyond the hold she has on his other hand. Her daughter is beautiful, but Isla doesn't think beauty can account for so much.

The boy is not beautiful. His hair has grown longer than she remembers it from that day in Goldie's. His eyes, without the horror and panic of that crisis, contain a softer horror and panic for this one. He has narrow lips, a small chin. He is not ugly. He is no less than ordinary, and no more, either.

He should have been marked by what happened. He should be scarred, or broken, or openly bleeding. Even his clothes are tidy and clean, his blue shirt neatly tucked in. He's even wearing a tie. He could be a valedictorian, or a boy putting grocery bags in the trunk of her car. If she hadn't seen for herself his monstrosity, it would be hard to believe.

These young people, he and Alix, too, have mysterious hearts.

She lets go of his hand, which holds no useful clues. This time, he is at her mercy. What should she do with power like this? If she wants to see scars, she will have to carve them herself. If she wants blood, it's her job to draw it.

She glances at Lyle. She sees he is staring at the boy with perfect, dry-ice hatred: a man in a rage, and in despair, at the demolition of his own life. She looks at Lyle's two sons, the handsome, thriving, useful William and Robert. They are watching their father, too. How unfair they must think it that through no fault of his own, he's been captured by all this, by her. Through no fault of hers, either, but that wouldn't matter to them.

And her own son? Jamie is gazing into the distance, a muscle in his jaw clenching and working, only his profile turned to her—what does he see? Various sorrows, she supposes. Or maybe various vengeances. She looks from him back to this boy here, this Rod. There should be more to him, more substance, there really should.

He has made Madeleine cry. She is standing at the bottom of the porch steps, Bert's arm around her shoulders, his hand making comforting pat-patting motions, with silent tears running down her face. Just for that, for causing an old woman, a mother, to cry, this boy should suffer.

He is suffering. He's surrounded and, except for Alix, he is surrounded by contempt, rage, and grief. He has gone from severe discomfort to anguish. He looks as if he could weep.

Well, good.

Could this possibly be what Alix intended? Has she, alone among all of them, set herself to revenge, is she the clever one who has figured out, and put into action, a plan to torture this boy so exquisitely, so subtly and carefully, it can appear, even to him, like an act of love, or even redemption?

Alix looks stern, and sturdy, and maybe also serene. She stands beside him, but is leaving him to whatever fate he can manage.

Normally with a new guest this would be the time to offer a drink, an hors d'oeuvre, a place to sit, some kind, welcoming words. Certainly they can't remain in these frozen postures, with the boy in the centre like a highly debatable lawn jockey. "Perhaps, Lyle, you could get the young man a soft drink?" she asks. And when Lyle, that deeply civilized man, shakes himself out of what-

ever state he's been in, and stands, she says to the boy, "Sit down,"
and nods to Lyle's chair. Turning her attention to William and
Robert, she says, "How were those horseshoes coming? Who was
winning?" which they take, as she intends, as an invitation to
return to their game. "Mother, when you're out in the garden,
would you and Bert mind collecting some flowers for the dining
room? A couple of small bouquets for the table, maybe, and a nice
big glorious one for the mantle? Maybe Alix could help."

She's rather good at this. It's with some pride that she
watches the general dispersal. Those leadership qualities that
used to come in handy running a household, and organizing
advertising campaigns, have not deserted her.

Lyle comes out with a cold pop and a glass, and looks surprised to find the boy in his chair and almost everyone else
wandering off. The clink of horseshoes resumes. Alix and
Madeleine are in lively conversation—angry conversation?—
with Bert standing by. "Thanks, Lyle," she says. "Maybe Martin
and Jamie could give you some advice on that problem you're
having with the back lawn." She is unaware of any problem with
the back lawn, and Lyle raises his eyebrows, but it's not a difficult point she is making, not a hard one to twig to.

"Okay," he says slowly. "All right. Guys?" Jamie's the most
reluctant. He stares hard at the boy, while speaking to Isla.

"We won't be far," he says.

Does he think this boy would hurt her? Could hurt her further? The danger here is to him, not to her. "Pull your chair
around," she tells him, "so I can see you better," and awkwardly,
setting down his pop first, he does, hoisting with difficulty the
unwieldy wicker beneath him. An obedient boy. Perhaps it's
partly her fault, for not calling out "Stop!" at that critical
moment in Goldie's.

"Well," she says cheerfully, "this is awkward, isn't it? What do
you suppose we should talk about?" If Alix has by any chance
committed an act of deliberate cruelty today, it's no mystery
where she picked up that keen, slicing skill.

"I don't know." Like a twelve-year-old, he looks at his feet. Which he must suddenly become aware are kicking back and forth. Which he must realize hers cannot do, so in mid-swing he stops.

"Why did you come?"

"Alix, I guess. She said I should. I didn't," and he glances up with a wild look in his eyes, "want to." Obviously not. But if he is looking wildly to Isla for some sort of maternal reassurance, he's banging into a rocky-hard bosom here.

"Then I expect we're even. No one but Alix was keen on you coming, either. Ordinarily of course I wouldn't say that to a guest, but I'm sure it doesn't surprise you. I don't suppose there's too many things we need to dance politely around, you and I, the way we maybe would with other people."

Probably he would be grateful for any dance of politeness that was offered. So there's that hope dashed. The funny thing is, what she said turns out to have its own sort of truth: this boy is actually someone from whom she needs to have very few privacies. They have, the two of them, seen each other in each other's rawest form. Removing clothes, exposing histories, is nothing next to that moment in Goldie's.

"But now that you are here, against everyone's better judgement including yours and mine, what do you think we should talk about?" He shrugs, helpless, lost. Well then. "I know, how about how we've each spent the past year? You tell me all about jail, then I'll tell you all about the hospital. I bet they're not so different in some ways. I mean, that you can't do what you want in either place. Mind you, I still can't and evidently never will. How about you?"

Too cruel? She didn't exactly mean to make tears come to his eyes. She thought he'd be tougher. He had a gun, after all. He shot her, didn't he?

She thought she'd be tougher, too. Maybe this is what Alix meant: that in person, right up close, he is no monstrosity.

Then who will haunt her, what looming figure can she call on, who can she reliably regard as a representative of doom grand and powerful enough to have cost her her legs, crucial movement, necessary sensation? This boy? His insignificance, his meekness, his frank fear, altogether make her doom seem small, her suffering minor, her struggles paltry. What an insult, what a blow.

Is this what Alix found, too? And so did she set out to build him up, make him larger, help him grow into a role he has already played? This is a worthwhile project, if so. Isla's sly, clever child.

"Tell me," she asks, perhaps too open-endedly, "how you feel. I mean, besides scared and not wanting to be here."

"Well," he says, taking a moment to consider, or maybe just to wonder what answer she's looking for, "I feel sorry." He raises his head again, small dull eyes still glittering with tears. "I'm sorry."

"About what? Getting caught? Going to jail? Trying to rob an ice-cream store? Screwing it up? Shooting me? You feel sorry for yourself, or for me, or what?"

His voice quavers. Heightened fear, if he's smart. "Everything, I guess. That it happened. I didn't mean it, any of it. I couldn't believe it."

"Me neither," she agrees. "I couldn't believe it, either. Still can't, really. Although here you are, and here I am, and we did have that, what shall we call it, that encounter together, you and I. I guess we have to believe it. Do you think about that moment much? I do. I can't tell you how many thousands of times I've gone over and over it. Every time, quite a shock. How about you?"

"Oh yes," he breathes. Now he's regarding her with some strange kind of hope. Peculiar young fellow. "I think, just a little difference, that's all it would've taken. I never even ever shot a gun before. So how could I have hit something that one time?"

"Not something. Someone. Me, in fact." Oh dear, that sharp tongue of hers. "So you're not one of those boys who goes hunting all the time, with their fathers, say?"

"No. He goes with his friends. Not me, I never even shot a bird or a rabbit! I like animals, I had a dog, or my grandmother did, except he died when I was away. The only dead animals I ever had anything to do with were already dead when I found them."

An unpalatable image. She tries to set that one aside. "Then why? What were you looking for? I was at Goldie's for ice cream, but what were you doing there? With a gun? What was your purpose?"

"We had a plan. We needed money to go away, get an apartment, that kind of thing. I thought it'd be easy. The plan was so clear." He speaks in bursts now, like a gun. "I wasn't supposed to use it, except for a fake shot. So it'd look like a real robbery. And then you came in. Just when I was going to do that. Shoot into the wall. So I had the gun up and you startled me. And, I don't know, it just *happened*. It just *happened*."

Isla knows, and he slowly realizes, what he has told her: that it was a plan, that there was a *we*, that some gunshot cover was needed to make it look like a real robbery. "Oh geez," he says. "I was so careful," and she understands that what he means has nothing to do with firearm safety, but with having been so careful about protecting his friend.

"Yes," she says, "you certainly were. He should be very grateful. I suppose in many circumstances loyalty is a virtue. Not in this instance in my view, but often. I can see how you might have made that mistake."

"What will you do?" Puppet-like, his limbs have gone limp and dangly. As if only loyalty, the only good thing he had to say for himself, has been holding him up.

"I don't know." She isn't lying; she really doesn't know. "I'll have to think about it. It was a very terrible crime. And as you see," she gestures towards her legs, "it still is. And will remain."

"I know. Oh, God. But," deep breath, "I'm the one pulled the trigger."

"Believe me, I'm aware of that. But would I be right that on your own, you would not have been standing in Goldie's, or anywhere else, that day with a gun?"

Yes, she can see he understands that that's true. Is it good news or bad for him? Does it imply some kind of innocence on his part or some kind of gutlessness? He has been for the past year an armed robber, a gunman. That must feel quite different from hapless follower. Not quite a dupe but certainly a fall guy. "Well, no," he says. "But I was." Now it's her turn to interpret ambiguity: is he insisting on ownership of his big, bold, bad deed, or claiming penitence all for himself?

She can't believe she's even wondering this. That she has the slightest interest in these tiny details of his criminal concerns. "You shot me," she says in wonder. "Does that stagger you? It still staggers me. Or it would if I could stagger." Time for him to begin learning about dicey verbs. He flinches as if she'd just slapped him. "Does it?" she asks again, more gently; more, in a way, companionably.

"I guess," he says slowly, "I'd give anything for you to be fixed. You too, I guess. You must hate me." This does not sound like one of those occasions when something like "You must hate me" is spoken in the interests of hearing the other person say, "Oh, no, not at all, of course not." It sounds like a fact. Which it must be.

But hatred is huge and requires a huge object, surely. And there is nothing about this boy that is big. The gun was big, and so was the moment, but he is not. "I don't, you know," she says, just as slowly as he. "I hate what you did, but that's a slightly different matter." How much does an eighteen-year-old understand about these distinctions? Also, does he understand the difference between his saying this was something that happened, and her saying it was something he did to her? "And I'm very angry, as you can probably tell." She sees him glance past her and turning slightly, sees Alix, with Madeleine and Bert, watching them from the garden. The conversation out there seems to have calmed down. Alix nods towards the two of them on the porch: telling them what, that they're doing all right? Alix has no idea. None at all.

"I am, too," he says unexpectedly. And looks as surprised as if that's a new thought to him, as well.

"You're angry?"

"Yeah, well, I did one stupid thing, and everything got wrecked. One minute, if I could have it back, it'd make all the difference. But I can't, so yeah, I'm mad. I mean, at myself. Everything. You know what I mean?"

He has been hitting his fists on his knees to the beat of his words. His expression is, oh, filled with regret, real anguish, true self-loathing. And some horror, too, at this array of awful sentiments. Has he not said them before? He seems to display, anyway, the particular shock of hearing them for the first time in the air. "Honest to God, I'd kill myself if I could only start over." His voice veers upwards. "I could kill myself anyway."

Does Alix have any idea what she has on her hands? And what she has done? Also, does Isla?

"I know," Isla says quietly. "I've thought of that, too." So she has. He must know she is not patronizing him. "You know, for a while, in the hospital, I was totally paralyzed. No feeling, not my arms and hands, not my legs and feet, nothing. Couldn't move, couldn't feel. Unspeakably strange state to be in, so help-less. There were times I believed that I would probably need to die. Except that wasn't happening by itself, and I couldn't think anyone was going to help me and I had no means to make it happen myself. I was so furious, and in such despair." Of course he has to hear this as reproach; but also, perhaps, as an experi-ence she, too, knows a good deal about, one, she supposes, they have in common.

It would be terrible to be him. To know what he has ruined, all by himself. And he is only eighteen. He must want to tear his head off his shoulders.

"Now, as you see, things are better in many ways. Only my legs are lost, although that is a great deal to lose. The strange thing is that I sometimes feel real pain in them, but that's all, only pain, nothing good. It's not that they'll ever be any use to me. But now, I *could* kill myself. It's no longer out of my reach. And I'll tell you something nobody else knows: after the surgery, I did reach to do it. I held knives, I held pills right in my hands, considering it. It's tempting, isn't it? Just to reach out and do it? But," her voice hardens, "as you see, I haven't. All those possibilities, and I still haven't done it. Although," a quick, sharp smile, "you never know about tomorrow. At least I don't."

He is leaning forward now, elbows on knees, hunched and close and looking up into her face. "Why not? Why didn't you?"

She can't lie. But also she cannot be as careless and unwitting about this young man as Alix.

"Because it was very hard to get here. Even this far, it was too hard an effort to waste. Also, these people." She gestures vaguely, but doesn't take her eyes off his. If she lets go he will fall, she knows he will fall.

"These people here, how could I do that to them? There've been times that didn't matter, but mainly it does. My children, well, you know Alix, at least. And my husband. You probably don't know this, or maybe you do, but we haven't been together so many years, and I was finally very happy, very safe. So right now, although I suppose I may decide differently at some point, I couldn't punish him that way. On the other hand I don't want to be his burden, either. I don't want him weighed down."

This, surely, is beyond an eighteen-year-old. Or none of his business. But he is listening carefully, carefully. As Alix says: he seems to crave filling up.

"But you know, my children are young and my husband's a capable man. They'd survive. My mother, though—well, you see her over there in the garden. She's been a rock for me, and sometimes she's saved me, in a few disasters you know nothing about." Or does he? Hard to say what he and Alix may have discussed. "Aside from anyone else, I couldn't do that to her. It would be like killing her, too. She's my mother, so...." She shrugs.

"My mother," he says softly, "left me. Or she got taken away, I don't know, I was little. I guess she was sick. Then after a few years, she jumped off a bridge." Hostility rises sharply between them, the thick consistency of her suspicion: is he seeking her sympathy? Giving some half-assed explanation for having gone off the rails? Repeating a dreary perception from jailhouse therapy? "I guess my grandma would mind a lot, though. And my dad. I guess I didn't think too much about that, how they'd feel. Like, if I killed myself."

Yes, she recognizes this: the self-absorption of the victim, the carelessness of the damned. "But you're not going to. And neither am I. Having come this far." That's like a bargain, a pledge.

"I guess not. I don't know what to do. I've found the bridge, though. I tried to imagine."

She sees the men, Lyle and Jamie and Martin, edging around the corner of the house. Looking towards the porch, gauging events and their place in them, deciding in some soft way to detour to the garden to join Madeleine and Alix and Bert. Robert and William are no doubt getting tired of hurling horseshoes around. Everyone is behaving with considerable delicacy, it seems to her. Or fear. Or confusion. At any rate, they are behaving well, and with respect for mysterious events they're not part of. She is a very lucky woman, although in a remarkably unlucky way.

"So," she draws herself up as straight as she can, signalling to them that she's all right and to this boy that they are now some-what changing the subject, "if you're not going to kill yourself, what are you going to do? What are your prospects? Will you be going back at some point to live at your grandmother's?" This is of interest to her. She doesn't want to be running into him, as it were, on the streets at unexpected, haphazard moments.

"I don't think so. Everybody knows. They'd look at me." One of the circles of hell, no doubt. They look at Isla, too, rolling around in her wheelchair. She is not entirely happy that people are much friendlier now, feeling free to bend over her and fall into conversations about things like weather, shopping chores, even community events that might interest her. Nothing about being crippled, they are far too polite; or uncomfortable. Still, only a couple have spoken to her slowly and loudly as if she's gone deaf and stupid, not legless. She supposes that says something marginally good.

It's a hard way, though, as she has remarked to Lyle, to get accepted. Standing up, walking about, it could have taken decades.

"Alix has been helping me. I got my Grade 12 inside." He stumbles slightly over *inside*. "So I guess I'll get some kind of job. She says it won't be much to start off, even though my marks were pretty good. Probably in fast-food or some kind of a store." He should hope, then, that he never finds himself facing a kid with a gun. "I wouldn't mind landscaping, she's mentioned that, too. I used to mow lawns and do garden work for people. I like being outdoors."

"Yes, me too. Before all this, what did you have in mind doing?" Well, how would she have answered that at seventeen, eighteen? Some vague notion about words, about advertising, she remembers, not exactly a goal or a prospect or a plan, just an idea. Because by then she had James in mind, too, that older young man, full of promise.

Oh dear, those are tears again. And she has upset the boy, now regarding her anxiously. She shakes her head. "Never mind. Just something I thought of. Go on."

"I didn't know. I didn't have any big ideas. I guess if I'd had better marks then, I could have thought about college, but I wasn't paying much attention to school. Anyway, I don't think there was enough money for that. But inside, we did different tests about what we'd be good at, maybe, and mine said I could think about working with plants, or animals, or numbers, something like that." Too bad Jamie abandoned that florist shop; he might have handed his job right over to Rod.

"Alix has all these college books, you know, where they list courses? She says that's what I should think about in the long run, but that I'd need to save up the money. It's different from how I thought." How chatty he's becoming. "All we thought about before was getting a good apartment and having a really good time."

With money from Goldie's. Did they expect so much from the till of one ice-cream store? Luxury and freedom both? What infants, what hopeless hopefuls.

"It's not like that, though."

"No, I don't imagine it is." Isla, of course, has no way to visit Alix's place. She can hardly climb narrow staircases. But as Alix describes it, it's considerably less than luxurious. Alix, involved in her ill-paid good works, seems to feel those good works require a certain rigour in her environment. But at least she is earning her way, and without any uniformed, doe-eyed pan-handling on behalf of the ghastly Master Ambrose. She seems to have the right idea, mainly, as long as she doesn't lapse into extremity or martyrdom, always a risk, apparently, with Alix.

"I like exploring. I used to do that around here, but now I'm where I would have grown up if my mother hadn't got sick, so it's kind of interesting to see how it might have been there, if that hadn't happened. Like, all the stuff I would've known already. I'd kind of like to find some people who knew her. I found the bridge okay, but I don't know anybody yet who knew her." Isla is finding this confiding a little annoying. Has she slid in his fearful esteem? Does he now regard her as just a friendly, stationary woman he can talk to?

"But you haven't held up any stores or robbed any people."

"No!" He looks shocked. "Oh, no."

"Why not? You're not very good at it yet, I'd have thought you might have come out of jail figuring you needed more practice." It's so easy to make him shrink. She can scarcely believe she feels badly, but she does. "Sorry," she says, and can't believe she has also apologized to this young criminal whom she has brooded on, pictured and fantasized vengeance on, for a year.

What happened to the woman eager to scar, keen to draw blood?

Oh, she's still here. She may well always be here. Only, this particular target is a poor thing.

"I guess," he says cautiously, "you should say whatever you want. I mean, if it was me I'd want to kill me, for sure. But I don't know what to say. Like, *sorry* isn't much. It's probably not anything. But I can't fix it. So I don't know what to do." This emerges as a cry of sorts. He really is at a loss. Because of course he really is right. And they are going in circles. They are stumped, because there is no answer to her lost legs, his lost heart.

"Would you feel better if I shot you?" she asks kindly. "Just winged you, disabled you, fair's fair, fifty-fifty, eye-for-an-eye, legs-for-legs?"

For a moment, about as long as the moment in Goldie's only perfectly still, no turning, no twisting, he just looks at her. And then a smile begins to flicker at the corners of her mouth. Then at the corners of his, too.

They're not exactly laughing. They are not exactly twinned souls. Nor are they twinned exactly by circumstance, nor has she ceased regretting his existence. As, possibly, he regrets hers. But it's far more than she could have imagined.

In this moment, this glimpse, the terrible bitterness of punishment, the onerous weight of revenge have lifted to make a space for—what? The word for this might, she thinks, after all be *grace*. She is not sure what that is, the entirety of what it is supposed to embrace and encompass, but it is the word that comes to her: she feels, briefly, graced.

She is astonished in fact, quite bowled over, by her own, not precisely benevolence—she neither expects nor wants to become a benevolent person—but by a fervency not to cause harm. Not necessarily to create light, but not to bring down darkness, either.

Grace is not sustainable in any perpetual, permanent way, at least not by her. It's hydroponic, not rooted, but it's something to know. And to cultivate. How does a person cultivate grace?

Like anything else, she guesses. Like the exercises to strengthen her chest, back, and arms: by repetition, through practice, by doing the same thing over and over to the very edge, and sometimes over the brink, of difficulty and pain.

She reaches out to touch Roddy's knee. Not from affection, and not with forgiveness, but because, however clumsily and inadvertently, he has given her this.

Lyle is now leaning against the far corner of the porch, speaking quietly with Martin and Jamie. "Is it time for another round?" she calls out to him. And, "Come on back, everyone. You should all meet Rod properly." By which she means, she guesses, in conversation of sorts: stumbling questions, awkward answers, a ritual of acquaintanceship made onerous and possibly terrible by the weight of grudge, mistrust, dislike, fear, resentment, ineptness and, it must be said, very deep anger.

Which is in fact more or less how it goes. Voices are strained and unfamiliar and scarcely relaxed, but like the good hostess she steers them towards each other, drawing links and points of common interest beyond the obvious one, which is herself, and drawing them apart when voices grow sharp. She tells Jamie that Rod passed his Grade 12 in jail and has an interest in the outdoors. She tells Rod that Jamie too went back to school, and for a time worked for a florist.

She tells Robert and William that Rod's mother also died when he was young, and tells Rod that they are, between them, an eminent scientist and an eminent practitioner of public opinion. She tells Martin that Rod's dream was to move from small town to city, and tells Rod that Martin's desires have become more universal, and that he has recently returned from a journey to India. There are many possibilities, she is trying to say. A true multitude of outcomes.

She tells Madeleine that Rod grew up mainly in his grandmother's home, and tells Rod that if it hadn't been for Madeleine, she doesn't know what would have become of her, or for that matter of Jamie and Alix, in some very bad times. She tells Bert that Rod's father sounds like a man of few words, and tells Rod that Bert is as well, but that his words are always intended to support and give solace.

Much of this amounts to quite a creative conversational stretch. But having done her best, she leaves them to it.

Solace is an interesting notion. It returns to mind as dinner is ending some hours later, as soiled dishes and napkins litter the table, the candles burn down, the flowers wilt and droop low. On one side of the long table, Jamie and Martin are at the moment in low-voiced conversation, and William and Robert, book-ending Bert and Madeleine on the other side, each bends inwards, towards the old couple, all nodding in some shared amusement. Alix is beside Rod, who is beside Jamie, a bold configuration that in the course of the meal, before Jamie turned away towards Martin, became, if not warm, at least cordial, and for a while even animated as Jamie and Rod compared jails, guards they met, views of police officers and of their individual lawyers. Isla heard Jamie say, "I was lucky," and so, she thinks, he was.

She and Lyle are at the head of the table, side by side although her chair takes up more space than his. Beneath the cloth, they touch hands. She has no large faith this affection, however deep at the moment, can now last them another one, two, three decades, but right now, they touch hands.

Right now the day ends as she pictured it ending: in dim light, after good food and drink, in this company, in this house. The day also ends, because of that slim figure between Jamie and Alix, utterly differently from the way she imagined.

She sees she was longing for not only revenge but, more vastly, for consolation. But she is incurable in too many ways, and so is grievously, fundamentally, inconsolable.

This is a moment, however. And a moment, as she learned swinging through the front door of Goldie's, can be very long, very large.

There is endurance, that hard, unbending oak of a word, and within endurance there are these sturdy two-legged moments, strange and nearly sensual, of joy. This joy, rare and unfamiliar, is not compensation, not by any means; but it is, in the end, and at least momentarily, consolation.

And this, she imagines, hearing the voices rise and fall around her like music, like water, might be grace: a consoling joy, flickering like candles, embedded in endurance, flaring now and again into a brief picture. Like this.